CW00455806

KING

KING
RIAD NOURALLAH

QUARTET

First published in 2013 by Quartet Books Limited
A member of the Namara Group
27 Goodge Street, London W1T 2LD
Copyright © Riad Nourallah 2013
The right of Riad Nourallah to be identified
as the author of this work has been asserted
by him in accordance with the
Copyright, Designs and Patents Act, 1988
All rights reserved.
No part of this book may be reproduced in
any form or by any means without prior
written permission from the publisher
A catalogue record for this book
is available from the British Library
ISBN 978 0 7043 7318 1
Typeset by Josh Bryson
Printed and bound in Great Britain by
T J International Ltd, Padstow, Cornwall

CONTENTS

PROLOGUE

The god glowered down at us with one fiery garnet eye; the other, empty and passionless, stared at the wind-whetted dunes glinting in the distance behind our backs.

Hewn from the white quartz of some alien quarry, the monolith stood high and forlorn in the square of the oasis town, shadowless beneath the noon sun. His bulging arms were folded under his pallid beard and over his massive chest, his feet resting on a basalt plinth which may have served as a stand for more than one ancient idol.

Beneath him, to the left, stood the priestess, diminutive, but graceful as a gazelle and mysterious as fate, her great eyes swathing my companion with their dark glow, her rippling red hair aflame in the glare. A hot breeze fluttered about her, pressing against her breasts and belly and thighs enticed and snubbed by her gauzy robe.

Even before Emru's broad hand touched my shoulder fleetingly but firmly, I had already slackened my pace. Conscious as I was of the imposing spectacle before me, my gaze was drawn to a tiny scarlet anemone eying me with its black iris from a small crack at the base of the pedestal.

Emru advanced towards the god and the woman. A slight swagger in his gait spoke of a seasoned nonchalance, an innate confidence in conquest. One or two uneven steps whispered of a wayward unease. In days past, he would have stridden towards the woman, rare and revealed, and worshipped at the altar of her splendour in ways he was most skilled in. Now, the once-perpetual fire in his loins was sojourning in his head, meeting the combined energies of the god and the woman with the fierce serenity of a honed, transcendent flame.

Suddenly, the god spoke, though his inhuman, otherworldly voice seemed to issue from the priestess's slender throat, his own quartz lips remaining solidly sealed.

'You have come to our sanctuary to seek our judgement. Man's cunning is keener than that of the desert fox; fleeter than the hurtling oryx. But even *he* will have to empty his quiver before the gods. Even he must grovel, begging to borrow for an instant their far-seeing eyes perchance he might be granted a glimpse through the tumbling mist...'

1

'I grovel to none and beg no one!' Emru hissed through his teeth; but the priestess persisted, unaware or heedless of his profane intrusion.

'Only the gods can read the runes dispersed in the mist, teasing the prying ken of mortals. But even the gods cannot erase what has been written.'

Then the voice wilted, perhaps humbled by the enormity of its last statement. It went on to shed its unearthly tenor for a vaguely human voice, mournful but cautionary:

'King and mendicant, hunter and prey! In your wish to travel with the god's arrows you shall be granted a vision of the course you must pursue. Endeavour not to stray from that course, unpleasant as it might seem to you.

'*You* have chosen to consult the god, so you must resign yourself to his judgement. And you must show civility and draw *one sole* arrow! The god will not be trifled with, sorrowful as He is for pitiful man!'

With a petulant shrug of his shoulder, Emru stepped forward, closing the gap between him and the idol. His immense eyes surveyed the woman, who fluidly pointed to a stone quiver I had not noticed at the side of the monolith's left leg.

Emru drew nearer, ascended four steps, and eased his right arm into the mouth of the quiver. He paused for a moment, sifting the occult mind of the god. Then he lifted his arm clasping an arrow.

He raised the object towards the sun then lowered it to study the inscription along its shaft.

'The god forbids!' his angry voice rang out. 'The god forbids! He says I must *desist*.'

Emru paused for a moment, forcing down the demons hollering in his dark fire.

'But let us try again! The fellow may be recovering from a hangover. His feet smell of stale palm-wine and sperm and the blood of wasted sacrifice! Let's give him a breather to find his voice!'

As I mused for a moment on the curious anemone and whether it was roused into its scarlet growth by such blood, such lusts, Emru jerked the divination arrow back into the stone quiver. He stirred his hand inside the hole then brought out an arrow. He glanced at it and quickly yanked it back into the cylinder. He again shuffled his hand in the hole, somewhat desperately, before brandishing another arrow – the same arrow? - for a third time.

Emru then turned to face us, we twain, and the gathering folk of Tabalah. A conjoined smell of camel dung and lamb roast suddenly drifted into my nostrils.

The priestess was shaking her head, with its carmine cascades, muttering in a half-alien, half-human voice, 'You can draw only once; only once can you draw...'

The crowd were visibly agitated. Some mumbled words of annoyance; some shouted in undisguised dissent. Did the rumour of an army behind the dunes deter them from open violence?

Emru was impervious to all.

He stabbed the sky with the last arrow before lowering it to the level of his smouldering eyes, squinting in the sun to inspect its inscription.

Soon he was roaring out, 'The god forbids, again! Why, you stiff-necked, one-eyed lump of quartz! Had it been your father who'd been murdered, O bastard of the Chaldeans, you wouldn't have forbidden me to avenge his death!'

With a grand sweep of his sinewy arm, he turned round and smashed the arrow against the flank of the idol. He then fished out the two remaining shafts from inside the stone quiver, hurriedly inspected what was written on each of them, then, reaching up, shattered them one after the other against the beard of the god.

'Here's your 'The god permits' and your 'The god urges prudence!' Stick them up your arsehole, if you have one! And lick your mother's *bazr*, if you have a tongue!'

He jumped, not ungracefully, from the plinth to the ground, stretched up to his full height as if loath to be dwarfed by the monolith towering behind him, and walked towards me without glancing at any of the faces retreating from his fuming march.

But he suddenly stopped and turned to look at the priestess.

She was now kneeling on the ground, her face hidden behind her hands (weeping? laughing?) the horny breeze butting its rut in vain against her lower belly, veiled and exposed by her lucent robe.

Then, gently, musically, as if a songbird instead of a white-hot blade had emerged from the forge of his fury, Emru said: 'Forgive me, fair maiden. I meant you no disrespect. You deserve a better, bolder, god than *Zul Khalasa*, though I can think of none fit to be your footstool amongst them – *gods!*'

He brought out of his belt a small bag of yellow cloth tied at its neck with a black ribbon and sent it flying in a slender arch to land, tinkling, in front of her opal-white knees.

'For the privilege of beholding your eyes, fair one, a small offering to the temple of your beauty!'

Then the priestess stood up, the yellow bag pitiably disgorging some of its gleaming innards beneath her toe, and spoke in her own voice.

Emru's songbird faded in the dawn chorus of her syllables. But she did not look long at him, only to say, an enticing foreign cadence interlacing her words, 'He is not so bad; but I *do* have better gods, *goddesses*!'

And then, most unexpectedly, her night-sky eyes, scintillating with distant suns of their own, bored into mine.

I staggered back a step or two, pierced and almost blinded. But I could hear her words deep inside my head, rasping under the melodic stream of her public voice.

'The god is struck, and the time for summoning has come!'

In that instant, I felt Emru's grip coil round my upper arm steadying my steps and leading me away.

Soon we were back on our dromedaries trotting over their earlier tracks, already being obliterated by a surging wind.

As we rode on, my thoughts assailed by a spectre that had risen from an old prophecy, a simoom-like gust thumped us in the back. I wondered whether this was the breeze in the town driven into a frenzy of lust for the woman or the old god snorting at men who have swords and tongues and arses but would, before long, yield them all, steel and spit and shit, to the oblivion of the sands.

PART ONE

A KING SLAIN,
A KING ENSNARED

Oblivion-bound, I trot to a gallop upon fading tracks of time. In my face stares the naked China paper, dreading, lusting after, the barbed reed-pen.

Ten months earlier, Emru,
>> the fire in his loins,
>> a Jinn-Muse at his lips,
>> a bounty on his head,
>> a smothered Shah on his chessboard,
>> disowned,
>> disowning,
>> a host to a band of tramps and outcasts, jesters and bawds,
>> a mate, a slave, to them and to the feral laughter of the fleeting day,
>>> became a king.

We had been playing the Persian game in high Hadramot, seated at a western balcony of a dilapidated fort called *Al-Ahqaf*, clad in the vermilion of the afterglow.

The sun had just dipped behind the rows of the dark blue mountains in the distance, spiriting away their tenuous crowns of reddish mist. But the pink stone houses on the nearby slopes, though robbed of the freely given light, still stood proud, four and five and six floor tall. Lamplight was beginning to flicker through their ornate latticed windows, their *barjeels* breathing in with relish the cooler, unencumbered air.

We shared it with them, that air, scented with the tangle of the jasmines and roses and basils of the gardens and balconies, the fruit trees and vineyards of the more distant terraces lapped in their own reveries.

The dark red wine in the flask and the cup beside me, and in the cup swaying in Emru's hand like a dancing girl, had itself started off from some great forebears of the berries on the darkening vines, famed in the region for yielding the best grapes ever crushed into liquid ruby.

It was then. It was then.

A late serin had just let out a tinkling cry as he flew through a sky beginning to be streaked by bats. A *sa'luk*, limping as he chewed a cheekful of *qat*, had just brought in two oil lamps and placed them on the parapet, their slight flames cavorting in the breeze.

It was then that a messenger arrived to tell Emru that his father, King Hojr, had been slain by the Asads.

Emru's response sealed his fate and mine.

I had been poised to checkmate his Shah on the diminishing acacia board.

A brisk match it had been under the retreating sun. Emru did not seem to be giving his bone royals much consideration, exposing them to the dumbest of reposts. He was mumbling some raw verses about a night of debauchery gone and another awaited, the wine cup swaying in his left hand.

But with his imperial piece smothered and about to be checkmated by my horse, Emru suddenly revived and surveyed my face with his vast eyes.

A sly, quizzical smile rose to his sensual mouth, banishing the Jinn-Muse fluttering at his lips. Was he trying to charm me away from clinching the game or, instead, lead me on to claim a win to which he may have manoeuvred me?

In any event, I was not inclined to be generous, being in a treasonable mood.

The black bone horse had mutated in my imagination into an instrument of retribution. It snorted and whinnied loudly inside my head. It squealed and grunted against the house of Hojr and its chaining of my father's life and mine, the death of my mother and the wrecking of my happiness with Sofia. With a flick of my hand, a kick from him, my equine avenger, I would topple the whole accursed dynasty and send it reeling beyong the world-aping board.

I paused, ever a coward, even when seized by a wayward humour.

Then a half-stoned *sa'luk* who had been appointed by Emru as the sentinel of the now departed day declared the arrival of an old man with a message. The man had negotiated the climb to the fort herding a pack of bedraggled thoroughbreds, one of which carried a bundle of antiquarian shields, the *sa'luk* was able to observe.

Moments later, I was transfixed upon my cushion. The messenger was none other than my father, lined but unbent in the eyes of my exile.

Half acknowledging me, his own son, he blasted Emru with his report, delivering it in one grim, breathless volley.

'Your father, the king, has been killed.'

The tremor that went through me brought to the surface to my mind the face of Hojr as I last saw it.

It was not unlike that of his handsome son, but cold, severe, careworn, the eyes burning with an occult fire of their own. Then the features convulsed and dissolved.

They were replaced by the ever-radiant and carefree face of Al-Ward, Emru's pal and chief of the *sa'luks*. He had been residing with us at the fort - a walled residence which Al-Ward had tolerated to humour Emru. A roving nomad by choice, he had always said, 'a Jumping spider needs no web.' Now, in the tremor of my mind, he was dismissing yet another urban superstition, as was his habit.

Some three weeks before, a hunting dog kept at the fort had spent a day and a night howling. As it did so, it held its head down and howled and howled and howled.

A local old man delivering a sack of dates to the fort said that the dog's behaviour meant that someone was going to die. He added that a dog holding its head up and barking was a sign of rain, but a dog holding its head down and howling was definitely, most definitely, a portent of approaching death.

Al-Ward, who believed in earthly powers but scorned any authority beyond them, made light of the old man's reading. But he did not show him any discourtesy. He only said, merrily, 'Ah, death is just a name we use when we think life has jilted us. But life is a lover relentless. She will continue to shag us even in the grave. Even with the roots of her tamarisk and vines snaking round our bones and into our cracks and sockets.' A practical man, he went out in search of a mate for the dog. The ruse worked. Al-Ward was never wrong. Rarely so.

My father was pressing on with his onsalught.

'The king was leading an expedition in Sumayra. This was to punish men of the Asads who had butchered his tax collectors. I had appealed to him not to go. I had pleaded with him before not to impose taxes in the Persian and Roman fashion. But vain was my counsel. He needed the silver to fund his dream. Then, he was enraged by the words of an Asad slanderer. The words were conveyed to him by the one man who had escaped the massacre. Words I would not repeat. They vexed him to no end, casting a dark, dense aba upon his judgement, rousing his demons. Your sister had implored him to stay. To send someone in his stead. But he went, spurring his noble *Adham*, still not sufficiently watered, ahead of the other horses. Hend had seen a dream, an eagle, its heart being eaten by a crow.'

'Ah, my sister and her dreams! Always wings of one sort or another! It's time she grew a couple of her own!' Emru interposed. My father continued, somewhat resentful of the flippant interruption.

'We rode for a day and a night. Then, without rest, without even sending a scout ahead of him, the king swooped on the Asad encampment. He rounded up the men who were there. They were few and strangely unprepared, limp after the butchery they had revelled in.

'On the testimony of our man who had escaped the slaughter, the king winnowed out the killers and put them to death, along with the slanderer. So seized was he by his *efreets*. He then decreed, from the saddle, that the women and children of the tribe be driven to exile in Tehama. He gave them an hour to collect their chattels. Then he herded them like cattle before him.

'Yes, that he did. But some two hours later, the king had a change of heart. The women had raised the wail and lifted up their babes appealing to his mercy. Their cries and the blood he had spilt helped dull his rage loosening the demons' hold. He gave orders for the whole party to return to Sumayra.

'Soon thereafter, at a place called Al-Abraqan, we set up camp. The king retired to his travel-tent. He had been having one of his headaches - doubly dazing, crippling. He wished to lie down for a short space, the lavender-oil cloth wrapped round his head.

'Before too long, we were attacked by Asad horsemen. Many of them had been away when we raided their encampment. They had followed us slyly, biding their time, and our inattention.

'One of them, Elba, son of Al-Hareth of the Kahl clan, and brother of the slanderer, rushed the tent of the king. I was after him in an instant, my sword half freed of its sheath. But Elba stabbed the king in his left side with a spear. He did so even as the king lay on his rug, his head bandaged. I slashed at Elba, fast and nimble as he was, hyena-eyed. His shoulder hacked, he dropped his spear and fled the tent. The other horsemen galloped into the desert, spiriting the assassin away.

'The king bled like a fount. Even then, he ordered forty of our men to go with the Asad women until they had delivered them safely to their kin in Sumayra. To me he turned, his pallor rising, and entrusted me with his will and testimony. He made me swear to deliver his dying voice to his sons. He let go of his last breath in my arms.'

'Where does his body lie?' Emru asked, his voice unruffled.

'I wrapped the king in his white, once-white, *aba*. The Asads had rallied round. More of their horsemen appeared in the distance. They were emboldened by whatever news Elba had given them. They tarried to harry us as we moved back. Some of them peppered us with arrows. Others made lightening attacks on our rear. In time, we were reduced to a handful of men. Still we were hotly pursued.'

'And the king's body?' Emru asked again.

'His body, his body, I had placed in front of me on the saddle of my horse. His own horse, the noble *Adham*, had collapsed with injury and loss of blood. All the while, I tried to shake off our pursuers. But we were shorn down to four riders. So I asked the other three to take the road to Yamamah. I veered in the direction of the setting sun, fastening the king's body to mine with strips of my *aba*, which I had torn in the middle.

'I carried through until I reached the small oasis of Akrabah. There my horse buckled for the first and last time. His gallant spirit expired within a yard of the water.

'The pounding of hooves filled my head. I laid the king's body in his *aba* behind an *arta* bush and covered him with orchids and *ghaf* leaves. I would have carried him on my back; but I had no sufficient strength. Unaided, I feared the pursuers. My one spur to life was to convey the king's last wishes.

'By some miracle, namely that of a roundabout route I took and the gift of the water I carried in my water-skin from Akrabah, I reached Mushakkar - two days later.

'The three men I had sent had broken the news to the tribe. The women had bruised their throats with wailing; ripped the necks of their gowns. Some of them brandished spears and swords. Most of our men, you may not know, were away on an expedition in the Persian Gulf.

'When I saw your sister she had her braids loosened, carrying a spear, shouting for vengeance. But she was drained, her sparkle sunken. Young men, prancing and posturing, rushed about with impotent blades. We were leaderless. I did my best to instil some order, some hope. The king's voice had to be listened to, be it out of devotion to the memory of a father, to me a brother. A new leader, yeah, be it a king, had to be chosen. The tribe was in mortal danger. The Asads were on a march relentless.'

Even then, Emru, who had stood up to welcome my father, betrayed no visible emotion. The flickering light from the two lanterns continued to cavort on his finely chiselled face. My father's words and the scenes they had depicted, frightful as they had been, seemed to have stirred up no passion in him. They seemed to have cast off their sting, their nightmares, in mid-flight, flailing down upon the *sarooj* floor like stricken flies ere they reached his ears.

'Ah, dear uncle,' he said, 'So good to see you, to listen as of old to your tales of derring-do! But your trials and the insanities of other men have laid upon your shoulders – magnificent as they are – a cloak of unseemly dust. Weariness itself, sweet at times, wouldn't have dared aspire to such a lofty place. You must wash and be adequately nourished. The horses must be fed. And your son must win his game.'

He gave orders to a swelling throng of his motley guests, himself a guest of the local lord, for my father and the horses, whinnying pitifully in the courtyard, to be attended to. Al-Ward and a pack of his finest *sa'luks* were away on an ibex hunt.

Then he turned to me, still transfixed upon my cushion, beads of cold sweat tingling on my forehead. 'Your move', he said.

He squatted back onto his cushion, the cup in his hand tilting but not yielding a single ruby drop onto the *sarooj*.

I remained seated, wondering whether I had wetted my cushion and too embarrassed not to reach out, in double anguish, for my father. A drop of sweat fell just behind my bone horse splashing his base with the salt of my confusion. A minute or so earlier, I had been about to brandish him, that horse, as a tool of a fanciful mutiny against a royal house, the death of whose head now caused my knees to quake, the wine in my stomach to rise, sickening, to my lips.

When I regained some of my composure, I leant forward avoiding my horse to pick up the chariot on the left. The piece was not required for a direct kill. Emru bent towards me, his eyes flaring, and grabbed my forearm. 'Your bow is cocked; your arrow must find its mark and your horse his leap', he said, guiding my hand to the bridled slayer.

12

My father, in the meantime, having swollen with the blood and fury of the tale, now seemed shrivelled. He looked like a sail bereft of wind or a water-skin emptied of its liquid.

His purpose, I thought, had been to depict the horror of life-taking, all life-taking, rather than one that had claimed the life of his king.

For years, he had served Hojr as a loyal minister and a caring, though not always prevailing, adviser, infuriatingly loyal. Nonetheless, sharing his wife's loathing for war, he now had boldly portrayed Hojr to his son, Yeah as a resolute and chivalrous ruler, but also as a man of moods and demons, fiends and *efreets*, that needed to be exorcised by a more sober and forbearing headship. Also, the crime, hideous as it was and already spawning more butcheries, had roots in the king's harsh taxes.

Yet, my father was not finished with his gales and salvos.

His king's last and most imperative voice had to be given tongue, now that its author had changed his throat.

For, from the king's body, drained of its life-blood behind the *arta* bush, there would have emerged the spectral bird whom the Arabs call *Al-Hamah*. Clamouring for revenge, it would cry out in one obsessive refrain: '*Ousqouni, ousqouni, ousqouni*' - 'Quench my thirst, quench my thirst, quench my thirst!' It would continue to hoot into the dreams and nightmares of the murdered man's kinsmen until the crime was avenged.

So my father continued.

'The king, your father, said that I was to proceed and call on his sons, one after the other. I was to tell each of them what had happened. But I was to hand over his signet ring along with the stud horses and the Shield of Ishmael and the other four shields to the son who took the news of his death like a man, like no other.

'Yes, he made me swear to this - absurd, canny, as it may be - by all the gods he did not believe existed and by the memories we shared.

'Still, none of your brothers were at Mushakkar. Each resided with the clan he was elected to govern. I advised the tribe to leave for Al-Anbar through the Nafud. I further counselled them to make their way to Hadramot, but only when it was safe for them to do so. I then collected the studhorses and the shields and proceeded to fulfil the king's wish. I tracked your brothers, starting with Nafi' onwards to Zuhair. Each broke down and sobbed like a babe or was flustered with fear and loss of nerve. All, except you.

13

'So to you I surrender my charge, the ring of Kenda. The horses, those who have survived the journey, await your further attention. All are descendants of the legendary *Kohaylan* and the more worldly, *houjja*-necklaced, *Sabal* and *A'waj*. The Shield carried by Ishmael also awaits, as do those wielded by the first kings of Kenda. They all tarry, the horses, the shields, with their own woes of sinew or steel. You are your father's successor. My mission ends, yours start; may it be attended by reason. Men kill, often on impulse and without hate, which may be brought in later to fan the flames; but it is a folly to allow such men-made fires to consume yet more men.'

Here my father stopped. The blood-tinged wind decidedly deserted him, but only for it to wheel round and erupt within Emru, animating the rake with its ferocity and gloom.

Palming off the white Shah from the chessboard, he tossed him farther than I would have done in my imagination - over the parapet of the balcony and into the darkening chasm below.

He then raised the cup in his left hand, hoisting its vine-blood to the dying light, and spoke in a tone whose solemnity and reach I had seldom heard from him before.

His words mourned his carefree life of past years and the life to come, though cleaving unto it with the resolve of a doomed lover.

'My father'-
he said -
'disowned me with his bile in my youth,
and lumbered me with his blood in my manhood.
No soberness tonight
and no drunkenness tomorrow.
Tonight is for wine,
tomorrow for war!'

CHRONICLER

I write in a language not my own about a man beyond my grasp.

Doubly at a disadvantage, I must however persevere. Perhaps in the telling I may yet capture more of that man in whose blaze I am fated to walk and whose words I must set down, albeit in a speech forever alien to him and only less to me.

But there are always many other reasons for writing   reasons that impregnate my mind from beyond it or are miraculously born within its restless, lustful womb.

Of such reasons I have a passing acquaintance but no settled or clear knowledge. Yet I know that I must be truthful and unswerving, though truth has many faces and the world of nature and men many seasons and moods. My own feelings about that man, my friend and king and subject, are themselves in a perpetual ebb and flow of comradeship and jealousy, loyalty and treason, worship and apostasy.

And why can't the shadow, which is I, illumine the sun, which is Emru, even as his face obliterates my fitful existence with its lethal beams, joining me to the darkness at the core of his being – and mine?

And why can't the story of one man tell the story of a nation, and that of a nation speak of the men and women of *all* nations, as they conquer or crawl or copulate their way through history, breeding the mongrels of future days?

My own truths and myths may in times to come sit too naively or jostle too grossly with the prevailing tastes of the day. But I am unable to view men and women existing now or in ages yet to come without that shudder in the loins which confirms their humanity and that half-baffled half-nostalgic gaze at the stars which hints at their mystery and promise. Nor without that mix of dread and daring which haunts man and drives him to slaughter or glory, silence or song.

And as I travel with these unruly lines of ink as though on the hump of a runaway camel or in the guts of a flash flood or as a ghostly dhow over the archipelago of a vast shattered mirror, I can only offer glimpses of a madly careering reality and a sprawling clutter of shards that mock evenness and finality.

With such a mount, and with the scars and hobbles, flights and rifts, of my own soul, I fear that I may not have the power to rule any reins or wrestle any rudder. I may not hear a pulse other than the hurly-burly of elements being transformed into blood and sweat and semen and no speech but a babble of men and beasts and demons howling and groaning, with strains of nymphs and sirens singing and sighing beyond reach.

All may prove to be beyond reach.

Yet I shall labour, be it across this cracked glass of visions and frenzies, and in the swirl of rot and perfume, to impose some shape or order, perhaps through a device, an interplay of past and present, a *marwaha* dance, imposed upon this unfolding narrative. My pages, like the tales of the Bedouin, shall welcome all voices, my pen all hands, be they human or non-human, cultured or coarse.

I shall write when an opportunity (and paper) present themselves; and I shall abide by the truth as she reveals her faces and fancies to me, in the heat of the event or in the cool oasis of remembrance.

Whether such encounters will come out to soothe or torment, enlighten or mortify, I cannot tell.

I am a hybrid plant of the land of the Cedars and the land of the dunes, torn between the legacies of my Christian mother and pagan father. And like my rebel priest and missionary of an uncle, I am a devotee of the doughty saint of the *Confessions*; though I do not claim to be fired by his searing purpose or desirous to reach his numbing heights. And yet, his God of 'sweetness without deception' may look with favour upon whatever wild interludes my tale might unfold with their transports and torments. And as he has done for the saint, he may have to put up with the sins and duplicities depicted here, by design or accident, by myself or others. And he may have to put up with all those that may gatecrash my narrative or take possession of my pen.

Too long has the face of the shadow been veiled, his voice muffled in the loud and glowing histories of kings and nations. Might not some smudges of the dark stalker and some of his growls trickle through the cracks of this narrative? Why should the loud shout of the caravan leader forever muzzle the whimper of the discarded dog? And why should the tilt of a gold-tipped staff, drowsy in its self-worship and dubious glory, forever send thousand after thousand after thousand of men to their doom with lordly impunity?

16

And beyond men, what riposte to the millstone of time have I?

Will I be able to gather the strength and the stratagem to scatter my grains over the gullies and alleyways snubbed by that millstone which knows no rest nor tolerates a deserter?

Will the spectral hand that plants spores into the breasts of beautiful women show mercy to my grains, maimed and fugitive as they are?

Wouldn't it be better if they too withered into everlasting muteness, stirring up no scandal, making no bitter bread?

And yet, again, why should the loud-mouthed and the heavy-handed and the deep-pursed always have their way, like the gods that seem to favour them?

In truth, I fear that my very pen, now released like a dagger, long famished and brooding in the scabbard of years, may be but a trinket in their armoury, a pawn on their board, a loop in their ever-blaring horn.

The very prophecy which had shepherded my birth and defined my life may have been voiced but for their benefit and double power.

And what if the priestess's blinding shaft of late was no more than a sly distraction, a bustard released to lure a hawk away from his comforting hood?

But if that was not the case, and even if it was, why should I not seize upon the gash in the darkness and the gasp in the fanfare? Why should I hold back my own shudders and shrieks, profanities and follies, in deference to their monopolies and decorums? Why fear the censure of my contemporaries should these pages be read in an age when my dust would be as dumb as their own?

And yet should this record so endure, might not my dust stir a little and let off a chuckle or two if the fading ink could yet tell of the shifty and lecherous sand seeping and crackling into the thoughts of the living?

AVENGER KING

Emru woke up the following morning into the alien skin of his vow.

Tossing away his hangover and past life like a pair of frayed sandals and wearing a sepulchral face, he called for my father.

From him he received the signet ring of Kenda, forcing its sapphire stone upright on the index finger of his right hand. He then inspected the heirloom shields. His fingers circumnavigated the Shield of Ishmael as if it was the tender breast of a bedmate. Then, down in the fort's courtyard, he stroked the arching necks of the horses, restored to some of their former lustre by a *sa'luk* groom.

My father had led the precious herd from Najd across desert trails and mountain passes, losing several manes on the way. The purebreds, the purest in Arabia, symbolised Kenda's power and her drinking and saddling of the wind.

Then he, Emru, set about preparing for the whirlwind ahead.

He sent couriers to his brothers in Najd and to his mother's tribe in Al-Anbar. Nearer to home, he dispatched messages to Kenda's Arab and Jewish allies in the parts of the Yemen free from Oksum's occupation.

At times, he seemed hunched, weighed down by the role laid upon him. More often, he seemed to have grown taller than he already was, acquiring the stature of a god.

He had clearly broken loose of his carnal compulsions, no longer eying the world from the pupil of his penis as had been his habit. His was now a broader and higher outlook, one which required a different pace, a larger though breathless immediacy, a fellowship and a quarrel with deities.

Fourteen days after the simple ceremony of investiture, the local lord, Karmal Ben Al-Hameem, not bothering to make an appearance, Emru was to meet a delegation from the Assads.

They were led by Kubeysa Ben Naym, their chief spokesman, a man of a great age and of a stately, seductive eloquence.

My father personally saw to their reception and comfort, putting them up in a western wing of the fort. Even as my father was escorting him to their quarters, Sheikh Kubeysa requested an instant audience with Emru. They were on a mission of peace and diplomacy which could not be delayed, he said.

My father was asked to go back to the Asad delegation with the statement, 'The king is preoccupied with shining Kenda's shields'.

Kubeysa was alarmed. '*Hu-Baal* forbid!' he declared. 'We have travelled all this distance so that we might put the lunacies and woes of the recent past behind us. We offer reconciliation and recompense, a stemming of the blood-flow let loose by senseless men. They'd foolishly nursed an injury that could've been healed with prudence and patience. Sadly it was made worse by a madman once counted as of our fold. He has since melted into the desert. May her jackals chew on his wretched bones and the bones of his vile accomplices, loathsome as these must be even to hyenas. Would that the young King of Kenda respond to us favourably and with gracious speed!'

My father, his tenacious spirit spurring his sinking body, went to Emru with that appeal.

Once more he put to him the Asads' case, and his own.

Emru, in his new skin, had already sealed his transformation.

Dressed in black from head to toe with a crimson sash round his waist, signalling the intent to avenge a murder, heeding the call of the *Hamah*, he came to see the envoys.

My father shuffled behind him, a grim bird of his own perched unseen on his high shoulder.

'Vengeance', he had once told me, 'is sweet as honey on the lips of a day. It will however linger long and deep in the soul, scattering seeds bitter as the Vine of Sodom.' He may have been expressing a sentiment dear to the heart of his much-loved wife. For the pagans, however, the *Hamah* will dissolve into its cosmic essence and leave the graveside of the slain man and the fitful slumber of his kinfolk *only* when its thirst for blood has been quenched.

When the Assad envoys saw Emru in his garb, their faces paled even as they rose to their feet. Old Kubeysa also stood up, with some difficulty. His old age seemed to fade away as he began to speak:

'Greetings, noble King and son of a noble king, sorely missed', he began his speech.

'You do not need me, ancient as I am, to counsel you on the guiles of fate and the fickleness of fortune. Already you possess, young as

19

you are, much knowledge of the world, one adorned by your rank and lineage. These and the reverence accorded your house by the Arabs give you the clout to forgive a wrong and scorn a fault, however grievous these may have been.

'Verily', he continued, 'now is the time for men who dream of true chivalry to turn to you for the fulfilment of their dream. Yeah, and for the fulfilment of the dreams of wisdom and mercy and charity. For it is in the vast misfortune at hand that these grand virtues are most needed. This is a calamity that has joined to Kenda the whole of Arabia, from Nezar to Hemyar, in sorrow and grief over a man of such exceptional nobility and rare distinction. Hojr possessed all, together with the graciousness and dignity which distinguished him and most of his rule. And if it were possible to ransom the dead with the lives of those that still breathe the air, even our worthiest women would not shy away from offering their babes in such a barter. But Hojr has journeyed upon a road whose end stretches too far beyond its beginning, a road that leaves us all blind as to its final purpose.'

The snow-bearded Kubeysa paused to gauge the effect of his words on Emru.

Emru, clad in his blackness and splash of scarlet, betrayed no visible emotion. But I could see his lower lip twitching.

Kubeysa continued on a more urgent and practical course of reasoning:

'Hence, we await your judgement. But we ask you before you dress it in silk or chain-mail to reflect on three offers we shall put to you thereafter to choose what appeals best to your prudence and sympathy.

'The first, that you name a man of Asad, highest among us in lineage and rank, and we shall deliver him to your door to die by your sword. Then people will say that you were a man tested by the loss of one eminent in your judgement and that of the world, and you found some comfort in avenging his death by the death of one equal to him in rank.

'The second, that you name a ransom of whatever amount or magnitude. We shall drive it to you from our coffers or pastures with gladness and contrition. By such amends, however deficient in the scale of your loss, the swords will stay in their sheaths, and the innocents will be spared the randomness of revenge.

'The third, the third, that you allow us, O King, a grace period, a respite, until the unborn in our women's wombs have been delivered.

Then, you will find us girding our loins and hoisting our lances with the wedding veils of our women fastened to them.'

Emru's eyes had been glistening, but they smouldered fiercely when he answered:

'The Arabs know that there is no man equal to Hojr in blood, and I shall not barter his for coins or camels, reaping unending shame and self-defeat. As to the respite, it is surely needed for the benefit of the unborn, whose injury I will not tolerate. From then on, your folk shall see the horsemen of Kenda and Hemyar on every horizon, the points of their spears glinting with the flames of their eyes.'

And he extemporised the following verses:

When Kenda rides, her blades shall whisk a mighty wave-
A timely purge for Death; ablutions for the brave!

He paused, somewhat unsure of his sudden eruption into the prosody of combat outside bedchambers. Finally, he asked: 'Are you abiding or leaving?'

'We are leaving, though with the worst option, one from which nothing but war and ruin can issue,' Kubeysa rejoined, genuinely saddened, a man of vintage wisdom and grace. My heart went out to him, perhaps meeting my father's heart on the way.

He rose wearily from his cushion. His advanced years and the long ride of the previous days had clearly taken their toll. But he perked up as he quoted a line of verse by Asad's chief poet.

Abeed Ben Al-Abras had been a long-standing imitator of Emru's love poetry; but he had of late been pawning his rhymes to the service of a maniacal war god.

A thought crossed my mind: Had Abeed's bellicose verses, which had reached us in our exile, played a part in rousing the hotheads to their mutiny and the murderer to his crime?

But here was Kubeysa replying to Emru's challenge as required by tribal custom.

At Death's face our foe can only gape in fear
As joyous Asad hurls her Death-anointed spear!

'Nay, *I* shall not gape at his face! Not in *fear*,' snapped Emru. 'But take your time, and you shall see through the dust, clearing, rank after rank, the horsemen of Kenda and Hemyar and their kinsmen and allies in Arabia, pushing back the murderous darkness of the Asads.'

Clearly, Emru had mortally snubbed a liberal peace offer. In my mind flickered Al-Ward's lines on the follies of kings. Furthermore, Emru was indulging in unseemly banter with his guest. Was he, the master poet, also incensed by the superior verses of his imitator?

I felt my father's eyes on me. They burned through the mist of his grief at the news I had conveyed to him the night before. But I could do nothing. So he cleared his throat and leaned towards Emru. The breach of the hallowed rules of hospitality was as vile as murder itself. Fortunately, by chance or a meeting of minds, Emru had by then recovered enough self-possession to say,

'Forgive me, Sheikh Kubeysa and you honourable men of Asad. It was most ill mannered of me to address you, esteemed guests and Ambassadors, with such thoughtless words. I must have been waylaid by the juice of an impish grape in an otherwise fine flagon I had emptied of late. But I also beg to blame Sheikh Kubeysa for stirring up my poetic demoness, exciting her jealousy with his most excellent speech. Would that the occasion had been different, Ah! I would have celebrated the Sheikh's eloquence with a feast for all the tribes of Arabia, boasting that we have such a man amongst us. All the same, a camel shall roast for your dinner tonight. I entreat you to forgive my trespass!'

'We thank the king for his temperance and generosity. But what awaits us in days to come is beyond words, whether kind or unkind', Kubeysa said, gravely.

'That is indeed the case. But you are most welcome to stay in *Al-Ahqaf*, though unfit for your indulgence, until you have recovered from the discomfort of your journey. Nothing shall be spared in entertaining you or in providing for your ride back whenever you wish to set forth', said Emru.

'We travel when the eye of *Algol* starts to blink. Our tidings are eagerly awaited in Najd. But what we are made to bear will gladden the hearts of none but the warmongers.'

'I bow to your wish', said Emru, slightly tilting his handsome head, crowned by the ominous turban, and placing his hand upon a heart no longer his own.

SUMMONING KENDA

I did not recognise in time the Seeress, who had recognised me.

Already a sea of dunes separates me from her and her mystery, tangled as her words and ways are with my own life's riddles and roads. And yet the peal of the summoning is upon me.

But where do I begin, with every step and every thought being a new birth, and a possible death?

I call upon the power of the prophecy to help me 'summon the bygone runes' and give them the breath of life, as the prophecy had commanded!

The prophecy! The prophecy!

It may be no more than the word-juggling of a sham sibyl, the ravings of a drunken Bakkhe. But terrible has been its threat of instant punishment if I tarry - alluring its promise if I comply!

Saint of the *Confessions*, I seek and call on you even as you seek and call on none but the ineffable ravisher of your heart!

And yet, I am, above all, a chronicler of footprints in the sand, and above and beyond that, a scribe of the mind, and of the heart. And from these two dissemblers I must draw my inspiration and strength.

And yet, and yet,

Like the pages which I unfold and smear with my ink, I am, as I have pledged, ajar to every pen and every muse, every murmur and gust.

And yet I find myself at this gasp of time utterly alone. The dark satchel strapped to my body weighs heavily upon my soul. And instead of the promise of a new dawn flickering from the ink, I feel trapped, caught in the midst of an infinity of dunes and memories, jostling in a cosmic *kashkoul* too wild and riotous for a measured *marwaha* dance!

Kenda is the tribe to whom I belong by an accident of birth or a design of fate and whom Emru has of late been leading to further glory and ruin.

How can I tell her story?

Can a frail reed-pen relate all her work songs and battle cries, her pleasure moans and death rattles?

Will it dip into enough ink to trace the footfalls of her dune-beading scouts or the foam-trails of her wave-cleaving dhows; Aye, or even the hems of her women's skirts kindling the earth with perfume and desire?

Will there be a sufficient amount of the sticky stuff or the scarce China paper for tales of her bloodletting and tears?

Might the reed-pen sprout wings of poesy or break asunder on account of her savageries and blunders, disgraces and desolation?

Beyond the omen and the promise, what powers have been vested, invested, in me to lure her untamed chronicles and flights of fancy onto my pages? Do these powers truly exist? Woe to me if they do not and if they do, for dare I set them in motion unpredictable or consign them to a rest perpetual?

Have I in me the means to summon the ancient sagas, give them the required mouthful of life, and seize them to do my bidding?

Other than my rage and lusts, hitherto Solomon-sealed, have I the 'spell' of a master scribe, a master mage, laid downd by the prophecy?

Dare I say, like the Saint, tainted as I am, I summon thee Kenda, Kenda, come into me?

But how can I or anyone else contain Kenda, who has filled all Arabia, though remaining unfulfilled?

Kenda rises in my head. She swells up, dilates, pressing on my temples, my chest, overwhelming my page, bursting out with her conceits. My ears are struck with her thunder, pounded by her surge, even as the ramparts of my reason and rancour resist, doubting, mocking!

'Great granddaughter of Ishmael, I, Kenda, mother of all Arabian tribes. He who knows me shall know all Arabs for aeons to come. But never shall we be revealed. Never shall we be truly known', she proclaims, and turns away, disdainful, dissembling.

I rush to honour my pledge, climbing over my barricade for her voice and memories. They boom and clatter, stalk and chase, across the coliseum of my mind. They don the armour of her scorn and dangle the veils of her pretence.

I feel her sneer crackling through my thought-veins. I hear her bragging of her dominions.

'My first realms are well known to you Arab, you an Arab? a mongrel of the loins, of minds? My first realm, the kingdom of Sheba, *my* kingdom; the Queen of Sheba, Belqis, *my* queen, *my* maiden! My Yemen, *Happy Arabia* to the blue-eyed mariners. I hear, and I know. I see them as they inhale the aromatic breeze wafting to their foredecks and fantasies from my shores! And, higher, much higher than their beryl-eyed masts can see, grows *my* Myrrh. It grows on *my* slopes, Aye, upon *my* Myrrh tree!'

Kenda invites me to see that tree.

I see the tree, detached, windswept, unkempt! Ugly! Like a woman veiled, her charms hidden under a scruffy caftan, standing still, then hurrying, unknown, unsung, in a darkening alley, hurrying, her caftan fluttering, to her house, or her lover's. I see her there glowing, her true light revealed; I smell her as she exudes her fragrance now released, intoxicating, in her lover's embrace, his desire pounding hers and his into ecstasy.

I can see many lovers and suitors of the tree, teeming, sprawling, in their courts and cloisters - robbers, emperors, traders, slavers, poets, priests - all partaking of each other's trades. I see many a city, one I know so dearly, some advertising themselves to my ears and fancy – Kashgar, Ktesiphon, Alexandria, Almeria, Bayroute, Byzantium, many – a net extending, ensnaring, trading, whoring, warring.

Kenda tries to block the unlicensed drifting of my sight.

But I can see only the rich and the powerful affording a feel of her parcelled balm.

This, the tree's essence, her resin-gum, assaults my nose and taste with its tartness. But, touched by a flame, it rises to spread a canopy of sweet smoke. Underneath it, the wealthy and the powerful burn their offerings to their gods of healing or malice. Ah, let it be of healing!

But, lo! a healing is denied!

All the same! The resin is moulded, re-aroused, in the deft hands of a stern-faced man, an embalmer.

It sinks, melts, into a cloth, a shroud, woven on the anguish of the loom.

I see, but do not see, the holy infant being anointed with it.

I see him on the desolate hill, a man, a god, magnificent in his desolation, bearing a gift Adam and Eve had been given in compensation for the loss of their garden.

And here he is, again, my mother's eternal lover and restorer, shedding his death-garment, its Myrrh-scent forever in his nostrils, a Phoenix pulsating in the shroud, flaming into a new, unearthly life.

'But beware! Beware the gifts of the gods, Myrrh added to wine is nectar to the immortals, madness to lesser men! Myrrh added to your ink, a poison!

'Behold my Tree, a goddess to kings, a mere chattel to me!'

I see the tree, again, in her lofty sanctum on the terraces of the southern mountains. I see her farmers and priests, making ablutions and putting on ceremonial robes before they draw near to her with their consecrated blades. I see her resin (her very blood and milk, her teardrops and pleasure-flow) carried along the high roads to the workshops and seaports of the Phoenician-now-Roman sea. A goddess cheapened but enlarged by trade!

And I see another goddess, through Kenda's eyes, one with wings, keeping watch from her elevated station over the slouching caravan!

But who keeps watch over the indigent farmers when they take off their pious robes and sheathe their sanctified razors, the few *drachms* of their labour multiplying a thousand times into the coffers of the sheikhs and the merchants?

I ask.

Kenda scorns the question!

She wears the insolence of a god. She boasts of trafficking in other deities and delusions of men (wines, swords, horses, silk, salukis, cinnamon, ivory) sanctioning their passage from China and India and Africa, through her ports (Mocha, Kana, Aden) on her own booms and dhows onwards to Syria and Rome, ploughing the waves, cleaving the dunes.

She boasts of her conquests, south and north, westward, eastward, her triumphs over the Persian banner (I see it fluttering in red and pink and yellow); over the Roman Cross (aquiver in gold and red). I see the subordinate flags hoisted by Arab minions in Iraq and Syria and Yemen. I see them fleeing, scattered like autumn leaves before the falconine sirocco of her black standard.

'Minions frantic to keep their minion-hood! Frantic, even as their paymasters are, to keep Arabia weak and divided!' I hear Kenda's voice, the voices of her great kings, Hojr the First, Scarface, Amr the Victorious, Al-Hareth the Seeker, all united in their impossible dream, their incurable madness.

Kenda boasts of her Hemyar king, the proud Zu Nuwas. Undiminished even as his army is harvested by the Cosmic Scythe. He casts a cold eye as column after column of war elephants draw nearer and nearer, archers in turrets on the elephants' backs letting off volleys of arrows, elephants trumpeting. I glean a glimpse of his thoughts, laughing in the rising foam as he spurs his stallion into the sea. A grave of coral, even seaweed, is nobler than death by a foreign blade, nobler than a life as a puppet king in the Iraqi or Syrian fashion. He laughs as molluscs flood into his lungs and turn into pearls.

Kenda boasts of the honour conferred upon her, alone of all Arabian tribes, to drape the walls of the temple in Mecca. I see the temple, the Sacred Cube, bare but brilliant with the whiteness of Abraham's touch, the celestial sapphire in its eastern wall dimmed by the sins of the innumerable fingers that touched it. The hundreds of stone idols around it gaze on, unblinking.

Kenda, the Great Weaver, weaving together the hired hands that weave ream after ream of black silk - the colour of her insignia, The Black Falcon, hoisted on the Ka'ba, interlaced with gold threads in designs meant to confound the pilgrims into awe and submission.

But what price holy art?

Kenda in her guileless prelapsarian wanderings had survived on a nomad's diet - camel milk and locusts, dates and *sidr* berries? Her belly now swells up with royal banquets, with the fussiness of kings and queens. It puffs out with *dinars* and *byzants*. Her mouth reeks in my nostrils – the stench of young cadavers she sent out to die for her swelling gut?

Where are the spine-melting embraces of her maidens, their horsemen-tumbling glances? Where is the womb-stirring musk of her sporting youths?

Ah, Kenda, Kenda of the many faces and many masks, Kenda of the many mammaries and masteries, now dons a goddess's beatitude!

She declares that she has been 'a Guardian deity as none has. A warder of caravans and water wells, a warden of trade secrets, a vanquisher of quicksand and robbers, storms and pirates, a guide through every gully and gale, a joiner of every *zakar* and *han*, a rocker of every cradle.'

Kenda uses her reclaimed motherhood, her reasserted grace, to let loose a torrent of grand tales. Against them I struggle to shield my mind; for these speak of large events, too large to be missed by the usual historians.

It is the history of the hidden and the unsaid, the slight and the slighted, the feared and the unfulfilled, that is more of value to me, though the broader, louder proceedings may yet maintain their shrillness, shackled as I am to them and to their authors.

So before I take my yet-to-be-born reader on to the archipelago of broken mirrors and the head-turns of the *marwaha* dance, might I be allowed to summon the reason of my narrative?

But what if I am summoned elsewhere?

HOUJEIRA

Somewhat confirmed in my given powers, I do not wholly trust to their gallop nor to my mastery over their mane.

Did I summon Kenda by the power of the prophecy? Or, was I summoned by her? Or was it the wild-eyed word-slinger raving inside me who conjured up that encounter? Did he also spin the web on whose threads I am wriggling like a captive fly?

Captive or not, I must persist, doing so in a world where all threads are intertwined, as those of my birth and destiny are with Emru's, hero and reason of this history.

Emru and I, I and Emru, a twain entangled with the untold other threads of life and death. Clammy threads that tighten around me even as I struggle to break loose from them!

But why should I break loose? Might not these very threads take me back to Sofia's bosom, her orchard body, sea-blue eyes and sunny soul?

Hence this appeal, this incantation, which I must make and not tire from making! Let it be as a preamble, a refrain, to a song I may not have the skill to compose or the throat to sing, an invitation to a dance I may not have the head to steer or the feet to sustain!

So I appeal to the prophecy which has promised me the power to 'summon' and the power to 'bind' - though at a cost.

I appeal to the Saint of the *Confessions*, that master tamer of the 'bitterness of remembrance' and all 'multiplicities of things'. I appeal to him to help me with my remembrances and entanglements.

But lo! it is the Venus of the prophecy who seems to appear! A goddess whose charity I do not deserve having betrayed one of her kind!

And yet to be called to the heaven of her face be it for a liquefying glimpse is a dissolution to be coveted.

But this is not Venus! Nor is it Silvia, and certainly not Sofia, whom I see! It is Houjeira who rises, summoned and summoning, and, for the moment, possessing all!

A maiden, lean and lithe! A doe and a panther! A stately mast of golden honey! Breasts a pair of collared doves about to take wing and confound the air!

She leads me by a domestic but alluring hand to her enclosure in the house, a house ominously empty.

Where is everyone else? Gone on an outing to the pond of *Asjad*!

But I'm supposed to be trudging to my uncle's hermitage. Waiting for me there are my daily rations of Greek and Latin and a mix of the seven arts, flavoured with the gentle herbs of Yesu, the stirring *memres* of Ephrem and the scorching spices of John Chrysostom.

However, my father had insisted I stay this time in the care of Houjeira and wait for further instructions. What is he up to?

Behind a curtain of Damascene cloth, Houjeira sinks onto her honeyed haunches and stretches on her back pulling me on top of her body, warm, cool, and pillow-soft. The scent of wild lavender dizzies the late afternoon.

But then Emru wakes me up.

AN ARMY ON THE MOVE

How does an army move?

It strides, it prances, it lurches, it slouches. Its belly scrapes the rasping sand. Its gob drools over imagined loot, fancied honour and vain glory. Its rump fills the desert's ripples and drifts with streaks and piles of shit. When it halts, it dishes out its cooking pots and carving knives, throws up a pall of smoke and bawdy tall talk, masking for a moment the stink of its sweat, the reek of its droppings, the villainy and innocence and doom of its men. When it dozes, it rolls out a carpet of soggy dreams and foul wind. When it wakes, when it wakes... I hate armies.

But what if ours is different?

Compared to the legions of Alexander, Darius, or Crassus in the histories of Xenophon and Plutarch I read in Bayroute, Emru's army was small in size. But it was meant to be a lightning strike-force. The Asads were most probably expecting a larger army, lumbering and loud.

So we proceeded, six hundred and fifty men, with their horses whinnying and snorting, and three hundred camels, roaring and snarling and gurgling. The latter, of the prized ruddy breed of *hurrahs*, are the chief means of transport in the region, a mainstay and a mainsail across the oceanic desert.

For despite its raucous sound (to the unlettered in camel-speak) and ill-temper (to the ill-informed about camel-etiquette), the camel is most wondrous and generous to an Arab. Not only does it give him and his household its back to ride and cart upon; it also gives many other things, both in life and death-milk, butter, meat, a shield against sandstorms, a shade against the sun, a snook at the dunes, a step nearer to the stars, a marvel, a type of 'long-necked, long-legged beauty' unlike any other; skin, hair, and bone to redo into a thousand things...

The horses, more romantic icons of 'good looks' but the chief fodder for the war-dragon, are used for close combat, the beautiful mares often reserved for the dubious honour. But the *hurrahs*, who more often than not are *daluls*, as unerring as homing pigeons, also have a good foot for mountain passes which even a *tahr* cannot rival. Some of the camels, invariably bulls, also carried our water as well as armour, tents, and cooking utensils. A retinue of some fifty servants and attendants also came along – to serve our last meal and cheer our death?

HOUJEIRA STRETCHING

The Great Bear, all the length of him from *Dubhe* to *Alkaid*, is low but resplendent in the pre-dawn sky.

I ride, with my unfinished sleep behind Emru, holding sullenly to the back horn of his saddle. I feel cheated out of a good dream, a memory, bitter-sweet but real nonetheless. Rocking to and fro in the starlight, I try to entice the experience back, embarrassing as it is.

Houjeira, in the first bloom of her youth, eases away in one fluid movement her saffron-yellow cotton skirt, her only article of clothing. Slaves are spared the inconvenience of having to cover their upper bodies. Houjeira, like all our domestics, has been given her freedom by my parents, both intolerant of slavery. But, proud of the two winged beauties on her chest, she has been availing herself of a slave's license, disdaining the rudeness of a hunter's net.

She lifts my own boy's robe to my waist before she eases me onto her satin belly. She then takes my small face between her strong hands and draws me close to her plump jasper lips. Her large jet eyes bore into my eyes, daring the little *efreets* inside them. And with her tongue pushed between my unyielding lips, she anchors me further to her.

Where did she acquire all that art?

She then moves her hands down my belly like a sand viper gliding towards a petrified gerbil.

We ride, Emru and I, under the shimmering constellations. For a week now Najd has been battered by a fierce heat wave unbroken by the nightly setting of the sun. Emru turns aside to reveal we are heading for Dar Jouljoul.

Ah, Dar Jouljoul! That fabled palm orchard (a quarter of a *farsakh* to the east) owned by one of Emru's uncles, the ill-tempered Mu'awiya. The trees are famous for their extraordinary height, their dates for their exceeding sweetness.

'We're going flamingo-watching. The highborn birds are flying inland this summer. The coast sizzling is too barbarous for them. We're in the luck. We'll have the chance to see them dip perhaps doff some of their feathers into the gentle water of my rough uncle. I've been looking out for them.'

But I'm reclaimed by my memory.

Houjeira, on that lavender-crazed afternoon, drapes my boy's body with the glow of her freshness.

However, another memory, a dark, harsh, image of some two years before, cuts in. It trips the rush of my fuzzy, unripe lust, scattering it like a wolf laying into a flock of sheep or a fox thrashing about in a hencoop: My small head seized by the hands of a giantess, a seamstress about the house - the house also empty of my mother - my ears muffled by sagging elephantine flesh - my face needled by, choking against, a thicket of some reeking vegetation, a wound? oozing with blood? puss? inducing vomit! A memory repelling, crippling.

But the enterprising Eritrean is already too committed to back away. She gets hold of my hips and positions my limpness on top of her own hardness. She begins to move my smaller body back and forth, her scimitar-like eyelashes shut and twitching, perhaps invoking fantasies of a more deserving lover. A minute later, she heaves a tremulous sigh and drowsily releases the night of her eyes. She smiles, pensively. Soon she is rising from under me to fix her skirt and pull my robe down with her toe. Then she wags a half-playful half-reproving finger at me, 'You have to be man enough before you go about seducing girls with that look in your eyes!'

Emru and I draw near to the orchard's wall.

Dawn, heralding the sun, has unrolled for his queen a streaming carpet borrowed from advance strands of her radiant hair. He is attended in his labours by a chorus of song-birds and a guild of frenzied cockerels behind the high mud wall that now faces us - an unusually high wall, a sign of the new meanness and mistrust among Arabia's men.

We come up against the wooden gate. Some seven or eight camels are tethered to the left of it. The tinkling of female laughter behind the gate eclipses every other songster.

The laughter takes me back to Houjeira's own.

For some months earlier I had indeed been taking a puerile fancy to the girl. I followed her around with vagrant looks, which women seem to notice even when their gaze is engaged elsewhere. All the while Houjeira was prancing about like a gazelle with her wide eyes, slight waist, playful haunches, tapering legs, aerial breasts. Menial domestic chores she performed I saw in my hazy infatuation as acts of peerless grace and mystery. The scorching sun of Arabia is ever in the business

34

of quickening the seeds of puberty within boys and girls. It is also adept in brutally chewing the adult leaves into an untimely decay.

More laughter behind the wall; but I continue to be seized by Houjeira.

The wild lavender of the afternoon surges within me. I walk back to her, shuffling my feet with a mix of gall and remorse. She sits outside the house, nearer to the purple of the lavender and perennial salvia, humming an incandescent tune. Her statuesque legs are apart as she milks a she-goat. I stand before her unable to articulate my litany of blame and supplication. Without a word, Houjeira jumps up. She releases the udder of the she-goat she was milking, inadvertently knocking over a bowl of frothy milk into the earth. She rises to her full honey-golden height, her breasts leaping to the fuchsia-tinged afternoon sky, her broad, beautiful, fierce eyes needing no *kanab* ash to grant them *kohl* nor a sun to make them blaze, She drags me, stumbling, behind her, and glides across the empty house back into her enclosure. But I must cease. I must not reveal my shame.

I must not!

I!

She rises, her collared doves heaving as if trapped under the hunter's net they had scorned. She spits out a volley of words, reinforced by a kick from a honey-hued toe.

Ah, that kick! I shudder with the rage of it.

The shudder grows with the rage, summoning.

It summons the green expanses in Houjeira's soul, spaces from which her parents had been plucked, spaces grafted into the marrow of their dreams and etched onto the rack of their days' nightmares.

I see and I become part of the skin, s-t-r-e-t-c-h-i-n-g, pulled about by its robbers and ravishers.

Flayed across vast distances, the skin o-o-z-e-s. It drips clots and oases, archipelagos and whirlpools, scar tissues and sagas. It drips them over wastelands and seas, citadels and prayer rugs, daubing, nourishing, and enraging them with vintage sentient blood. Whole geographies and histories rise and holler in their manacles. And then, shattering their walls and centuries, they come together - with their own map-melting fury and fearlessness. They come together to mock and nudge their ravishers' skin, which retreats and cowers inside its terror, its presumption of mastery and mission sinking into the quicksand of its own lie. They glide across it, dancing and singing.

35

GOOD AND BAD KINGS, INVADERS, INSURGENTS, AND A PACIFIST GOD

Of kings and men and gods and doings that came to pass before the army moved I must now speak.

A GOOD KING

Old Marthad Al-Kheir was the goodly King of Hadramot. His very name suggested the goodness that he personified. Rooted and towering in his charity and forbearance, he had a soft spot for Emru and his liberal verses and had invited him from his exile in the Hejaz wilderness to his eyrie in the blue mountains. He was a friend of Hojr's, the angry father who had cast out his degenerate son into the desert. But Marthad feared no retribution. He was unassailable in his mist-turbaned, boulder-fenced dominions. He did not even fear the legions of Abyssinia marching along the lengths of the occupied coast and eying the heights with castrated greed.

Marthad was goodness overflowing; but he was not immune to the axe of death! He died suddenly - shortly before my father arrived with his news. Indomitable as he was, he may still have been whittled away in his last years by a procession of axes, and axe-wielders.

INVADERS

The Abyssinian Negus Kaleb was one of them.

A score years earlier he had led troops to invade Yemen blessed in his crusade by the emperor of Rome and her Bishop. The Hemyar King Zu Nuwas had converted to the faith of Abraham, and in his zeal to spread his belief had conducted a massacre of Christian rebels in Najran. He was offered to give up his faith in exchange for suzerainty under Rome. He refused and elected to stand and fight. Faced with defeat, he chose the sea as a nobler sepulchre. A local sheikh, Semyafa Ashwa, who agreed to convert to the creed of the invaders, was appointed as a king on a foreign leash.

Trade had suffered by the disruption of sea routes with Persia. Under their kings, Hemyar had long traded with the Persians to the mutual benefit of both.

Marthad's heart may have cracked under the strain. Was it Emru's 'curse' that had invited the final axe?

The old king had died childless. His successor, Carmal Ben Al-Hameem, was a dour, cheerless man. In no time he asked Emru and his *sa'luks* to move from the palatial fortress of *Menah*, assigned to us by Marthad, to the out-of-the-way and derelict fort of *Al-Ahqaf*.

He did not seem too keen after that to bridge the chasm between him and his precursor's guest. Some unhelpful reports about Emru and his cronies may have reached him. In fairness, though, he may have been too busy trying to get his beleaguered kingdom back on its feet, weighing the options of a treaty with the Abyssinian forces in the south, who, when their steel was frustrated by Hemyar's cliffs and darts, chose to creep up with smooth-talking Ambassadors offering gifts and trade deals.

INSURGENTS

Whatever his reason for the earlier disdain, Carmal later showed remarkable tolerance. He put Emru's case to his people. Five hundred of them volunteered to travel with the king to help him avenge the murder of his father. An old Hemyar merchant, Eliakem, also opened his coffers to these men, bolstered by Emru's band of *sa'luks*. These had joined without hesitation or petition. Their readiness for indolence as for exertion was one and the same, their love for Emru and his cause supreme. Their leader - Al-Ward Ben Zayd - had long before conveyed his philosophy and theirs in the lines:

We are but one body under the sun.
We move to breathe as one or die as one.

As free, as gay, as life we move - one breath,
Unbound, untamed, unbent, even in death.

My father, a descendant of the noble Ofair Ben Adi through his great grandmother Kabsha Bent Okba, and close to the Kenda royals by virtue of his office and friendship with Hojr, had nonetheless long harboured deep sympathy for the *sa'luks*.

These were young people, some coming from rich families, who scorned the growing pretensions of their various tribes. The new airs, which had wafted from Persia and Rome into the tents of the Arabian chiefs, they saw as a betrayal of the freer and fairer ways of the Arabs.

Al-Ward himself was an exile from the wrath of his own father, a sheikh of the tribe of Abs. He had been sent as a youngster to Mecca to be trained by the *Homs*, austere guides of the pilgrims who flock to that city. But he was confronted by their own hypocrisies and lust for wealth and power as they began to form a pact with the Koreysh, self-appointed 'custodians of the holy places'. He railed in his poems against the corruption of kings and priests, maintaining that a true Arab was a child of the infinite spaces and a votary of none save the will to remain free - free, even within the fraternity of the *sa'luks*, though not from endless sympathies.

Such sympathies had already been gently dinned into me by my father, the secret of his own loyalties and discontents not always clear to my mind. But sympathies and vexations were intertwined with my family's tradition. My dear mother, adept in loss and exile from her early childhood, had found some comfort in cuddling her own restlessness, itself nourished by the restlessness of her rebel priest of an uncle. *He* had had to flee his beloved Lebanon with his orphaned niece to escape the persecution of a church against whose duplicity he had roused a section of the populace. But as he persisted in his zeal to change the world, my mother pursued her quarrel with that world by taking a flight, worthy of the Platonic Origen, beyond its confines. Her surrender of my daily schooling to Ephraim implanted yet another wing for freedom in my soul. But it was a wing doomed to dash against the bars of an ambivalent cage.

My father had also advised Emru to travel in quest of help from the Taghlebs, their lands lying in Al-Anbar on the western banks of the river Euphrates. Emru's mother, who died when Emru was a boy of three, came from that grand tribe. His sister, Hend, acting on my father's advice, had already taken refuge there with many of Kenda's womenfolk. The Taghlebs were Christian of the Nestorian brand, persecuted by Rome and protected by Persia. Still, they were secretly unhappy with Persia's deputy in Iraq, the pitiless Al-Munzer, who for years had been pursuing a vendetta against their tribe and Kenda.

As he later reflected on the great distance to the land of the Taghlebs and the dangers to which we would be exposed, my father changed his mind. He advised Emru to send a letter instead. No word had come from Emru's uncles. Rumours suggested that Sheikh Kubeysa had visited them one after the other.

I was able to talk my father into staying at *Al-Ahqaf*. This he needed to do, I pleaded. He needed to nurse his failing health, made worse by his grief at the news of my mother's death which I had conveyed to him the night he arrived there. He was also needed to watch over Kenda's five heirloom shields. First amongst those was the shield carried by Ishmael, Abraham's other son, who had helped the Patriarch build the sacred Cube in Mecca. My father was also needed, Emru himself argued, to help protect Kenda's womenfolk, who had recently arrived from Al-Anbar. They had arrived without Hend, who was lost on the way.

ANOTHER GOOD KING

Emru's aunt, Mariam, had chosen to stay with her cousin, Hend Bent Amr, mother of the Taghleb King. But she, together with the other Kenda women who had opted to remain there, sent with Hend all their jewellery. They wished to help the refugees in Hadramot.

As luck or rather luck's opposite would have it, the King of the Taghlebs, Amr Ben Al-Mundher, died a few days after receiving the letter from Emru.

He had gone out to hunt wild deer in the early morning and was fatally wounded by an arrow shot by a young son of his. The lad, one called Ghaleb, was taking part in the hunt for the first time, his eyelids still courted by sleep.

The late king, chivalrous by nature and much moved by the plight of his nephew, had made preparations to send Emru a contingent of two thousand horsemen. He would also dispatch an envoy to the young

Persian king at Ktesephon arguing that Emru was a worthier ally than the perfidious Asads.

A RELUCTANT KING

Amr's eldest son, Yazd, had now succeeded his father. Yet another 'succession'! The young king harboured his own jealousies towards Emru. These were made worse by gossip going about in the Nestorian tribe that the advent of Emru's letter, and earlier his sister, had somehow brought about the death of the king.

Emru, the slanderers whispered, was a man with a jinx and a pagan at heart.

Yazd went through the motions of trying to raise the troops promised by his father. His formidable mother was at his back, making sure he fulfilled his father's pledge. But he pestered her with his need for fighting men to deter any aggressive intents by Al-Munzer. He claimed that news had reached him that Persia's agent in Iraq was planning a punitive expedition against the Taghlebs on account of the late king's sympathies with the cause of his nephew. Al-Munzer's spies, everyone 'knew', he said, were atop every palm tree and in every adder's hole. Yazd vowed to send the two thousand men promised by his father when the threat had passed. In the end and as a gesture (half-hearted but calculated) to his mother, Yazd sent a hundred horsemen with Hend and the other women who chose to leave for Hadramot. Interestingly, seven Kenda beauties, 'the Flamingos of Jouljoul', all opted to stay in Al-Anbar.

I mention them today as I may not have a chance to mention them tomorrow - Oneyza, Salma, Hafsa, Horeytha, Rabab, Nawar, Khawla, and Buthayna.

A PACIFIST GOD

In the meantime, my father had summoned up the guile to urge Emru to consult the god *Zul Khalasa* of Tabalah.

The town was on our way to the Assad pastures in western Najd. Emru hoped to reach them in two months. Tabalah could also be reached sooner if we were to take a perilous shortcut through the vast desert known as Al-Rub' al-Khali, the Empty Quarter.

Zul Khalasa was famous throughout Arabia for the accuracy of his divination, inclined to peace and reconciliation than otherwise. His oracle was delivered by means of three arrow shafts and the slender throats of his comely priestesses.

My father must have concluded that the odds against Emru were great. The odds were greater now that the Taghlebs and Emru's uncles had no stomach for a fight with the Asads, particularly as the Asads were presently in an open pact with Al-Munzer. Riders across the desert carried reports that the Iraqi chief had played a role in the killing of Hojr. This, the reports suggested, had been achieved through a militant faction among the Asads, one spearheaded by Ghitrif, Elba's brother. It was Ghitrif who led the attack against the tax collectors and was the throat of the slander against Hojr. The slander was so terrible that Emru, who was central to the slander, was never told what it was. He did not seem to care to know.

In any event, though Ghitrif himself had been slain and his brother Elba had disappeared after his deed, their faction survived. It had now won over the ripe wisdom of elders like Kubeysa. The vintage wine of the old sheikh seemed to be pouring into the ascendant cups of the hotheads.

So my father hoped, I suppose, that *Zul Khalasa* would dampen Emru's impetuousness. He knew Emru enough to realise he did not care a shrivelled fig for the gods. But he may still have reasoned that a public oracle, if it advised against vengeance, could weaken the avenger's resolve. It could also sap the support that might be given to him by others, thus knocking the wind out of his sails. Otherwise, if the oracle was in favour of action, it might give Emru and his people's army the authority they needed. In all this, my father must have taken my interest and personal safety into his calculations.

For the success of the scheme, Emru had to agree to the idea of consulting the god.

My father may have hoped that his own closeness to the murdered king and mine to Emru might influence the new king's decision. He may have also hoped that the famed glamour of *Zul Khalasa*'s priestesses might tip the scales. However, Emru had taken an added vow - not to lust after a woman or knock at her portals until he had avenged his father.

41

An alien presence, one alien even to the desert Jinn, had by now taken possession of his body.

After bidding farewell to my father, we paid a courtesy visit to Carmal in his splendid fort. We also paid a sincerer visit to Marthad's graveside and to the gracious Eliakem in his palace. Then we started the descent from the blue mountains.

THE FLAMINGOS OF
DAR JOULJOUL

'Hey, dreamer!'

Emru's voice pulls me back into the pale threads of pre-dawn.

I hold tightly onto his waist, my grip on the horn of the saddle becoming too tenuous.

But he suddenly stands up in the saddle. I almost keel over.

He has manoeuvred the camel next to the gate, which is lower than the perversely high mud wall.

He strains to scout the scene over and beyond the jagged barrier. 'These accursed trees! We're going inside!' he grunts.

He deftly turns the head of his mount to the right and drives it along the wall to a cluster of tethered camels, eight in number, their jaws rollicking, chewing some fodder. He jumps to the ground, and, with a rope wound round the front horn of the saddle he ties the beast's front legs. Then he climbs back onto the saddle bidding me follow him over the wall.

He drops inside the garden, landing comfortably on the soft earth.

I follow, leaving my heart suspended two *qamat* above my head and spraining my left ankle.

A minute later, I trail, with a limp, behind Emru's crouching figure, slithering through the columns of trees.

Dawn has by now done his work, sweeping the prickly stars out of his mistress's path. Even the planet Venus, who maintained a solitary reign for some time after all the other stars had been broomed away, now makes a dignified exit. Dawn himself waits to be made redundant by the blaze of his queen.

Emru zigzags fox-fashion between the fat tree trunks. The giant palms rise to a height of more than thirty yards, each with a canopy of fronds a dozen yards wide, each tree sporting a dozen bunches of a thousand dates. But also rising is the heady smell of a well-watered soil, irrigated by the ancient system of *aflaj* which harnesses and regulates subterranean rivers and rainwater. Customary laws ensure a

43

fair distribution of water among the local farmers, the sun clock and the stars used to measure the time due to each farmer. But the brothers of Hojr have been lately siphoning off more than their share, inflaming the spirits of the dead and the rancour of the living.

Then, from a clearing at the centre of the orchard, the shimmer of the lake assaults our eyes. And the nakedness of the maidens.

Ringed by a low and uneven fence of dwarf palms, the lake (more of a lakelet or a sizeable pond) gleams like burnished glass. It gleams with the rising glow from the east, perhaps also with memories of the starlight, the blaze of our eyes contributing!

But why look for other sources of light with the naked maidens aglitter in the water?

'Here are our flamingos, landed nearer to home and ahead of season! Blessed heat wave!' Emru whispers.

I turn to look at him in the growing brilliance, his vast eyes smouldering, lust crawling on his face, darkening and igniting it.

Suddenly, the gravity of what we are doing descends on me. It tumbles down onto my consciousness like a camel settling upon a clump of wormwood. I mumble some words of caution; but Emru knits his brow and raises a finger to his lips.

Behind the trunk of a massive palm, I pull at the sleeve of Emru's *aba*. My heart pounds like a hunted rabbit's. Emru pulls away without turning to look at me, his gaze a hostage to the scene on the lake.

Eight of Kenda's loveliest maidens are gaily playing in the water, the light of their unrobed flesh an envy to every other light.

Emru edges forward. I follow, half stumbling, in his hungry trail, my soul increasingly crippled from sharing in his wolfish frenzy. The teachings of my uncle drum in my ears. The admonitions of my mother claw at my heart. The fear of a scandal chokes the tingling thoughts the memory of Houjeira and the sight of the maidens had kindled.

Emru devours the distance between him and the edge of the lake. I freeze, sweating at the side of another tree trunk, my legs unable to move, my hands powerless to restrain Emru from his insane lunge.

Soon he is crouching behind a clutter of dwarf palms on which the maidens have hung their frocks. Their female musk hangs in the air overpowering the tangled perfumes of the orchard.

For a fugitive instant, I watch them, bathing water nymphs, bobbing in and out of the lucent water, their youthful breasts bouncing up and down and their long black braids loosened but dense with wetness, scattering silver spray as they twist and turn.

I recognise at a glance almost all the maidens. But I dwell, furtively, on the form of Salma. She is a friend of Hend's, Emru's younger sister, and outmatches the rest with the size of her bosom and the heartiness of her chuckles.

Hend is not here, but Oneyza is. She is Emru's proud cousin and authoress of his recent torment as he has been claiming. I avert my eyes from the sight of her virginal bosom in consideration for Emru. He turns to look at me with a grin. 'That Salma! I should ask Hend to introduce me to her, properly.' I feel my face burning, a sense of shame washing over my fear and arousal.

And then, suddenly, I feel at peace. The proverbial camel of guilt rises from the proverbial clump of wormwood. A breath trapped inside my chest breaks free. I see myself settling down to another dream, a free dawn peep at the illicit charms of some of the fairest and most arrogant maidens of Kenda's *despotes*. So I might as well enjoy it and take my own illicit revenge.

Suddenly Emru too rises, less proverbially, from his cover behind the dwarf palms. He strides with a swagger towards the edge of the lake, prompting a rooster and his hens to scatter, flapping their useless wings and cackling most shrilly, and the illicit dream to flail inside my head and the sky to drop on top of it.

The giggles stop abruptly. Even the hens scurry away with dumb beaks.

A moment (an eternity?) of stillness follows.

The universe holds its breath.

Then the shrieks begin.

Then they stop.

The maidens have all vanished under the water.

MARCHING BY SHEBA AND THE PROPHETS

We left the cultivated terraces and lumbered down the mountain passes trusting in the surefootedness of the *hurrahs* and the skill of their master drivers. Cascading streams tinkled by us as we began our descent. Herons and kingfishers flew above our heads. Those perched on the glistening rocks gazed menacingly at us, but more intently at pools sparkling with iridescent sunlight and the backs of unsuspecting fish.

But it was the menace of human eyes that we feared.

As we descended, vineyards and plantations became scarcer and scarcer, their place taken over by the wild *sumr* trees and *senna* bushes, and by clumps of the coarse *khuweira* and *dhoweila* and *harmal* plants. Prudently, our camels and horses avoided the last shrub, its leaves and seeds lethal to them. In the *wadis*, however, the *rakh* plant was everywhere, and offered itself to the appetite of our camels and horses. But it left a sickly stench on their breath and a revolting reek in their droppings.

We did not take the trade route through the towns of Hawra, Hurayda and Shabwa, leading to Ma'rib. In that last town, now in Abyssinian hands, our great grandmother Belqis had her seat of power. It is said that Menelik, the son she had with Solomon, is buried there with the Arc of the Covenant.

No, we did not take that route. It would have led us to Sa'da and then Najran. There, in the latter, as I may have mentioned, Christians were put to the sword some score years ago, their churches and palm date groves torched, providing an excuse for the invasion. The Abyssinians may have had the added temptation to get closer to the Arc. Carrying it off to Aksum, their kingdom in Abyssinia, would seal for all time their link to Menelik.

So far this has been denied them.

We were denied the road.

We proceeded in a north-westerly direction, careful to avoid human settlements. But the danger of discovery was everywhere. A single rider or goatherd could unwittingly betray us. So we skirted a string of towns and hamlets, at times binding the mouths of our tolerant *hurrahs* with leather straps. The towns which we avoided included Shibam, Seiyur, Aidid, Atfah, Qubhudh, Hanin, Sur, and Thukmin.

The tomb of the prophet Saleh was on our right as we moved through the passes; but we avoided it as well. The few remnants of his tribe, the Thamoud, still visit the site, declaring their belated belief in the prophet's power. Their forefathers had perished for slaughtering the wondrous she-camel sent to them as a proof of Saleh's mission. Their once prosperous town lay farther to the east, buried under the dunes that had rushed like fabulous giants to inter the doubters.

I had visited the prophet's tomb before - shortly after my arrival with Emru and his band of *sa'luks* at *Al-Ahqaf*. Al-Ward had graciously accompanied me.

The two of us had climbed to the tomb, which perches on a hillside, and I intoned a prayer for the prophet. But Al-Ward, who does not believe in God-sent prophets, deeming each man a prophet and each woman a prophetess, if not a god and a goddess, said I was wasting my breath. The body of the prophet was not there, but in Sinai, the story itself having had its origins in the town of Al-Hijr near Tabouk. He whispered this information to me. The whispering he did out of regard for the feelings of the tomb's keeper. The old man had insisted that the prophet could be seen on some nights giving water from the nearby fountain to his giant she-camel. The beast could also be heard grunting eerily in the night, he insisted. He also claimed as he stood by a clay Hemyarite inscription shaped like a flower and placed at the head of the tomb, that the prophet, himself a giant judging by the size of his grave, was powerful enough to reclaim any object taken from his tomb. I instantly saw a gleam in the eyes of Al-Ward. A *sa'luk* is one to rush into the lap of every temptation and the fists of every challenge. So, no sooner had the keeper turned round to point in the direction of the attendant village of Khonab that Al-Ward palmed a small seashell placed on the tomb. For half a breath he seemed about to separate it from a leather pouch tied to it with a string. He paused and winked at me, as if to assure me that this was only a prank and not a test of the prophet's mystic powers. The pouch, I assumed, contained a petition to the prophet by some frantic or jilted lover. But then and before the keeper turned to face us, his finger which had been pointing at the other village in the distance shaking with age, Al-Ward had replaced the seashell with its comet's tail back on the tomb. Later he told me, 'I could not find it in my heart to cut in on a petition from a desperate man or woman, bet it addressed to Oblivion, which may yet answer - who knows?'

Further to the east in Wadi Maseila lies the shrine of the prophet Houd, believed to be Saleh's father. I had visited that shrine too, also with the sceptical but obliging and good-natured Al-Ward. The shrine lay high on the side of a gully and we climbed the rough slope up to it. But I was rewarded by the scene that met us. For there was the famous cleft in the side of the mountain into which the prophet is said to have disappeared. A huge boulder there is believed to be his she-camel, the one he had ridden for years. Pursued by an Adite mob intent on killing him, he tied the camel to a shrub, and stood before the side of the mountain and said, 'Open by the permission of Allah.' The prophet had long berated his tribe for their cruel and evil ways. Now he paused before an opening that miraculously appeared in the mountainside. He looked back to invite his camel to follow him; but she dithered, and held her ground. Behind them the mob unleashed their arrows; but before they touched the rump of the camel, she had turned to stone. Houd disappeared into the mountainside.

May the mountain passes open their gates to us, but not close upon us, nor offer us the gift of turning to stone, I silently prayed.

And there we were, driving away from the failed prophets and their victims glad to feel the vibrant warmth of the *hurrahs* under us. We were not too happy, though, to skirt the beautiful Wadi Hadramot. This is the valley which receives the rivers from the heights and turns them into the golden dough for the date palm groves and wheat fields of the region. This time round Emru would not watch from the cliffs the comely women of the *wadi* working among the vegetation under their high straw hats, their skirts rolled up to their waists. This time round he would not feast his eyes on their nether charms, nor hear them across the distance singing songs to the deathless gods of the soil and the rain. But, not far from the *wadi*, birds and pigeons flew about, and we could still see the occasional heron lapping up its lunch from a stream and the enterprising goat perched on top of a bush browsing on its upper branches.

Then we left all this behind us to canter through the desert of Raydat Al-Sayyar. The vastness of that desert was not too overpowering. The stings of its sandstorms not too cutting. The groans of its buried cities not too loud.

This was because we were soon to plunge into the greatest desert of them all. Eleven days later we paused in reverence and awe before its first spectral dunes.

THE FLAMINGOS UNDRESSED
AND TRIUMPHANT

O Saint of the *Confessions*, unto whose eyes the wiles of my fettered soul are bared, help my words break free, but do not look or listen further!

An old woman emerges from a shed not far from the water's edge. Squinting through her ancient eyelids, she sees us. Frail and stooping as she is, she raises a scream shriller than the shrieks of the maidens combined. For a moment I wonder how a slight frame like hers can unleash such an ear-splitting bolt.

Her scream, which has elicited cackles of terror from the hens scuttling between the trees, sinks into her wasted lips when she comes up against the towering figure of the intruder and recognises who he is.

The bathers' faces now pop out of the water, one after the other, mouths gasping for air.

'My compliments on your high notes, Om Mahbouba, dearest of nannies! How I miss your lullabies and fables! More precious than all the pompous verses and sagas of Arabia! But I promise you, soar as they may, your notes will not reach the ears of the girls' fathers. The brutes are snoring away in yonder town, raising in their dreams what they could not raise for real. But you don't want them to hear your sweet racket, do you? And you don't want someone passing by to hear it either? I assure you, beloved nanny, you'll have no better sentinel of your fair wards than that gallant youth stroking his fine scimitar behind that palm tree. Nor of course ME!'

'My *e-m-i-r!*' the crone chews on the raider's title. But, with one last ember inside her, she casts scorching glances at me as I emerge from behind my cover.

Never before has Emru showed me up in the presence of others or alone.

I realise he is carried away, and I feign boldness in playing the role assigned to me. My appearance is greeted with gasps of double outrage from the maidens, covered to their necks by the darkly shimmering water.

50

Emru ignores the old woman. Nonchalantly, swaying his shoulders, he begins to gather upon his arm the bathers' frocks left on the fronds of the dwarf palms. He then strolls to the edge of the water and addresses his female audience:

'Be not alarmed, my beauties! We mean no harm. We have been drawn to your light as moths are to a shining lamp. It is we who will be scorched. *Your* flame will live to singe scores of poor, besotted moths like us! So do allow us, half blinded by your night-scattering blaze, to flutter around your fire for an instant in time. But, if you wish us to be utterly consumed, irretrievably charred, come out of the water before the town awakens. Come out, and claim your scented robes, treading upon our ashes!'

Some of the maidens seem impressed. They giggle without reserve. Others pour more scorn on us three, the old woman included for her shameful toadying.

We wait under the gathering light as the sun climbs behind high hills in the distance, my eyes burning, my legs wobbling.

Then capitulation to the inevitable begins.

Cheeky Salma is the first to start rising to her feet, unfolding from her crouch like a lotus flower.

Liberal breasts float on the surface of the water.

They emerge more fully as their proud owner stands up and glides towards the bank, unbothered with Christian prudery, Salma not being a follower of the Nazarene as some of the other maidens are.

Her bare buxom body drips ululating pearls in her glide towards the soggy bank.

Once there, she strolls leisurely, shaking off the wet soil from her plumb feet.

Clusters of fond, desperate droplets hang on to her heaving bosom, nipples stiff and unabashed.

She snatches a rue-yellow frock from Emru's hands and veers sideways with a ringing, defiant laugh.

Thereafter she makes a show of sliding her frock down the swells and curves of her luscious body.

Soon the rest follow:Hafsa, Horeytha, Rabab, Nawar, Khawla, Buthayna.

As they amble to their garments they treat Emru's bold gaze (and my furtive one) to a dazzling array of feminine splendour otherwise concealed by coyness or conceit or claims of exclusive possession by a parent or a god.

51

One maiden remains behind, water-draped to her neck - gloriously rebellious.

'It Is Your Turn, Now, Oneyza,' Emru, like a pompous actor, calls out, modulating his great voice.

'Now is your turn, Oneyza! Now is the time for thee to send forth the all-annihilating, all-liberating flame! Now is the time for thee, slaver and liberator, to toss our ashes to the four winds! To toss them so that they may travel over the lands and the seas whispering to plodding aaravans and home-parched mariners about the superlative beauty of the daughters of Kenda!'

'I see no merry ashes where you and your scarecrow of a buddy stand. Only sad irons on heat! Irons fit to make footwear for old mules! Go and take your miserable lackey away, and take back whatever shreds remain of your honour and civility, if you ever had them. No need have I or my Kenda sisters for our names to be mentioned to the vulgar who reek of the sweat of the roads or the salt of the sea. Such men can only wait at our doors to sell us slippers and anklets, never daring to dream of touching our toes!' Oneyza replies in a sweet but rage-ruffled voice from her watery tower.

'Lo, my gentle lantern has turned into a fire-mountain! Still, lash on, light of my life! You can only confirm my wish, my desire, to be incinerated in that dear little furry furnace of yours setting this lake alight!'

There is universal merriment from the maidens standing in their colourful frocks on the bank. But Oneyza, who has moved, squatting in the water, closer to the shallower part of the lake, stretches out her gazelle-neck and retorts, 'The kiln you speak of is reserved for precious metals, not for base ones which have been filed away to a wick in the whorehouses of Yathreb and Tabouk!'

Emru, thrown back on the defensive, summons up all his rake's cunning in one last toss. 'Pure gold, which is my substance, needs no further promotion. Yet it will gladly enter a holy fire, therein to be moulded to the shape of an earring, An earring hugging one of your little earlobes. Or let it be a locket, one to snuggle between your little breasts!'

'Little breasts indeed!' Oneyza suddenly stands up in the low water, the water cascading down her shoulders sighing and splashing.

She jerks her head to the side to fling strands of her long black hair, clustered over her chest, thus uncovering her firm upright breasts.

These immediately become the centre of attention of everyone on the bank as if to gauge the truth of the offending remark.

By her action, Oneyza is able to capture and hold all eyes upon that part of her anatomy while she glides swiftly, a water nymph, to the bank. There she snatches the last robe from Emru's defenceless hand and disappears behind the palm fence.

Just at that moment, the disk of the rising sun breaks free from the distant hills to the east and begins its unfettered flight in a sky of unblemished blue.

But whoever has summoned the scene whispers to me of yet more triumphs for savvy women over lascivious men and of greater humiliation looming for the latter.

PLUNGING INTO THE GREAT EMPTINESS

I bowed in awe and homage to the first dunes of the Empty Quarter.

They seemed like giant Jinn elders sitting in council to decide the fate of our breaths and sanity.

Then they seemed like enormous breasts jutting into the sky, their proud lift vibrating with the exuberance of the wind, their drabness with the boredom of the ageless earth.

Later, I was to know that the drabness was only a speck in my eyes.

Not only were the dunes of the Great Desert so varied in their sizes and shapes and the textures of their sand, but, endlessly whisked by the wind, they revealed, as if under a lover's caresses, other tones and shades - gold and silver, purple and red, orange and oryx-white, in bold and subtle variations.

And on their slopes and crests and precipices and in their dips and hollows bloomed bushes and plants in infinite shades of green and yellow and white and lilac. We were fortunate that the rain had fallen a few weeks earlier. One shower can sustain these plants for years, Al-Ward told me. Just one shower! So enduring is the memory of joy and charity shared, the memory of love! The roots and leaves of these tender plants, even as they sleep, even as they shrivel out of sight, continue to dream for years of that downpour of a day. In the baking sun or in the folds of the dunes, their little hearts continue to beat, however faintly, nourished by that one sparkling memory - sustained by hope for another.

Forbidding they seemed to be from a distance, those colossal sand mountains. But they offered with the green islets and clumps on their slopes a haven and a granary to a host of small animals and birds and butterflies. Their capacity to bar the progress of men and heap sheets of sand over their lips and ambitions, however, remained implacable.

But not when a man like Al-Ward stares them into compliance and charms them into coition.

Like a seasoned lover, he, unabashed, wooed their harshness, inclined to their aloofness, and stroked, like a master lutist, the cords of their memories.

As he did so, he gazed into their secret sorrows, forgave, laughing, their ancient sins, and rode the surf of their lusts.

They, trusting to him and crumbling to his gaze, bared their long-veiled frailties and lifted the skirts to their hard-to-get portals.

But he was not a faithful lover to them; for he had pledged himself to a more urgent tryst.

He had pledged himself to Emru, Emru the *sa'luk* rather than the king.

He had pledged himself to the fraternity of the outcasts, to the quarry rather than the hunter, the hurt rather than the blade.

And he had pledged himself to the free and the exultant, vowing to restore Emru's sparkle and humanity, perhaps the sparkle and humanity of Arabia as well.

Silently, instinctively, he had vowed, as a migrating swallow or stork might ineffably vow, to lead us across the dune-ocean without stopping to dally with the mounds, though they were pouting to his gaze and melting to his touch.

To that end he had put heads together with his fellow *sa'luks*. Several of them came from Hadramot and had crossed the Empty Quarter from one point or another, losing comrades in the crossing. He himself, though a native of Najd, had traversed the Great Desert at the nearest point between Najran and Sa'da. He had at that time been fleeing a party of Abyssinian horsemen, and a fellow *sa'luk* from Yemen had acted as his guide. But the memory of a *sa'luk* is as vast as the great desert itself. It hovers over the colours and contours of life, recalling and cuddling them with the power of a true enchanter, a life's paramour. So, he had proposed that route to Emru, who readily approved.

Not long afterwards, the glare of Death soared to preside over the interminable distances.

But every time Death stared, Al-Ward and his men stared back.

When Death stared through the wildly rolling eyes of the bull camels, maddened by thirst and fatigue, the *sa'luks* knew when to unburden the beasts and where to loosen them to graze on the *abal* and *zahra* and *qassis* of the hollows and the slopes. And they knew how to coax into their thick-lipped mouths dregs of noxious water from buried wells when no other water was to be found. And they knew how to couch them and groom them, and how to wheedle them up yet another dicey slip-face and over yet another crumbling dune crest.

And as we rode on the flats between the rows of dunes, Death stared through the eye sockets of flayed skulls and plucked his eerie melodies on the ribs of bleached ribcages. Then, Al-Ward's voice rang out in celebration of man's tenacity and the courage and brotherhood of the five hundred warriors and their attendants and camels and horses. And his voice rang out in remembrance of his wife Zeinab and his son Orwa in faraway Najd. And his voice rang out in fraternity with Death as a brother, a twin, to Life, promising him a final consummation in the fullness of days.

And when *Algol*, the demon's eye, winked in blue and yellow to mock the vanity of men, Al-Ward told stories round the cooking fire of heroes laughing as they held up demons' heads for children to gaze upon them and learn to triumph over terror. And when false oases gleamed with liquid illusions in the distance, he sang of the dreams of men and women and how these dreams populated rough mountain terraces with infants and draped them with vineyards and with fig and almond and pomegranate trees.

All along, Emru chose to wear the muted side of the Great Desert upon his lips and her elusive blankness in his gaze. Stooping in the rocking saddle of his *hurrah*, he seemed to see and hear none but the spirit-bird of his slain father, beckoning to the pastures of blood beyond the horizon, seizing the thirst of his heart with its ghoulish refrain, '*Ousqouni! Ousqouni! Ousqouni!*'

A PHILOSOPHICAL DEBATE

What do the gods want with us, humans? Are they exacting revenge on us because we made them?

And the seeresses? Why don't they turn the other way when asked and allow us to go through our lives in blissful blindness? And what would a mere glimmer they dole out do against a legion of darkness?

But if we have made the gods, then our suffering at 'their' hands must be of our own making too!

But what of my own making?

Emru, carrying the name of a god, grows up to shed all thoughts of gods.

A whirlwind in the shape of a young man, he will not stop to explain or justify. Nor will he deliver or tolerate sermons. In the lessons my mother makes him attend at the Hermitage, he has no patience for my uncle, nor my uncle, sometimes, for him.

I yearn to share with his merry, runaway wisdom my thoughts and troubles.

He can summon words readily and exultantly. He sings as the deep sea might sing to itself, caring for no shore swooning for it or a ship swaying in its perpetual orgasm. Or as the nightingale sings, indifferent to the star-audience or to the dawn prowling behind the garden wall.

Tribe or war or glory is nothing to him. Neither the heritage of his Christian mother, whom he was not given time to know, nor his pagan father, who has no time for him, can woo or chasten his mind.

I contrive occasions to draw him into serious talk. We both have attended meetings in which Ambassadors and missionaries spoke to his father and Kenda's dignitaries. But Emru always seems impatient or has something else to do. He sometimes asks awkward questions. At other times he simply slips out on silent sandals.

In any case, engaging him in a conversation is like standing in the path of a stampede or a flash flood. Young and impetuous as he is, he sounds as wise as Solomon.

'But wasn't Solomon himself a young fellow who rose to his wisdom in his harem?'

So begins Emru as I coax him into a debate, he humouring my desperation. He does not mind me throwing my thorns and thistles across his path of lilies and myrtles.

'I'm yet to rise to my hundredth queen, nine hundred short of Solomon's thousand,' he continues. 'But wisdom isn't the object. Nor is pleasure as such. It's perhaps the sweet agony of being in the arms of the divine, as your uncle might phrase it, be it for an hour.'

'This god of our mothers, of your venerable uncle,' he persists, perhaps relishing the challenge, 'Didn't *he* choose to pitch his tent in the womb of a woman for nine months? What was he doing there? The Church in far-off Rome has worked out a few clever answers. But, if god he was, if god there is, I may suggest he was revisiting his first home, the womb that gave birth to all there is. Re-inhaling his primal element, he may have been bracing himself for a new birth, a new creation, in which he is both man and woman, the latter being the better. Hence a true Christian is one who, when he sees a beautiful woman, falls on his knees or rises to his feet in worship. He can worship with his words, his eyes, his hands, or his rod, or with all combined. In my *church*, a word I hate, an *infidel*, a word I despise, is one who turns away from beauty. His arrogance won't be forgiven. Indeed, he'll be worse off than your uncle's Satan, though what that amorous angel does in the yarn is no more than commit a crime of passion. In the process however he helps Jehovah's latest toy stand on its feet!'

Eager to keep him talking, I enquire as to whether people who are not beautiful have any role to play in his 'church'.

'Of course, like any other maker, baker, potter, basket weaver, ship builder, your uncle's god will create, let us say, objects that may not be so beautiful. These surely have a place and deserve his love and ours. But they're artefacts of his boredom, his rush, his heart not being in the job.'

'What if God is subtler than that? What if these were meant to make beauty seem dearer, more inviting, the night surrounding the moon?'

'A perfect assumption. You see, you're thinking like a poet, which is as important as thinking like a god, a creator-god. However, you can also argue that it was the night that created the moon to draw attention to night's own beauty. You can even argue further, for you love arguing, that beauty is like death. Both are vital for a true enjoyment of life. Both bring out life's flavour. Both are life's twins, condiments and aphrodisiacs to life's banquet!'

I am drawn to these images, fascinated by them, conjured up so artlessly. But most, I am cheered and emboldened by his comparing me, rather charitably, to a poet. So I enquire as to whether a poet's 'mission' should involve him in drawing our attention to the beauty invisible and the beauty within.

'You're being too 'philosophical'. Give me a *qabbadah* and keep your philosophy to yourself. And certainly your 'mission', though I'd rather have you share your bed with a *qabbadah* than a scroll, little brother.'

'This brings me to another point,' I rejoin, somewhat cheered by the breezy sash of affection he often throws on my shoulders. 'If we were to worship God through his beautiful creation should we not offer our devotion to one sole object, say, one woman, instead of many?'

'You're dragging me back into the bog of your philosophy, which is not my thing. But this is important, little brother. You see, men are a selfish lot. They love to own and keep. Though some women are similarly afflicted. They love hoarding. But they are better off whoring than hoarding. Hoarding is bad for both man and woman. It's the way of the miser. The coin stays in the sack. But if a skirt, or the fine velvety promise underneath it, can entice the coin out of the sack, then there's a good bargain. The contract of an hour is best. In it the two parties get more than their hour's worth. Anything beyond that is likely to turn into bondage laced with bitterness. For, after the fineries and perfumes of the bridal night a married woman sinks into the blood of childbirth and the smoke of the oven. In this state she can be saved by the love of a man other than her now grubby, flabby, jaded husband. Surely, she can come back to him after her new bridal hour is consummated, if she so wishes. But, since we live in free Arabia, she can always show her husband the non-door and pick her man from the scrum of scrotums at her door or on her bed. But an hour is best, though people are free to renew the contract. And yet a love recalled in sweet dreams, if you have time for them, is better than one chewed to a sour mush in reality. Love is best on the wing, on the branch, at the gallop!'

'I need to master the trot first,' I say, trying to be clever, but needled by anguish at my shortfall.

'You *will* do well, little brother. But a man needs to surrender to the surge of his charger - surrender to the wind, to beauty and Oblivion.'

And then he becomes irritated with my questions.

'I really don't know. Don't know anything. You're forcing me into saying dull and stupid things. Ask someone who knows. Put your questions to your uncle the great priest who never talks about his god's harlot-wife, your mum the holy abbess, your dad the wise counsellor. Put them at the doorstep of Time. *He* might answer them, when he chooses.'

I am in the grip of a contentious mood, so I quibble:

'Are you suggesting that Time dwells in a house and does not move?'

'Perhaps he does, perhaps he doesn't. And we do all the moving inside him. But I'm inclined to imagine that he does move. Everything else moves. Do you think your uncle's god rests? The moment he sits on his bottom he turns into stone, like those lumps they call gods in Mecca and out of which they make a roaring trade. Yes, everything moves. Unless Time is like one of those strolling actors I saw once in Dawmat Al-Jandal. A sort of a clown, a jester, who keeps changing his masks to con us into some bad barter. But whatever we give up, we must not give up on life. Life is greater than all the deities, and more generous, she being the supreme one. And we need to meet her generosity with one of our own. So scatter your stars as you go, lover lad, and don't hoard straws for a nest in the storm.'

'But how can the hatchlings grow without a nest? And is not a nest life's own way to care for her children?' I persist, peevishly.

'Life will find a way. And I must find you a way, a rope, out of this philosophical swamp of yours. And mine now. A rope that pulls but does not bind. Go and grab a nap, for we're throwing a rope up to a window tonight. We together; if you deign to join me. You take the lady, who'll love to have you. I'll take the maid, if she stoops to take me.'

Emru, as always, has been the better man, the better swimmer, even in the quagmire of philosophy.

MARCHING AGAINST
THE GOD

It took us some fifty days to cross the Empty Quarter and reach Tabalah.

The story of Emru's encounter with the god there, having unleashed this history, will not gain from a re-telling.

I may however note that the story did something to illustrate Emru's humour at the time, while letting loose upon me the full force of the prophecy, real or fancied.

The prophecy! That cascade of dark rhymes shelled out by the red haired Zelpha, who, in the Land of Cedars, had gone under the name of Silvia, Silvia who had served in the temple of the wild goddess Astarte and in the church of the Virgin Mary!

The fateful lines had been seared into me more intractably than with a branding iron. Even now they twitch upon my lips and quake at the point of my pen, crucified as I am upon the map they have drawn for my life.

How I became thus crucified, thus groomed, for a 'mission' I cannot tell. My pagan father had petitioned the prophecy out of his feverish worry for his dearly loved wife and for her newborn child. She, dismissing the augury out of hand, later saw me as the real, superior 'star' of the oracle. It was I who would carry the 'peace' of her beloved Yesu and the 'spellbinding pen' worthy of her adored Saint Ephrem of the dazzling *memres*.

The concluding lines of the prophecy had suggested dire consequences if I slackened when the hour arrived. When it did, on that noonday in Tabalah, I had but a few of the writing sheets, the sea-borne leaves of the prophecy.

Now that more China leaves and more Assad infants had been delivered, the naked innocence of both waited to be soiled by our follies and crimes.

And now that we had trekked in our hundreds against the dare of the Empty Quarter, we had to march through the knitted brow of a god.

61

A LAMENT FOR THE UNYIELDING MUSE

I cry out for the Muse who will not mate with my tongue, singeing my speech with her aureate fire!

Never will I journey between times and realms, a mystic mariner, a leper and a prophet, a harvester of moods, a plucker of hidden strings, a sculptor and mourner of faded beauties and withered loves, a god!

This is not to be. Even the prophecy has assigned me the prosaic role of a 'scribe'. My mother's conferring upon me the radiance of her reading has done little to comfort me.

And much that I love Emru and take pride in his gift, I secretly bemoan my loss, slyly coveting that gift, shamelessly jealous of its brilliant recipient.

I have endeavoured to learn by rote all of Emru's verses, enunciating every line, tempting the Muse to visit a path already glowing with her own alchemy. But, apart from the borrowed tunes, I could only eke out the refrains of a clumsy parrot and a paltry crow, never the soaring airs of a lark or a nightingale. I knew then that I was forever barred from the forest of stars and could only wait at its edge beside the woodcutter's log-pile for a spark given away in charity or carelessness.

It was then that I began to seek some solace in the role or commission of a historian of sorts. I continue to doubt my fitness for the task, but I hope, however forlornly, that the unleashing of the sign will carry with it the power to thrash my self-doubt and nourish the wick of my expectations.

Meanwhile, Emru has been launching a torrent of fearless verses that have no precedence or equal in the utterance of the Arabs. They roam wide, unfettered and untamed, compelling and amusing. Life in them is no idea to reflect upon or a goddess to kneel to, but a lover to wrestle with and yield to and pierce to the very sucking core, a wild mare to ride in the rushing breeze or, on occasion, to be thrown off her feral back.

Ah, that back!

The tribal Elders have wished to spread the fable that the dangerously attractive poetry of Emru and his band of *sa'luks* is the creation of the non-human Jinn rather than ordinary men's wants and discontents. Emru has spurned the appeals by the Elders to sing of the greatness of Kenda and advertise her lusts for more pastures, more powers, and more odes and alms to her vanity. Playfully, though, he lets it known to those who crave the pretence, that he has his own exclusive Muse, whom he calls Akesa.

On her back he rides to heights no other poet has reached. A perilous ride it is, the ride of a male grasshopper that can have his head chewed off in the act. But, clasping her flanks from behind, he sees her change from a brunette to a blonde, to a negress, to a redhead, and from a woman to a man, to a mare, to a she-goat, whose horns he clasps as she bucks under him milking him dry. All the while, he will be shouting verses of rare and fierce attraction.

I never see him with his chameleon-Muse. He speaks about her with masterly make-believe, moving his hands like a rapt actor, like the poet he is, a maker of images, an author of new truths and legends, a king, a tenant, restless with eyries and ravines. Moving his hands, softened and braced by the bodies of beautiful women, he moulds and remoulds the muse's demonic contours and our rapt fantasies.

No, I have never seen the fair blighter. He winks at me when he talks about her to the dunces; but I hear the poetry he claims to have flowed with his essence. I hear and I am speechless with envy.

THE FOILING OF THE
FIVE HUNDRED

Emru thrashed the only god he came within a yard of, unintentionally offending the Seeress who had put my life in irons with his life, even if iron dissolves like dew to his touch.

But Emru has changed. A smelter of iron, his very heart now seemed to have inclined towards that metal.

As soon as Emru had rejoined his small army, which he had instructed to remain out of sight, we resumed our march, thrust along by a renewed dark fury in Emru.

We had snaked and crawled down from the wooded highlands of Hadramot and the northern slopes of the Hemyar Mountains. We had marched and halted, halted and marched, across the dunes and flats of the Empty Quarter. We had prevailed over the dubious, lethal chastity of the sand giantesses, over the razors of their crests, the snares of the quicksand, and the guiles of the mirages. We had marched into the scowl of a god, undeterred by the derision of the grinning skulls, the madness of the parched camels and the bites of the horned vipers.

Now under our feet and those of our camels and horses the loose sallow sand gave way to speckled gravel plains with frequent shrubs and grasses, hinting at the cultivated places behind them. But we kept our aloofness from human settlements fearing their treachery. Emru, acting at the suggestion of Al-Ward, posted armed guards ahead of us and on our flanks and at the rear of our drawn-out procession to ward off opportunistic raiders.

The Asads, we had heard, were on the move in the region of Tehama, north of Mecca, their destination the encampment of the Kenanas. These were their cousins. But the Kenanas had long lived in peace with their neighbours spurning the rude expediency of *ghazw*.

We rode at greater speed. Our mounts, revived by fresh water and fodder, trotted and cantered at intervals, puffing into the glare the labour of their large hearts. It is less bumpy to ride a camel at a canter than at a walk.

It took us a day and a night to reach the outskirts of the Kenana encampment. Already, more than nine months had gone by since the Asad delegation came to *Al-Ahqaf*, and the truce had overrun its insidious course. We were now slicing through busy lanes inevitably advertising our presence to passing riders. In my mind, silent upon the world, I was reciting time and again the incantation for Binding All the Implements of War, which I had often heard recited by my mother. 'May they be bound', I implored after her dear, desperate fashion, 'by means of the living God who sits upon the throne of heaven. May they be removed and destroyed from the east and the west and the north and the south, all the arrows and the swords and the daggers of wicked men, by the prayers of my Lady, the blessed Mary, Amen!'

Two Bedouins volunteered the information that hundreds of Asad horsemen were at the Kenana encampment, though many more had journeyed elsewhere. A Hadramot warrior advised Emru to make his move during the night. Emru regarded this as un-chivalrous. He would launch his attack in broad daylight. The veteran warrior finally convinced him of an early morning assault.

We left the camels and the attendants behind us in the last quarter of the night and trotted on our mares and horses for half an hour before we spurred them into a gallop at the edge of the sprawling encampment. I was on *Shams*, son of *Najm*, the splendid thoroughbred my father had assigned to me when I left my boyhood. Did I ever?

The sight of a sea of tents unruffled by the storms of the world met us.

Emru was the first to break the stillness ahead of us on his stallion, his sword drawing loops in the crisp morning air, he shouted, 'For the blood of Hojr, for the blood of Hojr!' Hundreds of horsemen behind him picked up the refrain.

Wakened by the shouts and the hoof-beats, people began to emerge from the tents. Their eyes were wide with incomprehension. Their hands held no weapons. Even so some of the Taghleb riders began to cut them down, randomly and savagely. It was an ugly sight. A gaunt old man in a loincloth had his right arm chopped off by one of our warriors swinging his sword about like a wild boy at play. I felt faint and nauseous in my saddle and was about to keel over to the side when I saw a lightly clad woman come out of a large tent and dart with no regard for her safety towards Emru as he shouted, 'This is for Hojr, ye swine of Asad!'

The woman raised her milky arms in front of Emru's fuming steed, boldly seizing his reins, and yelled at the top of her voice. I pressed the sides of *Shams* with my remaining strength, my stomach about to disgorge its meagre contents, to get closer to the scene. And I heard the woman scream, 'We're Kenana, we're Kenana! The Asads left last night! None of them are here!'

Emru froze in his convulsing saddle. The woman, a most comely creature, one of her iridescent breasts half-exposed under her flimsy shift, still clung desperately to the reins of his horse. The steed, full of the lust of the charge, neighing and grimacing, his eyes bulging, continued to jerk the woman's hand, swinging her slight but resolute frame this way and that way. But Emru steadied him, even as his nostrils flared widely, sending jets of excited steam into the dust-speckled air. The plucky woman had clearly recognised Emru, and realised his purpose – and blunder. He too had recognised her, and his own mistake. He hollered for his men to stop the carnage.

'The Assads left the night before. They decamped in a hurry without asking leave of our elders. They may have received a warning of your coming,' the woman shouted. But the noise around her was already dying out, except for the keening of women over the slain, and the moans of the injured. The maimed old man, now on his bony knees in a pool of blood, had somehow picked up his severed arm and was trying, even as he swayed in pain, to join the severed limb, bloodied and soiled as it was, to his oozing stump. I struggled to keep my battered eyes on him as he closed his own before he crumpled to the ground like a sack emptied of its contents.

'I thank you, fair Hafsa, for your intervention.' Emru's words sliced into my mind like a cold blade. 'Had I known you were here, I wouldn't have disturbed your sleep. Not even if my father's killer was lying at the foot of your bed - unreachable as that heaven is for the likes of him. A train of camels is following us. A hundred of them shall be given to the Kenanas in some recompense for the error of our swords. But we must be on our way. Fare you well, my *sayyidah*. I leave you to the protection of the gods. May they guard you from their own envy of your beauty and the idiocy of men like me!'

BLIND JUSTICE

Ah, the litany of trivialities summoned, summoning, in the midst of our grand trials! But are not grand trials the offspring of the commonest and most mundane of acts?

O Saint of the *Confessions*, help me with your mastery over the 'many chambers furnished with many goods'! Mine are filled with futile imaginings and trifles of all sorts.

A date-stone, a palm kernel, is thrown into the little lake!

The kernel, long and slender and grooved along the middle like a woman's *han*, sinks down to the lake's dark-green bed. Ripples form on the surface. I travel with the ripples.

The outermost ripple, a little curving wave, sails upon the surface of the water like a bow; it takes to the air like an arrow, a bird, one of a sort worse than that of a *hamah* – a rumour unfolding its pernicious wings!

It hovers for a few breaths over the bank and over the palm trees.

It eyes with suspicion the male branches tied among the sprays of the female trees for pollination, now long consummated.

It gathers unto itself the smells and sounds of the garden and the subtle, scheming silences of human minds:

The whiff of roasted meat,
The voices of the maidens feasting and trading jokes with Emru,
The splashing of date-stones into the water,
The merry banter of Emru and Oneyza,
The ruse simmering in Oneyza's mind...

In its rush to fly off and disgorge its freight, the creature makes its own conclusions.

It sweeps beyond the orchard
across the distance into the nearby town,
into the fancies of maidens in must and lads on heat,
into the pretensions and prejudices of the Elders,
into the very marrow of Emru's life and mine.

As it does so, it is transforming and being transformed.

It multiplies into many shapes, many minions, serving a single, hydra-headed master.

It goes from house to house thumping and flapping, whinnying and crowing, nibbling and nuzzling. It makes sure that whoever opens their door will not direct it to their neighbour's door before they have decked it out in a new set of feathers or a new hide, a new head, a new jest, a new horror; not before they have put on it their own mark to tell it apart from its already innumerable siblings.

It reaches Hojr confirmed in its grim ripeness, anointed by a deadly sanctity, a drooling consensus.

It reaches him a swarm of locusts, a whirling flock of starlings, bent on nothing but ravaging the leaves and berries of his tree of life, and that of his son. The wings, the beaks, the mouths, flap and drone about holies defiled, privacies invaded, virgins violated, the crone alone being spared.

'Honour…Honour…Honour!' I hear the Elders bellow in the tribe's assembly. But I hear my father murmur to himself, 'Behold Honour's self-appointed champions! Behold them ramming Honour in every orifice, whetting their blades to slit her own throat in her very name!'

Oneyza's father, Mu'awiya, is on his feet ranting against Emru. My name is mentioned but only as that of an underling, denied the tainted glory of equal partnership in crime, un-deserving of a full-blood spill. The privilege is reserved for Emru.

Oneyza's father is an envious, scheming one-eyed bigot and coward. He has his one hale eye on the signet ring of Kenda. He threatens, spittle dribbling on his beard, to rise against his half-brother if the offender isn't put to death.

Other parents discharge growls and farts in proportion to the size of their cheeks above and below.

At the fringe of the assembly, the young and the merry are amused and fired up. They marvel at the alchemy which has transformed a young man's lark into a tribal saga of assault and battery embellished with stories of wild couplings under the palm trees.

Petty rhymesters have been jumping on the back of the story (how many backs?) with their own lurid flourishes.

I am drawn to two poetic accounts by none other than the author of the event. But the lesser known ode rises in my ink as I see Emru rise to his feet in the shade of Dar Jouljoul's palms to recite the poem to the maidens after they have merrily feasted on his camel's roast:

To what can I compare a maid?
A Persian pearl? A Hindi blade?
A Christian hermit's lamp at night?
A Jew's Menorah, bright, upright?
A star remote, a palm unbent
Whom none can tame or scale or dent?
A *Wajrah* deer? A flask of wine?
A cross no martyr can decline?
The deep blue sea? The perfect ode?
The dream of China's silken road?
A spring flash flood? A sweet earthquake?
The finest twine no man can break?
The spur, the prize, to life's mad race?
The Great Beyond's more comely face?...
All idle words! A man must learn
To go beyond the words - and burn!
And when he's burnt, to rise and swear,
'A maid is well beyond compare!'

Need I splash more of Jouljoul on my China paper? Need I say how Emru and I, fooled by Oneyza, are made to race naked in the pool?

I racing Emru! He has given me all the races he has made me enter. Not that I ever consented to my fake triumphs! But this time the reward is so superlative that its promise has overwhelmed the charity of his heart. More importantly, it has overwhelmed the judgement of his mind.

Here he is, having done the seven loops required by Oneyza, I struggling with my third! Here he is, standing up from his watery exertions, his magnificent arousal rearing up in anticipation of the sweeter exertions promised by his lovely tormentor!

But she is nowhere to be seen! Nor are her intrepid accomplices. Only old Om Mahbouba is left at the bank, grinning and showing her two lost front teeth.

And here we are, the two of us, victims of the ruse, in worn-out frocks donated by the crone, trudging to the town on foot under the jeering stars.

But I am happily, sadly, drawn elsewhere.

I see Hojr turning an irksome signet ring round his finger, the left side of his head crying out for the lavender bandage, the juice of *rihan*.

He has sent word for his son to come to his presence. Emru has set out alone, promising to join me at chess in less than an hour.

He goes alone, but I can see all.

Hojr hauls his son over the coals for the incident at Dar Jouljoul. He also scolds him for the error of his ways acted out in boudoirs and *howdahs* and whorehouses up and down Najd.

Emru snaps back, 'I have done nothing worse than visiting the shrines of beautiful women, where I was welcomed as a pilgrim and given food as a supplicant and allowed visions of divinities. Isn't this better than luring young women into the cages of men twice their age and with a slither of their endurance in bed?'

I am swept into the veins twisting like vipers in the king's head. He has of late taken the young daughter of a northern chief as wife. This he has done to seal a valuable alliance rather than to put new flesh on his often deserted bed. To add insult to injury, a story has already reached him of Emru having recited some verses describing the bride's charms, suggesting he has had intimate familiarity with them.

Hojr, always in a rush to be somewhere else, dismisses his son. Before he calls for the lavender bandage, he orders my father, who has been at his side, to slay Emru before the day is past and bring him his eyes. He singles out the eyes which have leered so lustfully at hallowed maidenhoods and glared so insolently at their own sire and king.

Luckily in the event, he omits mention of the other organ of trespass, the poet's tongue!

THE ASADS BLOODIED

Emru went after the Asads as soon as he had settled the matter of reparations with the Kenanas.

Behind him, he left an ally of a day, one that might rise the following morning an enemy, perhaps a rouser of more.

The Asads had left clear tracks in the earth, footmarks of men and beasts. We could make those out in the light of the moon and, effortlessly, in the sun's glare.

Around noon of the second day, we saw the dust of the quarry and smelt their wind. But our horses, forced to canter without rest with only a fraction of our fleet camels keeping pace, were worn out. Our throats gasped for something other than our sweat.

When the Asads became aware of us, they made exceptional haste. I thought they were hurrying to increase the distance between them and us. But Al-Ward, riding in front of Emru, shouted, 'They're heading for the water of Sa'd!'

The word threw our party into a frenzy – 'Water... WATER... WATER!'

It was our right and entitlement to get to the water first. Were we not on the trail of murderers and brigands?

Throwing caution to the wind, we rushed towards the stockade of blades the Asads had by now formed round the pool.

Al-Ward shouted a warning. But few seemed to hear. The air was thick with dust and crackling with the neighing of horses and the bellows of men.

In the end, we were thrust helter-skelter into the mesh of swords and spears fringing the pool.

Even as the men fought (for the blood of Hoj? for the water of life?) the pool quivered and winked like a seasoned whore through the lattice of steel.

The lust for life prevailed. If the Asads had thought holding the pool would yield them an advantage they were proven wrong. The desperate charge of our men bested their designs and numbers.

Before long, we had both the water and the field to ourselves. Scores lay dead or dying around the pool, some half-sunk in its liquid silver, pouring into it a dearer liquid. I prayed, shutting my eyes against the horror and pushing down the vomit frothing in my throat, that the fallen had not all died thirsty.

The Asads were in full retreat. Though more numerous than us, they were but a small group of a fairly large tribe. Their womenfolk were not with them. Chieftains of note were nowhere to be seen.

Emru nibbled at the heels of the mangled columns. The surviving *sa'luks* and Hemyar horsemen kept pace and sword with him. For the others, the dead, the dying, and the wounded, other distractions held sway. The hundred Taghlebis were whole. None of them had come to harm. They wore Persian armour, and indifferent hearts.

DELIVERED UNTO EXILE

My father does not try to argue with the king.

Hojr wears the stone mask he has long carved for himself. But the fine, hard sculpture is chipped by chisels and mallets without and within – public slurs and threats, private aches and discontents, the hammering of an impossible dream his grandfather, the first Hojr, had cursed him with.

My father strolls out to do the will of his liege. I can read his thoughts and I can hear his footfalls.

He returns, emerging from the dusk that drapes the sprawling town of white houses.

He carries a bloodstained bundle, which he opens and lays at the king's feet.

Hojr looks down, unbelieving, his chiselled indifference coming apart.

He is overcome by the horror of the order he gave.

He struggles to find words, his face contorting as if by a stroke.

And then he howls.

And howls.

And howls.

The women of his household batter the walls with their screams and tear at their hair and clothes.

He swoons, the cracks of his face revealing defenceless flesh.

The flesh speaks of a moment of insanity that made the stone, not the flesh, not the flesh, have a son murdered and mutilated in the grisliest of fashions.

The flesh glowers menacingly at my father, the long trusted adviser, for carrying out the depraved order so readily, so unquestioningly.

My father, weighs the depth of the tyrant's anguish.

Satisfied, he tells him that Emru is safe under his custody, awaiting the milder judgement of his father and king. The eyes belong to a slaughtered sheep.

Hojr sways on his feet.

He feigns displeasure at my father's cheek. But a sigh of relief escapes him. A breath aglow with the surging stars of the night sky fills his dark chest.

But he too is a condemned man, trapped by his own demons and inherited ring.

He sends my father on another assignment, just as deadly, though not spelling out Death's name.

I am with Emru at my uncle's Hermitage. This is the Ka'ba my father circled in his youth. Built by a Syrian missionary of an earlier generation, it was in time occupied by my uncle upon his exodus from Lebanon with his orphaned niece, my father's youthful, enduring love.

Made sacrosanct by that history, the place had suggested itself to my father as a safe haven for Emru.

The dear rebel priest, tall and lean and impatient to fill God's heaven with saved souls, is rambling along on yet another sermon of his, this time about the wages of sin and the torments in hell. Hell, he says, is not a place far-removed. He quotes a *memre* by his illustrious namesake Saint Ephrem. He recites the verses with his usual passion, his large Phoenician eyes filled with tears, his thin, long arms scooping up invisible cosmic waves, plucking yielding feathers from angels' wings:

The world was fixed with two eyes, twined;
But one, the left eye, Eve made blind.
The right eye Mary filled with light
To ransom us from Eve's dark night.

How curious, I reflect, for my uncle to mention eyes and blindness at this time! But the world made dark by sin is a much-loved subject of his.

Ephraim had been Emru's 'cleanser' and 'baptist' as he had been mine. At least he had performed the ceremony of baptism requested by our mothers shortly after our births, Emru preceding me by three days. As we were thus anointed, he calls us 'sons of God' and 'children of the Heavenly Womb', our entry into heaven assured, our Eucharist sealed, though needing to be regularly inspected and catechised.

Ephraim's own greater baptism had already come to pass. For him, bread and wine had unquestioningly transformed into the body and blood of the Saviour. And like the Jews fleeing Egypt for

74

the Promised Land, he too had undergone his exodus when he left Lebanon for Arabia. The sea of sands he had to cross was his Red Sea, as it had been his Jordan. He had escaped from bondage and had entered into Paradise, fenced against the world's assaults by dunes encrusted with vipers and belching with the rusted spears of empires. No matter! 'The best prayer is the one offered on the altar of the heart,' he often said.

Ephraim ends the sermon with a gloss on miracles. Having enacted his own miracle, ambivalent as it has been, he remains hopeful of more. But it is the turn of the wonder brought about through Elisha. The oil is made to flood the jars and is sold to release the widow's sons from the bondage of debt. Bondage has been my uncle's nemesis, freedom his transcendence and philosopher's stone, hard and barbed, but with an inner glow that can transform the world.

The *memre* of Jacob of Serough with which my uncle concludes his homily tells of old mysteries and new possibilities:

The Virgin's Son removes the veil.
The Stammerer, healed, is loud and hale.
All ancient prophecies stand revealed,
With Moses' brilliant seal unsealed.

After the sermon, I try to make light of Emru's ordeal. But I am seized by fear, the fear of what awaits us at the hands of a fuming father here and now rather than that of the heavenly Father at the end of time. But what if the two patriarchs are working in fearsome harmony?

Emru does not need my fake courage. He has graciously tolerated the sermon and the pious verses. But the latter have roused his wanton Akesa. Invisible to us, she has been driving a new bawdy ode from his loins to his lips. He mutters profane lines in the sanctuary. 'Doesn't our holy man say the best prayer is offered between a woman's legs?' he whispers.

'On the altar of the heart!' I want to correct him, cultured as I am in the *memres* of the Saint from Serough as in those of Saint Ephrem and Saint Narsai.

A horse at full gallop comes to a halt outside the door. The sound brings upon me a fit of cold sweat and light-headedness. But my father strides in with a hint of a smile on his face, his loving eyes beaming.

But as is his habit when on official business, my father dispatches his message in a terse and forthright manner, keeping a tight rein on his emotions.

'Ah, my stern father has a sense of humour after all. He has wisely chosen to practise it on his youngest son before unleashing it on an unsuspecting world! Too long has he kept it hidden behind the headstone of his face! Arabia has been *impoverished* without it! But he needs to chisel away at its jagged edges, for they gash the heart!'

'Affairs of state freeze the blood even in our sun-baked land!' my father rejoins. 'The king, sadly, isn't merry-making. He expects his command to be followed to the syllable. So I repeat. You're to leave Najd before tomorrow's sun has set. Should you be found within this upland thereafter, your life would be forfeited and the king would be obliged to pay the weight of your head in gold should it be brought to him. He doesn't wish to tempt those who seek your death. But they will not relent. Nor can the king restrain them without great harm to Kenda ensuing. So take you the fleetest dromedary, the best *dalul*, you choose. Take her from the king's herd or my own smaller but no less enabled one. Take the companions who may wish to share the banishment with you, and leave. Leave before the king is forced to reduce the day to an hour and the hour to the suddenness of another insanity, fanned by another incitement. Go, my *son*! I pray you! Things may still change, for the better. Be patient! You're a *man*. And as a *poet*, alone you never can be. And with your comrades, your soul-mates, you can continue to explore the infinite spaces!'

My father's voice falters. It shakes, a *sidr* leaf in a *shamal* wind. The man tumbles from the high crag of a king's confidant into the eddies of an anguished father, doubly buffeted by what this will mean for his beloved wife, my mother. But he recovers, sustained by his infuriating self-mastery as by his desire to save Emru's life, and mine. He may have concluded that exile is not such a bad option after all. It will deny the enemies chances for further insult, or murder.

While he was addressing Emru, he was also glancing at me every now and then. But as he wraps up his speech, he enfolds us equally with his eyes, the word 'son' embracing us both.

I know I am to share Emru's exile. Had I not been marked a sharer and a camp follower by a higher power, even before I was born?

But there is to be an embellishment. In my father's thoughts I can hear the word 'Bayroute... Bayroute... Bayroute'. Her time has come!

I walk out with my father and see him get on the back of his horse rather wearily. I remember the days when he would whirl into the saddle with the lightest touch of the saddle horn.

In a minute, he is galloping away, his horse's hooves kicking up small puffs of angry, confused, and desolate clods behind them.

MUTINY

When Emru returned, he was still brandishing his naked sword, blood congealing on its blade. His eyes too were bloodshot and steel-cold as they surveyed from the height of the saddle the bodies of the fallen.

Many of the fallen were Hadramot lads. They had outwitted and survived the Empty Quarter, and now they lay broken and sliced open, re-claimed by the vast void. No more would they rise at dawn to join the ibex hunt and return at dusk to sing the *zamil* and dance the *marzaha*. Was this why their mothers had borne and suckled them and hung amulets round their infant necks? What comfort could be bought for the mothers bereaved? What honour was there for the youths butchered for the blood of an old tyrant and a bad father, his cadaver long torn by jackals and crows? And for the murdered *sa'luks*? Was not the fellowship of the howling wind and the languid moon, even of the tittering hyenas, fairer than soldiering for an unhinged prince who betrayed them into death? And for the slain Asads, grimacing among the senna and the wormwood like the heads of slaughtered sheep, what wrong did they do to be driven this way and that way then to be cut down for the crime of one or two killer rams?

But weren't they, dead as they were, better than me? Better and more alive for having done or suffered their deed with a conviction I lack, for having dared to be what I am not?

Emru, his cheeks flushed and his brow bathed in sweat, led his obliging mare towards the pool, and slid off her back to allow her to drink.

There flashed in my mind a memory of that mare, the beautiful *Jarwa*, as a young playful filly. Emru had ridden her when he came to inspect my *Najm*, the horse presented to me by my father as he presumed I had left my boyish years. Emru helped me clamber on *Najm*'s astral back, to which I never did justice.

Emru's voice rang out, his throat spiked with sand, his speech slurred by a gathering fever:

'When the horses...and the...riders have...have had their fill... ll...let them...let them be...ready! Ready to...hh...hunt...hunt down the…slayers of Hojr, to…hunt them down…ll…let them be ready…let them…be…be ready!'

The men who rallied to his words did so sluggishly. Everyone was worn out. Some sported gashes from Asad swords and stabs from their spears. Several of those with deeper cuts asked to be taken to the nearer encampment of the Kenanas rather than suffer a further march into the unknown. Emru turned to Al-Ward to ask whether some *sa'luks* could escort them back. Al-Ward hesitated. He did not want his mates to be delivered unto a new uncertainty.

We marched into the breathless night, stirring up the carpet vipers and the scorpions and the wolf spiders in the bushes and under the rocks, trampling on some, some of our horses bitten, Al-Ward dipping again into his pharmacopoeia. Sleeping wagtails and bustards scattered ahead of us and around us. Only the flies, gallingly tenacious, kept company with us. Where do they come from, and how can their faint wings keep up with such distances, such speeds? The stars maintained their muffled chatter as *Al-Rami* continued to train his arrow at the Scorpion overhead.

The dubious water of Sa'd had long dried up on our lips. Emru's rush to follow the Assads had left only a few of our water-skins sufficiently slaked. I wished the dawn would dole out some dew. But, unlike the vile flies, the moisture did not keep pace with our canter.

When Emru, bending through the night like a hunchback in his saddle ahead of us, turned to inspect his men, his face was blazing, more by the fever than by the sun rising to the right of his face. It was a stubborn face, though. And like a night creature, it seemed surprised by the sunrise, resentful. Perhaps it had hoped to sink its teeth into its quarry in the darkness, hidden from the meddling daylight. It then turned away stabbing the horizon ahead.

I followed, as did the others, listlessly.

The tracks soon divided into two branches, a third stretching forward. Emru paused. Al-Ward rode up to him even as he leant to the side scrutinising the marks. I spurred my horse to get nearer.

I heard Al-Ward say to Emru, 'The sand boa leaves its forked tongue sticking out to lure small birds.'

Emru turned to face the men. 'We…shall not be…side…tracked. Their main…body are going…going…forward. To…the…high ground…ahead. We…follow!'

A voice went up in the sultry air. It was that of a Taghleb horseman, one of the hundred sent by Yazd.

'The horses are all-in! They won't survive the journey back to Kenana, nor onward to Hadramot. Surely not across that foul desert. The whole of Najd must know about us now. Kenda is dying. The reek of her death is everywhere, inviting all the carrion birds of Araby,' the Taghlebi mocked.

In an instant, Al-Ward had prodded his horse closer to Emru, his fellow *sa'luks* rallying to form a ring around the twain.

'There'll be no going back! Not until I've...had Elba and...his paymasters taste...my blade! Not until they've...eaten...the dust where my...my father fell! Kenda shall not...shall not die! Kenda shall live...forever! This is the moment of her...triumph. There's no...reek in...the air. None...save the reek of treason...and...cowardice. The...frankincense of a...new...wedding shall fill Arabia. The wasp shall be...evicted...from the beehive,' Emru roared and croaked and hissed, swaying in the saddle.

'When might we reach the high ground? Another hour? two? three? What if the two other parties ambush us as we gallop blindly after your *sa'luk* and your fever?' the Taghlebi reasoned.

'Let it be. I know this region. We must keep going,' said Emru, suddenly calm and collected, his will-power seizing his weakness like a vice .

'No. It's against the tribal law. Nor is it a sound plan. The Asads will in time realise how few we are, and round back on us. They've obviously overestimated our numbers. And we'll not have upon our heads the 'curse', the 'curse' which caused the death of Fatima, and Hojr, and our King Amr. We shall go no farther. You've shed sufficient blood for blood. Let it stay thus, though forgiveness would've been better from the start.' The man was a Christian. His comrades had all converged at his side now. Yazd's handpicked men they certainly were.

The mention of a 'curse' causing the deaths of Emru's father and uncle swept through the men. It preyed on their human susceptibilities. The charge of bad leadership gave the claim more talons, though the notion that Emru was responsible for the death of his own mother was blatantly absurd. She had died three years after giving birth to him, though not before she had given birth to his sister Hend.

80

But let it be so! Why bother? Let fickleness and superstition triumph over the lust for war! Let them conspire, tainted as they are, to take the ground out from under the foulest of human endeavours! Let them prevail, though they too are often hirelings and victims of war!

So, in the face of the mutiny of the Taghlebs and the buckling of the general will, Emru, his fever rising, could do little.

Ah, he still wanted to charge into the distance alone and slice the haze with his sword. But Al-Ward and I restrained him. We drew him to our chests, scorched by his fire. As his men bent down their heads in shame or exhaustion or in fear of the 'curse' (to which the *sa'luks* were immune), he cursed them. And he cursed the gods. And he cursed me and Al-Ward before he went on to curse himself into further delirium.

BAYROUTE

Bayroute rises before me, within me, like a Venus from the tumult of my depths and the offing of my dreams.

Summoned, summoning, she dares me, draws me, into her embraces. The caravan pace of forty-five days to her green gate quickens into an instant; the many years of my schooling by Ephraim for her desk shrink into a shimmer; the seasons within her expand into a lifetime.

Submerged in her lulling, stirring, folds, how can I see her as she truly is?

I fumble about for my first impressions of her, but they're inseminated by later, timeless ones.

Cradled between a wall of dark green mountains and an ever-beckoning sapphire sea, Bayroute has been a mother to many empires and a harlot to many more. Her symbol, the dolphin coiling round an anchor, is half betrayed by her anchorless lust for pleasure and adventure and profit.

I coil with her thoughts as she reprimands and rewards her schoolchildren; as she writhes and moans with genuine or fake pleasure under endless conquerors and clients; as she sways with her cypresses and feeds her violets and roses and narcissuses with her wells and tears and latrines. In her murmurs and modulations I hear the rustling of the cedars and the clatter of the looms of her mountain hamlets, the whining of the ship rigging and the din of the oyster factories on her shoreline. I hear her *mawwals* and *walwalas*. I become one with her mariners as they sail upon the Phoenician (now Roman) sea dotting its shores and islands with colonies and alphabets, pottery and purple dye, granaries and labour camps, Aye and with altars to gods with wide staring eyes. I lose sight of them (mariners and gods) as they disappear beyond the Pillars of Baal (now named Pillars of Hercules) leaving the lucid turquoise waves to sail into the dark mists of nameless alien seas.

More sober, tolerant, and devious than her sister cities, Tyre and Gaza, she did not defy the young Macedonian as he stormed his way into the Birth-Continent of the Sun. Rather, she readily supplied him with ships and soldiers and spies to help him lay waste her hot-headed siblings.

Her names cavort around me to claim my ear and pen - city of Wells, El's First city, Neptune's Betrothed, Julia, Felix, Augusta, Bayroute, Berythus, Mother of Law-Making, Nurse of Legislation...

City of many names and many masks and many loyalties as are her people!
City of bargains and deals and commissions!
City of fortunes and fakeries, fairness and fanaticism, rootedness and restlessness!
City of cisterns and circuses and cloisters!
City of veils and revelations!
City of clinging webs and fugitive horizons!
Beloved Hydra of many heads and hearts, honest and bought devotions, scented tongues and soiled sheets!

But, buried (to be reborn) in her embraces, I see that her allures and riddles, lusts and schemes, schisms and harmonies, will outlive the struts and sneers of all conquerors. Their deities will trade courtesies and curses in her temples and sepulchres and in her palaces and hovels, brothels and abattoirs; but her own secret gods will cock a snook at all and go about doing their business in their own ageless way.

Yeah, Bayroute will go on trading and praying and whoring and giving birth to martyrs and murderers, mariners and middlemen, lovers and legislators, to the end of time and in a merry, gory, regal, and ever-fecund free-for-all.

HEND RETURNS

There was a curse in the air and in the minds of men.

I did not have any of my childhood amulets to chase the curse away from my own mind, where facts and fantasies growl at one another like wild dogs. The last of my mother's talismans round my neck I had given to Sofia before I left her temple.

The two women receded as I travelled with the feverish Emru and the ever-feisty Al-Ward back to Hadramot. They receded though I had summoned them to enter, in the manner of the Saint, the mansion (in my case the hovel) of a soul clamouring for salvation.

In my desperation I repeated loudly what I could remember of my mother's prayers. Even the doubtful incantation for 'Binding All the Implements of War' I again recited, loudly this time, risking the silent ridicule of those who could hear me. The binding incantation against 'Fever' I intoned for Emru's comfort, pleading, 'From the east and the west and from the north to the south, may there depart and be removed the hot and cold Fever from the afflicted body and soul of Emru; so be it, Amen!'

As our diminished party of men and beasts trudged the dicey road back to Hadramot, I kept reciting the prayers that continued to resurge upon my lips binding the chasers and the wild dogs and the scorpions and the false dreams.

Ah, the false dreams, sourly, sweetly false!

The Taghleb warriors had abandoned us with sullen disdain after the battle of the pool. And despite the binding prayers, we were further reduced along the way by murderous human jackals. Their kind can sniff out blood in desolate veins and booty in starved saddlebags. And they would not let go of their prey until, like leeches, they were gorged to a daze. The amazing sa'luks never failed to conjure up means to foil the raiders and save lives, often at the expense of their own.

All the while, Al-Ward struggled with his plants and herbs to haul Emru out of the fire pit into which his body had sunk. Fever it certainly was, with all the relentless rapacity of the type. And yet it seemed a strange affliction, utterly resistant to all prayers and herbs and fanned by flames deep within its victim - flames possibly fiercer than the fever's own ferocity. Emru seemed to have succumbed to it as if it was an all-consuming mistress.

When Emru began to recover, Al-Ward and I assured him that he had done enough for his vow. He had also redeemed his name and that of Kenda (for which Al-Ward did not care a fart) throughout Arabia (which Al-Ward believed deserved her slavery). But he was inconsolable.

As the fever relaxed its hold on him, he kindled new fires of self-blame. He was furious with himself for not challenging the mutiny of the Taghlebs. I suggested to him that the revolt had been planned in Al-Anbar by the two-faced Yazd, and there was no way of preventing it.

Still, he prated on about not having seen any of the Assad notables at the water's edge. Silently, I thought, had he accepted Kubeysa's offer he could have had those notables driven like cattle to *Al-Ahqaf*!

Kubeysa, Kubeysa, did the old fox ever mean to deliver what he promised? Was Elba really swallowed up by the desert?

I reflected on the recent events. The thought of my once fun-loving mate surveying those killed near the pool so coldly from his ornate saddle sickened me. I imagined him trotting like a hyena to smell out the fattest and tastiest cadaver on the battlefield! As we rode across the desert, I wanted to cry out to the dunes against all kings, and against all wars. I wanted to serenade the wisdom of my mother, and the wisdom of her God who submitted so sheepishly, so supremely, to the harsh Roman cross. I wanted to mourn with her lost throat the death of her young father, one life seized and flung so callously on to the path of human folly, a single life, a single death, shaping other lives, other deaths.

But I did not.

I held my peace.

Rather, I spoke of poetry and wine and women, professing some experience in them all.

I claimed, wishing to soften Emru's hardening heart, that I had caught a glimpse of his Jinn-Muse swaying in grief over his head as he raved in the delirium of fever. She keened as she rocked this way and that way, I told him. Her long ginger hair was braided with pearls, her breasts were perfume-pots of ivory, her navel an amethyst, her tears of lace agate. He smiled wanly, and asked, joining in the charade, 'and what of the carnelian between her jasper thighs?'

But he went on to speak of plans that needed to be put in place, a new army, a new stratagem, alliances new. He was pulling back onto himself the skin somewhat loosened by the fever.

Before we passed through the gate of *Al-Ahqaf*, we had shed most of our men. The scores who had survived now disbanded to return to their Hemyar families. Cries of joy and anguish boomed in the tall buildings. But neither touched Emru's heart. His head had cleared of the fever, but not of the madness.

I was happy to see my father again. He had unbuckled more of his feelings, and embraced me with the wedded-widowed passion of a father and a mother. Hard and long he clasped me to his chest, I the son of the woman he had loved so totally and was now searching for her in my face. I wished Emru might be visited by such tender feelings. But the grip of the new skin was tightening.

Will Hend help him wear it more comfortably? Or will she speed up a welcome moult?

For Hend had arrived! She had survived!

I may have said before that Hend had led a group of Kenda women out of Yazd's dubious hospitality. She had roused them to rally to the cause of her brother, though many did not need such prompting. The women were escorted by the hundred horsemen Yazd had begrudgingly provided. They had arrived in Hadramot just before we set off on our campaign. But they had arrived without Hend. We all mourned her sorely, even as I wondered how Hend could ever lose her way anywhere.

Now we knew the story.

Halfway through the journey, at a place called Mubarraz, Hend, restless and resentful of her Taghleb escort, had wandered off on her camel. She was however caught in a sudden sandstorm which led her adrift. When she managed to emerge from under the whipping tabernacle, her camel strayed into quicksand, and she had to leap from her *howdah* with her jewellery even as the poor beast sank deeper and deeper into the still eddy.

She was to know later that her women companions had refused to move until she was found. Several Taghleb horsemen had to gallop off in search of her. Then a band of Jadilah scouts allied to the Asads rode by. The Taghlebs, fearing a larger army, were forced to move on, even as the Kenda women protested.

Incredible as it may sound, it was one of the Jadilah scouts who helped Hend reach *Al-Ahqaf*.

Oweir Ben Shajanah was his name, a name that should be inscribed in gold.

A lover and a hunter of riddles, he had left his companions in search of the lone camel whose tracks he had spied in the sand. When his curiosity was stirred by the marks of a woman's feet and he came upon her, she, undaunted by his rough appearance, appealed to his gallantry to help her, intoning the plea for *aman*. He responded in the noblest tradition of the desert, and pledged to take her to the haven she sought. Though she told him who she was and he had not been an admirer of her late father, he vowed to protect her with his life.

For twenty days and a night he walked ahead of his camel, having given its back to Hend, never complaining. He did not complain, even when the girl, flying into tantrums on account of the detours he was taking in order to escape hostile tribes or find water wells, made fun of his spindly legs. He simply answered, 'These legs, unsightly as they seem to you, are not the legs of one who'll betray you.' When he brought her within sight of *Al-Ahqaf*, he bade her farewell, refusing to respond to her tearful entreaties for him to stay. Nor would he accept any reward for his legendary labours.

On this paper which crossed the typhoon-tossed seas from China, may Oweir Ben Shajanah, in his rags and on his gangly legs, move like a Kohaylan and a Pegasus, agile, majestic, and triumphant, across the typhoons of Time. Unlettered as he may be, may he inscribe his calligraphy of chivalry and charity in all the colour schemes of the stars for eons to come!

Hend had grown from the mischievous and tousled-haired girl I had known in Najd into a fine young woman. She was younger than her brother by three years, her mother dying after bringing her into the world. She still had, everyone said, her mother's splendid eyes and proud, provocative look; but she also had some of the brooding nature of her father. Now she stood tall and straight as a *samhari* lance, her breasts as arrogant as the look in her eyes, the black silk of her hair streaming down her back like the night defiant behind the full moon.

There was a hint of adversity shading the sneer of her eyes; but this retreated before a razor-thin grin when she saw me.

My eyes looked into hers and pulled away; but they strayed, unbridled for an instant, onto her bosom. Acknowledging my gaze, her grin swelled with conceit and a dash of mockery. Is the lust for conquest and the gloating that attends it forever carved into her line?

I am ashamed to say that when I stared into her eyes, or was drawn into them, I thought of her *han*. Eyes are the most seductive in a woman, being the casements of the soul. But they also lead the onlooker unto other covert zones.

What was her *han* like now? I mused. Was it trim, straight and tall like her, attended along its progress by tiny slaves with tousled hair of their own? Was it tightly sealed in self-sufficiency, winking in playfulness, pleading in desperation? Was it perched on a hill or crouching in a gully or lolling on a plain? Did those long, slender fingers of hers ever fondle its lips, murmured to them as she grew up disdaining suitors? Did those lips murmur back to her? Did they ever whisper my name?

I am ashamed to note down these thoughts; but that was what came into my mind at that time.

A distant memory had floated back as I stood for a passing moment staring into her eyes.

We had been playing 'story telling'.

This was a game I was truly fond of, being so bad at every other game and sport. Not that I was so good at that game either. But, like a *houbara* bustard, timid and secretive, I could yet perform an unpredicted dance with an erect crest and a revived throat in my courtship of the imagination.

So there I was, with Emru and few other boys and girls, sitting in a circle under the balcony of Hojr's house in Al-Sharaf. Houjeira had just offered us roasted *kilit* berries to nibble and retreated with a giggle, my eyes hazily following her taut rounded buttocks under her fragile skirt. She had not had her sad lavender encounter with me yet.

A light rain had fallen on the town and there was a fresh, pungent smell of the coming autumn, a season celebrated for its rain and horse races by all and sundry.

Hend had seated herself, by chance or choice, next to me. I had finished telling a story, a fanciful cast-offs about an emir who travels to the Island of the Blue Jinn. He brings home to his clever but doleful people the elixir of madness. He wants them to be happy, and less clever. I may have picked up the bare bones of the story from my father and embellished it as is my wont. I cannot remember how the story ended at the time. It had a number of good possibilities. But one boy in the circle said his grandmother told better stories.

In any case, I had finished my tale, and Emru, sitting opposite me, started on one of his own. This was the rule of the game.

Never had Emru tried to outdo me in public. He did not need to. However, his cousin Oneyza was in attendance, and he wanted to impress her. This became a habit of his.

Hend sat cross-legged next to me. The hem of her frock had slipped across her thighs towards her lap. As I finished my story she turned towards me, smiling in praise or commiseration I did not know. But as she did so the frock slid further up, and I was entertained to a glimpse of her hairless crotch – the slender bud my mother had said if touched would explode into a fountain of blood, drowning the sinner.

But as the girl adjusted her position, she somehow came closer to me. The whole sweep of her right thigh rested against my left thigh, also exposed by my retreating boy's caftan.

As Emru progressed with his precociously bawdy tale, I began to feel the warmth and smoothness of Hend's thigh rubbing against my thigh. She was rocking back and forth as she listened to her brother's tale, laughing at its ribaldry. Though there was a nip in the air, I broke into a sweat. I was enjoying the friction, forbiddingly delectable.

What if the others had noticed? Let them notice, let them stare, let them sprout a thousand eyes, but let Emru go on with his story-telling, and let his sister move her thigh, so innocently, so deliciously, so desolately, against mine!

She was here now, thighs and all.

DOROTHEUS

Beloved Saint of the *Confessions*, attentive to the heart's frailties and cravings, grant me your amnesty!

Bar me from your garden-fortress for a little while! Allow me, 'unformed clay' as I am, to roam freely in my wilderness as you roamed in yours!

Scarred Saint, dear to my uncle for his own scars and flights, dear to me for mine!

The calling to which you set your spirit has eluded me! And yet, you would not have arrived at your garden, fragrant and fortified as it is, had you not waded through the pastures of the flesh, where I must wade, and dwell.

Timerider, slacken for me the reins of memory and spur me, the Judas that I am, to cleave to the 'flesh that passeth away and cometh not again!'

The flesh of human fellowship!

The heat of the flesh!

Young flesh converging before a giant building! Bayroute's School of Law. A building *of* giants, *for* giants? White marble gleaming in the sun! The liquid topaz of the sea in the distance a-shimmer.

The clamour of the young bodies, rising, making up lines as it goes:

Dorothĕues, judge and sage,
Wonder of a wondrous age!

And,

Captain of the ship of law,
The ship's without you's like a straw!
And,

Dorothĕus all pure sunlight,
Not like that glowworm of a night,

Not like that foetus with no soul,
A quarter snake, three quarters mole!

And,

Half-moons grow big, but not Helâl,
Congealed like wax in the ear canal!

And,

Dorothĕus the Lord adorns,
Helâl the devil made his horns!

'Who is Helal?'

'Ah, a man whose name means 'the crescent moon' but calls himself
Helius, the Sun. In origin, a Bedouin of a clan of brigands, yet a man of
airs. And they all smell horribly.'

'He was plucked from the thistles and weeds of Elusa in Palestina III
by one of Senator Climacus's caravans.'

I had heard, somewhat furtively, of the Senator, believed to be
Persia's agent on the sly, helping her designs on Syria.

'The Senator saw *possibilities* in the boy, then a prickly little urchin,
and paid for his education. Even then, Climacus sent him below the
windows of his political adversaries to shout out obscenities.'

'Yeah, many a pail of shit was poured on his little head in those
days.'

'A baptism of sorts. Befitting his smelly career.'

'More glories lay ahead. Climacus made him study book-keeping
and then Law.'

'This was for the minion to cook the Senator's books and defend
his deals at court whenever needed – the Senator's trust in him so
unshakable!'

'At the start of the year Climacus used his influence to appoint Helal
to teach the Civil Code, Dorotheus' own speciality.'

'Climacus' pretext was that Dorotheus was absent for the term in
Rome, invited by Tribonian.'

'Also, the Master's assistant, Paulus, had fallen ill!'

'Climacus and his faction are buoyed up by news of a possible
Persian invasion of Syria!'

'Yeah, but Helal proved to be such a bad teacher that we can't stand him anymore. His cockiness and the foulness of his mouth know no limits.'

'In the last few weeks he's been maligning Dorotheus himself!'

'He boasts he'll replace Dorotheus, permanently!'

'He's also been spreading a rumour that Dorotheus is a secret agent of the Persians, planted to subvert the Roman state and its laws!'

'Which is so absurd, given what we know about his boss!'

'Dorotheus is back from Rome, and Helal and his paymaster feel threatened. Dorotheus had been on a case against Climacus for bribing a judge!'

'Which is remarkable as Climacus covers his tracks so well!'

'Yeah, but for Helal to slander the Master!'

'The upstart has enough rough skin, 'Roughness' being his second name, and a tongue venal enough to slander his own mother if paid to do so!'

'Dorotheus' sandals are worth all the smart togas Climacus puts on the slither's shoulders!'

'Yeah, but a dozen sessions with Dorotheus, celestial as each one is, won't cleanse the rank memory of one session with Helal!'

The shouts continue:

Helâl will lick his keeper's oil
To spit, when told, his sick vitriol!

And,

Helâl is paid to lick and spit,
Without reflection, sense, or wit!
A tongue, when ordered, turns to wag,
An adder's hiss inside a bag!

And,

Helâl a teacher? What a joke!
A bit of coal, a lot of smoke!

And,

Helâl to teach? What? How to skim,
Then stand in court and speak from whim?

And,

Helâl to teach the Civil Code!
So uncivil, the vulgar toad!

And,

Helâl a scandal for our school!
A teacher's robe worn by a fool!
A Philistine who apes a sage!
A grey baboon, maroon with rage!

And,

Helâl the rough will huff and puff!
He wants his bite, we say 'Enough!'

And,
Dorothĕus the Cedars' pride;
Taller we grow, wider we stride!
Dorothĕus for us the guide;
A guide we will not be denied!

My rebel uncle would be cheered to hear of this youthful protest in
his beloved city.

But I'm sweating in my shame.

It's my first day of term, the second term of the year. I stand, terrified
of being associated with the riot afoot. Two senior students on my left
and right have been drawing me into their conversation and biases.

No one else seems to be sweating. They're busy hollering against a
man I do not know, and in favour of a man who is my benefactor and
guardian in the city. And yet I don't want to be seen as a lackey of my
patron's, incorruptible as he is, spineless as I am.

I shiver in the naked, sea-lidded sun!

Sweat beads quiver on my skin; they come together and stream,
flickering, all the way to Najd, where my mother's tears wash over
me.

I am embarrassed by my mother's desolate cries. What will the tribe
say? My uncle offers her words of comfort. He turns to me, half-choked,
with a last homily. His precious copy of the *Confessions* he slips into my

hand. Inside the book, he reminds me, is the letter of introduction I am carrying to Dorotheus. My father, fine looking with greying temples, seems emotionless. But his lower lip is twitching. There's a mist in his eyes and his chest is buffeted by gusts inaudible.

And there is Emru's leave-taking!

Astride a mare from my father's stable, the beautiful *Jalwa*, a niece of my *Najm*'s, and in the splendour of a new silken *aba*, he holds up a date, yellow as a yellow beryl, in his hand for all to see. He makes a show of putting the date inside his mouth and chewing it. He then takes out the stone and throws it in the direction of the town he is leaving. Then he flings at the town the lines:

I pay you this, a pip, no more,
And ride to shag a better whore!

I hear the gasps and I hear the curses. But I also hear the women and the maidens of Kenda weeping at his exodus. Some swoon in grief. Many are shearing their lustrous tresses in mourning.

Who but my mother weeps for me as I am handed over, like a bundle of dried figs, to the leader of a caravan about to leave for Syria?

Arrangements have been detailed by my uncle, negotiated by my father, sealed by Hojr. I am to study in Bayroute under a *Grammatikos* then a *Rhetor* before rising to legal study under Dorotheus. Dorotheus's father was a friend and a covert supporter of my uncle's. Dorotheus will see to my lodging and tutoring in the city.

For many years my uncle had, by chance or design, prepared me for this task.

Single-handedly, he had led me through the three stages of Roman education, progressively teaching me to read and write Latin and Greek along with the hallowed, Yesu-blessed language of this history. In his august but caring presence I sat at times for hours my tablet and stylus rising to his every word. He taught me the essentials of the seven liberal arts, but could not bore into my skull the runes of counting or the abstractions of arithmetic.

My ambition to become, to school myself to become, a poet like Emru had sprouted no feather or leaf. No Jinn-Muse cared to begild my tongue or yield her back to me. Could the sedentary, austere life of a scholar ever make up for the enchanted flights of a poet, an in-between creature?

BLOOD PURSUED
EMRU DELIVERS
A WAR SPEECH

Emru spurred his mare, the beautiful *Shaqra*, onto a little hillock and addressed his new fat army from the saddle. The tentative fingers of an autumn sunrise stroked the left side of his face, handsome as ever but glowing with a feral, self-possessed inner blaze:

'Men of Kenda and Hemyar! Men of Ghatafan and Bakr, Hanzala and Abd Al-Qais, Darem, and Ruqayah! Descendants of the noblest race to have come forth from the First Womb! A race of men and women who wrestled with angels and made covenants with an ineffable god, then went on to make gods of their own. gods to place on high and fatten up or tear down and trample upon when they sit on their arses and expect us to do all the work for them!'

This elicited a few murmurs, but wider laughter, particularly from the younger warriors.

Emru continued, addressing the traditionalists for a start:

'The gods *will* be with us today, fear you not, silver beards. For, if they don't, they won't get their supper tonight [laughter]. Which will not please their priests. For it's they, the shamans, who gulp down the mutton and pocket the coins. So it's in their interest that we prevail today. It's in their interest that we are free, and that we give freely.

'The yoke might be a wonderful collar for an ox in Syria or in Iraq. But it's a noose of death for a true Arab. For a son of the infinite spaces will not draw breath inside a loop etched by the sword of a tyrant.

'Yeah, we've come together, a guild of brothers, a fraternity of equals, to avenge the murder of Hojr. Perhaps some of you think Hojr was not as good as the elegies have made him to be. I, his son, did not think he was such a paragon. He had too many dreams. Dry dreams. And too many headaches. Which made him angry. And always in a rush. I suffered from his anger, and from his rush. Perhaps not unjustly. No doubt, he wished to be better. Wished to see some of his dreams sparkling with the dew of a new dawn; more of his headaches laid to rest. But he was denied the chance. And his murder has touched us all; for it has also denied us, we too, the chance to be better – better men, better Arabs.

'Long denied and denying their inheritance, their destiny, the Arabs have become the laughing stock of the world. They've been diminished, demeaned, by despots. Despots within Arabia, cheaply bought hirelings. Despots without. Bullies drooling for your unguarded riches, yet fearing your unity.

'They don't mind us being numerous. They certainly don't, as long as we remain divided. Let them breed till time has shed all its feathers, they say. Let them shag day and night so long as they give birth to rabbits and rats, they say. Let them be as numerous as the grains of sand in their wretched deserts. But let the rabbits not roam beyond their warrens. Let the rats take all the breaths they want in the assholes of rotting camels. Let the sand lie flat and not dream of rising to a storm, perchance to a star. Yeah, let the cocks and the hens copulate and cuckold and cackle. Let them riot to their hearts' content inside their henhouses. We can always stretch forth our arm, they say, and pluck out the chicken we want for our table.

'Who would deny them? Who would blame them, weak and divided as we are? Would you not do the same, you who love the soft flesh of chickens?'

'Our hands joined, our heads held high, our brotherhood mocking crowns, will frighten them, sneer as they may. I tell you, as we stand under the dawn of a new splendour, I tell you that when the frailest of sticks come together they will not break easily. A big stick will make a stout cudgel. And it will scare off the big bad wolf. It might even smash his skull should he come too close. And I'm not talking here about the over-exercised sticks our fabulous women know how to revive again and again on the mat [General laughter; women ululate].

'I admit, I own up! Wonderful as it's made to be seen by the likes of Abeed Ben Al-Abras, a killing field is not the best place for a man of sense and reflection. A far better place is one between the breasts of a loving mistress. What better mufflers against the ill winds of the world? Though further down, there is, for those skilled in the arts of *Lazzah* and *Bah*, a sweeter, all muffling, all melting, reward [cheers of approval].

'Still, some will prefer to be in the company of their snivelling children or on the trail of the black-rumped oryx or at the ruby lip of the cup. Whatever the choice, there will be plenty of this and that and the other when we're through with today's job.

'So strike with one mighty sword and one nimble wrist. Strike so that the great tribes of Arabia and the not-so-great ones become truly great and greater as *One Nation*. A nation that is also a brotherhood.

'There's nothing behind your backs, should you turn tail, but the desert, and everlasting shame. That is, if you can get past our doughty womenfolk at the rim.

'Before you, there is a freedom to be won, a dignity to be restored. And a languid hangover the next morning.'

The men laughed and cheered. Some wept in a jumble of emotions. Emru held their lives in the palm of his hand and their swords in his own scabbard. Their loud pledges to fight to victory or death peppered the creeping sunrise.

A DAY IN *NISAN*

O Saint of the supreme *Confessions*! And you, supreme Saint of the *Memres*! Vast is your knowledge, combined, of my soul! Vast are the wingspans of your words! Help mine, limping in their fetters, to break free; but, yet again, do not look further!

Priestess of the prophecy, by which I am defined and doomed! Restore me into the constellations of your eyes! Then hurl me, like a fistful of shooting stars, upon the waves panting beneath the balconies of Bayroute!

Who but the Jewelled city can pluck me out of the rush of events at hand? Who but she, aided by the grace of the Saints and the power of the prophecy, can summon me from the gathering tide of blood?

She need not pull, I need not resist.

In truth I need not solicit any guide or muse, imagined or real.

Never did I need to cast a fishing line for memories of the beloved city. The faintest breeze on the surface of my mind raises them from the stillness of the deeps and the underbelly of the waves.

And they rise, bedazzling the sea, as pearls might rise, though needing no diver's plunge or basket.

They rise as the face of a mermaid might rise to a wistful mariner, though mine are not of the fabric of dreams, unless life itself is of that stuff. And if that was the case, then Bayroute and Lebanon would be the rarest and dearest tapestry in that dream.

Be it the dream of one spring day.

A day in *Nisan*!

I rise from a fitful sleep to join my hostess at the gate of the villa.

A large carriage tethering two stout mules, and surrounded by five gaudy horsemen, waits outside the gate. Two lanterns flicker on both sides of a heavy-eyed but burly driver.

The light of the lanterns and the chill of pre-dawn retreat before my lady's iridescence. She stands beside the carriage with her friend, Lady Marta.

A chorus of sparrows and shrikes and nuthatches clamour in the garden; a gull calls from the sea, an early riser. The birds are celebrating the coming of spring. They're effortless, fearless, as I cannot be.

Shhhh; shhhh; shhhh... The waves swish upon the pebbles below the cliff, faint but exasperating in their monotony and conceit. Who are they shushing, mocking? What are they dispersing, gathering?

The kindly professor sends us off with a prayer. He is impatient to return to his own unwavering lanterns and indulgent tomes.

Lady Sofia's friend and confidante, Lady Marta, wife of the city's Prefect, had asked my hostess to come with her on an outing to Afqa. This is a mountain hamlet some forty miles northeast of Bayroute. There, they're to attend some mysterious gala put up by the locals.

Lady Marta is a renowned saloniere, and a buxom beauty to boot. The amplitude of her black drawn-out eyes is outshined on her figure only by the amplitude of her bosom, itself outpaced by the span of her joviality and generosity of spirit.

She is a dutiful Christian who attends Sunday church without fail, occupying a front seat on the women's balcony. There she can watch her husband and other city dignitaries sitting below in the nave of the church. But, even on the most austere religious or state ceremonies, Lady Marta has a loud exuberance and a lust for life that is seldom abashed by official sneers and pretensions. Her glowing presence bestows on any occasion, be it a dreary memorial service or a stuffy formal ceremonial, a brightness for which a man of a liberal spirit cannot but be grateful.

Nonetheless, the expedition to Afqa has been planned with an air of strict secrecy.

I was whispered to that the gala to be performed there belongs to a bygone age, an age harshly suppressed in its latter days then surgically removed, and dumped beyond reach with its viscera and libraries and altars. This had come to pass after Rome had swapped the Eagle for the Cross and her relative tolerance and accommodation in the west for extremism and exclusion in the east. More recently, the cult, lying low, even under the rubble and the offal of the past, but entrenched in the souls of the people, has boldly risen to the sun. The Prefect has chosen to give a deaf ear to the reports reaching him. His vivacious wife has expressed an interest in attending the pageant.

'If, as you say, it's only a *pious* celebration of the coming of spring, then heaven has chosen you to make it *less* pious and *more* of a celebration,' he replied to her in good humour – Lady Sofia's dear lips have disclosed to me.

The dear lips have also told me that the Prefect has arranged for an escort, helped in his choice by his wife. Similarly, the Professor has suggested that I, his devoted pupil and protégé, might, for my own education, chaperon the two ladies on their expedition.

Lady Sofia has seemed quite happy with her husband's suggestion. But, like her friend, she may have helped manoeuvre it into place. In any event, the Professor has been hard at work on a legal opinion required in Rome.

The carriage, drawn by the two mules and shielded fore and aft by four cavalrymen led by a tall, ruggedly handsome officer on horseback, clutters along over the cobblestones of the road leading away from the villa. The two lanterns on both of its sides splutter merrily through the dark neighbourhood.

Lady Marta, ensconced inside the snug carriage, banishes once and for all the chill of the hour with the sweet redolent steam of her body blended with that of Lady Sofia's.

Her lively chatter also nearly banishes the bumpiness of the road.

After a brisk breakfast of cheese and bread and olives, 'too early for figs and grapes', she says, her first talk is of the eye-catching cavalry officer, one named Kahlil.

She had first seen him in the city's main basilica at her husband's side. And here he is outside, sitting upright and easy as he must be in the saddle of his black stallion cantering ahead of the convoy.

Lady Marta rambles on with dancing dimples and a charming lisp. She gossips about scandalous priests and corrupt politicians as about her intolerable in-laws and noisy neighbours.

She mentions the ongoing case of Senator Climacus, now threatened with imprisonment but retaliating with threats of insurrection. He has a well-armed and well-funded militia in the mountains to the east, one capable of wreaking havoc on trade routes with the Syrian hinterland. The man is powerful and rich enough to bankrupt the province should he choose, this at a time when Rome has neither the money nor the will to help.

Lady Marta admits her husband is easily intimidated. She talks about problems he encounters on a daily basis as he tries to govern a country torn by conflicting loyalties. She describes the country, quite imaginatively, as a seasoned chameleon and, in the second breath, as a Hydra with many heads.

On a daily basis, her husband, she says, receives headmen and gang leaders, priests and brothel-keepers, informers and gladiator trainers, asking for money in return for continuing loyalty to the Roman State. He knows that they all go to Climacus demanding similar handouts in exchange for continuing loyalty to the Persians.

She jokes: 'When God created Lebanon, unmatched in the splendour of its landscape, the other lands became envious; so He created the Lebanese!'

'In fact', Lady Marta babbles on, 'The Romans ought to be grateful that the heads of the beast are more often in battle with one another than with the Romans.'

Lady Sofia rejoins, 'But the Romans, true to their policy of divide and rule, have been busy feeding the Hydra's heads. Each head they regale with a dark diet of mistrust of the other heads. This has created a lot of rumbles in the country!'

Lady Sofia adds that it may benefit the Roman Administration to learn from the advice the wise Chiron gave to Hercules, 'We rise by kneeling; we prevail by surrendering; we gain by giving up.'

'But this is not to be', Lady Sofia continues. 'Everyone wants power. Big Hercules finishes off the creature and goes on to loosen his juvenile arrows on others. Why don't they leave the poor guileless beasts alone?'

Lady Martha quivers with silver laughter and promises to convey this to her husband. But she inquires, glancing at me cowering in a corner of the opposite seat, as to whether her friend will partake of this advice in the hours to come.

The topic then turns to the subject of the clandestine fête we are meant to attend.

I learn that the event commemorates the death and resurrection of Adonis, about whose fortunes Lady Marta seems to be well acquainted. I too have read about him in Apollodorus and Hesiod. I also know him from an ancient Kenda trader of the Yemen who associated him with the Myrrh tree.

Adonis's father is Phoenix (the Kenda man called him Sinar), King of Phoenicia. His mother is Myrrha, the beautiful daughter of the king. Cursed by a jealous Ashtoreth (Aphrodite the Greeks call her), Myrrha sleeps with her father during a drunken festival of the corn-goddess. She runs away when he comes round and is about to kill her. Baal takes pity on her and turns her into the crooked but munificent

Myrrh tree. Nine months later the bark peels off and a babe emerges. He is named Adoni, 'my lord', and Ashtoreth is so moved by his beauty that she places him in a basket and entrusts him to the goddess of the Underworld Ereshkigal (the Persephone of the Greeks) who nurtures him to manhood. However, a tussle follows between the two goddesses. Ereshkigal refuses to give up the handsome youth. Baal mediates in the conflict. Adoni chooses to live one-third of the year with Ereshkigal in the Underworld and the remaining two-thirds with Ashtoreth on earth. Who can blame him?

However, as with all headstrong lads, Adoni will not give up a dangerous sport of his, hunting wild animals. A wild boar, goaded by another jealous god, Rashef, kills Adoni. The goddess is beside herself with grief. Her tears mingle with his blood, as her fluids had with his in life. The blood, so endowed, nourishes the coming of Spring. It flows with the river in Afqa named after him, rinsing its waters with a joyous tint. The scarlet anemones of the region also derive their dye from the wounds of Ashtoreth. She had walked barefoot on the thorns following the death of her lover in her arms inside the very grotto out of which the river gushes forth.

Our kindly mules trot patiently for some three hours down the paved road which extends from Bayroute to the famed city of Byblos.

We pass by a string of ancient villages and castles. Some stand tall and prosperous; others lie crushed and scattered on the coast and on the rocky slopes to the east.

To the west, the sea heaves with the blueness of Lady Sofia's eyes and the sighs of drowned sailors.

But less than four miles before we reach Byblos, we come to a jangling halt. Captain Kahlil, or Catallus as he is also called, directs us to an inn. He insists on us having a repast and a brief rest before we ascend to Afqa.

Later, the obliging Captain invites us to another banquet - the sight of the river of Adonis at its estuary. The river, having tumbled from the heights of the cliffs, pours into the sea in tumultuous crystals, restless to don the mantle of further mystery.

THE COMING TOGETHER OF
STEEL

My father had advised against the war.

He did not approve of another campaign against the Asads.

He pleaded with Emru to return to the Muse and her party now that he had bloodied the guilty tribe. Al-Munzer, with Persia's might behind him, was too awesome an opponent.

My father argued his case long.

He appealed to me not to take part in a fight looming in Emru's mind.

News had reached him, even before we returned, of *Zul Khalasa's* warning. He had counted on the god's benevolent guile.

But warnings, god or man given, were like straws before Emru's flash flood.

I could not leave Emru, chained to him more by love and pity than by the prophecy.

But I was happy for my father. He was sinking into old age, though with a lofty head. He had finally freed himself of his self-forged bondage to the house of Hojr. He had served them loyally for many years, even while his soul soared beyond their pretences. Even the dream of Arab unity, which he had shared with Hojr, he had now banished from his pillow. He did not care for the storm whipped up by the hotheads and met its lashes with towering indifference. Privately, he was immersing himself in his memories of his wife. And though an inveterate pagan, he yearned to join her in her Christian heaven. When I bade him farewell, he prayed with emancipated tears that the Saints his wife had loved would watch over me.

Did I need that much protection? I wondered.

For during our absence from *Al-Ahqaf*, some momentous things had come to pass – the scythe of Emru's curse at work?

Hojr's two ever-quarrelling brothers, Shorahbil and Salamah, had finally reconciled their differences, in death.

The third brother, Mu'awiya, Oneyza's spiteful father, had, at an Asad ambuscade, preceded his two brothers to that levelling realm.

His beautiful palm grove had fallen to the triumphant Asads.

His daughter, whose petite breasts had kept Emru awake for many a night but had now suckled half a dozen babes, was safe in Al-Anbar with her children and philandering husband – and no doubt her now sagging breasts.

But to continue.

Remnants of the uncles' armies had converged on Hadramot. There they met with the fighting men of Emru's four older brothers, Nafi', Alqama, Zayd, and Zuhair. They had flocked from high grounds south of Shammar to seek protection on securer heights and submit themselves to the prudence of their kin.

The presence of all those troops prickled the young *emir* of Hadramot. But it ignited the passions of the Hemyar youths, who clamoured for revenge upon the Asads. Emru's arrival, with his few horsemen, scarred by an inconclusive 'victory', had earlier stirred up a fever for retribution. The *emir* withdrew into his fort and abandoned his province to the firebrands.

The lovely, fearsome Hend came along, leading a band of women from the tribes.

Now, three quarters of Arabia's sands were behind us. The quarter that remained held its breath.

TO THE TEMPLE OF LOVE WE RISE

We climb to the higher mysteries of Afqa.

The Captain and I ascend on foot. The two ladies are royally seated in sedan chairs borne by four local porters.

At the coast, Lady Marta had asked the Captain to instruct his soldiers to guard the carriage, he to proceed with us. He seemed content enough.

We trek along a winding path cut in some places through slabs of rock and fringed by oak and cedar and juniper trees. The more modest orchids and myrtles, thymes and thistles, peep curiously at us from cracks in the rocks and the undergrowth.

Afqa itself rewards our expectations. It gathers unto itself the surrounding mosaic of summits and terraces, ridges and ravines, but shines with an allure of its own.

And it roars!

The ancient shrine of Ashtoreth has survived after a fashion. Captain Kahlil's military career has in no way dimmed his intellect or compassion. He tells us that the shrine was rededicated under the Romans to the worship of Venus. 'Not a bad thing at all! We're all for love, whoever wears the crown', Lady Marta declares gaily. The two goddesses are deities of love, and in the stories they bond in their passion for the slain youth. Kahlil's disciplined demeanour relaxes into a smile. He adds that the Emperor Constantine, in his own interpretation of the Christian creed of love, had the building destroyed as a vile pagan relic. Later, a dark wave from Constantine's Capital, one unleashed by none other than the redoubtable John Chrysostom, hurled itself against the remaining columns of the temple. It aimed to knock down every trace of the obstinate cult. Its followers, in desperation, fought back with spears and rocks. Those who survived were crucified. The priestesses were disembowelled, their entrails thrown to pigs.

'I admit that neither law nor sword can shake away this sort of thing,' the Captain says. 'Not even earthquakes', Lady Marta rejoins. 'Unless made by big handsome men,' she adds merrily, her dimples dancing a jig.

The temple stands before us, its rose-granite columns and walls seem to have been freshly restored. Lights flicker in its windows as night descends.

And the night roars more loudly.

A massive mouth in the sheer rocky face of the cliff has been disgorging a thunderous torrent of water. This is the source of the sacred river. Its roar, suddenly amplified, shoots up like a giant *efreet* breaking out of its *qomqom* and overwhelming the valley, the cold spray needling us. The two ladies retreat, their wetted dresses clinging to the curves of their bodies.

Thunderous and untamed, the cataract bears little kinship to the waters eked out of wells in the arid parts of Arabia or those civilly harnessed from the *aflaj* there. It does remind me though of the killer flash floods that build up in Najd without warning and surge through the gullies sweeping away unwary children and sluggish cattle.

We recoil in awe.

A dying dusk still manages to light up a cluster of russet-coloured stone houses bordered by walnut and olive and fig trees.

We continue to hear the plunging water beating its fists on the boulders in its path as we retire to a small house provided for us by an agent of Lady Marta's. Tired as I am after a long land journey and a hard, winding climb, my chest is animated by the crisp air of the night as it slides over the heights and the valley. The prospects of further mysteries and revelations conspire to delay my sleep inside an alcove near the door.

But I wake up to a double radiance: the early spring morning and, more dazzlingly, Lady Sofia's gleaming breasts partly exposed under the neckline of a linen frock. She is bending over me, her cherry-lips scolding my indolence with a melody shaming all mountain warblers, 'Wake up, lazy bones! The carnival is about to start!'

RIDING TO THE
FINAL BATTLE

So we marched, three thousand strong, to the plain of Al-Sada.

Swords rattled like snakes in their sheaths, horses neighed, camels growled, women rehearsed their war chant, men rehearsed their death, not believing in it.

Emru was on his blond mare, surrounded by his four brothers. The four were reluctant avengers. But they appeared so self-assured now, erect in their embroidered saddles like swollen penises. One final strike and they would trot back to grassy Najd, having justified a longer lifespan of idleness and excess.

They had finally woken up to Kubeysa's schemes. The grand diplomat was now unashamedly serving his new master in Iraq, who would brook no diplomacy save one which would uproot every tree and sapling of the Kenda line.

Al-Munzer's enmity for the tribe had never abated. In fact it had flared up like a *soheet* bonfire in the face of Emru's quest to avenge his father, in whose killing the Iraqi despot may have had a hand. His arm was long enough to reach and grasp treasured cities under the very shadow of Roman ramparts. The rise of Emru from the pursuit of poetry and romance to the hunting of armies and political rainbows Al-Munzer must have viewed with concern, fearing the rise of a star that might eclipse his own seasoned flare. A poet and philanderer turned warrior seemed a greater threat than a dour king with a headache and a people's hatred.

He must however have looked on Emru's reversals and half-triumphs with relative relief. But news of our large army marching on the Asads where they had redeployed south of Al-Anbar he could not but have received with disquiet.

And possibly with anticipation!

For here was a chance to do away once and for all with a power that might rival his own in Iraq and Syria and in the very heart of Arabia. More importantly, it might, with enhanced pinions, soar higher and range more widely with further endorsement of his own Persian master. It might even wrest the Roman Emperor's trust in his own vassal in Syria.

Both the threat and the opportunity were equally balanced. Emru's own grandfather, Al-Hareth Ben Amr, had seized such a moment when he learned of Kavad's change of heart towards Al-Munzer. Al-Hareth's cynical act of getting in with the new Shah by converting to his new religion of Mazdakism had been swiftly and harshly punished by the Iraqi warlord as soon as Kavad was succeeded by his son Khosro, who rewarded Al-Munzer for not converting to the cult of Mazdak. Now the act could be re-played.

Seizing the moment, the Proteus in the sea of change, is what politics about. Seize the blue imp-god and he will tell you all the truths you need to know about the world. And all the falsehoods you want the world to know about yourself?

And so we marched, buoyed up by Emru's war speech to face the Asads. Their villainy had ebbed and flowed in my mind, but not in the minds of those around me. In theirs, it had surged and surged and surged. To what bloody peak?

THE TEMPLE OF LOVE

I walk behind two cloaked and hooded females on the path snaking up to the temple.

Thus, the ceremony begins; and I am bemused to see a pagan gala unfold in the heart of a Christian country. But why should I be surprised, the mongrel that I am?

From inside the temple, a procession issues forth. It is made up of a column of maidens dressed in long sable cloaks with wreaths of briars round their heads. They carry on their shoulders a litter with an effigy of the stricken god. They are intoning a hymn, probably timeless in its anguish:

> No sap has blest the garden's rose,
> The tamarisk bewails her bloom,
> The willow droops in grief and thirst,
> The daffodils are sunk in gloom.
>
> And Earth, in mourning, rends her veils.
> 'My child,' she keens, 'is dead, Adon!'
> She cries for homes, for streams, for fields,
> That see no babes, no fish, no corn!
>
> She mourns the cypress, bent by drought,
> The cedar, sulking in the heat,
> The vineyard, bare, the honey, spent,
> The bridal gown a winding sheet!

Lady Sofia leans against my shoulder. I feel the heat of a sigh upon my neck, a nectarous shiver rippling through my body. This exquisite pillar of strength teetering by my side! I don't know what I should do or what is expected of me. I want to shout at the maidens to stop their sham lamentations which have made my mistress so upset. But are their dirges really fraudulent with all these tears flowing? I half wonder about this as I place a trembling arm round Lady Sofia's satin shoulder, consoling, protecting, soliciting? I know I'm taking liberties, but I assume (perhaps foolishly) that I'm being invited to them, though I don't know through what door. One thing I know for certain, that I'll be fumbling with the key.

A swelling crowd of votaries follow the procession with us upon a descending path. We walk next to the course of the hurtling cataract and see it grow into a stout river bound for the sea hundreds of feet below. Then we come to the edge of a lake formed by a tributary of the river and ringed by fig trees. Kahlil explains that the ribbons and parchments dangling from the branches are petitions to the goddess. Here the leading maidens in the procession lift the effigy, a red gash on its side, from the litter and ease it into the water. Then something remarkable happens. The pace of the water pouring into the lake seems to quicken. A dark torrent rushes to overtake the sparkling whiteness of the stream, staining it with the colour of blood!

Distracted by the transformation, I do not follow the actions of the maidens. They have deftly exchanged their wreaths of briars with crowns of red anemones, which they must have removed from the litter, into which I now see them throwing the sable cloaks they had on their shoulders. They are revealed to be wearing sheer robes of a bright red dye. Also revealed under the sheerness are the curves and thrusts and hollows of their sinuous bodies.

Now they chant, to the complement of a chorus of flutists, who had been plodding behind them almost invisibly in grey, their flutes unseen. They too have now exploded into loud colour and sound:

> My lord has bled, but now is hale,
> The sea salutes his crimson sail,
> The earth with joy lifts up the song:
> My child is back and sings along,
> He's filled the cups with ruby wine,
> The granaries with corn divine,
> The olive's juice, in jars, awaits
> To join the bread and mead and dates;
> The streams and brooks now flow with mirth,
> For death has yielded a new birth.
>
> My lord is hale, and though he's bled,
> His blood anoints the marriage bed.

The ceremony, the Captain whispers to us, is part of a ritual that is acted out not only in Byblos down by the sea but also in cities and towns across the Mare Nostra, one being the great city of Alexandria. Here in Afqa the height of the rite will take place in the temple itself.

We re-ascend the slope behind the beguiling haunches in red gauze and the swaying male phalanxes of the flute players.

As we proceed in this fashion, I turn the story of Adonis in my head. A very handsome lad fought over by gods and goddesses; but is he truly a member of the celestial family? Does he deserve to be treated as one? But why shouldn't he? Isn't he a sa'luk of the Land of Cedars, a lad of the people's dreams and fancies? And what are gods but dreams, or nightmares, of men and women? And of the two, the dream and the reality, which one deserves the higher praise and devotion? Can the one exist without the other? Is not the life and death and rebirth of Adonis but an acting out of the cycle of seasons and seeds and the dramas of men and women? Is it not also an acting out of the dramas and cycles of empires and creeds? And of the gods, yielding their temples to newer gods so that all continue to live in bold or subtle ways, sharing their stones and votaries, their effervescence and endurance?

Both, reality and dream come together in the temple of Ashtoreth and Adonis. So do the women and men, priestesses and supplicants, entwining in the darkly perfumed alcoves of the building, all doing the pleasure of the goddess, and their own. Lady Marta, escorted by Captain Kahlil, withdraws into a darkness welcoming.

Lady Sofia whispers to me, a fever on her lips burning my cheek and liquefying my thighs, as she leads me by the hand from the portico of the temple towards the little cottage at the lip of the hamlet,

'My real name is Ashtoreth, and you shall be my Adonis tonight!'

111

KENDA'S WAR CHANT

A scout Emru had sent ahead of us returned. He reported that Asad tents were filling the plain. He had seen no sign of unease. He was panting like a parched saluki.

Emru was elated. The quarry was in his grasp.

Despite the sun, rising somewhat sluggishly, I felt an inner chill. Then came the sinking heart, followed by cold sweat and queasiness, the marks of my fear of conflict, a legacy of my mother's helpless vendetta against war.

I urged my horse, a fine thoroughbred though not as fine as my long lost *Najm*, closer to Emru. I was hoping to gather an ember from his fire.

His half-brothers, imbeciles in silken *abas*, bejewelled swords at their ponderous hips, were riding some of the finest horses and mares in Arabia – so undeservedly. They had fallen behind. But Nafi', the eldest, kept pace with Emru. He was unhappy with Kenda's signet ring round Emru's finger. He was trying to show the cool-headed dispassion his father had wished to see in his successor.

Emru had seemed to me dull and distant during much of our trek from Hadramot. But I was so much moved by his speech of the last hour. It unmasked him as a rabble rouser, a gambler with the lives of men, and a chaser of the dream of pan-Arab unity, which Al-Ward, *sa'luk* as he is, deemed both unnatural and unworkable. However, the speech restored him to my affections. Here was my Emru, my mate and nemesis, bawdy and brave, funny, outrageous, reckless, a lover of freedom and life! And yet, I forlornly wished that matters would not go beyond the dash of words.

Walking my horse next to his superlative *Shaqra*, I blurted out a flattering remark about his speech. He brushed aside the compliment. 'I must have been drunk. It was the Hadramot wine!' he said, once more. He had not tasted that juice or any other since the fateful night at *Al-Ahqaf*.

Suddenly, the encampment sprawled into view.

I wanted an ember, but Emru suddenly sent sparks flying at me. His gaze scorching my eyes, he hissed, 'What are you doing here? Go back and stay with Hend. Foolish girl! She wants to fight and get herself killed. She's to guard the shields. I trust no one else with this, with them, except her and you. And Al-Ward of course. But he's here to stay. Find her this very instant and get her back to the black camel. This is an order. Do it or I'll run you through in your fancy saddle.' He drew his sword.

It was a great humiliation to be seen galloping to the rear of the army just as the men and some of the women were about to surge into an all-out charge. It is the custom of the Arabs (should this record outlive the practice) to go to a decisive battle with their womenfolk. Some of the women will carry swords or spears and ride with the men in the front lines. Others choose a more perilous assignment. They stay at the rear of the army carrying slings and spears and the like, which they would use to prevent anyone fleeing the fray. The presence of the women, some of whom also act as nurses, helps to shore up the resolve of the men to face their enemy - especially when the women start chanting. Thus for an Arab to flee and leave his womenfolk behind, slain or captive, insures a lasting disgrace for that man and his tribe. In any case the women at the back would make sure that no deserter, man or woman, passed through their ranks without being turned back or pelted or killed. Their chants vary from tribe to tribe. That of Kenda goes like this:

We are our mother's carers,
Our Kenda's standard-bearers;
To those who turn and flee
We are their undertakers,
To those who charge the foe,
We grant our beds and favours.

I overcame my sense of shame and spurred my horse into a gallop curling from the left flank of the army to the column of women arrayed at the rear with murderous looks. Their spears and slings pulsated in their hands like cocks and balls. I shouted out that I was carrying a message for Hend from the king.

I had in fact overheard the exchange that had taken place earlier between Emru and Hend. Emru had asked his sister to be in command of those women who had chosen to guard the army against itself. She had answered, shouting, 'I don't want to stay with the Shrill Throats, damn good as they may be to you! I want my sword to taste Assad blood, my teeth to sink into the liver of my father's killer! Hojr was my father as he was yours, after a fashion!'

Emru had answered, 'The dear women will have no reason to assault your ears. None of my warriors will turn tail. Should anyone do so, let your sword drink freely from his blood. For indeed he would be an accomplice of the Assads! As for the livers of men, you have no need for them. Spare your sweet lips for more deserving men with other aching organs!'

But Hend wouldn't relent. She kept up a volley of protest.

So he reflected for a moment, and said, in jest or earnestness I couldn't tell, 'Carry the shield of Ishmael and you shall fight by my side. But only after you have made sure your women are in line!'

'I shall be there,' she snapped back.

Now, the women were in line. Some were atop their camels, some on their horses, some standing. Some waved the flags and banners of the various tribes warring alongside us. Almost all had their weapons at the ready. Hend was on top of the black dromedary called *El-Pheel* for it looked like an elephant. But she was not seated. She was grappling with a bundle of shields under a steel net. The net had been strapped to the animal's body by none other than Al-Ward, at Emru's request.

The dromedary had accompanied us from Hadramot. All the way through he was regarded by Emru and the Kendas with the reverence accorded the camel that carried Kenda's gift to the Ka'ba. I had regarded the bundle, wobbling and rattling under its steel mesh, with a mix of feelings. The memory of my father rescuing the shields and conveying them from Najd to Hadramot evoked tender thoughts.

Ah, would that he alone, with the exquisite mares and stallions, had survived the journey! Would that he had left those accursed relics to sink into the sullenness of the sands, seasoned as they are in swallowing up men and their vanities!

Hend was furious, ranting against Christian saints and pagan gods. The net securing the shields and which she had been tearing at would not break loose. She was livid with rage, and refused my assistance. I delivered my message, which she did not seem to hear, and dismissed me with a cuss. I galloped back, but turned, dithering, recalling Emru's orders for me to stay and guard his sister and the heirlooms, to whose net she was now applying her dagger, to no avail.

And then the thunder began.

SOFIA

I write with much of Arabia below the precipice of my China leaf.

Let the deserts of Nafud to the north and Dahna to the east howl and hurl their dust across the sunken ravines and the serrated ridges below. They will not touch us here, on the green highlands of Shammar - an eyrie for the freeborn spirit, and the fugitive one.

The battle of the plain howls in my ears. But my soul takes flight to a haven in distant Lebanon, a heartbeat away.

Dear Saint, as in your ears, in mine also hums the 'cauldron of unholy loves' - but why unholy?

For though in my soul also howls the 'famine for incorruptible nourishment', the body too howls to be fulfilled – a creature of a day as it might be.

And O Saint, just as your own soul was 'besprinkled' with a 'sweetness' that cast out the 'gall of sorrow-bringing bonds', so let it be with me, though the spring that flooded my veins may seem different from the one which inundated yours.

When I arrived in Bayroute to sit at Dorotheus's feet and take the morsels, nay the generous helpings, of knowledge from his hand, my mentor had been recently married. His wife, Sofia, came from one of the noblest and wealthiest families in Phoenicia.

Artless in her loveliness like a gazelle of the grassland, she yet possessed to the highest degree the urban refinement and graces of Bayroute's society freed of its affectations and hypocrisies, though not blind to them.

And seemingly unconcerned and unhurried as a lioness, she was gentle and kind to the poor in the city. When I came into the zodiac of her brilliance, she had lately founded a refuge-house in a southern suburb of the metropolis which she dedicated to the destitute and the ailing.

And though as generous as a desert sheikh, she towered like an Olympus over her suitors. They, besotted by her beauty and goaded by the apparent apathy of her husband, hovered around her like flies circling a jar of honey. However, taking no pleasure in disdain and genuinely devoted to the good name and interest of Dorotheus, she calmly spurned their petitions and pleadings, whether brazen or discreet.

This she did, not because of any religious scruples. She seemed to follow a moral code of her own, one that flew with wings not nursed in the yolk of any specific church or creed. Indeed, she had a remarkable independence of mind, which I believe held many men, including her husband and myself, in much awe, perhaps crippling both of us in our different ways.

In all her manners, Sofia was splendidly composed and dignified. Only on one or two occasions did she go into the kind of tantrums some married women are prone to go into from time to time. And though graced to perfection with that sun-brushed Lebanese complexion, she had the most striking blue eyes. Did they hint at a foreign connection in the long history of her family or rather at the sea her Phoenician ancestors had tamed even while carrying its wildnesss and snares in their veins?

Women in Lebanon, when granted the luxury of education, are fed a diet of religious texts which assigns to them roles of silence and tasks in corners and kitchens. They are chaperoned to churches, where they are jealously guarded from the leers of young men under the dome. The priest will berate their sex from the pulpit as the agent of the Fall and the gateway to Hell. He will not grant them the license of taking a bath for fear of the bather seeing her own nakedness.

And yet, the opulence of the human body, undraped, unashamed, unblemished, male and female, is everywhere in the villas of Bayroute, including that of Dorotheus.

When he offered me, in an act of unprecedented honour, a lodging in an annex of his magnificent residence, the great man cited his respect, and that of his late father, for my uncle. Ephraim's fame, I was happy and embarrassed to note, had survived his exile from the city. To his admirers, he was a glorious rebel, one who turned his failure to a triumph and his flight from his hometown into an epic mission to spread the faith in barbarous Arabia. To his detractors, he was a doubter and a fool.

I recall one statue, a marble copy of a Greek sculpture depicting the goddess Aphrodite, whom the Romans call Venus. It was placed near an incessantly chattering eight-pointed fountain in Dorotheus' garden.

I recall the perfect posture subtly inclining to the right,
the elegant head faintly tilted,
the look in the blank eyes dreaming of gods to enslave and mortals to
set free,
the delicate breasts,
the slight waist,
the smooth belly,
the wet (wet?) robe clinging so intimately,
so revealingly,
to
the rounded hips,
the precious, perilous, mound,
the tapering thighs,
a sigh of the flesh meant to live in immortal marble for a thousand
mortal years!

I spent hours gazing at the image from the sea-facing window of my room on the first floor. This is where Lady Sofia lodged me in preference to the annex in the garden whose only window faced the pine-carpeted mountains to the east.

It was in this room that one autumn afternoon my host and mentor let fall upon the mosaic floor a law book he was holding. He had been kindly clarifying a legal matter I had found too obscure earlier at the School. As I bent down to pick up the book, he placed his hands upon my shoulders and, lifting me, drew me close to his body. The sorrow in his brown eyes was mixed with a look of desperation as he took me into his arms and I felt him grow against me.

THE BATTLE OF THE PLAIN

'Wake ye up, ye Asad curs! Breakfast on the blades of Hojr!' Our men shouted as they galloped into the sleeping plain. Their rumble promised no shower but that of blood.

As the men rode down with swords held aloft my sinking feeling climbed with a surge of curiosity. I seized the halter of *El-Pheel*, Hend thrashing about on his hump, and pulled him behind my horse towards the edge of the slightly higher ground on which we stood.

The towering beast strangely yielded easily.

I was now able to view the scene unhindered save by the cloud of dust kicked up by so many hooves.

The hamlet of tents lying before the hurtling army remained a fresco of utter calm. Emru had hesitated with the order to charge. He had walked his *Shaqra* restraining her from leaping into a gallop. A descendent of the noble pedigree of *Al-Haroun*, she had whinnied and convulsed beneath him, turning one side of her beautiful face to look at him with huge, questioning eyes.

The eyes of his half-brothers had also been upon him. 'When is that poet boy going to give the order and give us the necks and the *hans* lying down there?' their eyes seemed to say.

But killing people, especially as they slept, had never been Emru's game.

For a long while, the blunder at the Kenana encampment had preyed on his mind.

Before he snapped his brief, searing order to me, he had been soothing his restless mare, leaning forward and patting the luscious mane on her arching neck.

But he had also been in deep thought. 'What if…' I heard him murmur just as I spurred my horse back towards the fragrant forbidding line of the guardian women on the gently elevated ground.

I wondered if it was Nafi' who had given the order to charge.

As the waves of our horsemen thundered towards the tents, scores of women emerged, old women, wailing and screaming. No men were seen.

At least they did not come out of the tents.

They came out from behind the ridge of the high plateau to the east mounted on horses, their spears and swords glinting, the green Asad standard beaming. They stretched in many hundreds, the rising sun behind them, and into our eyes.

They had waited until all our men were roundly in the plain, twisting and turning between the tents and the screaming women.

I saw Emru in the distance wheeling the neck of his mare towards the Asad horsemen and galloping up towards them on a somewhat steep but tractable incline while hacking the vast sky with his slender sword. Hundreds of riders, Kenda, Hemyar, and *sa'luk* stalwarts, swept up behind him. His half-brothers dawdled in the plain with their followers, snaking their way between the tents and the women.

But both groups, the brave few who had charged and those loitering in greater numbers in the plain, had run into a trap of steel.

For from behind the crescent of hills to the north there emerged a shimmering column of hundreds of horsemen, fanning to the east and the west. As they rode in tight formation down the slopes towards the plain, another column fanned behind them, and another and another and another - rows of shimmering terror.

Surely those were no ordinary desert riders, but the cavalry of Al-Munzer, distinguished by their black Iraqi cloaks and light Persian helmets, round shields and slightly curved swords. These were the scourge of Rome's imperial troops in the buffer lands, hounding them and tearing at their flanks and rears, and on occasion their very hearts and spleens, mocking their studied routines and rehearsed manoeuvres. Battle hardened and trained to a combination of desert warfare and Persian discipline, they were a formidable adversary to any regular army.

Nor were their imperial masters too far away. For as the Assad horsemen descended from the crest of the eastern plateau to meet Emru's charge, they revealed behind them a rising then cascading file of heavy Persian cavalry, the fearsome *Asvaran*, perhaps four hundred strong. These stood out with their high steel helmets, full body and horse armour, javelins, battle-axes and swords, their booming drums suddenly drowning the sounds of men and horses. Then came, without pausing, their volleys of armour-piercing arrows shot with stubby bows from high pommelled saddles.

120

The women around me, sensing the looming disaster, frantically raised their chant as their men-folk were being primed for the carving-up in the plain below:

We are our mother's carers,
Our tribal standard-bearers;
To those who turn and flee
We are their undertakers,
To those who charge the foe
We grant our beds and favours.

What beds? What favours? I almost laughed as my head spun and my heart could plummet no further.

The men of Kenda and Hemyar and the fun-loving *sa'luks*, encircled by a massive ring of blades and spearheads, were being systematically pierced and diced and skewered as for a banquet, a very big banquet for King Death. They certainly were no passive lamb joints, and were fighting desperately, cutting down wave after wave of their butchers. But it was obvious that the banquet was to be at their expense.

I wanted to shout to the women, now true undertakers in the making, to call on their men to turn and flee, promising them all manner of perfumed indulgence if they could come out of that carnage alive. But it was of no use. Even if some of the men who had an hour earlier pledged their lives to Emru wanted to renege on their pledge, the route to escape, to beds and favours, had by now been almost completely sealed off.

Even then, I should have rushed into the fray like a man to die next to Emru; but I did not. There was a whirlwind in my head, and I did the only thing I could think of as necessary at the time. I turned my horse's head to the south, forcing with the lead rope in my hand *El-Pheel*, the frenzied Hend on his back, to turn behind me. I turned again and gave the buttocks of the beast a loud slap with the broad side of my otherwise useless sword. As he jerked and shot forth like a mountain possessed, I galloped next to his heavy air-gulping and his passenger's shrieks into the gaping desert.

The women, braver than all my coward's reasoning, had taken their shrill throats, their slings and spears, and galloped, banners flurrying, down into the plain to join their men in a final, more intimate, chant to King Death.

SOFIA SUPREME

Sofia's sunny voice radiates from one of the wings of the vestibulum. '*Dori*! *Dori*! *Dori*!', she calls out the pet name she has for her husband. Her voice glides nearer and nearer across the corridor until she stupefies the room with her radiance.

She pauses, dazzling, in a white silken gown accentuating the felicity of her form, the delicate thrust of her bosom, the night-stream of her hair, with the glow of her skin and the sea of her eyes adding to the dazzle.

She stands at the door of the room and observes her husband bending down to pick up a book from the floor.

I gaze at her loveliness, feeling a strange power dawning forth from her body and soul, enveloping mine.

Somewhat singed by the sparks of the earlier encounter, I shiver and break into a cold sweat, beneath which a flame licks at my heart. My legs flutter as though by a tremor. I half hear the lady quietly but icily (how can ice form on those lips?) tick her husband off for forgetting that they have a Prefect's ceremonial to go to.

I feel sad for Dorotheus. In some ways I empathise with his predicament; and as his staunch pupil and follower, I am very much within the radius of his appeal and power.

Though steeped in Roman law and an avowed Christian, Dorotheus is a fervent Graecophile. He speaks with passion worthy of a true pagan (a pagan of the mind) of ancient Athens, her triumphs and tragedies, her gymnasiums and Academy, her artists and philosophers, playwrights and orators, gods and goddesses. I count myself privileged to sit with sons of Lebanese notables at the feet of this celebrated scholar. His zeal and learning as he digresses from the legal texts to stress a point of rhetoric or culture or myth, are infectious. I learn to root for Achilles and Odysseus, pity Hector and Paris, adore Helen and Penelope, and tearfully celebrate the martyrdom of Socrates in the cause of freedom. Aristotle's dictum 'Plato is dear to me, but dearer still is truth' leaves an indelible mark on my youthful mind, a mind already contested over by the assorted passions of my parents and uncle as well as of Emru.

Something of Socrates, and of Zeno, who spitted out his tongue to the tyrant, was already instilled in me by my father's political preferences and his empathy with the *sa'luks*. Arabia itself had the song of freedom as her chief of songs, even though that song was being gagged by the rising despotisms. In older times, every grown-up member of a tribe was consulted on its affairs and no man or woman would be forced into doing something they did not wish to do. At least that was the case before the new fashions were imported by the bloated, and the arrogance and exclusion of walls began to eat into the native 'democracy'.

Dorotheus himself is a patriot of sorts. Much as he loves the ancient Greeks, he also speaks passionately about his bubbly Lebanon.

Hearing him talk about Cadmus makes you think that Greece had languished in barbarism for centuries before it discovered the arts of writing and farming and navigation, which Cadmus brought to the Aegean as he searched for his sister, Europe. In like manner, without the voyages of Hanno and Himilco, the continents of Africa and Europe would not have been mapped. Without Hiram, King of Tyre, Solomon's Temple in Jerusalem would not have been built. Without Pythagoras of Samos, Thales of Miletus, Mochus of Sidon, and Zenos of Sidon, the Greeks would not have been launched on their philosophy, atomic theory, mathematics, poetics, and so on and so forth. Even less remotely, without the blood of martyrs like Perpetua of Carthage, Theodosia of Tyre, Barbara of Baalbeck, and Aquilina of Byblos, the tree of Christianity would not have taken root or breathed a convivial air in the Levant.

Perhaps without Sofia being there, I would have been led with little resistance down my mentor's lonely path. I have heard tales whispered at the School of boys offering their flesh for a superior kind of pleasure not unknown to monks in their forlorn monasteries nor to patrons of the city brothels, about which students spoke with revulsion or fascination, some bragging about their experiences with the accomplished courtesans on offer there. A student, one named Yuhanon, spoke of Senator Climacus as one who forced his boy-favourites to yield their backs to him.

The Professor's wife was on hand to guide me onto another road, her splendour providing the greater hazard.

It isn't that I did not notice Lady Sofia before.

She had been very kind to me when I first arrived at the gate of her villa with the gaucheness of a peasant boy despite my earlier education in the city. The sea-facing room in the villa which she invited me into she made cosy and comfortable with an abundance of cushions and curtains and a suite of elegant furnishings. Later, I came to know that it was the lady of the house who had been overseeing the tidying up of my bed and infusing the room with sweet smelling herbs and incense, the sea breeze itself wafting its own heady contribution to the potpourri. The delicate dishes which were sent to me in my room or which I was invited to partake of at the master's and mistress's table were often the loving handiwork of the lady herself.

More boldly, she initiated me into the high society of Bayroute. A 'desert prince' she called me, which, I felt, cast me into the role of a noble barbarian. But I knew she did not mean to embarrass me. Rather, she deemed the title lofty and exotic enough to act as a rite of passage for me into her city society. It was also a defence against potential gossip, as I was also presented as a nephew of the legendary Ephraim and a living proof of the success of his mission in Arabia. This Lady Sofia reinforced with talk about my scholastic and otherworldly zeal, creating the impression among her lady friends that I was more of a hermit and a bookworm than a simple youth in need of initiation into manhood.

As to why the glamorous and sensible lady should be interested in me, who is no Joseph in looks or a Solomon in wisdom, I do not have a clue. Nor am I ever likely to, save to attribute this to fate or to a streak in Sofia's nature, the same streak which made her consent to her marriage to Dorotheus. She certainly had in her the strength of character and the obliging family to have freely chosen any of her many other suitors. I suspect that she was drawn to him as a thinking man, a quality she always valued and respected.

And, since I have made a reference to Joseph, I need to say that Lady Sofia is certainly no Potiphar's wife, at least not in the way in which that Egyptian lady is portrayed by the religious zealots - a mountain of lustful flesh wobbling and scheming and browbeating its way into the bed of the saintly youth. For in truth that lady of the Nile may have been as proud and sensitive and praiseworthy as Lady Sofia is; but, caught in a passion she was unable to elude, she had to resort to stratagem. Perhaps she prevailed and the zealots changed the story.

Do the heavens have anything to do with these entanglements? I cannot tell. People say that an alignment of planets brings odd bodies and souls into similar arrangements on the earth. Others speak of halves that float in the ether in search of one another.

Do we align and cohere, or rather drift and collide, sucked into our ruin by our nearness to one another? Are we pawns on the chessboards of the gods, polo balls on their playing fields, jokes on their lips, teardrops from their stony eyes? I do not know. Nor do I wish to.

RESPITE IN SHAMMAR

We are safe here in the heights' haven under the Emir's *aman*.

Unassailable are the ramparts of Shammar and Al-Mu'alla's valour.

And yet, the rancid dust of The Plain of Death howls and tears at every pore in my routed soul.

I had returned after my flight with Hend and under the sickle of the moon to the field of slaughter.

I had returned, transformed into a night scavenger, my crouching body dimly mirrored in the betrayed stares of the dead. I moved with jackals and hyenas, who too were pilfering the sickly but welcome light of the crescent moon to tear into the doubly murdered flesh. But I had come back for the living, or had been recalled to them by the silent keening of their wounds, their dark, gluey blood glistening in the moonlight as it clung to the fresh corpses or sank into the ancient sand.

Hend, half-healed of her frenzy, was by my side. The sheen of her fingernails and the sweat of her armpits crackled in my senses, shielding them against the horrors around me. From the distance drifted the drunken songs of the victors.

Spectre-like I moved through the mounds and clumps of bodies being ripped and gnawed. These were bodies that had sprouted from joyous loins, cherished in anxious wombs and swaddled and nurtured and trained in the ways of the world before they were entrusted to the unblinking gods. They had tasted needs and ecstasies unknown to the gods themselves. Now they lay, surprised by Death (does Death ever come but as a surprise?), mangled victims of the man whose body we sought.

Then we found it, that body, O joy supping with woe! Life had not altogether trickled out of its veins. Emru had fallen, under his beautiful mare, a drinker of a wind no more of this world, the mare's equine divinity desecrated by a porcupine of arrow shafts.

Emru and his mare had stumbled not far from the spot where I had last seen them charging the cascading columns of horsemen like some crazy pebble hurling itself against an avalanche.

The pebble had somehow managed to stop a few big rocks, now scattered around it in death.

The victors had retired to the other side for the night away from the cloying smell and the tittering hyenas. They had however posted guards around the sprawling terrain to prevent Bedouin robbers from looting the corpses. But I was astonished to see that some of those human jackals were already there. They slithered about, their eyes gleaming like their daggers, like the Martian eyes of wolves, eying me with murderous intent and Hend with lust. They were too careful however not to raise a sound that might alert the guards drowsy with their victory or fear of the grim pasture they had helped sow. Their comrades, Persians and Iraqis and Asads, would return at first light to retrieve, finish off, rob, rape, impale, gloat over. So we had to act quickly and stealthily. The camp lights were flickering under the ever-malevolent twinkle of *Algol* and the grinning yellow sickle.

But long before these fires had died out, Hend and I had managed to pull the battered Emru from under his golden-haired equine shield. With the help of a man who had risen from the dead and who walked with the stealth of a fox and the strength of a horse, we hauled him to the high ground. There we lifted him onto the back of the black dromedary and strapped him behind the shields of long-dead Arab kings.

GODDESS IN BAYROUTE

O Saint of the bold *Confessions*! The soot and fire of your ink have anointed and seared my soul even as I curled up in my mother's lap and cowered before my uncle's tablet.

But let me, a crow-throated outcast from your garden, sing the praises of a goddess, yeah, mortal as her dewy flesh must be!

For, even as your own goodly mistress was a grace and a shield and a spur to you for the span of fifteen years so has Sofia been to me. Brief O brief has been my sojourn in her temple. But to me the memory of that sojourn is forever a grace and a shield and a spur, redolent with jasmine, riotous with ecstasy and anguish!

At Afqa, Sofia was a goddess who invited me to heaven. But like Etana riding the eagle, I was terrified at the fellowship of the stars and pleaded to be returned to earth. She was a spring basket, a banquet, a cornucopia, into whose sweet succulence I should have sunk my whole being, my whole life.

As I pen these letters in Shammar I see her as a fruit of virginal ripeness, standing so divinely revealed in that small cottage on the hallowed heights, the moonlight streaming through the window in concert with the incessant cicada music, the chatter of the waterfall in the dark distance, the smell of the moist mountain soil, the jasmine of her perfume, and the gleam and pull of her body.

She was an Astarte, but I was no Adonis. And though my very blood would have been too little to give to her, what I offered was a mean libation, which, on the floor of that blessed room, sprouted no anemones or wheat stalks.

Was it a failure of the stout heart, one that had never been stout? A triumph of the fantasy of marble over the reality of the flesh? A hidden lust for lasting pain, for martyrdom in the jaws of concocted demons?

If I were to stand before God, what would I plead? That my fear of Him was greater than my love for His creation? What would He say? Would He not see through my pretence and self-deceit?

Nor was Sofia blind to my troubles. She administered to me with the fierce devotion of an Isis and the stubborn patience of a Job. But while the goddess of the Nile managed to piece her consort together, my dismemberment proved too wilful for the Bayroute goddess. Each fragment of mine was in endless battle with the other, and each fragment secretly worshipped and dreaded a different deity.

What does Empedocles say about the four body elements that can only come together by the power of love? For only then can they triumph over the power of strife. I cannot call his words to mind.

Love was certainly there, in Afqa, not just her infant courier with the meddlesome bow. All-supreme, she could have plucked me out of my dispersal with her strong hands and brushed away the civil war from my body and soul. This was a place where barren women came to become fertile, where ailing children were brought to be cured and the insane to be restored to what men call sanity.

But Love stayed her hand. Perhaps she had concluded that I was no true pilgrim, no true worshipper. Perhaps she was delaying her beatitude. Perhaps she was waiting for me to steel myself to the contest of her heights and the rack of her healing!

Surely, I was not strong enough to scale her mountainside or take her flaying medicine.

But now in Bayroute I am recalled to her perpetual present.

Sofia chases my demons away. She reveals to me that Hojr of Kenda is in correspondence with Dorotheus, entrusted with the job of training me in Roman law and the arts of diplomacy – particularly those connected with the Roman court. I am to serve in a grand scheme Hojr has put together. The king of Kenda is considering an alliance with Rome. But both Hojr and Al-Hareth Ben Jabala, Rome's long-standing surrogate in Syria, share a history of jealousy and mistrust. Meanwhile, the Persian claw in Lebanon, the scheming Climacus, has his spies everywhere. One of them, none other than the hapless Helal, as the Professor suspects, may have intercepted a letter from Hojr sent while the master was in Rome. Sofia also reveals that Hojr has been preventing my mother from leaving Najd to visit me in Bayroute. No explanation for this is given.

'Be your own man. Do not pawn your life at another man's shop! Nor at any woman's! Not even mine, though I run no shop,' she tells me, laughing, with a ripple of sadness in the sea of her eyes.

I tell her about the prophecy, that rope from the past with its attendant noose. I am hoping she will toss it away from my neck with a flick of a suckable finger and a silver laugh.

With her exquisite tools and talismans, she's been whisking into exile many of my demons. 'Fear is a thief; and though thieves are locked up, it may be best that this one is just released, sent away, far away!'

I give her the amulet my mother placed round my neck many years ago. She will not have it, out of reverence for my mother's love. But I insist, raucously. She lifts it to her lips investing it with the profane sanctity of her own love.

But fear is such a sly creature! And so is guilt, which I had watered into a spiky bloom. One fear or many? There was the fear of the 'rose'; the fear of betraying my tutor and host in an act far worse than that of Helal; the fear of betraying my mother and uncle; the fear of God!

'The 'rose', as you call it, loves to be inhaled and cuddled. It loves to be broken into, its solitude overrun, its destiny fulfilled, populating the garden with pollen and petals and perfume.' She picks her words to ease her way into my mind. 'Dorotheus will fulfil his own destiny and pasture of choice. He will populate the School's library and many other libraries and courtrooms with his tomes. He will be happy. And he *is*. Have no fear,' she insists. 'As for your mother and her beloved Yesu, if you truly believe in his mission, he is all about love. He has redeemed all the sinners of his day, if you regard yourself in league with them. And he has most decently done so for all future sinners, all future years. All sinning redeemed, he riding Time itself and repealing all sentences,' she adds – humouring and overwhelming me.

I recite to her once more the lines of the prophecy, first spoken by the Time-surfing Zelpha on the day of my birth in Najd. Sofia smiles, somewhat bored by the repetition. She already suspects that the whole story is a contrivance of my fancy, fooling around with words and realities. But she continues to humour me, 'Be of good cheer, a rope can be useful as long as one end of it is not tied to your neck. You can use a rope to your benefit when the need arises. You may find that you can use it to pull a man out of a well, or climb out of one yourself, or perhaps tie up your own demons with it. That is, if you continue to have any of them, demons, after I'm finished with my exorcism,' she says in gay earnestness.

Ah, there is no pleasure in the world that comes near to that of lying down and conversing, coupling and eating, dozing and rising, with a beloved and loving woman, savouring her body, blending with her soul.

All the voyages of discovery, all their perils and rewards, the plumpness of the sail, the kick of the wheel, the sigh of the wind, the wink of the land, pale, all pale before the voyages lovers together make. The alphabets they learn and the treasures they unearth in their lovers' bodies and souls they also learn and unearth in their own. The heights they reach with one another and the depths to which they plunge in each other's arms are done with the tireless wings of eagles and the vast lungs of dolphins and pearl divers. These, I believe, shall serve them in the storms and glooms of life as well as under her bright skies and at her board and cups.

And yet that level of intimacy and shared affection and understanding can be reached only by a shared history and entwined memories, which requires time. And much that I want to keep faith with the ideal of being loyal to one woman, one's hallowed wife, as my father has done, my association with Emru and what I know of Sofia's marriage makes me hold on rather feebly to that ideal. I begin to see marriage, when joined by convenience or compulsion or misadventure, as a prison for both parties. Women of the *sa'luks*, preserving ancient Arabian traditions, would not fetter themselves to one man, but would pick and choose at their leisure. If they gave birth to a child they would freely assign to it the father they deemed to be most fit or most dearly loved. A man can be cast away by the woman by moving the door of her tent to the left, signalling his dismissal from her heart and mattress. A man thus spurned suffers no loss of face. Rather, he is free to court other women and taste other pleasures or woes.

When the sea in Sofia's eyes is misted with tears, proud and exultant as that sea is, I view marriage as another name for death in life. Even the happily wed would be severely tested if they were to be eternally paired off in the Christian heaven with their same earthly spouses. But these are thoughts that roll from side to side and back and forth upon a fickle tide.

Nonetheless, I come to see that a meeting of minds is a requisite for lovers. After all, courtesans of all cultures, like the Hetairae of ancient Athens, trained themselves in the arts of conversation and literature and philosophy. As such they could age gracefully in the eyes of the men who sought their company since they would offer more than a fellowship of the flesh. And in their advanced years, a man or a woman would I imagine require a steady and trusted companionship. But even

131

they would die a lingering death if they did not dream from time to time of their limp brook surging into a flood.

What can I say of the moment when my own brook burst into a deluge and a delirium it had least expected or imagined?

Emru had told me once that a man who entered a woman with just his organ would attain a shiver along the length of that organ. But if that man were to plunge with his whole being, seasoned and disciplined by the art of *Lazzah*, he would suffer the shudder which, in his reckoning, made the universe.

The mystery of that shudder, and why it visits us humans is beyond my artlessness to explain. Is it a chalice, an elixir, given by the gods from their own celestial cellars and star-studded flagons in repayment for the troubles and miseries inflicted on the mortals of this world? Is it, instead, a goad, a drug, to make us stay longer in the world's Coliseums in the hope of yet another round of cheers, another contest, another win, another reprieve, another intoxication to amuse the gods, the gods we created and gave obeisance to?

But what matters?

The goddess of Afqa has waited for me to come into maturity before she could grant me her own and her mortal-sister's rapture?

Yet, in the blessed room in Bayroute, under the gently swaying form of Sofia, unclad but for a mist over the sea of her eyes, I am not feeling particularly ripe or raw.

Nor is my mind being visited by any particular thought or fancy.

I am not feeling sorry (which I should) for Sofia's plush green robe spurned with the whole Silk Road upon the marble floor.

I am not reflecting (as I should be) on my lady's arts and games of love, which, bewildering in their range and humbling in their patience, have been nurtured only in the sanctuary of our union.

I am not even reflecting on Sofia's body of lilies and roses, honey and wine.

That fetching abundance is all before me; but I am not studying it.

My gaze is lost in the mist between Sofia's quivering eyelids, infinite as the blue behind them is.

I am blind to what her eyes see, as I am blind to what my manhood bears witness to as it grows in an orchard whose supple and succulent branches converge to seize the whole of me.

No! I am empty, empty like a dye-murex hollowed out and discarded on the shore of Tyre.

I am thus vacant, when another, higher, perhaps lower, world, an anti-world, an ocean, a Milky Way, suddenly pours into my unfilled shell flooding it with pearls and stars, tremors and silences.

Though no Adonis myself, I, the demigod's one time doubter, is swept with the power of a miracle, one enacted in a small room overlooking the Phoenician-Roman Sea.

As in Afqa, a river gushes out of the dark cavern, and life springs from stone, expanding, estranging, connecting, and, for a while, sweetening the brine of all the seas of the world and tingeing them with henna!

HEND SADDLING,
SAVING LIVES

Our path to Shammar's haven had been strewn with treachery and death.

Al-Ward was the man who had risen from under the rug of corpses moving with the pace of a fox and the power of a stallion. He is also the man with the eyes of a hawk and the wisdom of a shaman. To the crushed body of Emru he applied his herbs, ever close to his body as my writing tools are to mine. To the king's spirit, he, believing in no kings or spirits, applied the fortifying hymns and mysterious powers of the earth as they coursed through the tenacity of men.

As we fled southwards, we were somewhat comforted to meet remnants of our army who had survived the slaughter. They amounted to some ninety men, by no means cowards like me. Many were proud warriors who carried most of their injuries on their chests rather than on their backs and bore their defeat and flight deeper than the slashing of swords and the piercing of spears. Even the odd faint-hearts among them hailed the second life of Emru, and pledged to carry their wounds to another, fairer fight.

Well meaning or otherwise, they were doomed either way.

More men, but none of the doughty women, came out in later days from the exhalation of the desert. They were headed by Nafi', Emru's eldest brother. He had survived the carnage, most probably by running away at the first sight of Al-Munzer's horsemen, though I had seen no way out.

We sped, at the advice of Al-Ward, to the pastureland of Al-Baqums, a great tribe of High Najd and in the past an ally of Kenda's. Their present king, Aus, for they too had been visited by the royal disease, was a colossal man of some sixty years.

He received us with a courtesy that wobbled ever so faintly every time the name of Al-Munzer was mentioned.

Never the less, he assigned for our bruised party a few tents just outside his tribe's sprawling settlement.

Some six days later, we were to know, he was visited by emissaries of Al-Munzer. They announced that they were a vanguard and that their king was marching in a great army to round up the loose ends of Kenda and crush anyone that might give the fugitives shelter. Their king, they said, was a liberal man and would handsomely reward those who delivered the runaways into his hands. He would also pledge not to harm any prisoner handed over to him.

What has happened to Arab pledges? In older times a pledge was given in words, but was unshakable as the Mountain of Ohod. Even later, when Arabia was buffeted by contrary winds and unsavoury humours, a pledge was still sacrosanct though it had to be reinforced by a mixing of blood ritual. Now, no words or blood or parchment can hold out against the wink of a coin or the gleam of a blade!

Aus held out for the span of two days. The man remembered the old traditions. He mulled over the dishonour of betraying his former allies and present guests. The sanctity of *aman* was supreme in Arabia. But did Aus grant his *aman*? And why had he not rallied to Kenda's call before as others had done?

Still, Aus held firm. He towered high, straining, for two whole days, yeah. Then he tumbled down with the setting sun. No doubt he made a politically wise decision.

We were to be surrounded as we slept by the swordsmen of Al-Baqums, pounced upon and trussed up like fowls to be delivered to Al-Munzer's table.

To help him achieve his plan, Aus invited us to a banquet in his great pavilion. There he plied our men with the best date palm wines found in that part of Arabia. Emru, largely recovered from his wounds, but not from his vow, did not touch his cup. Nafi' and the other men were half drunk in the banqueting pavilion when I begged to be excused, taking Emru with me on the pretence of helping him rehearse a poem he had composed for the occasion.

Minutes earlier I had received a word from Hend carried by a little girl. Little girls make excellent messengers! The message little Amena carried was scribbled in the *Asafiri* code. This was a cipher Hend and Emru and I used when we were children. The message said that a great betrayal was afoot. We were to make our way to our guest tents without arousing suspicion.

Since Emru alone of our men was sober enough to be delivered on his feet from that web of treachery, I coaxed him out with Al-Ward's help.

I had of course taken the formidable *sa'luk*, who sat next to me, into my confidence. He had the strength in him to empty the wine cellars of a monastery and remain clear-headed. But he instantly pretended he was unwell and stood up to walk with us, staggering, leaning on Emru's shoulder. I promised our host to be back as soon as the poem was rehearsed to perfection, a poem Al-Ward wished to contribute to, I claimed. But we were followed with wary eyes.

At the spot mentioned by little Amena, we saw Hend, dressed for flight, and a possible fight to the death, a sword in her hand. She had saddled a number of horses and two pack camels, one being the black dromedary laden with the old shields. Hissing in our faces, she ordered us to mount.

'There's...no time...to get back...to the others,' Hend, breathless in the whirlwind of her agitation, tackled Emru. 'Al-Munzer promised... he wouldn't harm them. Nor would they...we...be able...to make a...dash for it...not all together. Al-Munzer may...or may not...keep his word. In either case, you...are Hojr's successor. To be taken...in chains...or killed...would spell the end...the end...of our father's line. His spirit-bird will thirst...will go thirsty...for all time!'

Hend explained the situation as we galloped into the night. Aus's young wife Lamis, had been friendly to Hend since our arrival. Young and beautiful, Lamis of the great tribe of Tameem, had suffered the taunts and jealousies of other Baqum women. Earlier in the evening, she had come to Hend's tent to warn her of her husband's intentions. The king's older wife, Al-Anoud, had minutes before boasted to Lamis about her own closeness to the king's ear. He had told *her* of the visit of Al-Munzer's envoys and sought her opinion as to what he should do, torn as he was between honour and fear of the ruthless Iraqi. The older wife, prudent and practically minded, had strengthened him in his panic. His first duty was to his household and tribe, their safety and wellbeing, Al-Anoud had advised.

Lamis acted swiftly. At a great risk to herself she proceeded to warn Hend. She reasoned that our escape was a better option for Aus. It would spare him both the disgrace of delivering his chief guest to his enemy *and* the wrath of Al-Munzer. It would also make the advice of his older wife somewhat superfluous.

So we fled that death, into another?

A TOMB IN A ROSEATE CITY

I sink onto my knees beside the grave. How I wish I can sink into the red earth to hug the body that lies there and had given me life!

That frail, brave, and dear, dear body!

How for many years it had carved out of its chronicle of loss and fear a battlement and a rosary against the legions of demons it believed clamoured for my body and soul!

Dear orphan whose young father was snatched from his marriage bed and offered as yet another human morsel to the bloated dragon of war! Snatched for his rebelliousness? for the coveted beauty of his bride? for the pride of the call-up officer? – I cannot tell!

All-loving frailty, loving all but war, battling war with your regiments of incantations and protection charms, talismans and *memres*! Banishing my childhood's fears with Solomon's power-signet and Mar George's gloom-dispelling Anathema!

Brave mother with wordless nightmares, and endless stigmata, invisible but to her!

Child exile! My father's hallowed Ka'ba!

My Monica! Tireless supplicant at your God's altar 'without the omission of a single day'!

Alas! the demons you have barred and charmed away have triumphed!

I have betrayed your ramparts and talismans and let the horned legions in! I have allowed them to enter through the cracks in my soul; and the demons have taken possession!

Yeah, they have triumphed even against the protection beads you had coiled round my neck! But the angels of the beads had long turned sullen, their shields (and snow-white wings?) tainted by the demonic blood they had spilt, though never to exhaustion!

But what if *another* woman has also battled my demons on the ramparts and in the alleyways of my heart?

No!

My mother did not die! How can a mother die? What use are the gods without mothers to work their miracles? What use are men, Life herself?

137

Where is the cypress that should have sprung and soared from her grave (her *grave*?!), and swept away the rude sun and the dumb stars?

Why is there only desolate sand, though of the colour of roses?

And this red pagan ghostly city outside the Christian monastery and its consecrated graveyard! Should it not leave its hillsides and drift on spectral columns to do homage to her, a saintly pilgrim cut down by godless fever?

But I can see only little black ants coming and going through tiny chinks in the earth!

Their traffic seizes my attention before the awareness bursts out inside me!

I bend down to crush the little monsters with my fists. Then I jump up to stamp on them with my feet! But I freeze, gripped by guilt. This is *her* sanctuary, she, who would not hurt a fly, she who never served the flesh of an animal on her table, she who in life gave food to all manner of stray animals and birds, conferring on them her *aman*!

And what if they have something of her in their ravenous mandibles, in the bristles of their tireless feet?

Ah, would that *I* were an ant to touch her,

to crawl upon her breasts that had nourished my fledgling, unwitting lust for life,

to snuggle under her armpit as had been my child's way, waking up with some vague terror and rushing, heart fluttering, to her sleeping form in the dark;

Ah, would that I could burrow to linger at her lips, her lips ever murmuring with supplications and protection charms;

would that I could linger, to listen!

Perhaps she has something very important to say to me. Something she has delayed saying all these years. A secret she had long concealed but had taken that fatal journey to reveal it to me – to me as I frolicked in Bayroute! A secret that now lies between the lips that had kissed me and kissed so many cold icons for my sake!

She could not have died!

Not with her zeal for my life, as it sustained us both!

Not with her knowledge of disease-foiling charms and harm-crippling amulets and her circle of saints and guardian angels!

But what if *they*, saints and angels, have conspired against her, driven mad by her supplications, her over-familiarity with them, her cheek in summoning them so casually and incessantly to her daily rituals?

What if it was Death alone who stalked her? Not so much to prevail upon her as to taunt the host who had long protected her?!

Would that she had made an amulet, a binding ban, against *him* with the virginity of her soul, to shame him away from his designs on those she loved?

And would Death have thus been swayed? He had not shown mercy to her young father who was made to march on the imperial road to the dragon's feast in Iraq. Nor did he, Aye Death, for the following three years come to her mother, though the young widow had pleaded for him to gather her to the coveted peace of her lost bed-mate.

But what if the stalker was blameless? What if the killer fever was a bonfire fanned to madness and self-murder by the excess of her own longing?

And yet my mother did not *die*!

I have *killed* her.

I have killed my mother.

HIGH HAVEN

The flight to the Shammar heights was also suggested by Al-Ward.

It took us nine days to reach the dark red slopes pockmarked with *arta* and *ghada* bushes. We paused to admire the boulder-strewn ascent to the higher violet-coloured upland and the blue sky above flecked with fluffy clouds. A furious sandstorm had delayed us; but it may have frustrated the Al-Baqums from tracking us down.

In any event, it was not only the lashings of the wind-tossed sand that harassed us on our journey. The battering of guilt at leaving our comrades in the hands of the Al-Baqums attended us all the way. Only Hend, practical and resolute in her purpose, scoffed at these 'useless sentiments'. She did so even as she continued to berate Emru for conspiring to exclude her from the Battle of the Plain.

The summits of Shammar seemed to lift us above all that history.

The heights are chiefly inhabited by the great tribe of Tayy, who trace their origins to Qahtan. Interestingly, some of the Tayy clans define their ancestry by their mothers' line. Hence, there are the *banu* or children of Judailah, Jundub, and Haur, among other great matriarchs of enduring fame. These clans had also formed part of the kingdom of Sheba, ruled by the formidable Belqis. They had migrated to the north when the great dam which had regulated their irrigation and political system broke down, inundating the land with lethal flood water. Before they had settled in the mountains, they had done battle with the Asads and the Tameems. The two tribes had preceded them to mastery over the flat lands to the east and north of the mountain of Faydh. In fact, before their retreat to the highlands of Najd, they had shared with Kenda control of the territories from the Najd foothills to the south of Palestine. There they had access to sheet after sheet of pastureland, which they still have in plenty on their elevated plateau. Their *abyar* and *aflaj*, wells and underground cisterns, never parch for water. Their present Emir is the formidable and munificent Al-Mu'alla Ben Taym, noted for his generosity, courage, and chivalry, as are his people.

On the first morning of our arrival, Emru stood before him. He stood tall, though somewhat chastened by his past reversals and present needs. He extemporised the following verses in praise of his hosts:

When Tayy opens her palm to give,
The rain clouds pour, the waste lands *live*.
But when she clenches it on steel,
The *constellations* seem to reel.

Later, having received the *aman* from the gracious Emir, he composed the following *qit'a* in praise of the Emir and his land:

An eagles' eyrie none can own,
While low Iraq and Syria groan,
Their kings held back by Tayy's high wall,
Whose lofty sweetness shames their gall
And whose free song incites their slaves
To rise and dig their tyrants' graves;
A wall of valour none can breach
Save Al-Mu'alla's gracious reach,
A wall whose prince defeats its height
By flights of bounty day and night!

Notwithstanding the extravagant claims of a panegyric so untypical of Emru, here on these highlands the Emir rules over his people as a kindly shepherd, even as an elder brother. He oversees them with affection and generosity, dispensing weal and justice among them and in counsel with them. Devout as his people are in the worship of freedom and skilled in the arts of mountain warfare, he sends a message to the human wolves and vultures beyond the realm that they would be skewered on the crags should they consider attacking this steely brotherhood. Around them are flats and hollows and terraces cultivated season after season with wheat and barley and millet. Groves of date-palm and fig and apple trees cohabit with vineyards waiting to wield their full clusters of rubies and beryls. A landscape of variety and revelation at every turn, a land of lushness and ruggedness, abundance and peace, a heaven!

'Recount to us, O Emir, some of the deeds of your forebear, the great Hatim! As children, we grew up being rebuked on his account. Either for being as wasteful as him or for not being as open-handed as he would have liked. Either way he was there to torment us,' Emru, regaining his good humour, addressed the lord of Shammar. He was keen to gain the favour of his host.

The Emir laughed loudly and riotously, upsetting a bowl of fruits and a jug of fine wine nearby, which he had not touched out of regard for Emru's vow. But after a day-long visit to one of the mountain's clans and a rich meal of roast mutton with his guests, he seemed somewhat weary, his laughing fit aside.

He was however civil enough to reply, 'O King, I am confident you know more about Hatim than I do. For tales of this generous man have acquired their own generosity, allowing what liberal men endlessly add to them. No doubt your own deeds will receive a similar treatment by admirers of courage and devotion and fine poetry, the finest.'

Ah, tales of Hatim! I too had been regaled to them as I grew up. They were always told with my father's passionate approval in the telling. How many to tell? The one in which Hatim's mother, the Lady Otba, is heavy with him and, when visited by a wish-granting spirit, she chooses to give birth to a delicate boy of unusual liberality instead of a hardy one who would grow up to rule over all Arabia? Another dream of Arab unity dashed! Or would it be the other tale where the boy Hatim gives away a whole herd of his father's milch camels to some casual travellers and, instead of being scolded, is rewarded by his mother with a herd of her own to give away to whomever he pleases?

I could have stood up in the assembly and narrated the tales, singing the praises of Arab women to the certain delight of the Tayy womenfolk surrounding Hend. And I would have gone on with a third and a fourth and a fifth tale. But I heard Al-Ward cutting in on Emru, who was about to respond to the Emir's courtesy.

'A generous act is like a vineyard,' Al-Ward said. He was in a poetic mood, one enlivened by quite a few draughts of the spiced Shammar wine.

'Yes, a generous act sweetens a season but travels to baffle Time itself. Yeah, like your excellent wine, it leaves the branch and rises from the cellar to bring merriment to the glad of heart and solace to the heavy hearted. It rises as the *zerutret* and the *rob* and the *kum* rise from years of drought to hand out colour and gaiety and healing. Yeah, I must say, some wicked deeds of men also rise under the downpour. They sneak up like *kutenun* and *zuger* to deal out thorns and spikes and blindness. The Emir, too modest to tell of the deeds of his forebear, leaves me with the duty of recounting at least one of them. But only if he allows a not so adept a storyteller to rise to that challenge.'

The Emir was pleasantly amused at Al-Ward's intervention. He pleaded with him to tell of what he knew, declaring that Hatim could not have hoped for a better narrator and a fine poet to boot.

The Emir did not need to plead. Al-Ward, who had in his bag a cure for itching, had an incurable itch to tell stories.

However, as if to back up his statement on Al-Ward's literary ability, the Emir asked, 'But, first, do us the honour of reciting some of your own verses. Your lines have crossed and re-crossed the whole of Arabia and scaled the heights to us here. Treat us first to your famous poem 'A Definition of a King'. Perhaps the lines that reached us did not do justice to the original,' the Emir entreated, goading Al-Ward.

And then he added, looking at Emru, 'Emru is our brother. His kingdom of art and valour will outlive all other kingdoms. The ring on his finger is but a small message from the stars of heaven to a kindred spirit, a kindred light on earth!'

Emru was moved by the words of the Emir. He went up to him and embraced him saying, 'Your words will suffice me for an honour. And the message from the stars you have spoken of I have borne only to hand it over to you.'

And Emru released the Kenda ring from his finger. It came off easily. He had lost a good deal of weight. But as he tried to place it on the Emir's finger, the Emir resisted, roaring with laughter.

With the ring restored to Emru's finger by the Emir, Emru tried foisting it on Al-Ward, who refused it with merry disdain. Then Emru said, 'Al-Ward's lines have indeed travelled the breadths and lengths of Arabia to the envy of many but the endorsement of many more.'

The *sa'luk* said, the dimples in his hairless cheeks waxing and waning as he spoke, 'Surely to no one's envy; rather to the pity of the master poet here. In any case, verses, like Hatim's deeds, are never the sole work of their author. As they leave him they lead lives free of him, unforeseen by him. But the lines that left my lips in the beginning are these.'

Then Al-Ward recited the lines that many in Arabia had heard and rehearsed round crackling camp fires and in floating saddles, even as those who recited the lines added more sparks to them or robbed them of some:

What is a king?
A leech that hugs, but does not heal!
A slaver to the slaves;
A traitor to the common weal
In favour of the knaves.

What is a king?
His court is pegged to human bones!
And filled with pimps and whores;
And as he laughs, his kingdom groans,
And as it roars, he snores!

What is a king?
A snare ensnared, a nightingale
Who sold his starry wing
And swapped his sky for a royal jail
And all the stars for a ring!

What is a king?
A king is not a *sa'luk*, no!
A *sa'luk* is born free,
And will with comrades roam or grow
Like branches on Life's tree.

What is a king?
A son who left our Mother's lap
To spread the silly lie
About 'pure blood', which is pure crap
No sane *sa'luk* would buy!

What is a king?
The dunes he can't hoodwink for long;
They mock his false belief
And wait outside his courtly wrong
To surge with gay relief!

The Emir said, 'You tell a harsh truth. May Shammar be never ruled by a king, though I must admit there are also good kings, however far and between – kings that are guardians rather than robbers of their people.'

Then Al-Ward, not losing any of his heartiness or pausing to receive praise on the finer points of his poem and impatient to canter along with his storytelling, recounted the following:

'Our hosts are famous for their extraordinary generosity to strangers and travellers. In this they go beyond all other Arabs. Stories of Hatim are many. They are the stuff of legends. I only choose one for your entertainment, one popular among the Abs, where I heard it when I was a child with an amulet round my neck, a most extravagant, most amusing, but edifying, story.

'A band of travellers from Khaybar happen to be passing by the grave of Hatim shortly after his death. They decide to spend the night near the grave. One of the Khaybarites advances to the grave and reproves its occupant for not providing supper for the night travellers as was Hatim's custom while he lived. The man's comrades rebuke him roundly for addressing the dead in such an irreverent manner. Later that night, the Khaybarite wakes up from a fitful sleep screaming. He has seen Hatim in a dream coming out of his grave brandishing a sword. He kills with it the Khaybarite's own she-camel. The man's companions, who have woken up at his screams, listen to his account. Humouring him, they go to inspect their mounts. To their astonishment, they find the man's camel flat on the ground with a grievous wound to her neck. So they slaughter her and feast on her roast, saying to their friend, 'Hatim has been true to his custom and has fed us, though from your own estate.' Then the company decamp and are on their way. The man who has lost his camel has hitched a ride with another man. Lo, they haven't gone a quarter of a farsakh when they're caught up by a young man galloping after them on a fleet camel. He's drawing behind him a superlative camel laden with provisions of all manner. It is Hatim's son, Oday. He has seen his father in a dream. His father asked him to track a traveller who doubted Hatim's ability to provide for his guests and give him the finest camel in his herd with provisions for a long journey.'

Thus spoke Al-Ward, mixing dream and rapture, to the delight and pride of an assembly weighed down by a day's work and a heavy dinner, though our party of four were weighed down by heavier burdens and less delectable memories.

AFTER LEBANON

SOFIA, AGAIN AND FOREVER

'Who brings this to my remembrance' as I 'cry...for the breast'?

'Woe to the sins of men!' And woe to their 'remembrances'! Summoned, they torment us, even though without them we are as dead wood. But will not dead wood reclaim its lost blossoms in the fire and rise to rejoin the stars?

It is the happy memories that are most painful. And they are so when we realise we failed to truly celebrate their authors and actors at the time; failed to heed their brave call; failed to allow them to make us live to the full.

It may be that we men are fated to fail. Whether we rise to celebrate our benefactors or foolishly sit on our arses sinking into our stools, we are doomed, doomed to fail. And whatever choice we have made we are bound to regret that it was not another.

I cling to Sofia on the night of my departure. I inhale the perfumes and aromas of her garden body. I gasp for her rousing breath. I sip at the surf of her soul, immense beyond me.

I have been playing a game with her, a bed game with her double name, Sofia (wisdom) and Safia (immaculate and endeared) as we were joined body to body and soul to soul. It was an invention of mine, this game, my sole invention. I was somewhat proud of it, though humbled by Sofia's many spontaneous novelties. But tonight I am incapable. The letter of the Abbot in Petra lies on a low table next to my bed. My body is crippled, heralding the desolation that lies ahead.

Still I lay my head at the fork of her thighs, kissing her warm belly, her soft, immaculate breasts, promising to come back to them, to Bayroute, to her wholeness.

Brief has been my happiness with my lady and hers in our nuptials. She has given me what she has given no other man, so undeserving as I am, so secretly needled by guilt – tutored as I am by the Master Jurist for the mantle of a Roman lawyer, only to be consecrated for the temple of his celibate wife!

146

After every supreme bliss, she used to cry. Her tears I selfishly thirsted for and stained with my own. But she also had the exuberance to scatter gaiety all around her - across her villa or in the sun or in her salon like a merry harvester winnowing the golden grain. The aureate dust would rain down and settle, glowing, in my heart, banishing the baser metal of fear, whether of gods or men.

Now, she sheds only tears, but bravely gives me the road to Petra, having given me Bayroute.

Like a fair and loyal handmaiden of Sofia's, Bayroute has danced and whirled and dropped her seven veils before my gaze, then curled into my bed to feed other cravings she created.

But, for all her allures, what is the maid without the mistress?

Without Sofia the city will be a maze of mute walls, her streets leading to no home, her libraries to no wisdom, her theatres to no delight, her stalls to no profit, her altars to no faith...

What is the meaning of this dear white villa on the hill facing the sea without Sofia being here, a sun among the stars of her jasmine tree; a dream of intoxication for her vine; to the swing of her sea, a cedar, to the marble of her stairs, a heaven?

Sofia has breathed from her myrtle-breath on the city animating it with life, fragrance and mystery, transforming its mercantilism into fair play, brutality into tenderness, disorder into harmony, and harlotry into sainthood.

I lay my head at the fork of her silken thighs dreading the fork of every dagger-toothed road that waits, ravenous, for me.

LEAVING SHAMMAR WITH THE SAND READER

Unlike the generous dead, the generosity of the living has its limits.

The Emir kept us diverted with his brave and welcoming face, and with his abundant rations.

But his people were closing up against us like a sullen clam.

They were troubled by the news scaling their heights. A massive army of invasion was being assembled in Al-Hera. Even then, and ahead of the gleam of spears and the thunder of hoof-beats, bags of gold and silver had reached various clans on the eastern and western slopes of Shammar.

One clan, the Tarf, received special mention. They had been entrusted, the reports suggested, with the task of spiriting assassins over the heights to slay our party or block our escape if we were to attempt it down the western slopes.

The Tarf, from their vantage point overlooking a stretch of the pilgrim road to Mecca, had always prospered on alternately plundering the pilgrims and protecting them. The choice depended on who was or was not paying the toll. They were sneaky and ruthless and knew both the mountains and the plains and the gullies as they knew the palms of their hands, eternally leased to the higher bidder. They were distantly related to the Tayys, but they had no compunctions about betraying them or their guests at the wink of a coin. Many of those were already tinkling in their saddlebags – the reports said.

On hearing this, Hend went to Emru, who in turn went up to Al-Mu'alla. He asked him to be allowed to leave Shammar absolving him of the obligations of his *aman*. Emru argued that his departure would save the lives and livelihood of the Tayys. The Emir would have none of that. He insisted he would defend Emru to the end, saying that the skewers of the Shammar cliffs would make perfect kebab of the Iraqi troops. The Tarf he dismissed as scraggy jackals who would turn tail at the first pebble thrown at them. Schooled in the lowly arts of treachery, they were, he said, bold only in pouncing on unsuspecting pilgrims and cutting off the arms of women to get more quickly to the bracelets they wore.

But Emru was already heavy with guilt for the loss of life he had caused among his own people and allies. He would not have the same visited upon his chivalrous host. He dithered, agonising.

It was then that a man by the name of Amer Ben Mazen came to Shammar.

He was of the tribe of the Fazaras who roam the Wadi Al-Rumma in upper Najd and are noted for their exceptional literacy of the land.

This particular Fazari had served Hojr on a punitive expedition against an Asir tribe some years before. Emru knew him well. He was a man who could tell the height and weight of a man or a woman, or if the man was carrying a sword or the woman a child, from their tracks in the sand. Yeah, he could do this even if these tracks crisscrossed with the tracks of a dozen other men and women. He could tell if a camel was lame or one eyed and what it had eaten and at what oasis. He could tell what the beast was carrying on its back and where it might be heading. This he could do by casually studying the contours, depressions, and symmetries of the prints in the earth and other telltale marks and droppings around them. His memory was such that he would be able, weeks or months later, to point out that same camel out of a herd of a hundred. A fugitive murderer was certain to be tracked down if he had Amer Ben Mazen on his tail. Even if the felon was to change his sandals or wear them backwards or hop over the back of a horse or an ostrich, Amr Ben Mazen would store the image and smell of the man and the manner of his gait in his vast memory, unerring like that of a *saluki*. The quarry would be hunted down to despair or death.

In short, Amer Ben Mazen had the gift to read the silent ciphers in the sands and in the minds of the hunted. He had come to Shammar having picked up the signs in the air and settled on the course to be taken on the ground. A very slight man with the bodyweight and suppleness of a caracal and the face of a rock hyrax, he came to Emru and looked at him with black owl eyes and spoke in the high eloquence of the desert:

'O King! I am not given to long or clever speeches. The fruit of the tongue is not my best choice for a repast. Its juice rises to my head and distracts me from listening. But I had served your father loyally. He was open-handed with his reward, though tight-fisted with the game I helped him hunt. Now I pledge my eyes and ears to lead you to another

149

master. He too I had served faithfully, his reward equally generous. Too generous for my needs. But now I can hear wolves yelping in the distance. I can smell their lust for your blood. Their packs will soon be on the march, howling in the wind, upsetting, gnashing at its easy flow and contented whispering. And they will come from where the sun climbs, and they will secure the path of the sun's dip. But I can lead you through their ranks and the clumps of their hirelings and render them sightless to your sight and senseless to your smell. But thereafter you shall need a stout ally and a fort impregnable. Samuel the Jew is the man, his fort in Tayma a shield unyielding. But the man's heart is even stouter than the walls of his fort. Nor will your verses deny kinship with his own. But you have to come to a decision about this. I shall abide here, in your *aman*, a guest of a guest, for three days, awaiting your verdict, needing neither your plate nor your beaker. I shall wait, even though the wolves below yap in their blood lust. Even as they have subverted many a heart around you here, more by terror than by coin. They yap now; but soon they will be howling.'

The third day saw the Emir away on an inspection of the eastern borders of his realm. As the day drew to a close, Emru asked a youth of the Tayy to deliver a letter to the Emir upon his return. The letter was accompanied by a poem.

Before the all-seeing sun had sunk below the western cliffs filling the distance with a fleeting blush, we were filing on our camels behind the slender but reassuring figure of Amer Ben Mazen. He drifted like a spectre in front of his sentient *dalul*, a needless head-rope in his hand.

Prior to that, we had called on the grave of Hatim. It is marked by a circle of rocks in the shape of weeping women.

PETRA OF THE SORROWS

'She acted in mercy, and from the depths of her heart forgave her debtors their debts. I implore Thee also to forgive her debts. Enter not into judgement with her on account of her son. Thou hast promised mercy to the merciful, that the merciful shall be rewarded with mercy. Let the scales of Thy Judgement be fixed in the scaffold of my heart!'

I loiter at Petra, belaboured by the timeless grief of the town, latterly forsaken by trade, my own sorrow and guilt and indecision adding to the gloom.

Visiting my mother's graveside is a daily chore. Another is tending, with the help of the monks, to my uncle's needs in his pitiful decline.

If there were angels in the world, the monks of Petra would deserve that title together with the wings that should come with it. In their modesty though they would decline both. They were angels sent to my poor mother on her deathbed. The kindly Abbot of the place, Abba Nahur, had attended to her last wishes and very last whispers. The latter were about green meadows she was seeing and sounds of brooks and birdsong and happy laughter of children drifting nearer and nearer.

But my name was the last name she sighed. It should have been her 'beloved Yesu' – a handier password into His Kingdom. But does He not reward all manner of love, however misplaced? The Abbot, himself a living testament of love, had written the letter she had dictated. He dispatched it to me with two monks setting off for Deir Sam'an. When the time came he performed the funeral rites of *ktaba dkurrasta annide*. Since then, he has looked after my uncle with the devotion of a doting disciple.

It was he who led me, shortly after my futile arrival, to her grave in the small Christian cemetery. My uncle tottered along with us. He swayed like a tower, lanky and gaunt, over the grave. Tears flowed from his dazed eyes, but he, her life-long protector and guardian, did not know for whom the tears flowed.

This is an ancient pagan town hewn out of hard mountain cliffs and strewn with pagan temples. Spectacular and grand in loud red, she stands defiant even in desolation! Her proud ancient builders have been betrayed by time as have their heirs by fading commerce. But the Christians have of late built a monastery, a lofty fortress of the spirit that pays homage to the One God, who is also two and is also three – baffling the larger pantheons, cutting them down to size!

I bow to the town in worship and gratitude. She offered my mother a bed braided with compassion when she was taken ill on her way to Lebanon. But the desolation around the small monastery proves too overwhelming for me. I yearn to go away, feeling guilty because of that yearning. I cannot find it in my heart to abandon my mother's grave nor my crumbling uncle, my solid mentor of many years. Am I fated to betray all my benefactors and teachers?

Reports of an incursion by Al-Munzer into Syria and the chaos it has spawned prevent me from taking the road back to Sofia. I bide my time, increasingly mortified by the thought of betraying my mother in her death, after causing that death.

I roam the ruins like a *majnun*, a man bereft of his reason by a vengeful jinni or unrequited love. I seek the company of the Jinn, who should dwell in such stricken and forsaken places. But there is only the hissing of the wind and the stillness of the stone. Even the awesome water cisterns and canals left by the ancient builders are covered in dust, the monks having cleared but few for their moderate use.

In my desperation, I turn for help to my uncle. His own wells and cisterns and canals are also clogging up, so harshly, so irreparably. He bravely tries to re-invoke some freshness, some mutinous sap, deep in his veins. He tries to drag back memories I craved for, names, faces, tales, on to the pages fading from his mind. Magnificent were those pages, filled with the languages of Rome and Greece and Syria! Filled with the words of the Christian God and the fathers and the saints. Filled with the songs of impossible freedom and the glitter of the unattainable City of God. The loving, gentle, austere, misunderstood Soldier of Christ is retreating into an armistice, perhaps a final peace, with the helmeted and hurtful world.

I linger for a few weeks in Petra, my mind a battleground. Going back to Bayroute, should the road allow, to be happy with Sofia, a married woman, seems like murdering my mother for a second time. Should I implore the Abbot to accept me as an apprentice monk, serving his and my mother's God in this stark wilderness rather than in the larger, alluring wilderness of the human city? How else would I earn my keep and that of my uncle? He is cowering into a room of a mind being stripped of its books and furnishings. Its very windows and door are steadily congealing into mental mud. Known for his temperate humour and kindly smile, though stern as a teacher, he is now subject to bouts of inexplicable rage. But in the curdling rooms there are fewer and fewer tomes and pots and spoons to throw at the walls. After the fit, he collapses back into his usual smile, now unmoored and rudderless with no harbour to sail from or return to.

With Al-Munzer pitting his fleet horsemen on behalf of his Persian liege against the Roman legions in Syria, my private war is overtaken by a war of the Titans. As for my mother, she has found a home for her soul with Christ and for her body with a cluster of fellow Christians consecrating a pagan cemetery. My uncle has fulfilled his life's mission and is achieving his salvation in blissful forgetfulness. And forgiveness? He has been moving the movables of his hermitage into the heavenly palace where the saints and soldiers of Christ sit and commune, having beaten their swords into daffodils, their wounds into roses, and their wise speech into wiser silence.

Meanwhile, thousands of young men have been marching to their life and death nuptials, their princes and priests promising them the rewards of earth and heaven.

Then a message comes from Emru! What hoopoe carried my news to him?

He is in Tabouk, at some six days' ride to the south from Petra. He is waiting for me to join him. He has sent a party of men with dromedaries and provisions to escort me to his impatient welcome.

My uncle, dazed as he is, does not wish to leave the monastery with me, much as I plead with him to do so. His older memories of the church are less dim than his memories of his nephew. He bids me farewell as he would to a stranger, the pupils of his eyes moving like worn swimmers in a rough sea. My own eyes do not shed tears as I hug him with an anguished heart and kiss his eyes and hands, my Good Samaritans and chastisers for many years.

I do not weep. My tears had run dry on my mother's grave earlier in the late afternoon.

The kindly Abbot says it will be a duty and a privilege for him and the brethren to look after their fellow missionary. This is probably for the best, as the state of his general health will not bear the strain of a harsh desert trek.

And yet, as I walk away, I hear a faint, forlorn cry behind me. I turn round to see my uncle stretching out his right arm towards me, tears welling up in his Phoenician eyes, a groan loitering in his throat. I race back and fall upon his feet, kissing them, wetting them with my resurgent tears. But when I rise to hold him, towering above me, in my arms, the blank tumult in his gaze has returned. The blessed, bittersweet surge of memory has sunk again under forbidding waves.

I don't have the courage to turn aside for a last look. I root myself in my high saddle and follow the messenger's *dalul*, sailing away from Petra.

We move, high cloudlets above us tinted by the blood of the setting sun perhaps also by the ruddy ruins beneath them. They seem to me like lambs tattooed but lost in the vastness of the sky and soon to be overcome by the wolves of the constellations creeping smoulderingly behind the waning blueness.

I feel the town behind my back recede into shadows, never perhaps to re-emerge for me into the light. Still I cannot summon the courage of a parting look. My heart is bound to be crushed, like a gerbil in a python's coils, by the enormity of the distances I am creating between my ever-faltering paths and the dwellings of the dear dead and the dear living behind me.

AL-WARD TELLS A BEDOUIN TALE

We rode down from Shammar into the blood-bath of the sun. Before long we were riding under the blood-shot eye of *Betelgeuse*.

We moved in stealth, stealth being a second nature to Al-Ward, carefree as he is. It is also a first nature to Amer Ben Mazen, though only when a higher whipser demands it of him as of a caracal stalking a sandgrouse or a *hubara* luring a wild dog away from her nest. All the while I was reflecting on the pain and shame our flight would bring the Emir. And yet I hoped he would forgive us and, more crucially, be spared the wrath of Al-Munzer.

Al-Ward was generally familiar with the ground. But owl-eyed Amer Ben Mazen could read its contours even in the darkest night, even with the stars blanketed by clouds. He could read the land, knowingly and warily, like a man familiar with the body of a mistress that can yet catch him unawares with new nunances and unpredicted challenges.

After a descent that lasted the night, we camped in a *wadi* at the foothills of Jabal Sana. Remarkably, Amer Ben Mazen took the watch. But when we rose late in the morning, he went to sleep under his cloak, which he had set up as a tent beside his crouching *dalul*. He had prepared for us a meal of milk and dates and dried hare meat.

We sat in the cool shade of the *wadi*, a small stream trickling along its fern-lined banks. A lime Swallow-Tail flipped from one wild jasmine flower to another. The world seemed to be at peace, biding its time. But then came the drone of a yellow-and-black wasp which was attracted to my inkwell, oddly enough.

Soon the yellow-and-black peril was distracted by the remains of our repast. So I listened with Emru and Hend to the irrepressible Al-Ward relate a Bedouin tale in praise of women.

Al-Ward was clearly heartened by the praise he had received as a storyteller in Shammar. This whetted his appetite for more. His appetite needs little persuasion in this regard.

But I believe the selfless *sa'luk*, who had suffered so bravely the loss of his dear comrades in Emru's enterprise, was mainly trying to cheer us up at a time when danger seemed to lurk behind every rock and bush.

Al-Ward has a bias for the desert and its people, the Bedouins, whose treachery I habitually fear. But he never fails to praise the nomads' native wit and gallantry. To me, trapped in that situation, theirs meant the wit of the jackal and the gallantry of the viper.

Al-Ward began his storytelling cheerfully, though he looked somewhat wistfully every now and then at the sleeping Amer Ben Mazen. He may have been feeling a bit jealous of the Fazari on account of the leading role the tracker was assuming, though a sentiment like jealously would have clashed with *sa'luk* principles. In any case, he obviously would have liked the tracker (and possibly me with my biases) to listen to the story.

'This is for my wife, Zeinab. I miss her,' Al-Ward began:

'Shan is a clever Bedouin lad. A very subtle one. He meets an older Bedouin on his way to an oasis. Having asked his permission, Shan walks silently alongside him. They walk for an hour or so, without saying much. Then the young man turns to the older man and asks, Will you carry me or I you? The man thinks the youth mad. So he doesn't answer, and keeps on walking, silently.

'Then they draw near to a village on their way. They see a field of barely that is ripe and ready for the sickle. The youth asks, "Think you that this crop has been eaten?" The older man, confirmed in his earlier suspicion of the youth, makes no response.

'Then they pass by a funeral. The youth wonders, "Is the man being carried away to his pit dead or alive?"

'Finally the two men reach the oasis, where the older man's kin are sojourning. He retires to his tent, where his daughter, a strapping lass named Tabaka, receives him with joy. As she prepares a meal for him, he tells her about the imbecile he has been travelling with.

'Why, she replies, this young man makes a lot of sense! And then she explains to her father what the lad meant. He simply wondered whether the two men could engage each other in conversation to make the journey less burdensome. By his second question, he wondered whether the crop had been sold. By his third he questioned if the man being taken to his grave had left children or some work by which he would be remembered.

'Her father, who knows how clever his daughter is, is nonetheless astonished. He runs out after the young man to apologise for his sullenness to him. When the youth discovers how the man came to understand his questions, he asks for the hand of his daughter. The girl accepts. After the marriage, the Bedouin youth takes his bride to his family, and when they learn of her intelligence, they say, Shan has found his Tabaka. And I have found mine, Zeinab!'

So did Al-Ward conclude his tale, promising to tell a more wondrous one. He wanted to keep our spirits up and my qualms down. 'The second tale will be about a Bedouin maiden who solves all manner of riddles.' Wishing to keep us intrigued, he made the mistake of looking at Hend as he paraded two sample questions. 'What is an eight and a four and a two? And who can tear a life crying out of another life crying?'

'*I* know!' Hend replied, confounding the challenger. 'The eight are the teats of a she-camel, the four the teats of a bitch, the two a woman's tits. And a midwife can tear a life crying out of another life crying.'

All were impressed with Hend's ready wit. Al-Ward was somewhat abashed. When he glanced at the sleeping form of Amer Ben Mazen he seemed happy that the tracker was asleep.

The wasp had by then left the pitiful slithers and drops of our meal. It began to forage for a dessert among a clump of oleander flowers, which swayed in the breeze with pouting lips and syrupy labia.

When Amer Ben Mazen would wake up, I hoped he would keep his sharp ears tuned to wasps of a different breed buzzing unheard, unseen, somewhere around us.

157

EXILE WITH EMRU

At Tabouk, Emru looks none the worse for his eternity of exile.

He jokes about it having been but for my absence the happiest and freest period of his life. He scolds me for not leaving my 'little cedar cage' sooner to join him and his new friend Al-Ward in his happy-go-lucky kingdom. He calls me a traitor. But he is sorrowful when he learns of my mother's death and my uncle's decline. I feel reassured by his closeness, soothed and revived by his gaiety.

In truth, exile has been a further liberation for Emru, though he needed none or little in that province. Nonetheless, the few bars of restraint he had allowed to dance around him in the past had melted down in the kiln of his banishment. Like a fabulous genie fabulously released from one of Solomon's *qomqoms*, he now towers over a vast dominion that echoes to his wild mating call.

His amorous appetite knows no bounds. It is as if he wishes to meet the expansiveness of the desert with an expanding lust of his own. It's as if he wishes to overwhelm the wilderness with one surge, one deluge, of passion after another turning the waste into a garden, a love bedstead, a burning bush of desire.

This is but Emru's nature. Carefree, adventurous, ravenous, he touches life and penetrates it at almost every hollow and funnel. And yet, one can see here a man trying to escape his hurtful memories. The wine-cup he holds so reverentially, so desperately, beneath the awning of a roving wine-seller or inside a ramshackle tavern, is a Eucharist held up in a church. He inhales the fermented juice, sips it with his eyes closed and savours it with his full sensual mouth, which has become more carnal, riper and deadlier than before. In the orgies and liturgies of his imagination and senses, the wine seller is a priest, the tavern a temple, the wine a divinity and an oblivion.

Ah, here he stands after the hunt, sweating, sparkling with the triumph and gaiety and folly of life, a leather sack of wine swaying in his hand, lines of verse streaming from his lips! He is paying tribute to his horse, the pedigreed, the splendid, *Al-Wajeeh*. The *kumayt* steed is at repose feeding close by among clumps of *arfaj*; but the horse is animated, perhaps for all time, in Emru's galloping hemistiches. In them, *Al-Wajeeh* is graceful and grand, lustrous and subtle, a mount and a master. He pours forth like driving rain, floats like a swimmer riding the surf, hurtles like a boulder dashing down a mountainside, breathes like a pot bubbling, whirls about like a spinning top. He has the slender waist of a gazelle, the tapering legs of an ostrich, the gallop of a wolf, the trot of a fox. Fleeter than any other creature on legs, the horse is a hobble to all that runs, to all he chases. Even before the oryx herd had time to scatter, he had spun round it, whizzed through it, and lo!, sweat-less, he had galloped merrily next to the herd leader, itself suddenly reduced to another helpless game, looped and lassoed by the horse's dash. Look at him in his repose, feeding among the blossoming *arfaj*! Don't be diverted by the mouth-watering smell of the roasting meat he has helped deliver unto us. Can the eye see anything more beautiful than him, more embracing and life manifesting, more worthy of study and reflection?

I never mention Sofia to Emru. But he senses a change in me, a confidence I did not have before. True enough, in my renewed closeness to the all-conquering Emru, I begin to feel equal to him, if not a bit superior. This is because one extraordinary woman in Bayroute gave me joys and powers a whole academy of sages cannot give; a variety and a commitment the legions of women Emru bedded could not give him. And she gave what she gave so lovingly, freely, and guiltlessly. A most wonder-full woman whom I ultimately betrayed as I betrayed her husband, my teacher, as I betrayed my mother, as I betrayed my uncle.

Even so, I am beginning to feel that I no longer need to hang on Emru's lips for words of worldly wisdom, never meant as such by him. Sofia has advised me against pawning my life to anyone, herself included. But I have already made up my mind to be back in Bayroute by the following winter come what may. Both my body and my soul howl for hers.

I no longer seek Emru as the *Mizar* in the night sky of my life's journey. But I remain fascinated and amused by his verses and anecdotes and antics. An envy for his poetic genius lingers on.

On my way back to Lebanon, I will of course stop at Petra. There I shall visit my uncle and pay my respects to my mother in her grave, the rose of her soul liberated from its mortal thorns.

The goodness of Abba Nahur often visits my mind. I am confident that none better than he can care for my uncle. His own worldly needs the Abbot has honed to a slender wick. But it is a wick that bursts into a bonfire as he bows his head to pray in the dimness of his room - and as he serves the world of his beloved God.

I talk, in my usual mix of earnestness and sentimentality, about the monks of Petra. They are the best of men, I say. Emru retorts that monks are men who are scared.

He elaborates,

'They're scared of life, scared of women, scared of other men, scared of their beds, and especially scared of their own *zakars*. They hide behind walls and icons and muffle the noises of the world with their loud chanting. Outside, upon their very walls the cats are in heat. They caterwaul, mill with their kind and maul one another to have the cravings of their little thingies satisfied. And these are a very small part of the choir, the orgy, that makes up the world, to which the monks also belong. How they manage to stay deaf and numb to the caterwauling and the scratching inside them, I don't know! Perhaps *they* don't know either!'

I reflect on the *memres* of Saint Ephrem and Saint Narsai my mother and uncle had often recited to me, at times within Emru's indulgent hearing. I argue that the monks, through self-discipline and exercise, manage to pluck the fire out of their loins and lift it up to a higher plane: a 'lofty flare of the freed spirit', a phrase my uncle used. As they do this, they scatter some light, some sparks, on people who need illumination and transcendence. 'Isn't this what poets do?' I ask, thinking myself clever.

'I agree,' Emru says, to my surprise, 'but a true poet should dwell on the flare between a woman's knees,' he half-concludes the debate, laughing, drunkenly. More soberly, he adds, 'Some of Ephrem's homilies with which your uncle graced our ears gave me a different impression – one perhaps unnoticed by your venerable uncle. For the shrewd Saint raised the flare of the spirit with one hand and kept the other well anchored between the dear knees!'

Whatever the case may be, with a price on Emru's head, life on the move is an allegory of the life of man. Man is under a sentence of death by the gods, even if these are an invention of his. He is hunted by the very spears he sharpens for them and which they hurl when he least expects – all in the game of life and death which he alone, of all other beings, traps and reanimates into words!

160

I dwell on the parable of children, who, like the gods that toy with us, toy with colourful beetles. Tying a string to a beetle's leg, they watch the insect take to the air and derive pleasure from feeling the string humming between their little guiltless fingers. No such pleasurable cruelties against animal, bird, or insect were allowed me by my mother. But, being a child, instinctively cruel and inquisitive, I had secretly hungered to join in such games.

Emru, carrying the name of a god and believing in none, will also declare, 'Let the beetle flap its little wings to its little heart's content. Let it brave the wind and land on all the leaves it can land on. Let it embrace all the joys it can embrace, and be embraced by them all. For soon, the leaves, the joys, and the beetle will shrivel and tumble from the conniving branch. And yet to drag out these joys, to hold them beyond the breathlessness of the moment or the freshness of the season only breeds the ultimate terror - boredom!'

A beetle, a ravenous beetle, of a kind, Emru makes use of his own wings in similar pursuits, and is further transformed in the act. Though a born hunter, with the mane and heart and tread of a lion, he has grown to be a more subtle changeling. Somewhat like his composite horse, he can now assume the silence of the spider, the briskness of the sandfish, the surefootedness of a *tahr*, the suddenness of a *saker*... He has learned and honed to perfection the manners and stratagems of the hare and the hound. But, underneath it all, he retains the heart of a lion.

But wasn't he all of that at Jouloul?

THE HOUSE OF ALLAH

Eighteen days later we entered Mecca as fake pilgrims.

The roving bands of Tarf had proved to be too erratic, too unpredictable, for Amer Ben Mazen. Alone, he would have drifted unseen through and between their blobs and blotches. But he had to take us into his calculations. So he suggested a roundabout route. He had spotted from the slopes a caravan of pilgrims en route to Mecca. He proposed we joined it. Emru instantly agreed. 'I can also perform my first *hajj*,' he said. 'And call on *Zul Khalasa*'s copy to check on any sympathetic bruises,' he added.

Over and above the *aman* an Arab gives to his guest, Mecca offers the safest sanctuary in Arabia. But unlike an *aman* that can be violated by a powerful enemy or a fickle host, the asylum Mecca offers binds everyone.

Even when not choked by the crowds during the month of the great pilgrimage, the holy city is never without visitors on their own personal or 'lesser' pilgrimage. So the Koreysh clan, who have set themselves up as custodians of the Ka'ba, are always profiting.

As we approached the dark, jagged mountains surrounding the city, we could see in the distance snaky columns of camels and horses converging from various directions. The city is a lodestone for both the *hajj* and the all important *tijarah*.

We alighted from our camels at a spot of *manakh* outside the temple complex. Emru, regaining some of his old self, was excited about the charade he was taking part in, short lived as it would be. Al-Ward, mingling with a cluster of merchants and travellers, soon re-emerged to announce that he had arranged for us to travel with another caravan heading for the north in a few hours. The caravan leader was a fellow Absite.

Emru and Al-Ward doffed their swords and clothes, Hend on top of her camel looking the other way. I too deserted my clothes with diffidence, my futile sword with alacrity. Amer Ben Mazen collected them and handed over to us the robes of purity which Emru had leased from the *Homs*. Amer Ben Mazen and Hend stayed with the camels. The black dromedary was too precious with its freight to be left unguarded. Hend was partly veiled. Emru's unshaven and drawn face provided a manly disguise.

The *Homs* are a clan of zealots turned brokers. Their business is to provide clean garments for use by the pilgrims. Clothes soiled by worldly pursuits, war and fornication are deemed unfit to be worn in the city's sanctum. While the *Homs* had the means and fanatical devotion in the past to give away such purified garments freely, they now offer them at a price. Emru had paid six silver coins for ours. Impoverished pilgrims who cannot afford the fee perform their pilgrimage with no clothes at all. Al-Ward had in his early youth fled to the attraction of the *Homs'* asceticism. It did not take him long to flee from its creeping partnership with money games and hypocrisy.

I glanced at a sullen-faced Hend as I moved away with her brother and Al-Ward in our purified robes. The wild thought of her ambling round the Ka'ba in her white nakedness sparkled in my mind. In it also shimmered the image of her hairless *han* next to my juvenile arousal in Najd so many years before. Her absence from the day at Jouljoul also twinkled in my thoughts, darkly. Strange and unruly are the thoughts of a man!

The droning of people chanting had reached our ears before, but it grew louder as we walked on. And when we entered the large courtyard through a high gate we saw the house rear up fully before us - some twenty cubits high. It was draped in the black, gold-threaded silk of the Yemen, provided for generations by the kings of Kenda.

Now Kenda's last king eyed the cloth, embroidered and embossed with his nation's dark designs and golden dreams. His eyes, like those of his great grandfather, Hojr the First, had the legendary hawk's gaze in them. But they also had the forlorn look of a hunted man. The heartbreak of the situation was not lost on me. Silly tears rose to my eyes.

The Cube was built by Abraham, the legend says. The Patriarch had come from Palestine with his Egyptian wife Hagar, and it was her son, Ishmael, who caused the dark waters of *Zamzam* to rise from the deeps as he paddled in the sand. Later, Ishmael helped his father lay the foundations of the Cube, a temple to the One God, Allah, in that otherwise godforsaken valley. Many centuries later, the miracle of the gushing well in the middle of the arid valley is still to be seen, a relief and a testimony to the parched pilgrims. Towering near it is Abraham's Cube, the Ka'ba. A simple structure, it nonetheless radiates with inexplicable power to its devotees.

Beside us hurtled a band of pilgrims circling the Cube chanting their halleluiahs:

Here we are, here we are, here we are, O our Lord!
None You have as a peer except Man, who is Yours.
Over him You have sway, over all that he owns!

The vast courtyard echoed to that refrain, repeated and modulated in other tribal dialects careering round the Cube.

It was a remarkable sight. Here were hardy and quarrelsome Arabs declaring their personal submission and that of their tribal gods to one supreme deity. Here they were bleating their homilies like flocks of sheep driven along by some invisible herder. In the season of the great pilgrimage, they must make an imposing spectacle, coming from all corners of Arabia. Then the demons of war are caught, muzzled and caged or are left free to howl outside the radius of the sanctuary, which extends to two *marhalas* in every direction. Hence, a man coming face to face with the slayer of his own father would not lift a finger against him. Such is the power of belief – pagan or otherwise! Such is the ultimate miracle of Mecca. Its ability to unite the Arabs, be it for a few days!

But there's a method here. The merchants, who drive much of the transaction between nations, have discovered in the ritual a useful lull and a stall to peddle their wares, bringing civilisations together in bales and parcels and jars.

We too, enacting a charade, were trying to barter the tide of blood behind us for an interval of peace, fooling gods and men with our rented robes of purity and meekness.

And there were the idols too – hundreds of them, ringing the Cube which Abraham had erected to Allah, the One prevailing God!

How it came about that the house dedicated to the One God became encircled with idols had been recounted to us on the way to Mecca by the all-knowing, all-eager-to-tell Al-Ward.

'This was related to me by my tutor, the most venerable Naufal. He said that hundreds of years ago a hard and cunning man called Amr Ben Luhay of the Khuza'a tribe came to Mecca. Before long he ousted the original custodian of the Ka'ba, one named Al-Haris, the 'Keeper', and placed himself in charge. He then fell ill. In that state he was told about a hot water spring in southern Syria where he could be cured. So he went there and bathed in the spring and was healed. Whilst there he noticed that the local people worshipped idols which they believed helped with their healing and protected them against their enemies. So, having made rich offerings to the gods of the place, he asked the town's elders to allow him to travel back with some statues, which he hoped to establish as guardian spirits among his people. The Syrians granted him his wish with alacrity. He returned to Mecca, where he set up the statues in the shadow of the Ka'ba.

'This did not go down well with the Arabs who had revered and stuck to Abraham's practice. Luhay argued that the statues were mere symbols of the power of Allah. He later claimed that some of Allah's power was embedded in the statues. As such they should serve as intermediaries between men and the supreme God. He further argued that even the Christians, who believed in one absolute God, divided their deity into three, and used icons and images to worship before them.

'To validate the new creed, Luhay had a set of Christian images and icons brought in from Syria and placed around the Ka'ba. They were later moved inside the Cube itself.'

Al-Ward said that when he was an apprentice-*Homs* he was allowed into the Ka'ba with his mentor during the ceremony of washing the interior of the Cube before the Grand *Hajj*. This was and remains a rare privilege accorded to few dignitaries. Al-Ward said that he saw inside the sanctum an immense portrait of the Christian goddess carrying the infant God in her arms. He also saw drawings of men with large staring eyes and of beings with outstretched wings.

The Koreysh are the present 'custodians' of the holy places. How they had prevailed over the line of Ibn Luhay though keeping his cult was a tortuous story best left to another occasion, Al-Ward had said when I had asked him.

He explained, however, that Ibn Luhay's reasoning had in time struck a cord with the Arabs, fiercely independent and differing in their ways. For soon, each tribe was having its own 'mediator' with Allah, stamping its own little godly hoof on the traffic between earth and heaven, the priorities of the former domain always tipping the scales.

For as each tribe brought a replica of its god and found a place for it in the courtyard of the Ka'ba or upon its roof, the idol acted as an advertisement for the tribe and a statement of its power and standing. All, especially the greedy Koreysh, benefited from the amnesty of the season and the trading opportunities on hand.

'My father hated the Koreysh, and I suppose I should love them, just to spite him.' Thus Al-Ward, self-appointed storyteller and chronicler, had concluded his narrative.

I recalled his as we circled the Cube seven times from a right to left direction. This we had to do before we could perform the other ceremonies associated with the pilgrimage. The know-all irreverent Al-Ward, who guided us through the rituals, mentioned with tongue in cheek that the tomb of Eve lay at some two days' ride to the east and was worth a visit. It measured more than a hundred paces, suggesting an enormous size to the First Mother believed to be buried there, he noted. Emru said, a bitter note rising to his throat, 'Little Adam must be lying curled up beside her like a fossilised worm, endlessly cursing the race of pigmies he fathered.'

As we were circling the Ka'ba we passed by the various tribal idols arrayed at the rim of the large courtyard. Al-Ward said they number some three hundred and fifty five, roughly corresponding to the days of the year. Emru was restless to finish the circumambulation. I humoured him and quickened my pace.

I was curious to know how his encounter with *Zul Khalasa*'s double would work out.

A TALE OF THE JINN

As Emru has become a citizen of the free and wild places, people say he has taken on the ways and manners of the jinn. He does not believe in the jinn's existence, but has discovered a poetic benefit in them.

The jinn, the jinn, demons and fairies of the desert, her *efreets* and ghouls, dreams and nightmares.

Al-Ward too does not believe they exist, but he does not mock those who do. He nonetheless believes in the powers of the earth as they course, seen and unseen, through the bodies and thoughts of men and women and all beings.

Al-Ward, sinewy and nimble, fast-talking, fast-running, surefooted as a mountain goat, eyes ever blazing, ever laughing, his joy-leaps as high as those of a caracal catching a bird venturing near the ground, dimples cavorting in his cheeks, is also an exile from the wrath of his own father. That father, a sheikh of the Najd tribe of Abs, had sent his son to Mecca to be tutored there by the renowned pagan scholar Naufal. But the youth took to the radical ways of the *Homs*, who later proved to be a disappointment to him. He in turn has disappointed his father further by refusing to assume his mantle in the affairs of the tribe. He snapped the last tassel with the old man by putting on the rags and manners of the *sa'luks*.

My own father always showed sympathy for that scruffy but high-minded fraternity. He hoped they would somehow save the old Arabian values being savaged by the new kings, many of whom lackeys of foreign gold. Did he not know that he served one such king, though one whose heart was yet untouched by foreign money but was raked by impossible dreams?

Astonishingly my father has introduced a group of *sa'luks* to Emru and myself. Now Al-Ward has collected around him a band of similarly minded youths. They look up to him as a leader. He hopes one day his own little son Orwa, whom he left with his mother in the Abs encampments, would be a *sa'luk* and a poet.

A *sa'luk* may not believe in the jinn. But the belief in them, counterparts of the spirits, demons and devils Christians believe in, seems to be widespread now among pagan Arabs.

But why am I being drawn to the subject of the jinn?

Other matters flicker in my mind, other scenes: the oryxes of Tehama, the taverns of Yathreb, the horse market of Khaybar, the festival of Oqaz... The scenes flicker, flutter, and fade away.

My pen quakes between my fingers. My mind dilates like a drop of oil in water and cannot find its centre.

Am I being punished by the spectral host for voicing doubt in them?

I will believe, I will believe, if they grant me one of their fabled fliers to take me back to Bayroute!

But, already, my pen has been seized.

Who speaks now?

'*We*!

'*We* were first in creation, in the being and the becoming. The angles came second. *We*, from Allah's passion, are pure fire. *They*, from His afterthought, are docile light distilled from *our* rage – *His* rage.

'We are the original breath, the pre-breath, and the primal leap of the Universe. Our laughter in the dark echoes its first terrible roar! Our silence mimics its pre-leap hush. Our aversion to light an aversion to a pathetic pretender.

'We are the creative spark. The pilgrims who come to our Wadi Abqar, in preference to sad Mecca, We lavishly entertain. Ever obliging, We dart off, when petitioned, to kindle inspiration in poets, architects, tool makers, shipbuilders, trackers, lovers...

'Hence, when these excel in their crafts or quests they are called *abqaris*. Their 'genius' comes from us. From the first fire now coursing through their sinews and the sinews of those they touch!

'When appealed to, We take up residence in the minds, evicting, when desired, what men call sanity. Madness after all is known as *junun*, a possession by the jinn. Madness, a twin to genius!

'Like your kind, we have tribes and clans, kings and queens. And our own *sa'luks*. Yeah, aerial *sa'luks*, some of whom the mighty Solomon punished, encasing them in *qomqoms* buffeted by waves, real or imagined. Should *we* not have the right to punish those who do us wrong by taking away the fire and leaving the smoke?

'And in your judgement, We can be wicked or good, ugly or handsome, profane or holy. But only in *your* judgement.

'Unlike you, though, we blaze for hundreds of your years. I know of one *jinni* in Jerusalem who served Solomon. He resides near a wall

168

of the temple which he had helped raise up though with human hands. And I know of another, a cantankerous fellow, who dwells, not so comfortably, inside a *qomqom* at the bottom of the Persian Sea – or so he thinks.

'We have been around long enough to see your Arabia forsake her fire mountains, or they her. We have seen her doff, leaf by leaf, fragrance by fragrance, shade by shade, the green gowns and parasols of her forests. We have seen her yield the sparkle of her rivers and the rainbow of her songbirds, donning sable garments and building mud walls.

'But in the caverns and on the banks of the rivers of Abqar all is restored. Even the golden lanes of Eram are, under Eram's golden sun and silver clouds!

'True, the long-buried woods shall rise and burn in an age yet to come. But it will be a prickly age.

'We hear the chatter of the vulgar, and we smile. But if the wise amongst you can truly listen to us, they will marvel at the tales we can tell, the gaps we can fill in your histories, the errors we can put right, the leagues of reality we can add to your count!

'But all this is idle work compared to what we can yet tell. For we can tell what the very 'Pen of Destiny' is writing, even now. Ay, we can hear its scraping on the Cosmic Tablet by *the* Throne. Faint as it may be across the star-islands, we can decipher its loops and flourishes through the quivering telltale strings of the universe.

'We, of the pulse of the deepest darkness, the litheness of the purest flame, the most virginal, most fecund blaze, can take infinite shapes. Thus we appear, our mystery unfathmoed, our fire-core untouched, as humans, trees, owls, snakes, cats, amber-eyed leopards... Shapes of long-vanished creatures – tigers with teeth like scimitars, deer with horns like *arta* trees, dragonflies with the wings of eagles... This we do to carry out certain tasks in the physical world. Tasks for the mind, tasks for the flesh. Tasks endless, as the imagination is.

'The imagination liberates, torments. Even as it weaves its fiery threads on the Great Loom and scatters them in the Great Dance. The imagination heals. It heals even the pain of parting, Ah, some of the pain.

'I will not stir up your male envy by dwelling on the prowess of our males in the beds of your womenfolk - their heart-milking endurance and instant revivals. You know one of your kind with some of our blaze in him! And you may know of our *qabbadahs*, kneading saplings into cypresses, spurring cowries into oceans, yeah, and urchins into kings? Ah, you know one of yours, but hers are the arts of total human love. How can a man turn to the embraces of other women, be they comelier in outward form? Do you not know of Amr of the Tameem and Bareka of the Speckled Jinn? Do you not know of their fire which still gilds the sands of Dahna to this day?

'But I shall not continue to impound your pen. Your deeper mind murmurs that I may tarry. But I shall go, and leave an ember, though not one to torch your precious paper!'

THE MANY GODS
OF MECCA

I cannot vouch for Al-Ward's accounts. He plucks too strongly the strings of his hearers' credulity, as I do sometimes, contrary to my and his pledges. But he's a poet. I'm not.

In any case, it was the echo of his words that attended my sham circumambulation and followed it

Seven times we circled the Cube from right to left. Now and then before us quivered the bare buttocks of women and men who did not afford or declined to don the robes of the *Homs*.

Emru should have been distracted by the female haunches. But his gaze was drawn elsewhere. A point, a spectre, in the north seemed to tug at his eyes, pulling his gaze way beyond the sanctum, even through the dense and jagged wall of the dark mountains surrounding Mecca.

His ears however may have caught some of Al-Ward's freely offered commentary.

We had by then finished our circling and were walking more leisurely at the outer rim of the courtyard where some of the idols stood. Other idols, mainly small replicas, were placed on the roof of the Cube.

'There's too many of them. Some three-hundred and perhaps fifty, fifty-five, perhaps sixty. Savants say the number replicates the days of the year. Some say it replicates the number of Arabia's tribes.

'They spin, like astral bodies, even as they stand still.'

We false pilgrims have spun, falsely but safely. The less false pilgrims, the fanatics, spin more dangerously, like flame-drunken moths.

Allah's house sits at the centre, blazing, in Kenda's colours.

It sits, unmoved, like Allah, who is nowhere to be seen. An absentee landlord. Yet the lesser gods at the rim revolve, in their stillness, round his absence - envy, mockery, subversion, in their hearts and eyes? In their hearts of basalt and marble, wood and wicker, agate and gold. In their eyes of amber and jasper, jade and amethyst, carnelian and lapis lazuli. Seeing eyes, sealed eyes. They watch. Even when the eyes are shut. Even when the eyes are not there. Crystallised dreams, congealed nightmares, sculptured lusts, originals and copies, they watch the circling of their supplicants. They follow them with disdain and pleading. Like traders in a market they stand. And watch. And hawk their wares.

And yet, together, spinning around Allah's untenanted house, too small to house his vastness, too fixed to arrest their invisible spin, they work their Arab miracle!

'There's *Hu-Baal!*' Al-Ward overwhelmed my reflections.

'The big red fellow to the right. In the shape of a man. He's made of granite. Has an arm of gold. Makes up for one he's lost. He's for the Koreysh, snooty custodians or rather hijackers of the Ka'ba. They revere him as their chief idol. Their prime go-between with Allah. Allah is too immense, too remote, for them. For everybody. Now and then they move him, the Baal, inside the Cube. There, perhaps, he flaunts his big red hard-on at the image of the Christian goddess inside. Today he's out in the sun. So feast your eyes on his big red godhood.

'He was brought into Arabia from Iraq. Pilgrims sacrifice camels to him. Big is his appetite. They consult him on a wide range of decisions they intend to take. He has seven arrows, outnumbering those inside *Zul Khalasa*'s quiver. So you may say he's a more subtle counsellor, more perplexing. Those who're fussy or foolish enough to want to know who the father of a newborn babe is seek his guidance. I don't know how he can pass judgement on this when a woman may have pleasured several men or have had more than one regular husband.

'And there's *Manat*. Also very ancient. See her enormous white boobs, her fulsome mound! Some assets! They stand so provocatively next to *Hu-Baal*'s red vitals. Coy goddess inside the Cube, eat your heart out!'

'Is *Manat* for the Koreysh also?' I ventured to ask.

'She's only a copy. The real one stands on the seacoast near al-Mushallal in Qodayd, north of Mecca. *There* she's worshipped by the Huzeil and the Khuza'a tribes. Pilgrims from the easterly town of Yathreb also sacrifice to her. Despite this buxom copy, her devotees will not be satisfied with their effort here. They must visit her in her wind-swept site on the Red Sea coast. Perhaps they hope to see her charms much enlarged. But every spectacle comes at a price.'

'I once heard, somewhat vaguely, that the Aws and the Khazraj of Yathreb, a gentle people, conclude their pilgrimage by sacrificing to her and shaving their heads at her feet.'

'They need to. As do the other tribes. She's the goddess of fortune, good and ill.'

The goddess held a human skull in her right hand, I thought that it hinted at a leaning towards grim endings. No wonder people feel she needs to be persuaded (or bribed) to change her designs on us poor humans.

'Riders to the sea sometimes pay up to ten silver coins to get a small replica of her. This would be a specially anointed copy, with dainty boobs but with the same quizzical look in her aquamarine eyes. On the seafront, she's not a silent idol. She has a haunting voice, which the sea wind must have a hand or a cheek in modulating.'

No wonder, I thought, her copy here some forty miles away from the sea had opted for silence.

'And here's *El-Lat*. She too's a copy. Her original stands in the mountain town of Taif, south of Mecca. This is a fair copy, though. But the real one, which I've also seen, is cut out of a colossal white rock. There she shimmers like the sun, which she's meant to stand for. Her mirror-like eyes emphasise the point. The high and mighty Thaqifs revere her. They've built a large sanctuary around her, and won't enter their houses after a long journey without first visiting her sanctum. They want to show gratitude to the white goddess for guiding them safely through their passage. An immense hollow beneath her in Taif is kept for the offerings and submissions made to her. These are never touched. The Thaqifs on their mountain stronghold are prosperous enough. And they'll not make a trade out of their guardian goddess. Perhaps more out of conceit than piety. But other tribesmen are impressed with this gesture. They take the trouble to climb up to her lofty dwelling, feeding into the Thaqifs' arrogance.'

And there was one with an even more radiant white face and a tiara on her head.

'That's *Al-Ozza*. She's exceedingly valued here by the Koreysh. They regard her, along with *El-Lat* and *Manat*, as a most exalted goddess, indeed, as a daughter of Allah, conceived in an inconceivable way! But her home is the oasis town of *Nakhlah*, on the road to Iraq. There, her sanctuary is surrounded by a hallowed palm grove.

'I remember a lady, fair as the goddess, who linked her to human sacrifices,' Emru said, wistfully, suddenly showing some interest.

'This must have taken place a long time ago; and definitely through no fault of the goddess. Can you see any sign of bloodlust on her face,

173

shining like the planet Venus in the early dawn sky? And yet I suppose excess of fondness can lead to murder as to madness.'

And then Al-Ward lowered his voice and said conspiratorially,

'When I was doing my apprenticeship here, misguided as it was, I overheard a whispered conversation between two men. One of them was a Koreysh notable, an honest fellow, head and shoulders above the rest. Shaiba was his name. It was to the effect that the scheming Koreysh had made a secret deal with the Shaybans, a deal about which Shaiba was not happy as it involved deception. In barter for gifts they would annually send to Nakhlah, the Koreysh kept the real goddess here. The Shaybans keep the copy.'

Al-Ward continued, and there was a spike of gloating in what he said next.

'Well, they managed to keep the morning star, but the moon god eluded them. For the *Wadd* you see yonder is a mere duplicate!'

Duplicate or not, the idol was a main attraction, his amorous favours courted by many pilgrims. These slowed down their circumambulation when they passed by him. The young had a dreamy look on their fresh faces. One woman's bare nipples rose up for the god's tireless marble erection, which an old man heaved himself up to touch. The vanity of human wishes, old age makes doubly vain!

And then a memory splashed upon the surface of my mind.

Of course, the Moon god! *Wadd*!

The memory took me to the time I was recalled from the side of my mother's grave in Petra to meet Emru at Tabouk. There, Emru invited me to go to the little town of Dawmat Al-Jandal, also to the south of Petra in the valley of *Serhan*. The town was home to *Wadd*'s temple!

Emru was then his usual fun-loving self. After we had embraced and he had patiently heard of my grief at my mother's death and had offered his sympathy, he mentioned the temple of the moon god in the town further to the east as a possible place of solace. I declined the offer.

But as we trotted on our long-necked mounts away from Tabouk, he told me, that he had been a regular visitor to the temple during his sojourn in Dawmat Al-Jandal before he came to Tabouk. He said that the god there was served by the Quda'as, who defend their choice of the god by babbling about a male force needed to stand up to the female fickleness ascribed to the moon-horned Ishtar. Fickle! Women fickle? Fresh from the bed of Sofia and the graveside of my mother, I thought

174

that trait should be the preserve of men, at least many of them, Emru chief amongst them, I following.

The original god, Emru had said, stood wielding a spear with the crescent moon at its tip, a bow slung on his back. Hewn out of a milk-white piece of rock by a master sculptor, he was represented as an older man, gigantic, with an enormous beard, but with a youthful and muscular body complemented by a huge hard-on. The left eye was half closed as to suggest an archer's squint or a swain's playful wink. He was ever surrounded, Emru said, by a large throng of men and women, some in a state of frenzy induced by the wine and the jostling of bodies, many clamouring for icons and cures, though never a cure from lust. The air was always one of festivity, soon to climax into an all-out orgy. On one occasion, a woman, Emru recounted, was being pleasured by two men, fore and aft, obviously to her great delight, as she was clasping each man with one of her hands and rousing them further with abandoned cries.

Emru had said at the time he would not mind at all taking the trip back to Dawmat Al-Jandal solely for my sake. I disappointed him by holding on to my grief and abstinence.

Now however as we stood before the god's copy in Mecca I valued the influence of the god on Emru. He seemed to be back to his youthful self which I had so much loved and envied. I too saluted the god, though in silence, whispering the name of Sofia. I did not dare mention my mother's name, knowing her devotion to her higher and austere Yesu, austere, though also a supreme god of love. But when I had earlier touched the cloth of the Cube during my circumambulation, I murmured her name. May be the Virgin and her God-son inside Allah's holy of holies heard it.

And the gods swooned and spun even as they stood in the heat. Al-Ward introduced more of them, those in humanlike forms: *Suah* of the Huzayls, *Manaf* of the Haurans, *Nuhm* of the Muzaynahs, *Suayr* of the Anazahs, *Am-Anas* of the Khawlans, *Al-Fils* of the Tayy's, *Dhu al-Shara* of the Azds, *Dhu al-Kaffayn* of the Daws, *Al-Muharreq* of the Rabi'as, *Al-Shams* of the Tameems, *Al-Jalsad*, whose original had held my infant body in his cold white arms, *Al-Qays*, after whom Emru was named...

And Al-Ward introduced us to gods in animal and bird forms as they stood spreading their wings or baring their teeth or sporting their manes: *Nasr* of the Lahyans, *Yaghouth* of the Murads, *Ya'uq* of the Hamadhans – names they had given to or shared with stars and constellations.

There is a belief in Arabia that Mecca lies at the very centre of the world, forming its navel and keeping its mass at balance. The black stone, said to have been placed in the Cube's south-eastern wall by Abraham, is believed by some people to have started its life as a shooting star that fell from heaven. The dour *Homs* believe it was a white quartz stone darkened by the sins of the hands that touched it. I must have added to it a dark shade of my own when I lightly felt it. To the side of the Cube was the massive rock marked with the footprints of Abraham as he stood on it to raise the walls of the house – so we're told.

The town's main source of water is the well I mentioned before called *Zamzam*. It has been serving the pilgrims since that day when Hagar's son caused it to gush to the surface of the earth in the middle of a wasteland. Al-Ward told us that the *Homs* believe that Allah had made a promise to provide for the descendants of Ishmael as to the issue of his half-brother Isaac. As for *Zamzam*, Al-Ward said the *Homs* believed that its water originates from a lake deep in the ground which Allah had created to cool a ball of fire at the core of the earth. The hint of fire lingers in the taste of the *Zamzam* water, and the pilgrims endeavour to carry some of it in their water skins as a blessing and a cure.

It is also said, and I was a witness to this, that the hundreds of white pigeons which fly around the Cube never soar above it. Also inexplicably, they never soil the sanctuary with their droppings.

I must admit that there are riddles in this world we cannot ravel out. It is best to maintain the mind of a seeker who is not blinded by his quest. Who knows whether it is best to have one God or many or none at all?

'It's all so silly!' Emru said as we left Mecca. 'Why should God give sanctity to one place at the expense of other places? Did he not mould the dough of the world with his own hands, as the story goes, rendering all holy?'

Here surged in my mind the Saint's exuberant praise of the 'Creator of all' followed by his anguished plea, 'Since creator and created are all good, whence then is evil?'

'I don't know', I replied.

'What use does Allah have for a house? And walls?' Emru mooted again.

'Perhaps to get the Arabs together for a few days each year,' I said, already doubting the miracle I had assumed to be true.

'A king should do that for them, and not just for a few days,' he replied, in a surprisingly serious tone.

I silently doubted if any mortal king could do that. But as I turned to cast a last look at an immense dark cloud that had been spreading like a mighty swarm of locusts over the valley behind us, Al-Ward sang out the lines:

Let the light of freedom shine!
Let it sweep all walls away,
Let it spur our warmer clay,
Let it be our only shrine!
Let dear freedom be our god,
One with whom we dance as mates
And sit down to eat our dates -
Equal gods, one brotherhood!

THE IN-BETWEEN CREATURE
IN EXILE

The *memres* of Saint Ephrem and Saint Narsai and the poems which the Saint of the *Confessions* quotes for his purpose have encouraged me before to quote poems for my own purpose.

And now the poetry draws me into its own. And as it does so, it draws a curtain, shutting off all other voices – and those of my pen's duplicities?

I hear Emru say to Al-Ward, Nay, both, saying to each other, round a crackling fire, their voices, their lines, racing one another, dovetailing, in a thrilling flight:

A poet is an in-between:
 Not a mortal, not a Baal;
  Neither human nor a jinn,
   Of no tribe except the wind,
    Of no Mecca but the heart,
     His own *Zamzam*, bitter-sweet,
      Guest and host to all he meets,

Sa'luk, king, of inter-realms,
 his own *Khidr*, the ever-green,
  Piping in the silent pit,
   Blossoming in the hourglass,
    Shuttling way beyond the loom,
     Teasing loom and sand and glass,
      Even as he gilds the dunes,
       bonding men to earth's song,
        Gasping in the unborn dawn!

And I hear him recite:

A poem is like a dark raincloud,
A poem is like a thunderbolt,

A poem is like a shooting star,
A poem is like a frisky colt.

A poem is like a spider's web,
A net of flailing wings like jewels,
A shaman's charm to fetter Time,
A fool's deception spun for fools.

A poem is like a bubbly spring,
A poem is like a cactus, hard,
A piebald mountain crowned by mist,
A poem is like a silent god!

I hear tribal voices, Elders, crying out to a young Emru, 'Tune your galloping lines to the glories of Kenda!' But he does not answer. He turns away. 'Invoke your jinni whore for the splendour of your tribe!' They shout. He mutters, 'A whore is not likely to praise another!' And he extemporises:

The jinn, men say, possess my ear!
Ah yes, I smile, the 'jinn!'
Together with a thousand groans
And, most, the groans within!

'We understand not. These are words beyond our care, beyond your years. Sing of war and the ecstasy of the blade, the expansiveness of conquest!' And he recites:

When War accosts young fools at leisure,
She wears a youthful face of pleasure.
She touts a prize of solid gold,
And juicy favours for the bold,
A feast of flesh unmarked by guilt,
Delights and glories to the hilt,
And best of all a quick release
A brief exertion crowned by peace ...
But once embraced and starts to shag,
She turns into a hideous hag;
Her silken braids spring barbs at you,
her old *han*-flow a crimson goo;
And rather than a love galore,

179

The fool collects a nasty sore,
And for the 'feather of the brave',
The fool secures an early grave.

And he adds:

No wonder wise lads choose instead
More trusted maidens in the bed!

And so he follows the call of his hunger, ravenous as it is:

I rose to her, her folk asleep,
A bubble surging from the deep,
A river-carp's dark, starving sigh,
Climbing towards her lily-sky;
I rose, I crawled, craving her light
An adder coiling for a bite,
A horny worm, if seen, in heat,
Would die under her father's feet;
A boy-Adam seeking a fruit
Arrayed to shake him to the root;
A boy who will yet ripe with lust,
Which, in the grave, will gild his dust!

A lady winked, and I obeyed,
What can a slave do, but get laid?

A youth lusting, lusted after, he declares:

She trailed a gown behind us twain,
Her hand in my damp hand -
'Fear not!' she said, 'the gown will hide
Our footprints in the sand!'

Behind a dune she spread the gown,
And stood, as do fruit trees.
And as I rose to pluck a fruit,
I plucked the Pleiades!

And he recites, riotously:

I shagged her hard, her necklace broke,
Its pearls, like argent doves, came loose,
And then they sank, like languid fish,
Her anklets round my neck, a noose.

And so I died for want of breath,
And she, in pity, joined my death.

And he grows up to recite, more boldly:

She came at night, shedding the waiting game,
And when she shed her robe, she shed all shame.
But wherefore shame? Who made the holy rules?
Unholy men hoodwincking bores and fools!

And yet more boldly:

She turned and gave her howling baby suck.
The blighter gulped the heaving breast;
And as I sulked above her trunk, she stretched
And gave me all the heaving rest.

And boldly and unsentimentally:

She wore her jewels and rouged her face
And daubed her long eyelashes,
But love had fled with his good flame,
And left my lust in ashes!

She, too, was toying with a spark
That would not smoulder higher
And ached to find a newer love
To start a fresher fire!

And daringly, in the ever-daring town of Dawmat Al-Jandal:

I sought her face, a silver moon to seize,
But loitered at the gold between her knees!

And gaily, desolately:

This was her home, now deathly bare
Without her jasmine in the air.
Wild deer are here, while she, most dear,
Is gone to charm another sphere.
But here I worshipped at her shrine,
And sipped her lips for holy wine,
An idol carved to cast a spell,
And trounce the eyes of a gazelle;
And here the marble of her form
Became alive to cool and warm,
And here the light of her clear face
Outshone the stars in their vague race,
Ah, here she swayed, life's sparkle sweet,
And spread a dainty field of wheat,
And here her husband snored till morn,
Sprouting yet another horn,
Vowing, awake, to shine his spear
Even if that should take a year!
Perhaps, in time, to lance my heart!
He could not fight or mime the part!
And when he sent his hatchet men,
They trundled back with 'Ne'er again!'
He knew I was the true bridegroom;
He held a branch; I held the bloom,
I held her heart and maidenhood,
Her very sap, and he the wood.
And yet the jasmine of his wife
Perfumed his sleep and spurred my life,
While Time, the ghoul, there stood aside,
Leering, daydreaming of our bride!

TO THE PIEBALD FORT

Our journey to Samuel's fort was a journey back in time, if such a feat was ever possible outside of memory and history, blurred and biased as these often are.

For, from the fountain of the Jews' tears had flowed the sparkling words of the Nazarene on the Mount, and in the forge of their tenacity his own passion on the Cross had been honed as was the Christian martyrs' grit in Rome's arenas. And did not the tablets which Moses had received on another mountain cast their tall letters, in shades bold or subtle, on many a law of the gentiles or stare them in the face?

The Christians have been going around pushing their faith on all and sundry, keen to drag souls drifting in the world's wilderness into God's garden. The Jews have chosen differently. They have been quietly tending to their own flock, mending every now and then the fence of the laws trusted to keep the wolves away.

But I am drawing here on the wisdom of my uncle Ephraim. Where are you beloved uncle and first teacher? In what storm or calm are you being tossed or nursed? May the fierce angels you have loved and exchanged breaths with shield you with their wings and give you some of the gentler memories they had shared with you!

Unlike his fellow priests and the Roman State, both of whom he had quarrelled with, my uncle harboured none of the traditional malice against the first worshippers of the One God.

My father was of a like mind. On his authority, the first Hebrews who came into Arabia were a priestly class of Rabbis called the *Kohens*. They were fleeing from the same monstrosity that has continued to harry that nation. Here was one kinship with the persecuted both my rebel uncle and secretly simmering father were drawn to.

An Arabian tradition mentioned by my father traces the first dwelling of Jews in Arabia to the time of David. That prophet-king led an expedition into the Hejaz, the story says, and established a settlement in Yathreb. To this day, the town or its neighbourhood is a stronghold of prosperous Jewish tribes like the Korayzas and the Nadhirs and the Kaynuqas. Further to the north, in the oasis of Khaybar, the inhabitants of seven forts there claim descent from Rechab, the charioteer. Rechab's own son Jehonadab, led the life of a hermit in the wilderness, but his offspring chose to settle in the lush oasis.

During our stay in Shammar, the noble Al-Mu'alla had casually mentioned Samuel as a ruler superior to others in every virtue. He had also declared that the family of Samuel trace their origins to Aaron, Moses' brother and aide in the Egyptian chronicle. But in the story of Abraham's visit to Mecca and the shrine he built there is further testimony to the traffic between Palestine and Arabia - a traffic already redolent with the incense of Sheba and the perfume of her queen.

In fact, it was in Belqis's kingdom, Kenda's first homeland, that the Jewish presence in Arabia reached its peak.

There, the faith of the Hebrews became the state religion after the Yemeni king Tubba' Asad Ben Abu Karib converted to that faith, receiving the *mikveh* and giving the *korban* and his foreskin away. The king, returning from a campaign in Iraq, had had a conversation with a Yathreb rabbi which convinced him of the superiority of Jehovah over the idols his people had long worshipped. If the story is true, the skills and accomplishments of the Yathreb community and the benefits of an alliance with them may have played a role in the king's conversion.

All the same, Tubba' must have discovered later that, even with the best allies, the Yemen was as ungovernable a country as a bucking camel. This was a conclusion Kenda herself was to reach during her rise to power there.

In Arabia proper, the Jews show no political ambitions. Apart from alliances made to prevent Bedouin raids, they live mainly behind walls overlooking the fields they cultivate. They produce excellent wine, which they sell along with the surplus of their agricultural produce to their neighbours and export to cities far a-field. They also are adept weavers and jewellers, their trusted craftsmanship having won them loyal customers and fame and wealth in the Yemen and throughout Arabia and Syria. And for a people averse to war making, their forges turn out swords that rival those of India and Rome, and shields, breastplates and helmets that defy the very swords both they and the Indians and the Romans make.

Amer Ben Mazen was true to his pledge. After we parted company with the caravan which was to plod on to Syria he led us round the roving blisters and rashes of the Tarf bands. They had hurriedly scattered after hearing of our desertion from Shammar but remained, thinned and determined, as perilous as concealed adders.

He spirited us under their very noses and at times it seemed to me, through their very eyelashes. How he managed to do this, I cannot tell. A lonely caracal of a man, he was not much given to social or light-hearted talk, the longest speech he had ever made by his own admission was the one he had poured out to Emru on his first arrival in Shammar. But he joked once, perhaps to calm me down, as he spoke about a magical powder he had in his possession and which he would throw up in the air causing lookouts to nod off or campfires to roar loudly muffling other sounds. I saw no such powder. Still, I imagined, rope-thin and clad as he was in his knee-high grey garment, that he had the power to bend down and make an incision with his knife into the ground, lift up a bit of the earth like the hem of an *aba* and disappear beneath it. Yeah, he was a man of few words, but I noticed that his lips, when not tightly sealed like the nostrils of a camel in a sandstorm, murmured unintelligible words. Were they incantations for secret passes to open up before us? Were they prayers to unknown gods or unseen jinn to shroud our progress with invisibility? Were they whisperings to an absent lover?

I am ashamed to confess that in the first few days following our flight from Shammar, I suspected at every bend that he would turn us in to a party of salivating Tarf. Perish the thought! So set in his devotion was he! And though destitute as he seemed to be, I came to feel that he would not be swayed against us by any promise or threat. He was implacable in his loyalty to Emru and Hend. Perhaps the gentle words and kindness of an otherwise rough Hojr had touched his heart and re-cast his mind, both unfathomable in their simplicity. He was a true son of the desert, honed by her sullen purity and indifference to life and death, her harsh regularity and infinite facility to surprise.

At the end of a four-day trek, during which he led us, the burden we were, onto rocky heights then descended with us onto the green plain of Tayma, we glimpsed the Jew's castle in the distance. Loud cheers rose to our throats as we caught sight of the hoped-for haven across a landscape of thickening vegetation. Our dromedaries too sensed our elation and leapt into a spirited canter. This went on for a time with the air, increasingly fragrant with a rich earthy aroma, rushing into our mouths and pushing any further cheers back into our chests.

I turned to Amer Ben Mazen to acknowledge his efforts.

He was not there! He had disappeared!

There was no trace of him anywhere around! Like a desert fish he had sunk into the earth. But the ground here was no sea of sand into which a skink, let alone a man, could plunge.

Shocked and bewildered, we scattered, riding in various directions to look for him. He was nowhere to be seen. Even the tracks of his *dalul* were not discernible. We called out his name. Hend too raised her spiky voice, chocked with rare empathy, tears a-sparkle in her large jet-black eyes. But as we finally turned the necks of our camels towards the fort in the distance, I thought of Oweir Ben Shajnah. And I thought that Amer Ben Mazen may have wished to avoid embarrassing us by our inability to properly reward him. I also thought that perhaps he did not want to see Samuel again lest the latter should think he had returned for further award. But these were mere thoughts of a baffled man in a frantic saddle.

Whatever his reasons, his disappearance, coming after so much effort on his part to ensure our safety, did not seem to have anything sinister about it. It had, though, the marks of a mystery not untypical of a wild son of the desert.

DRINKER OF THE WIND

The wind, redolent, breathes upon my page. Her long fingers snake round my pen. We bend and whirl and flutter; but we rise, pen and I, to move to her will, and her voice:

'When Allah wanted to bring the horse into being, He summoned me. And He said, I *WILL* THAT A NOBLE AND SPLENDID CREATURE SHOULD ARISE FROM THEE. SO COMPRESS THYSELF! So I compressed myself. Then the archangel Gabriel came and stood at the ready. At Allah's command, he took a handful of my substance, his wing brushing against it, and presented it to his Master. Out of it, a peal thundering from the sprinting cosmos in the background, Allah formed a most handsome creature. Its graceful body quivered with my essence, its eyes blazed with the keenness of lightning, its voice echoed to the pain and power and promise of distant nativities. It had the loveliness and the strength of the female and the male. And it was able to be of colours I had stroked and soaked up as I swept and swooned over the earth – black and brown and bay and chestnut and white and grey and roan and dun and other colours in keeping with the nobility and beauty of that being. Then I heard Allah say:

ARISE, O KOHAYLAN, KOHL-EYED, WIND-FOOTED, LIEGE OF ALL OTHER ANIMALS CREATED.

BLESSED THOU SHALT BE BY ME AND BY MAN AND WOMAN, WHO SHALL FOLLOW THEE WHEREVER THOU GOEST AND THEY YOU. BLESSED SHALT THOU BE FOR PURSUIT AND BLESSED SHALT THOU BE FOR FLIGHT, THOUGH NO WINGS ARE TO BE SEEN ON THY FLANKS.

UPON THY BACK SHALL RICHES AND HONOUR REST. AND UPON THY FOREHEAD SHALL BLAZE A STAR UNEQUALLED. A WHITE SPOT ON THY FLEET FOOT SHALL FOREVER BEAR THE MARK OF GABRIEL'S WING. THY BEAUTY AND GRACE SHALL NOT BE MATCHED SAVE BY THE MOST BEAUTIFUL, MOST GRACEFUL, OF WOMEN AND MEN. THY SWIFTNESS SHALL BE THAT OF

THE WIND AND THE OSTRICH, THY BRILLIANCE THAT OF THE LIGHTNING, AND THY FEARLESSNESS THAT OF THE LION. YET THY GENTLENESS SHALL BE THAT OF THE FAWN, THY FELLOWSHIP OF THE FAITHFUL HOUND, THY PATIENCE OF THE DEVOTED LOVER.

NEVER SHOULD THOU BE HARMED OR HUMBLED OR NEUTERED. NONE OF MY SERVANTS SHALL LEAD THEE BY THY FORELOCK OR MANE. NONE SHALL DENY THEE DRINK OR NOURISHMENT SAVE THAT WHICH HARMS THY WELLNESS AND ENDURANCE.

THE SOUND OF THY HOOVES SHALL BE AS DEAR TO ME AS THE CHANTING OF MONKS AND THE COOING OF TURTLE DOVES, THE ARCH OF THY TAIL AS SPLENDID IN MY SIGHT AS THE RAINBOW AFTER THE DELUGE! FASHIONED OF THE COMPRESSED WIND, *UNFOLD* AND DRINK THE WIND UNBOUNDED!'

SAMUEL

We remained seized with the mystery of our vanished guide even as we drew nearer to *Al-Ablaq*. It is so named, it became apparent to us, because of the white and black stones of its walls, which we were now approaching at a trot.

It was an imposing sight. The fort reared up like a piebald stallion atop a squat hill. Lower down meandered a dense palm grove with lush cultivated fields girdling the hill.

The air, suffused with the heady passions of a green, teeming earth, enlivened our chests with each lunge towards the upsurging sanctuary.

Emru released his she-camel from the trot he had allowed her, spurring her into a sudden gallop. He was buoyed up by his nearness to a promised ally at the heart of the Hejaz.

Soon Al-Ward and Hend and I were galloping after him. The dull hoof-thuds of the camels and the black dromedary mingled with those of his own, our resurgent shouts with his. How quickly did fade our anguished shouts for Amer Ben Mazen minutes earlier!

As we drew nearer, men and women working in the fields around the fort looked up from their tools to gaze at our party bounding towards them. Theirs were fresh faces, looking out with no anxiety, confident in the judgement of their sentries on two watchtowers flanking the gate of the fort.

Presently two riders emerged from the gate. They trotted towards us, their sheathed swords, bouncing up and down on the sides of their saddles. Emru slowed down his she-camel to a walk and raised his hand with a salute.

'A good day to the brave warriors of Israel! I am Emru El-Qais, King of Kenda. I have come seeking an audience with the noble Samuel. I bear goodwill and portly tidings. My sister and two friends, my brothers, are with me. We come in peace, trusting in the hospitality and wisdom of the steward of *Al-Ablaq* and seeking his *aman*!'

'A good day to the King of Kenda and his companions! Coming in peace, you are most welcome to share in our own peace inviolate. The master of the fort will receive you after you have rested,' said one of the two men. He was a young lad but possessed of the poise and speech of a veteran diplomat. I had an instant liking for him.

As we passed through a massive gate of heavy studded wood, we were greeted by the sight of a spacious courtyard bordered by small villas, their white walls crisscrossed by climbing plants in red flower. Men and women went about their business, carrying bundles and baskets or driving fat-tailed sheep before them. A large smithy echoed to the hammering by a burley man upon a blade positioned on a tall anvil, a forge hard by spewing sparks. An assortment of swords and hoes and sickles leaned on the smithy's walls or were piled on its floor!

Despite the acrid fumes of the smithy and the strong odour of the sheep, some of the soil-fragrance that had met us outside the wall still lingered in my chest. A watering well to the right of the courtyard held a file of men and women waiting with buckets in their hands.

After we were invited to dismount we saw our camels and pack-dromedary led away by attendants.

'We shall relieve them of their saddles and loads and we shall feed and water them', the young man assured us. Hend whispered to Emru and gestured in the direction of *El-Pheel*. Emru shook his head, dismissing her concern.

We were then guided into one of the small villas lining the courtyard. Inside, we were escorted past a small courtyard into a cool reception room with divans and swells of cushions. A door kept ajar seemed to lead into another room. An elderly attendant offered us fresh water in silver basins to wash our hands and faces, with a promise of a bath to follow. A fruit tray was brought in.

Emru however would not have us dally long in that luxury.

He had told our young escort on the way that he wished to see Samuel at once. But the youth took his time to make sure that three helpers, a comely young maiden among them, had assembled, carrying the tools and towels for our individual baths.

An hour or so later, a man of distinguished appearance arrived at our doorstep. He inquired as to whether we had taken our baths. When Emru assured him that we had done so, the man declared, 'A good day to you King of Kenda and favourite of the Abqar maidens! You have blessed our humble dwelling, and I have come to pay you homage as an admirer of your person and an apprentice in the seminary of your genius. I am Samuel Ben Ored Ben Adiya. *Al-Ablaq* has grown taller since your arrival.'

We were struck by the Jew's speech and graciousness, and looked at him with new eyes. He was a man of middle years and medium height, with a handsome face and a wide forehead. His jet-black penetrating eyes I felt could easily dart into the recesses of a man's thoughts and depart with one or two long-hid secrets. They however chose to flutter courteously around our minds not wishing to break in uninvited. As he unfolded his arms, Emru, moved by his stirring tribute, rushed to embrace him, tears welling up in his great eyes.

Samuel then turned to pay us, Hend and Al-Ward and myself, gracious courtesies, then escorted the four of us outside the villa and through the main courtyard into a large hall. There he introduced to us his handsome wife, Sarah, and three sons. One of them, to our pleasant surprise, was the fine young man who had met us outside the gate and walked with us to our quarters. He was called Hoth. He stood casually between his two other brothers, Shurayh and Monther; and though fine youths in their own right, Hoth outshone them both. I could see a twinkle in his father's eyes as he gazed upon him with special pride and fervour.

At the meal, and apart from instructing the servants to ply us with delicacies and titbits, Samuel remained silent, pretending to share our ravenous hunger.

Later, over bowls of fruits, Samuel proceeded to entertain us with a story.

It subtly reflected on our situation. A scholar travelling on a ship is asked by a group of merchants about the merchandise he carries with him. He says it is the best and the most enduring. Driven by curiosity, they look in the hold of the ship, but see nothing save their own bales. So they make merry of him. Then the ship is struck and wrecked by a storm and sinks to the bottom of the sea along with her freight. The passengers escape with their lives. They manage after much hardship to reach a foreign port. There, the scholar finds his way to the local synagogue, where he is appointed as head teacher and given decent wages. The merchants are in the meantime destitute without their bales and they come to seek his help, which he offers generously. They say to him, 'Verily, you spoke the truth. Our goods have perished, but yours endure.'

We all approved the sentiment, which made Samuel declare, 'It is recorded in our Book of Proverbs that a wise man is better than a strong man, and a scholar is superior to a warrior. However, when it comes to war it is wisdom and good counsellors that ensure a successful running of it.'

'I have had good counsellors. But victory eludes me; and I have need for your wisdom,' Emru rejoined.

'It is said that if a man does battle with the wave, it overwhelms him, but if he permits it to roll over him, it will pass on. It may be so with a sandstorm, or...a war...storm!'

'Should I then sink into a hole in the ground until the warhorses' hooves have faded into the distance?' Emru rejoined abruptly, a spike in his voice sullen and unfair to Samuel's parable.

The Hebrew prince took the outburst of his guest with grace.

'It is unbecoming for a lion to weep before a jackal, a wise rabbi said. By the same token it is unseemly of that king to give chase to a jackal if it snatches a bite from the king's dinner.'

'What if the jackal took the heart of the lion's father?'

'Then, it is written, to God belongs the vengeance. Verily, he who forgives his enemies and slanderers though able to exact retribution upon them makes himself a friend of God. This is so since God hears his enemies and slanderers and remains silent.'

'Gods seem to speak in many ways and through many throats. I heard a god speak a while ago, and smashed his three snaky tongues on his flank. I would have done the same in Mecca of late, but his pigmy of a copy was out of reach. It was taking turns on top of Allah's house!'

Emru could have said more. He could have admitted that the god was right; that the god had spoken the truth; that he had given him good counsel, a fair warning – as fair and uncanny as his priestess. It was true that *Zul Khalasa*'s effigy happened to be on top of the Cube during our fake pilgrimage, as were those of *Al-Jalsad* and *Al-Qais*. But an affront to an idol in the sanctuary can be contemplated only by a madman.

Even so, I rushed to restore the conversation onto a more amiable course, rallying to Emru's aid. He had been slipping as was his wont on occasion into a slinging match, though this time round with a most welcoming and well-meaning host, one who nevertheless took delight in repartee.

So I said, fighting for breath,

'Is...it...not the...duty of a...man...a man, of...learning, a man with a...vision...to go out and...strive...for...for...a...better world?

Perhaps…perhaps…his striving may…help give…his vision…legs. It…it then can…can walk…walk in…the marketplace and…speak in the…councils of…princes!'

Samuel turned to enfold me with his intense but kindly eyes, sizing me up with a benign smile on his sun-tanned face.

'When the angel of death stood outside Rabbi Ammi's door, the ancient man heard the rustle of the angel's wings. He wept. His nephew was in the room, and inquired as to why the rabbi was crying. Was it the fear of death? And why should a man of the rabbi's learning and goodness be frightened of the angel's embrace? Why should that be? The holy man had not been tainted by public office. Nor did he ever sit in judgement over people. The rabbi replied, 'It is for this very reason that I weep. I was offered the chance to establish justice in the land, but I cringed and shied away, to my pain.' I do certainly agree that men of vision should strive for a better world, but …'

Before he could continue, I butted in again. I did not wish to miss a chance to pay our host a compliment and consign our mission into his good books.

'Surely, what…we have seen in…*Al-Ablaq* speaks…of…a…kingdom, small as it may be…where a…vision…of…the…highest order…informs…the…the running of public life,' I stopped, and gasped for air.

I was flattering the man. But my words were heartfelt. What I had seen of the harmony and industry inside the fort and around it seemed like a philosopher's vision come into flower.

'Ah, my friend, I value the compliment. More so since it comes from such a learned and liberal young man. But, as you have so wisely noted, this is but a small kingdom, if kingdom at all. Hence it is but a small achievement. Nor is it the achievement of one man, but of many, men and women, present and past. The failures your forgiving eyes have passed over rest at the feet, and on the head, of *one* man though. This man, if truth is told, has his heart, most entrenchedly, in the pursuit of the perfect line of verse, vain as this quest may be. This he rates an achievement worthier than any other won by sword or trade or political husbandry. Yeah, he watches over men and women tending the gardens and the fields, and those at the battlements and those loading and downloading the camels. But he is ever distracted by the whisperings of the maidens of *Abqar*. Attending on their whispers should be his

193

sole calling. The king may share my sentiment. Indeed, in his superior kingdom of verse, I'm only a loyal subject and fan.'

'You are too modest, my brother,' Emru responded, 'Some of your very fine poems have reached me across the sands scattering oases as they travelled. They gladdened my heart and spurred me, as only the best of poetry can, to better efforts. I recall one ode. It starts with the lines...' Emru paused, then recited, somewhat tentatively,

> A man who...is of...malice free
> Anoints the land, an...olive tree;
> But one who is to...meanness prone
> Is spurned, a henbane, left alone...

'Ah! That was a trifle,' Samuel interrupted, a scarlet tint spreading across his face. He continued, 'But on your lips it has been transformed into something rare. Rather, *I* should be recalling your superlative lines; yeah, even though my lips can add nothing to their worth, nor take away from it. But I can recollect the long ode which starts with the quatrain,

> Here was her home, friends! Let me halt a while,
> Perhaps I might reclaim from Time a smile!
> Or else, unload upon his wing a tear
> To scald his heedless pinions one brief mile!

Now it was Emru's turn to break in, knocking down his own art.

'You are too gracious a host to remind your guests of their shortcomings. But do us the honour of reciting the rest of your truly stirring ode that starts with the lines I quoted. My memory of late has been jostled by the arrows and treacheries of men. Thus belaboured, it might do your perfect lines some injustice. I recall though that your poem next mentions a lady. How can it be otherwise? But she has spoken of your nation as a trifle too small, too light a weight in the scale of the world's nations. Will you grace and redeem us with the rest of the poem?' Emru pleaded.

Thus was Samuel coaxed into a mood he relishes, as one might expect of a poet.

A touch of vanity affects almost every rhymester. But Samuel was a man of great stature, in word and deed. He said, 'It is enough of an honour that my sluggish verses managed to reach your ear, O King. By climbing, or rather by being lifted, to such a height, they seem to have shed their baser elements on the slopes. Thus the four lines you recited were decked in a finer element. The rest I will recite only in deference to the wishes of a most honoured guest. May they also, their boasting forgiven, be touched by the alchemy that graced their preamble.'

Then Samuel loosened up in his seat and recited the following lines:

She says we are a tribe too small!
Perhaps we are, but we stand tall!

The young among us seize the heights
The old had scaled in former flights.

And though a few, we shield our friend,
Against battalions emperors send,

With swords deflecting evil darts,
And chain-mail made of our own hearts.

For us, death holds no fear or shame,
Only a shortcut gallop to fame.

To die in bed is second best,
Unless it were at a lover's breast,

Softer than down, whiter than milk,
Tented by strands of raven silk,

To die enthralled in her embrace,
But then reclaimed by her moon-face,

Or at her back, a freeborn mare,
No man can master; let them dare!

Let men hoard life inside a cask;
Our lives we give to those who ask!

MY DRINKER OF THE WIND

AN APOLOGY

His handsome face comes into sight –
  Broad forehead, a white mark on the grey-brown brow,
  Silken strands of the forelock, playfully tousled,
  Ears fine as those of a gazelle, pointing inwards, but turning around
now and again.
  The face tapers into a mouth small enough to fit into the palm of a
hand, my boy's hand,
  Deep, lean cheekbones,
  Chiselled, terse lips, the underlip longer than the upper,
  Veins running down the face,

running,

running,

a cascade of exuberance, a map, a
mystery, traced to the first sire and dame, or, earlier,
to a thought in the mind of an ineffable god?

  The rest of his body is not visible to me; but a hint of the arched neck,
the high withers, and the well sloped shoulder speak of the creature's
grace and power and speed.
  And then the eyes – probing, chasing; unsettling!
  He slices me with them, those eyes, black eyelashes curved like tiny
scimitars.
  His gaze penetrates my being, burning into my hidden fears.
  But it is a benign gaze. The eyes read but do not mock. They only
wonder as to why the fear should be there.
  The creature has been reared in the lap of human fellowship. Since his
birth, since he was massaged for the first time with butter and nurtured
on his mother's milk and camel milk and on wheat and barley and fresh
grass, he has had children all around him, both in the open stables and
on his back during exercise. He has had doting grooms rubbing down
his satiny coat, gentle fingers combing his mane – once a curious maid
touching, stroking, his root.

Inquisitive by nature, he probes my inner recesses. He detects in them a contrary, perhaps threatening, presence. But he is schooled in fearlessness. No man or jinn, no rumble of thunder or cavalry can unhinge the repose of his soul or the silent song of his spirit. But he moves the splendour of his head back, his fine ears turning more excitedly, his glossy coat rippling like a flowing stream.

He sees and he knows. He sees the humiliation of having a gauche rider on his back. He anticipates, he pre-feels, the pain, the embarrassment, of having that rider falling off his back time and again. In his native, celestial pride, he resents the indignity, the untidiness, of it all.

I recoil in shame.

But the core of my fear swells up, pushing the horse's unveiling gaze away.

My fear takes hold, as it does so often. Pushing the world with its eyes and arms and legs away!

I seek out my father. The creature is his gift to me. But he is nowhere to be seen, called on an urgent mission for his king.

Then appears a very young Emru, young, like me, and yet a fraction older, much older, and far more assured.

He approaches the questioning eyes, the neck arching more acutely than before.

He extends an arm towards the handsome face.

I feel the calmness of Emru's soul by my side. It touches me lightly, but it glidess beyond me to the calm lake at the heart of the horse's being, momentarily ruffled, though not by fear.

I hear Emru murmuring. His murmurs seem to rise from his own lake of tranquillity reposing in the depths of him, the confidence of his spirit, the satiety of his loins, young as he is. It radiates, even then, with the peace and certainty of a love-bed left a short time earlier. It hums with the stroke of a hand anointed in the mystery of a woman's body.

The horse shakes his head. He snorts lightly and blinks, as if to clear his throat and blow away the vision of a doubt that had loitered there for a moment.

The kohl-lined eyes accept me as Emru leads my hand on to the silken mane. The neck twitches slightly from the poll to the withers under my cold and clammy fingers. But it accepts. It accepts, with equine magnanimity, the coming humiliation.

I called you *Najm*, a 'star', but I never rose to your constellation!
Drained of time, I offer you an apology.

DISCOURSE AT SAMUEL'S COURT

So perfect they were, those lines, from Samuel's own lips, manfully spoken!

So perfect also for our purpose!

Did Emru steer the conversation towards that monumental pledge or did the gracious Samuel offer it unprompted - the offer having always been there for the taking to anyone who asked?

Emru sprang up from his cushion and went to Samuel hugging him, visibly moved, Samuel saying, 'You are the master bard, I am but a dabbler, a faint echo' and the like, Emru insisting that his host was the better poet.

I had long wished, my jealousies aside, to see Emru recapture his old humour. A smile rose to my face provoked by my better self. As my smile spread through my wayward soul Samuel urged Emru to recite some of his own poetry. Much of it Samuel said he knew by heart. But I secretly prayed Emru would not do so. It would have consumed the conference.

I was relieved when Emru said, 'Held in your memory, my verses are in the best keep they can hope for, though they were only meant for the hurtling wind. I am happy though to leave them in your care. But I've come to you on a quest, one that has proved to be more elusive than the maidens of *Abqar*, though these will shed all their shiftiness for you. You have been too civil a host to ask of our reasons for coming to your fortress. But it's time I explained.'

'News of your trials has reached us here. And though I was saddened by the passing of your father, I rejoiced in your accession to his saddle. I found in it an occasion for the two kingdoms of poetry and politics to be united.'

'Even as they are here, in your own dominion, united so perfectly. But my own trials, as you kindly call them, have been plagued by forces hostile to such a union,' Emru said pensively.

'Our holy men say that if a learned man engages in trade and is not successful it is a good sign for him. It means that God loves his learning and does not wish to distract him away from it by prosperity in the marketplace. The same may apply to affairs of state. I'm in no way suggesting that you're faltering there. Rather, as the proverb says, all beginnings are fraught with difficulty, and all is well that ends well.'

'I do not believe the gods love me, or I the gods.'

'Love may yet wear a mask of indifference, even denial,' Samuel rejoined.

He went on to tell one parable after another showing that god tests the people he loves. So the long-suffering Job was tested as a pitcher is tested by the potter, as a ship is tested by the storm, as an apprentice is tested by his mentor.

'In the case of Israel,' he concluded, 'one rabbi has proposed that God was gracious to Israel when he scattered her children among many nations. It was as a farmer might scatter his treasured seeds across his field. Another rabbi has likened her to a vine, trodden underfoot, but later raised, as wine, to the king's table.'

'I'm likely to share the fate of your people, though not their ascendance,' Emru said, dolefully.

In empathy, rather than conceit, Samuel extemporised the following verses,

We are a nation steeped in scars –
The bridge we cross to yonder stars.

But he added, 'As for myself, I must be content with the scars alone.'

Emru protested that his host had already achieved greatness.

'It is said that greatness seeks out the man who runs away from her. I will neither flee nor flatter her,' Samuel said. He went on to hint at Emru's situation. 'And yet a man should sometimes be yielding, like the reed, rather than unbending, like the cedar.'

'I have heard from my mate Jaber, of the cedars of Lebanon. They live to be a thousand years, I was told. Some of our gods are carved out of cedar wood. And many a ship can ride the waves thanks to her cedar beams. The reed pales in comparison.'

'But the reed can write, and can sing,' Samuel persisted.

'Aye, and, sharpened to a point, can kill!'

'So...let us...celebrate both...the cedar and...the reed,' I blurted in my rush to conclude this exchange amicably, encouraged by Emru's mention of me. I added, 'For, the qualities of…both…flourish in you… twain. And both…reed and…cedar…need to…weather the…storm… afoot.'

THE SHIELD OF ISHMAEL

The angel pays the youth another visit, bearing him yet another gift.

The youth looks up from the warm carcass of the ibex lying at his feet. Wide and lustrous are his eyes. They are the eyes of a hunter, fierce, unabashed, and stabbing, and by now used to the glare of the angel.

Even in the beginning they were not totally subdued.

Even when the angel brought him the horse with the thunder fresh in his sinews and the wind raging in his nostrils.

And he has since brought the bow.

And the arrows.

Ishmael pulls one arrow from the warm white side of the ibex, treacherously slain from behind an *arta* bush.

He raises the arrow, dripping with bright blood, for the angel to see. In his eyes gleam the pride and innocence and savagery of a child showing off some colourful pebbles won in a game.

He would also like to boast to the angel of his skill in riding the horse.

He wants to tell him how he puts the creature to an instant gallop;

how he clings his legs and heels around its flanks;

how he brandishes his bow in his hand, his *aba* fluttering behind;

how he turns right and left at speed, pulls up, then leisurely spurs the horse to a canter, then to a gallop;

then, floating, how he becomes one with the horse, drinking the wind, the distances, nostrils flaring, mouths gaping, together.

More, he wants to show the angel the arc he has recently built in the desert, the wild inheritance left him by his indifferent father.

He wants to brag of his cleverness, his handiness in bending the acacia wood to his will and the ostrich feathers to his sense of the beautiful.

He wants to crow of other skills, more those wrested from the harsh wasteland than those given by the angel.

He has not fared too badly since he was abandoned by his father, the heart of his sire going to another woman and her other boy.

Was he not himself the son who yielded to the knife, both at his loins, cutting into, flaying the flaccid, raw skin, and later at his neck, drawing a thin crimson line?

Or was it his half-brother Isaac?

He no longer cares, given his father's desertion of him and his mother in the blistering valley, given his father's reassurances, his father's lies, though these have been validated in part by the visits of the angel and his offerings.

But in Gabriel's gaze there is something akin to sorrow.

He offers the youth a round object, formed in an inhuman forge.

'A shield! To protect you from the arrows, as they rebound,' he says.

He has not told him that the bow and arrows, the idea of them, took shape in the hell of God's anger.

Nor does he tell him now that the shield, the idea of it, was formed in the hell of God's regret.

SAMUEL ON ROMAN AND ARAB POLITICS

My intervention, gauche as it was, helped ease the discussion out of the tangle of courtesies and wordplay.

Samuel already knew of the troubles of the king, and was willing to help.

He declared that he had good relations with the king of Ghassan, and suggested that Emru could seek his help. The Syrian king might see a benefit in helping Emru directly with his own troops. Otherwise, he might grant him safe passage through his territory should Emru decide to travel to Rome, which Samuel also recommended. The king, lampooned by Emru in Shammar, had some influence at the Byzantine court and was well known there. His auxiliaries were needed in any contest with the Persians. A fellow Christian, though, he was not of the sect favoured by the Emperor.

But Samuel had his own contacts at the court. Should Emru choose a sea route to Rome, which Samuel preferred, Samuel's agent at the city, one named Yonah, could gain him entry to the porphyry palace and an audience with the Emperor.

But Samuel was honest enough to warn Emru:

'I would not trust the Roman king. Long gone are the days of Anastasius, who held the sceptre with some wisdom and mercy, stood in the middle of the factional debate, and eased the yoke of taxes on the people.'

And Samuel went on to say the following, which I report here faithfully:

'Rome has her schemes in the region. These she will pursue with a cold heart. She is powerful and crafty enough to turn your situation into one of advantage to herself. Nor is her cold-heartedness reserved for use beyond her walls. There is a story that the old emperor Zeno was buried alive. When he recovered from the epileptic fit which had overwhelmed him, he pleaded with the sentry outside the sepulchre to let him out. The guards reported to the palace for instructions. They came back to tell him that there was already a new Emperor. He begged to be taken to a monastery, anywhere he could live his last days in peace. But no one in the capital wanted to upset the new order. After all, the old Emperor was of a barbarian origin. When, finally, an inspection was made some two weeks later, he was found truly dead. He had chewed on his sandals and his own arms.'

This was an account I too had heard in Bayroute but had thought overblown.

'Emperor Justin, the uncle of the present Emperor, started his career as a soldier. He was instated on a shield carried by fellow soldiers in the circus. He had come from the swine-herding stock of Illyricum and could not even spell his name.'

I knew that too. Dorotheus once joked darkly in class about an official in the archives. He said the man, like Emperor Justin, could not sign his own name. He put the first letters of his name to a document by passing his pen through the openings in a perforated plate.

'Justin was not graced with children. He placed his trust in a rough nephew of his, the Justinian of our day, lifting him to high office. He gave him, even as Justin sat on the throne, the power to rule on religious affairs as on the choice of games in the circus.

'When Justinian became Emperor, it did not take him long to combine the two activities in larger games of butchery and oppression. These he began against the one-nature Christians in Syria and the Jews in the Yemen.'

I had seen the scars of the first in Lebanon. As for the Yemen, Samuel continued:

'Here too he was following on the policies of his uncle. That man, some score or more years ago had helped the Ethiopian Negus with his invasion of the Yemen. He blessed the enterprise as a mission for Christ, fitted out with a fleet of Roman *dromons*.'

'Wasn't the situation in the Yemen provoked by Dhu Nuwas's campaign against the Christians there?' Emru enquired.

'Only in part. Dhu Nuwas had committed grave atrocities. But he was a recent convert, and gravely misunderstood his duties as a king to all his subjects. The fanaticism of a new convert took hold of him. It led him to force his faith on his people and persecute those who clung on to their own faith. But there is also reason to suppose that he was reacting to atrocities committed by the Romans in Palestine.'

I also had heard while in Bayroute of those massacres. They had been carried out by troops headed by the dux Theodoros and later the dux Eirenaios, infamous names in local memories. Whole villages, homes, synagogues, farms, had been looted and burnt to the ground, their inhabitants put to the sword.

Samuel continued:

'The purges in Palestine led to a new wave of refugees into Arabia. It placed more pressure on us here to provide shelter and rations for many thousands fleeing the carnage. Things became more complicated as the troubles in Palestine saw the Jews looking to Persia, and more closely Persia's client in Iraq, Al-Munzer, for help. The Jewish community in the Persian capital have wealth and influence.'

'So Dhu Nuwas may have been trying to put pressure on Rome to change its policies,' Emru suggested, his voice somewhat ruptured. No doubt the mention of Al-Munzer rattled his thoughts, as it did mine.

'Ironically, the remaining Judeans sent appeals to him, Dhu Nuwas, to end his campaign.'

'I heard he died *bravely*,' Al-Ward interposed. He had been largely silent since we rode into Samuel's fort.

I too had heard the story. The Abyssinian army, using war elephants, had wiped out the king's last troops. He was fighting from the back of his horse, *Al-Gedi*, to whose berth he had tied his legs, vowing to die in his saddle. Finally, turning down a last appeal for surrender, he rode his horse into the sea. Both disappeared without a trace. Esimiphaios, who was to be appointed by Ela Atzbeha and Justin as their deputy over Hemyar, camped on the shore with his officers for days. The bodies of the king and the horse were never washed ashore.

Yeah, Dhu Nuwas ruled like a bear, but he died a Chiron. Might he, like the man-horse tutor of Achilles and Jason, be weaned from his earthly agonies and transformed into a constellation?

Samuel did not think so.

'And *foolishly*,' he rejoined. 'He will be punished in Gehenna for his crimes and folly, and for providing Rome with a timely excuse to exterminate the Jews in the Yemen. Many of them were descendants of those who had fled the brutality of Hadrian. But his fierce spirit may be soothed, even in Gehenna, by news of the Hemyar revolt against the invaders. Yet, vain are such doings. For Persia, despite her ostensible charity, is bound to exploit the situation. Before long she will tiptoe or thunder her way back into the country.'

'But you speak of Al-Munzer as an ally of your people! The man has been at the heart of our troubles in Najd. He is Kenda's sworn enemy, the storm relentless at our heels', Emru suddenly burst out, alarmed and feeling trapped, perhaps betrayed.

'Al-Munzer, lion and jackal! Your nemesis, and probably mine now! But I must be truthful.'

Thus Samuel continued.

'Far from being a dark lair, his city of Al-Hera, glitters with palaces and bustles with trade. It's home to a population of Arabs and Persians, Nestorians and Jews, pagans and Zoroastrians. They live and work in peace and harmony. There, in his sumptuous palace of *Al-Sadeer*, Al-Munzer holds court and entertains philosophers and scientists, ambassadors and merchants, poets and theologians.'

'What faith does *he* profess?,' Emru asked.

'After the fashion of Khosro, his liege in Ctesiphon, Al-Munzer is truly a pagan. But he is tolerant of all faiths. The city itself has a magnificent synagogue and splendid temples for Zoroastrians and pagans and *Hanifs*. It is the seat of a Nestorian bishop, being I believe the city which many years ago held the first synod of the Nestorian Church. Its churches and monasteries are famous as architectural wonders. Its inhabitants speak Arabic, Pahlavi, Hebrew, Aramaic, Greek, as their tongues and interests incline.

Suddenly, our archenemy who had long towered over our miseries loomed as an even taller spectre.

And yet, what pride a ruler must take in such a city, if it truly existed, I thought.

Samuel continued.

'He's a deceptively simple man. But even in war he's proved time and again to be a brilliant strategist.'

As I recalled the tactics and discipline of his troops in the Battle of the Plain, I looked furtively at Emru. He seemed buffeted like me by conflicting emotions and cruel facts.

Samuel persisted in twisting a surgeon's knife.

'All along, and despite the odd bad advice he gave the Persians, he has been serving them royally. From his vantage point between the desert and the sown, he has been protecting Persia's rich agricultural lands in Iraq from Bedouin raids. He's also been challenging the lord of Damascus and his Byzantine backers across the Syrian Desert. But he has a will of his own and a subtle wit, which he uses to good effect.'

And then, interlacing his story-telling with frequent smiles and an occasional laugh, Samuel narrated the following anecdote.

'Two bishops of the one-nature faith visited Al-Munzer in his capital Al-Hera some years ago. They were hoping to convert him to their brand of Christianity popular in Syria. For long had the Nestorians been persecuted by Rome for saying that Jesus had two natures, human and divine, and that it was the man Jesus who died on the cross, not the divine logos, who was deathless.

'Clearly, it was not in Al-Munzer's interest to offend the Nestorians by seeming to curry favour with their rivals, associated, however cynically, with Persia's enemy.

'Hence, when the two rather brave one-nature bishops entered his court they saw before them a man of great dignity and distinction. But he seemed to be in a state of distress. He explained that he had just heard of the death of the archangel Michael. The bishops, falling for the trap set for them, rushed to assure Al-Munzer that it was impossible for an angel to die, being pure spirit. 'How then,' he exclaimed, 'can you maintain that Jesus, as God, died on the cross if he had but one divine nature?'

'The bishops were abashed, and retired with great unease. But Al-Munzer ordered that they be treated with the greatest courtesy. They were given presents and escorted by mounted soldiers through his realm when they wished to return to their base in Antioch.'

Ah, Antioch, Antioch, of the divided heart! City, devotee, of Adonis and Christ, victim of tremors and schisms! Home and tomb of the Sky-Dweller, Simeon! My young uncle's seminary for a year!

Samuel continued with his tale.

'The two bishops were left aghast when, two years later, Al-Munzer rode below the parapets of their city's walls with an army of thousands behind him. He had swept across a vast desert to reach the city without any of the Roman or Syrian garrisons knowing about it.

'I was told that when he was rounding up the city's inhabitants to take them to Al-Hera, he happened to see those two bishops. He dismounted from his horse, and embraced them. Not only did he set them free; he also allowed each one of them to ransom, by word, ten men and women from among the captives.'

'For an underling of the Persians, he seems to have a free hand,' Al-Ward wondered aloud.

'Such actions couldn't have happened without the blessing or connivance of the Persians. They had long abandoned Persepolis, their ancient capital destroyed by Al-Iskandar. In their new capital, Ctesiphon, they were closer to the Euphrates and to the Romans. This they had done to exact a historical vow Persia had made, a pledge to avenge the dishonour of Darius' defeat at the hands of the Macedonian upstart.'

Samuel went over a brief history of recent battles between the Persians and the Romans. In them yet again the name of Al-Munzei rattled and chafed. But there were also the names of Khosro and Belisarius and Justinian.

Samuel's oration opened our eyes to a side of our enemy we did not know or had chosen to ignore.

Samuel proceeded to enlighten us about the great man in Rome.

He spoke at length about Justinian's upbringing as the son of Justin's sister and spawn of a peasant father brought over to the city by his childless uncle. The youth was shrewd enough to orchestrate the events which led to the hoisting of his uncle to the throne of poor Anastasius. At his own assumption to the throne, he continued to exercise his guile, his lust for power growing. So he re-conquered Africa and Italy and part of Spain and pressed his authority on the kings of Gaul. Like the great Emperors of Rome of the West, whom he admires, he sees himself as a supreme legislator and legal reformer.

At this a stab pierced my heart as I again remembered my mentor Dorotheus, who was engaged by Justinian to compile with Tribonian and Theophilus the great law books of the Roman Empire. Where are you now my noble teacher? Might you be in Rome when we reach it if Emru chooses to travel that far? And where is your noble wife, my beloved Sofia? Might I be blessed with her sight in Bayroute as of old? Will we stop over in her jewelled city on our way to Damascus or Rome? Her city which I hope will be my everlasting home when Emru's quest is done!

Samuel then talked about Justinian's love of splendour and extravagant buildings. He spoke about his championship of Christian Orthodoxy and his zeal to spread that faith throughout the world. And he recounted strange tales of his sleeplessness.

And Samuel spoke about Justinian's wife, the Empress Theodora. He spoke of her humble origin as the daughter of a circus performer who went on to become a stripper and a prostitute. Her antics in the theatre he elaborated upon to the embarrassment of his wife Sarah and the loud laughter of Hend. He gave an account of her intimacy when she was a young courtesan with a Tyrian governor of a Libyan province. When spurned by him she travelled through Egypt and Syria, prostituting her way up to Rome but gaining knowledge of the people's grievances.

He also spoke (now in whispers) of how in Rome Theodora became the mistress of an Arab merchant and may have borne him a child before she went on to capture the heart of Justinian and become his wife, sharing his ambitions and saving his life and crown in a riot that swept through the great city.

Samuel was of the opinion that she was more clear sighted than her husband.

With her eastern (Samuel believes Syrian) roots and empathy with the Oriental Churches, she was better suited, Samuel suggested, to be approached as a possible patron to our enterprise in Arabia. In fact, Samuel surmised, she was more fit to save the Empire than her wasteful husband.

Samuel went on to declare in an un-typically pointed tone:

'To the two giants, the Romans and the Persians, the nations of our region are but clay on their potter's wheels, iron sheets under their hammers, and beasts they toy with and slaughter in their circuses. When we rise in their estimation, when we rise, we are corn sacks in their granaries, slabs of mutton on their plates, oars on their galleys. When we rise, and rise highly, we are incense in their funerals, purple dye in their garments, pliant horses they prance upon in their parades...'

His passion spent, my head reeling, Samuel spoke less heatedly, though more practically:

'And, yet, diplomacy is best. It is not always the fault of the victor that he prevails. Nor should a giant be blamed for walking with a wide stride or a heavy tread or with a vast appetite. Whoever is destined and doomed to be a giant will do the same. But, as you shall be petitioning the favours of the Emperor or the Empress should your road lead to Rome, know ye this. Despite the sheen of their armour and the girth of their legions, the Romans are more inclined to bargains and bribery than to war. They have come to the conclusion that the latter, however glorious and manly, is costlier than the former, however dull and gutless.

'We too have no love for war. But never shall we be mean or deceitful, be it for peace, our true love,' Al-Ward said, stirred up by the storytelling.

Samuel rejoined, 'I agree. And diplomacy will not succeed without honesty and honour.' He continued:

'Left to their own devices, the Romans would prefer to do trade and watch the races, with other distractions for the soul and the loins in between. But when their court starts weaving webs of intrigue, there is none to best them in the art. So parley with them gently, but make your cause agreeable even gainful to them. Solicit their genuine smiles, but beware of their false embraces – and of their gifts whether encrusted with diamonds or nails. Experience has taught my people that emperors, starry eyed or eagle eyed, with a sceptre of the west or of the east, care most and foremost for their throne. Yeah, even if its legs were embedded like spears in the flesh and dreams of others.'

'Even if our flesh is impaled, our dreams will not be touched,' Al-Ward again interjected, his passion further roused by the wine, the juice otherwise helpless to affect his reason.

'Yes, we have our dreams to protect and nurture into reality,' Samuel rejoined. Then he added, with a sense of purpose:

'Our common father, Abraham, has promised our two nations the greatest of all inheritance, not of land or cattle but of the spirit and a mission for mankind. And we, the children of Isaac and Ishmael, will in time leave the wilderness of Beersheba to claim our inheritance. This we will share with the rest of humanity in peace and content. Not in setting up Man as God, but Abraham's way, Man serving God and the human fellowship.'

'That is a noble vision, Emir!' Emru responded, 'but can it blossom or even take root in the howling sandstorms of our time?'

'A dream can travel far. Farther than the tumult of the moment. And many candles can be kindled from the parent taper.'

'Will this be enough to keep the flame alive?'

'The soul can carry the flame too, and the soul is deathless!'

'Ah, the soul! That is the stuff of theology. I have a quarrel with the gods and have no trade with the soul.'

'But those you quarrel with must be real! Shouldn't that be so?'

'A man can quarrel with an illusion, with his own nightmares, which is the essence of all quarrels,' replied Emru.

He went on to add, pensively, 'Quarrel itself is an illusion. Here we are, bred by the earth but doing battle with her and with one another. In the end we dissolve, we sink, with our quarrels, into the earth's ageing boredom, and the all-conquering Oblivion.'

'May you find that rest while you live,' said Samuel affectionately.

Then he added, 'King of the Mother Tribe, you may be interested to know that your thoughts hum with the thoughts of a great king of Israel and ripple on the same lute. He too had concluded that man's essence lies in the dust. But he enjoined us to eat our food with gladness and drink our wine with a merry heart. That's what I urge you to do!'

'I salute your king's wisdom and your empathy, Emir! But food, other than that served at *Al-Ablaq*, has of so late as though seasoned with seeds of colocynth in my mouth. And other than within these walls, my feet have been claimed by quicksand, my ears by the simoom,' Emru said, his voice breaking.

'Even the best of men are snared in an evil time. In such a time the shout of him that rules among fools is heard more than the words of the wise,' Samuel said soothingly.

Our host's agent in Rome had provided his master with a stream of information. But it was Samuel who wafted it into his garden of wisdom. Emru said:

'Knowledge is sweet, though it too may have a bitter aftertaste. But I thank you for the light you have cast on our path. It is best to walk with a lantern on a moonless night.'

'May this lantern never be taken away from your hand. But may the inner light and the greater light shine on your efforts and guide them,' Samuel concluded.

'We were blessed with a light, an unfaltering light, on our way here – a kindred glow of your own. Amer Ben Mazen!'

'Ah, Amer Ben Mazen, the richest and freest man in Arabia,' Samuel said, with sparkling solemnity.

THE PROPHECY

As the burning ink of our nights seeps away, I must pen down here the prophecy that has long crucified me even as I resisted crucifying it on paper.

It is seared into my mind like a firebrand. And I will not rouse it further with interpretation – neither the one given by my father, who had petitioned it, nor the one offered by my mother, who dismissed it, only to turn it later in my favour.

I shall record it as the red haired Zelpha delivered it on that fateful day in Najd and as it was told and re-told to me as I grew up.

I was told that the priestess had stood, dazzling in her flames, beside Tadweenah, the humdrum priestess of Kenda's chief god, *Al-Jalsad*, scorned by the tribe's Christians.

Yeah, she stood before my father, who, fearful for his newborn son and his much loved wife after a difficult birth, placed me between the stone arms of the idol.

There, the itinerant prophetess rolled out in her foreign enunciation a map of my life.

The lines she made up or lifted from some other oracle were to cast me into a role unsolicited by me or even by my father and were to chart the course of my life and my relation to Emru, born three days before me.

What if the lines were a fabrication by my father himself, an artefact of his frustration with his life and trade, of his fear for his frail wife and hard-won son?

But, I too have seen the mysterious Zelpha at Tabalah. What if that too was an invention of my own, born of my own frustration, spiked by my own fears and failures and fantasies?

Even so, here are the lines, be they the voice of truth or the echo of deception, consigned onto this sea-borne paper. I commit this uncertain act before I set out with Emru on our uncertain journey:

A star to trail an older star,
Who will unsheathe red Mars's sword
And bed with Venus, near and far,
With Death and Muses in accord!

213

A star less bright, though keen within,
A scribe of glories not his own,
Across two worlds to lose and win,
A voice of peace, at war, alone!

But when a god is struck at noon,
He must take up his pen and write
Upon sea leaves to make Time swoon
And pause, an instant, in its flight.

He must summon the bygone runes
And bid them breathe the hurtling air,
And make the puffed-up dhows and dunes
Succumb to his spellbinding stare.

He must, he must, or else he's doomed
And will not last the wink of day.
His words, in time, will be exhumed,
To don the fire of the clay!

LEAVING THE PIEBALD FORT

Thus will end the first part of this 'history'. Here, in the protective care of Samuel, I shall leave my manuscript, bidding farewell to its fellowship with a heavy or relieved heart I cannot tell.

Who knows if I will have the good fortune to retrace my steps back to Samuel's fort? Tomorrow I set out with Emru on a journey of untold miles and days and unforeseeable snares and promises, perhaps leaving no breath or ruse for a *marwaha*. I shall continue to write, though, my leaves having been replenished by the generosity of my host and re-animated by a new resolve in me.

But, departing from my old manuscript with its agonies and ecstasies, truths and fantasies, I leave a record of my life and imagination. More crucially, I leave a record of the life and imagination of my friend and sovereign, Emru Al-Qais, King of Kenda, perhaps the last of his line.

Should this 'history' come to an end here, never to be completed, let it be read as yet another record of human effort gasping for a conclusion. Let it be seen from whatever shore as a rudderless but stubborn vessel tossed about upon a sea of oblivion - this, written by Jaber Ben Rabi'a Ben 'Amr.

PART TWO

A PREAMBLE AND
A SUMMARY

This is the second part of a 'history' begun a mere three score months ago, but is touched and shaped by events of many years before.

Like the first part, this part too has to struggle to survive the designs of gods and the intrigues of men and gullies and waves that lie or surge beyond the station of the moment. Nor can I tell if it can be understood without that first part, which I have entrusted to the care of the noble Samuel Ben Ored Ben Adiya, Emir of *Al-Ablaq* in the Arabian province of Tayma.

The new sheaf of writing paper donated by the valiant Emir may itself succumb to the eddies of the voyage on which I am embarking with my friend and king, Emru Al-Qais of Kenda. Outwardly, he is on a mission to avenge the murder of his father, Hojr the Second, who was the ill-fated ruler of what was once the largest and most powerful tribe in Arabia, set to unite all Arabs. The crime is laid at the door of the Najd tribe of Asad and their Persian backers. Now the king's tribe has been overwhelmed and the king's fortunes, even his intents, are as dense as the sands that swathe his tribe.

No doubt I shall be haunted by the thought that I may never be able to return to the haven in Tayma to have this part of my 'history', yet a mere scribble, joined to the first part.

Will the powers that rule this *kosmos* and which I have offended allow me to bring that union to pass? Or will this bud of a tome wilt and die in the first shower of the new season?

A DREAM OF BELQIS

We stayed fourteen days in Samuel's impregnable and well-stocked fort, which can stand an army's siege for many a month.

Reports of such an army hastened our departure.

Samuel pleaded with us to stay. He had sent a letter to his agent in Rome, entrusting it to the leader of a caravan that had set off a few days after our arrival carrying produce and artefacts from Samuel's little kingdom to the mart of Gaza. Samuel's agent in that coastal town was to hand the letter over to the captain of a fleet ship for him to take it to Rome. A slower cargo ship was scheduled to sail days after the arrival of the caravan carrying the goods destined for the Golden Horn.

In the letter to his agent in Rome, Samuel asked the agent, one named Yonah, to advise as to whether Emru's visit to Rome was opportune and whether he could help towards its success.

Samuel's agent is Jewish. The Roman State is not charitable to people of this faith. But the agent, Samuel assured us, is a most astute man, skilled in the arts of diplomacy and had forged many friendships from within the trading and aristocratic circles of the city.

Whatever the case might be, Samuel had asked Yonah to make preparations for Emru's visit. It was a matter of great urgency, he had noted.

Accounts of an army being assembled by the Assads and their allies to march on the fort in Tayma had reached Samuel few days after our arrival. But he kept the news from us. It nonetheless reached the fine-tuned ears of Hend, Emru's redoubtable sister. She had overheard a guard who had come to speak to Samuel's wife, the Lady Sarah, about what the women could do ahead of a siege coming their way. Emru went to Samuel and begged for his permission to leave as he did not wish to endanger the commune on account of his stay. Samuel agreed to allow Emru and Al-Ward and myself to go. This was because a siege, however futile it would be as Samuel thought, would still delay our departure for Rome, whose priority was now unquestioned. But he gave a solemn oath that he would guard Hend and five ancient shields which belonged to the kings of Kenda until Emru returned. Any other argument he dismissed.

As the caravan had preceded us by several days, Samuel suggested we use three of his fleetest *daluls* to catch up with it, a lumbering albeit determined creature. He would have supplied us with gifts to take to the Emperor in Rome, but these would slow us down. He would instruct his agent in Gaza to provide for that.

Emru tried to protest Samuel's largesse. Its magnitude he found uncomfortable. It placed too much strain on Samuel and posed too much danger for him and his people. He proposed to take his sister with him, absolving Samuel of his portentous pledge. But Samuel would not be opposed, mild mannered as he was. In the end, Emru was won over. He had been impatient to proceed to his destination, drawn like a moth to the flame of its promise.

Samuel had also suggested that Emru could travel to Damascus to seek the help of the King of Ghassan, a good friend of Samuel's. Emru had satirised the Syrian king during a previous flight of ours to the Tayys of Shammar, where we were given refuge by their gracious Emir. Besides, a rider from Iraq had brought Samuel news that Al-Munzer, Persia's deputy in Iraq and Emru's inveterate enemy, was secretly calling up troops for a possible incursion into Syria. Should that take place, it might develop into a major action between the Roman and Persian armies endangering a land passage. It would also, Samuel noted, add meaning to the Asads' final push against Emru. The conquest of Arabia by the Persians or their allies would help any Syria campaign and confirm any possible victory there. The pressure on the Abyssinians, Rome's allies, in the Yemen would also grow. At this stage, however, all this was mere speculation, Samuel emphasised.

The caravan had left *Al-Ablaq*, Samuel's fort, escorted by some forty horsemen, the points of their spears gleaming in the setting sun. It carried bales of brocaded silk, mounted pearls, swords, and carvings made of ivory and ebony as well as jars of wine and oil and sacks of dried fruits, most for export to Rome. Two stallions and two mares with a pedigree traced to *Zul 'Iqal* and *A'waj* were also sent at Yonah's request.

Shortly after our arrival, I had seen the camels being loaded and the fine thoroughbreds groomed and exercised outside the fort. At the time it did not occur to me that those activities would be playing a role in our lives.

Yeah, forty horsemen accompanied the caravan, but were not its main safeguard.

Passage money is usually paid to the various tribes through whose territories a caravan passes. Some of these tribes may also have an added interest in the traffic, sometimes selling some of their produce or buying some of the goods left for that purpose. Nonetheless, an armed escort is a pointed reminder of the money paid and the pledges made. It is also a defence against human jackals. These will know that by interfering with the tribes' easy and lucrative business they will incur a rage that can pluck them up from whatever cave they may climb to and whatever ravine they may dive into.

But to catch up with the caravan, we had to make haste.

The ground was stirring to the hoof-thuds of warhorses.

Samuel introduced us to a trusted tracker from among his people. But Al-Ward, our mate and travel companion, said he could do the job equally well. Perhaps like Emru, he did not wish to trouble the gallant Samuel further. However, he went on to inquire from him about the route his caravans take to Palestine. Al-Ward already had a fair idea of the major trade routes owing to his experience in Mecca as a trainee *Homs* and, later, as a caravan-marauding *sa'luk*. But the times were unusual, and a caravan leader might take unusual routes.

We left without Hend, the beautiful, the fierce.

This was done at Samuel's suggestion and the insistence of his formidable and caring wife, the Lady Sarah. In support of her husband, she had argued that a journey of such magnitude was unfit for the girl, whittled down to a thread by our earlier travails. Hend was also developing signs of Melancholia, incompatible with her Choleric disposition, though not with her late father's excess of black bile. Her weakened constitution gave fever the license to assail her at leisure, time and again.

All that aside, what if Emru were to perish on this perilous mission? Who would preserve Kenda's royal line? Lady Sarah further argued.

When this was proposed at dinner the night before our planned departure, Hend flew into a rage. She thought this was a ruse contrived by Emru. At his grinning face, she threw bunches of yellow grapes from a plate on the dining table. He laughed and wept even as the grapes were spluttering against his face and chest. The thoughtful Lady Sarah hugged the raging maiden, restraining her with affection, their breasts under their robes heaving in unison, Hend's bosom much thinned and flattened. I too was a recipient of some grapes of wrath on my face and a look of scorn from Hend sharper than the sharpest of thorns.

Hend had seen a dream the night before, and was doubly concerned for her brother's safety. It was a sequel of a dream, a nightmare, she had seen before, even before the murder of Hojr. This time she had seen a crow perched on Hojr's chest only to spread its wings and fly over to alight on Emru's chest, pecking at his heart.

Hend did not appear when we set out on our journey the following dusk. She probably chose not to come to our farewell, an implacably proud woman. It is also likely that the prudent Lady Sarah had distracted her with drink or speech to spare her the pain and spare us another missile attack.

Nonetheless, as we three rode away from the fort's black and white walls, I kept turning round in my saddle to see whether Hend's face was shimmering on the parapets, her sternly beautiful Taghleb eyes needling the sullen horizon.

The chivalrous Samuel, along with his princely son Hoth, rode with us for a pace in the cheerless dusk. Emru had politely refused an escort of some thirty horsemen, but had accepted the three fleet camels offered by our host. The black dromedary who had long carried the Shield of Ishmael (Kenda's most precious heirloom) was put out to pasture, the Shield itself and four other royal shields of Kenda's were stored, at Samuel's insistence, in Hend's quarters.

Earlier, as we passed through the fort's gate, Emru had commented on the stoutness of the piebald walls. Samuel said, apologetically, 'Our sages had warned us not to make a wall more important than the thing that it protects.'

I prayed to all the gods I knew to protect that wall and what lay behind it against the storm brewing in the east.

As we parted, Samuel renewed his promise to look after Hend and the heirlooms. My own manuscript had been bound with twine and tied to the back of the Shield of Ishmael. Now Samuel put his hand on my shoulder and said, 'Your book is in my ward. More crucially, it is in the ward of Abraham's son.' And, smiling, he added, 'Most crucially, it is in Hend's keeping. But I will not be satisfied until you have made it complete.' And out of his saddle bag he produced one more sheaf of paper, 'For your satchel', he said, and added, 'I shall guard the ones you have blackened. Guard these from the waves of the sea, but not from those of your pen.' Then he lowered his voice so that Emru, who was exchanging a few words with Hoth, would not hear, and murmured, 'Your paper may still outlive the shields.'

Ah, how I wished that both the paper and the shields would survive. Vain is the effort of man to protect his chest with shields and his name with words! But given the choice, I would root for words rather than suits of armour that failed to protect their wearers from death and inheritors from folly.

During our last night in Samuel's castle I had seen (summoned?) a dream, and as we trotted away from Tayma I narrated it to Emru.

'I saw a woman who had the double radiance of a queen and a goddess.

'She had on her head a crown which was adorned with sapphire, little stars of blue gems. She was standing at the top of a flight of polished stairs. The gate to a palace or a temple towered behind her. At her feet, men in brocaded garments knelt in obeisance. She gazed skywards with great jet eyes, then lifted her right arm, silken sleeve sliding to reveal rows of golden bracelets round her lower arms. A bird settled on her wrist. It was a hoopoe. She brought it close to her face and seemed to listen to it with rapt attention. The bird moved its head with its cinnamon-red-and-black crest up and down near her right ear, from which dangled a chandelier of gems.

'Then I saw that same woman sitting in a palanquin, which seemed to float effortlessly over sweeps of land until it reached a great walled city. The woman alighted from the palanquin at the entrance to a grand palace. Its gate quivered as though with a welcoming smile as it admitted her. She walked, her head held high, into a spacious hall. At the end of that hall a bearded man who sported a gleaming crown round his head and a blazing sun in each of his eyes sat, flanked by generals and savants, on a throne of cedar-wood. Before she could reach the throne on which the man sat, she paused. She had seen that in order to get to the throne she had to wade through what looked like a shallow lake of shimmering water. Undeterred, she gathered up the enlaced hem of her gown and strode out through the water. But the water was a bed of soft crystals which tingled her bare feet as she advanced towards the man. His broad, handsome face broke into a smile, and he slid off his seat in welcome, bending to kiss her proffered hand.

'I then saw the twain alone on a large bed in a bedchamber lit by tall candlesticks. Fruit bowls and wine flasks and cups in gold and silver stood on tables of ebony and cedar-wood around them. Sticks of incense sent threads of smoke which twisted sinuously in the air of the chamber. Then two supple bodies, one virginal and demure, the other seasoned and self-assured, undulated on the giant bed. The bed began to stir and lose its edges as a red mist engulfed it. The mist clung to the bed's contours, which juddered and unfolded as the bed turned into a giant flower, a rose. Then, from the dark scarlet core of the rose a naked infant boy emerged. Round his temples sat a diadem, a combination of the two crowns worn by the woman and the man. Then more infants came forth, one after the other. They floated in a procession from the heart of the rose until they filled the room, itself now melting, the walls spreading out like a carpet into green and blue and tawny distances. This is what I saw or fancied I saw.'

'Ah, you are trouncing Hend with your own dreams now! This, I'm sure you know, is Sheba's queen, Belqis, our ancestral grandmother! She came to give us cheer on our journey to Rome. Ours is somewhat similar to the journey she made in the story. It's a good omen, if you believe in them, little brother, big fantasist. But your account neglected mention of the queen's hairy legs, which I wouldn't have minded at all,' Emru said, light-heartedly.

Al-Ward was riding ahead of us, but he had heard our conversation and shouted from his saddle, 'Give me a hairy woman anytime. They're the most passionate.'

I did not agree to that bias. But I murmured, 'May it indeed be a good omen for us!'

Privately I thought the dream meant something larger than our present travails and hinted at times beyond our own and possibilities not yet possible.

THE EYE OF THE NEEDLE

For two days and a night, with two token rests, we galloped and trotted, sweated and shivered, on top of Samuel's fleet camels.

Around us the scrub land, fringed by distant mountains, receded indifferently as we sped. What were we to them, hurtling shadows? Did I hear them snigger in the distance?

We hardly spoke, the three of us. Each was wrapped up in his own thoughts, Emru and I following Al-Ward's silent drinking of the road.

On the morning of the third day, we came to a high wall of rocks stretching from east to west. A narrow pass winked between two huge boulders. Al-Ward had been taking a shortcut.

The boulders seemed like two giants raising their arms to the sky as they yawned. Above them a solitary cloud hung motionless. From what distant seas did that cloud suck up its grey moisture, and upon what land or beast might it pour its cupful? I wondered. But what if the cloud was an ethereal parchment, a breath, of a goddess or a mother warning?

The pass was called '*Ain al-Hait*' or the 'Eye of the Wall', Al-Ward informed us. He added that it also enjoyed another name, *Khorm al-Ibra* or the 'Eye of the Needle'.

The two huge boulders making up the flanks of the pass were of a reddish-brown hue with bizarre streaks of blue and green in them. Red flowers in olive-green shrubs looked out with diminutive eyes through the crevices in the rocks. No other eyes were in sight.

We were to swerve, once we were through, to the west to catch up with the caravan, Al-Ward assured us.

Some thirty paces before the pass, Al-Ward checked the lively trot of his camel and raised his arm, signalling a stop.

When we caught up with him, he explained without turning his head or moving his lips that he had seen marks of two camels which had sharply veered to the right at this same spot.

He had noticed the tracks before, but had thought nothing of them, until they changed direction so sharply at this unlikely spot. He pointed with his finger from the hip at a double line of tracks swerving eastwards.

'There's no path to the right save the eastern desert, after an hour's trot. Until then *Al-Hait* stretches on. On the rocky slopes there's no living space except for lizards and snakes and the occasional old crow. Even migrating storks will not care to catch a breather on these forbidding boulders. The tracks are fresh. Two fleet camels of the Asads, I reckon!'

A shiver went through me, even as Emru said, rather nonchalantly, 'Then we must make a dash through the pass. The 'eye' may be brooding some mischief. We must outrace its blink.'

'But, in case it's an 'evil eye', if you believe in such a thing, we need to outsmart it; for it may not blink at all,' said Al-Ward, his back straight in the tall saddle, betraying no sign of anxiety.

Then he whispered, almost hissing as he bestowed a fake smile on the silent boulders towering in front of us: 'First we...walk...the camels...slowly...along the...arc ...and...length of the...marks, then...we turn and...gallop back...and dart into the pass. It may all be a...needless sport...but...all sport is good. Follow me...not only with your eyes!'

He lightly kicked the side of his *dalul* while forcing her long neck to the right with the reins.

Emru and I followed him closely.

In a minute, we were moving to the right of the pass and closer to the wall of the boulders, now rising directly above our heads.

As we were almost brushing against the side of the massive wall, Al-Ward whistled and kicked the right flank of his mount with force, turning the animal sharply with the leather reins in the opposite direction. He kicked again on both sides with all his might and the *dalul* shot forth under him like an arrow.

We followed her frantic tail as she made another sharp turn to the right and into the gawking pass.

I was the last to gallop into the breach, and the thunder of rocks was upon me.

THE SEIZING OF
THE CROW

When I came to, stars, remote and unconcerned, were twinkling around the silhouette of a man's head.

Inside my own head, assaulting its daze, was the rousing tang of some wild plant pressed by Al-Ward to my nose. Beyond it a gentler smell of roasted meat wafted into my nostrils.

'You'll miss your dinner if you don't wake up, dear Ambassador! We thought the extra rest would do you good!' Emru's voice chaperoned me into wakefulness as Al-Ward's herb pulled me up from a plumbless pit.

My whole body ached as Emru and Al-Ward carried me close to a fire blazing away, its homely sparks overwhelming those of the cold indifferent stars.

In the glow I made out the figure of a slight man, crumpled at the edge of the fire. A leather rope coiled round his arms snaking down to a knot round his bare feet. Even in the fitful light, I could see he had a swollen eye and a gash on his forehead. His left leg was covered with what seemed like dark blood. His hale right eye, under a narrow brow, gleamed with malice and sullen disinterest.

'Meet Elba son of Al-Hareth of the Kahls. He's our guest and will join us in our dinner tonight,' Emru said, with no resentment or sarcasm. He turned and bent down to release the part of the rope binding the prisoner's arms.

I was stunned. My wakefulness leapt like a caged wild animal, though only to slam against the bars of my pain and light-headedness.

Here sat the man whose very hands committed a crime that had engulfed Kenda and much of Arabia in a sea of blood. Here he sat, the man whose severed head would have been the best trophy and peace offering Kubeysa, the Asad's peace envoy at the time, could have presented to Emru. Here was the man whose wretched spear impaled us on a saga of misery and tumbling dreams.

And yet, there he was, beginning to receive the customary desert

228

hospitality, with what it implied. Here he was sinking his canines into the roasted meat with relish but no apparent contrition or gratitude.

Emru helped me eat as well, while explaining what had happened.

Elba and an accomplice of his, a man called Da's, had lain in waiting at the top of the pass. They had been tailing us since we left *Al-Ablaq*. Then, having deduced our plan, they had sped ahead of us and set the trap at the pass. The rocks were piled up by the twain to crush us as we negotiated the cut in the wall. But Al-Ward's manoeuvre distracted them. When they became wise to it, they rushed back into position. But they were able to release the rocks only after my two companions had darted through. My own camel tripped on some of the rocks even as others hit her. She tumbled and took me down with her, but her body shielded me from further injury, though some of its weight lay heavily on top of me. It took the combined strength of Al-Ward and Emru to release me from under the flank of the poor animal. This they did, however, after chasing the two assassins. The two had by now descended from the boulders and were about to mount their camels, tethered and gagged at a recess to the right of the pass. Da's was killed by Emru's sword in the fight that followed, and Elba was taken prisoner by Al-Ward after a brief scuffle.

Here Al-Ward pulled his knife out of the piece of meat he was carving. Raising the knife high, he said, in a theatrical tone, 'Is it not Elba's turn to follow Da's? The poor fellow must be waiting for his partner as the hyenas are. Or shall we allow the celebrated scorpions of *Khorm al-Ibra* to do the blade's work?'

Elba fidgeted and moaned, plummeting from his earlier nonchalance. He claimed he was only a tool, sent by the Asad elders to hunt Emru and finish the job he had been made to start at Al-Abraqan. The elders, led by Asad's chief priest Awf Ben Rabi'a, believed that since Elba's hands were already daubed with the blood of Hojr they would be drawn without fail to the blood of his issue. Thus Elba claimed.

The first murder, Elba alleged, had been ordered by the same elders. They may have been in contact with Al-Munzer, before or after the deed, he said. He had no will of his own. He may have been under a spell cast by Awf Ben Rabi'a, he pleaded, grovelling like a cur.

Spiked by my pain, I suggested it was his own hatred that had driven him to do what he had done, possibly in both cases. Brazenly, he admitted he had indeed committed the first deed to avenge the slaying of his brother by Hojr. Thereafter he was seized by a maelstrom of loathing which ultimately whirled him to this place. Cunningly, he averred that the killing of Emru, he had thought, would put an end to the feud between Asad and Kenda.

Upon hearing this Emru said sourly, 'Before you stand the last two of the Kendas, except for one in a gallant bastion and a handful scattered in the wilderness!'

Much to our distress, Elba revealed that the Asads had somehow guessed Emru's intention of seeking an alliance with Rome. They were busy trying to frustrate that effort in more than one way. Elba's was only one throw of the dice. The Asads themselves, Elba muttered, were a-jostle in the palm of a bigger dice-thrower.

Despite his swing between insolence and sheepishness, after filling his belly with the roast, Elba became resigned to death. He showed no remorse nor offered any clear apology for his acts of crime and treachery. He turned to sleep and was soon snoring away like a hedgehog.

At dawn, Emru stood by him as he lay trussed on the ground, then went down on one knee and cut his bonds.

'Take your darkness and fly. Your puny wings will not block the sun. Nor will their plucking ease my pain. My medicine, my quarrel, is not with you.'

The look in Emru's eyes as he delivered his sentence did not hint of scorn or magnanimity. It was, if I read it correctly, a look of unabashed indifference.

Thus, the crow of Hend's dream was seized, and set free.

He was allowed to walk away with a staff which Emru gave him. He limped away without saying a word, the apathy in his eyes almost similar to that in Emru's.

He was trying to reach the two camels he and his slain accomplice had tethered outside the pass. I would have liked to requisition one of those beasts in place of the fine *dalul* I had lost in the melee and on whose thigh-meat we had feasted the previous night.

I watched him as he clambered with his staff like a malevolent scorpion over the fallen rocks with which he'd hoped to seal the avalanche he'd unleashed so many moons ago – a diseased, pathetic creature. But I did not feel particularly cleansed of the loathing Emru had so fabulously transcended.

BEFORE THE PLUNGE

It took us a bone-crushing canter of a whole night to catch up with the caravan, and another two score days to reach Gaza.

There we were lodged at the fine house of Samuel's trade agent in the city, one named Aharon.

A jolly but highly organised man, he received us with beaming courtesy. He read the letter we carried from Samuel to him grinning and knitting his brow as his olive eyes leapt from one word to the next.

The caravan leader had preceded us to Aharon's office and delivered two letters. One lay open on the agent's writing table. The other, Aharon revealed, was meant for Samuel's agent in Rome. But this was made needless by the letter Samuel had given us to hand over to Yonah. In any case, the fast ship which was meant to carry that letter had not reported to Gaza for weeks. She was assumed lost to pirates. The weather, fine in the interval, was not thought responsible.

The letter we had carried to Aharon asked him to destroy the first letter meant for Yonah as it was superseded by the dispatch we carried. Aharon also told us that Samuel instructed him to command the captain of the cargo ship to take a shorter course to the Golden Horn in the event of us missing the fleeter ship. How Samuel could anticipate such contingencies was striking.

Aharon assured us that upon our arrival in Rome, Samuel's agent would be on hand to welcome us. Emru questioned him as to how the agent would know the date of our arrival since the ship would take a shorter course than usual. He said, 'As you draw near to the coast, the pigeon will tell him,' giving Emru and myself the impression that he was speaking in riddles or in the drivel of a madman, which he surely was not.

The loading of the goods on to the merchant ship was to take some three days. In the interval, the mart of Gaza invited us, our weary bones and bleary eyes notwithstanding, to explore its offerings.

A town of rich reddish soil, deep fresh-water wells, vineyards and palm and olive trees, Gaza curves like a crescent facing the Phoenician-Roman Sea with a smile. Its back arches against the eastern desert with its lethal simoom and ever-creeping dunes.

In the past, the east brought caravans swaying with the riches of Arabia and India and China as they passed through and were replenished at such towns as Gerrha and Petra. Now the heady days of trade from Gerrha to Rome were consigned to a faded past. But the link with Samuel in Najd was vital, enabling the coastal town to survive, though with a reduced smile and diminished means.

I had of course heard of Gaza during my study in Bayroute. It was the town which, like its northern sister Tyre, had so foolhardily defied the Macedonian conqueror. But I had also known of her as the home of such luminaries as Porphyry and Aeneas and Theodore. Porphyry's interpretation of the passage in the thirteenth book of the Odyssey, which describes the mystifying cave near Ithaca, had made on me a powerful and lasting impression. That cave, if I may digress, has the peculiar feature of possessing two gates, one reserved for mortals and one for gods. I shall digress further, as is my wont, to note that the Porphyry I have in mind here is not to be confused with the later and no less formidable Bishop of Gaza by the same name and who died more than a hundred years ago. In fact, Porphyry the philosopher was never forgiven by the church in Bayroute for his book *Against the Christians*. But, as a disciple and biographer of Plotinus, and a philosopher in his own right, he sits in a comfortable chair in the philosophers' hall, his work happily wedding the teachings of Plato to those of the Saint Augustine, my uncle's mystical mentor. My blessed teacher Dorotheus had made sure, just as Porphyry had done in his treatise on vegetarianism, to point out both sides of the argument in the case. So I was given the privilege to leaf through the rare manuscript, banned by Constantine, of the philosopher's harsh intellectual refutation of Christian unreason as well as his gentle and moving letter to his wife Marcella. Both compositions have left their dint on me. As to the image of the cave in Homer, Porphyry interprets the grotto as the world, through whose gate of desire mortals enter but have the capacity to emerge freed and purified out of the gate of the gods. A cheerful but meddlesome thought that continues to impound the fancy even as it claims to unfetter it.

Will the sea on whose waves we are to sail be a cavern of sorts, undecided and unbiased about our fate? Will it deliver us onto a blue death on its sunken bed or a golden life on its high shores? It would be enough of a triumph for us mortals to trudge at the end of our journey through the shingle or the sand with our skin salted and scorched but unbroken.

The tireless Aharon set the pace of our life during our three Gazan days. Tomorrow morning we set off on our journey. Al-Ward, Emru has decided, will stay behind. The noble *sa'luk* has however promised to ride back to *Al-Ablaq*. The caravan leader and Aharon had treated him with much deference though assuming he was merely our guide through the desert, whose most princely and heroic son he was. How can I bear to see his dear figure draw back and grow smaller and smaller as our ship recedes into the horizon? Will his ever-exultant eyes be misted over with a tear or two?

A day after we joined the caravan following the encounter at the pass, Al-Ward offered to take me to Petra. I had earlier expressed to him and to Emru my wish to visit the grave of my mother and perhaps that of my uncle in the town, be it for the space of an hour. The roseate town had been a customary stopover for caravans from Arabia en route to Syria or Gaza; and though it had fallen on hard times, I thought a brief stopover was still possible. We had by then travelled a long way beyond a mountain called Ramm and the caravan leader was about to veer with his camels and men further to the east. Encouraged by Al-Ward's offer, I solicited the approval of the caravan leader to change course for Petra at a distance of some fifty miles to the north and west. Both Al-Ward and Emru had been attentive to my entreaty. But the caravan leader, a robust man in his late fifties, refused to comply. A detour, he reasoned, would delay our appointment with the ship for a few days. He had considered himself lucky enough to have escaped Bedouin raids and possibly a crushing attack by the Assads while his caravan was plodding through the Hejaz. That said, he was a shrewd man. In the letter Emru had delivered to him, he must have noted Emru's importance to Samuel. He must have also sensed Emru's own impatience to get to the port, the king belabouring his ears with questions about how soon we would get there, this despite Emru's seasoned aversion to the 'blue vomit' as he called the sea. Nor was Emru's overt sympathy with my earlier appeal genuine I think.

I was left with no choice but to turn helplessly every now and then in my saddle towards the forbidden town hidden behind the eastern horizon with tears in my eyes as our camels plodded on disinterestedly in the opposite direction.

I may mention in passing that earlier today a very old man by the name of Zeyad Ben Hani, of the clan of Hashed of Yemen, came with his grandson to Aharon's house. Having somehow heard of Emru's arrival in the city and his intended destination, he sought to obtain his permission to send the youth with him to Rome. He said, rather cryptically, that his son, one named Hamed, had recently died but not before he implored his own son, Yahya, to travel to Rome, there to seek out a connection and an inheritance at the Roman court. The old man communicated this in the strictest confidence. He maintained that he did not know what that connection or inheritance was. Only his grandson had received his dying father's will and testimony. The grandson, an only child and by nature reticent, would not disclose what his father had told him. Still he would not be swayed from the quest though knowing that his fragile grandfather would be left in the mart alone. The resolve in his striking hazel eyes was as straight and steely as the blade of a sword. 'I seek something more than a connection or an inheritance,' he curtly declared. The lad's father, the old man informed us, had been a merchant and an adventurer, one who had traded in purple cloth for many years, but had returned, some sixteen years ago, from Rome, with an infant son, to whom he dedicated his remaining years. Aharon had known the father, and endorsed the story. At Emru's appeal, he accepted to take the old man under his wing until his grandson returned.

Yahya's strident almost demented assertion '*I shall return a king!*' amazed Emru. It somewhat mimicked and unwittingly mocked his own silent pledge. But the grandfather's tearful anguish solicited a sympathetic response in him. As we walked with the grandson away, Al-Ward trying to console the tearful old man with a joke, Emru improvised the lines,

> He wept, for time was short and distance long,
> And in his stinging tears there swam my song,
> Babbling of loves that would not lie apart,
> While far-flung lances pierced his ancient heart.

We sail with the indifferent dawn.

ROME

A CLANDESTINE MEETING

We were trying to finish off yet another extravagant dinner Chava and Yonah had regularly gorged us with since our arrival in Rome.

Our hosts were urging us to have more of the mutton *and* the fowl *and* the stews *and* the dumplings from the plates spread on the wide low table decked out for us and lit up with candlesticks in the cool of their garden. This the kindly pair were doing even as various sweet delicacies and fruits and pistachios were being pushed on to the edges of the versatile board. The aromatic wine liberally supplied was eyed by Emru but not touched by him. Somewhat similarly, the night breeze continued to entice the garden's flowers and fruit trees to indulge in their own scented lusts in the face of the approaching winter.

Then we heard the muffled but unmistakable clatter of a carriage coming to a stop outside the villa.

The snort of a horse came with the sound of a carriage door being shut. This was followed by the sound of two dainty but assertive feet trailing the hem of a heavy gown across the pebbled ground outside the gate.

Emru pricked up his ears.

Earlier in the afternoon, a woman who looked like a lady-in-waiting had told me to make my 'master' ready for a 'most important visitor' soon after sunset. But already the sun had laid her gold-threaded cloak over Marmara and trailed it behind her so indolently on her way to a bed in the distant west. With her had also gone the large seagulls circling the sky above the water tirelessly and somewhat mournfully. By now, Emru had given up on the proposal as a 'prank'. He went on to add jokingly, 'Or it may have been a well-meaning invite foiled by a husband staying home instead of going out for dinner at his mistress's.' So he had yielded to his hosts' appeal to partake of the garden feast. No female company attended it other than our gracious hostess and two old female servants waiting upon us. A garrulous Syrian cook came out from time to time to join her mistress in further goading us to more of her artful dishes.

But the petite, determined steps revived his hopes.

Earlier during the meal, we had been discussing our return journey. Our Roman mission had been crowned the previous day with an imperial seal of support and an appointment extraordinary. Yonah had even suggested we travel onboard the *Arada*, the ship that brought us from Gaza, thus avoiding the land route, now threatened with an Iraqi and possibly Persian incursion. But Emru's enmity with the sea was even fiercer than before. It had been confirmed by the rough sea voyage we had had, which involved a long-running encounter with pirates followed by a leak that forced our ship to ditch at the port of Smyrna rather than, more ceremoniously, at the Golden Horn's customs house in the shadow of the Acropolis. The experience made him renew his indictment of the 'wretched blue vomit' in front of his forbearing hosts. He however tried to put a rational shawl on the naked body of his unreasonable aversion. He argued that a calculated dash on camelback along the coastline should take him to his promised kingdom sooner and more safely, citing the pirates and the imminent winter as sufficient reasons to shun a sea route. All plans however were to be kept on hold. Emru had to wait for a formal invitation to proceed to Ankara, there to meet the Praetorian Prefect of the East on duty in that town. Still, Yonah argued, Samuel's ship, once re-loaded at the Golden Horn, can wait for us at Smyrna to take us back to Gaza and any other port on the way.

But the gate parted and we were swept by a gale of imperial perfume.

Empress Theodora was staring at us, her hazel eyes sparkling in the candle light like a cat's under the hood of her dark damask cloak. The cloak she abstractedly eased from her shoulders; but the sparkle remained.

I had seen her during the court audience the day before. She had sat in her throne largely silent and seemingly brooding; but her unblinking gaze seemed to slice through every thought and utterance of Emru's as he spoke and I interpreted, the few words she addressed me with unsettling then comforting me.

She was then in her full royal regalia, the splendour of her jewelled and pearl-garlanded crown and richly brocaded robe outshining those of her consort by her side. Now she was wearing, under her discarded cloak, a silken dress simple enough to escape the attention of strangers and light enough to slip out of for an impatient lover. Even so, she had a garnet-studded golden band round her short brown hair. The sleek dress, though slack and unfettered, did not hide the sensual curves and thrusts of her lissom body, her delicate upturned nose adding a particular charm to her features. And though entering an aroused garden, she wafted in with the fragrance of a thousand glowing roses. That alone would have upset any effort on her part to conceal her identity in her passage to Yonah's villa.

Emru stood up from his seat like a stallion raring; but at her commanding look, he went down on one knee, though still anchoring his gaze steadfastly to the gleam of her eyes. We all stood up and knelt.

'I must talk to you, O King!' she said, gravely, a sovereign, but also a woman pleading.

Yonah and Chava, pre-empting the word 'alone', gracefully withdrew into their villa. They were briskly followed by the two servants and the now-hushed cook.

Without taking her eyes off Emru's, Theodora pointed with a delicate but compelling finger at me, ordering me to translate.

'I am pleased that our often windy and cloudy city has slackened her dark passion for you and your cause, offering a more clement breeze. But she needs to summon a more reasoned passion to help your worthy endeavour. Anyway, you shall be returning soon to your steady sun, which is bound to shine more clearly upon the destiny you must fulfil there!'

'I shall certainly endeavour to do the Emperor's wishes, which will doubtless bring glory to us all, my Lady,' Emru said, diplomatically, having listened to my translation.

'Glory is not always the wisest goal for which to aim. Nor is the Emperor's course the best to follow. The Imperial heart leans towards the north, while the south suffers in silence. I give it my sympathy, my voice. But I fear that the neglected, the persecuted, will one day come together and roar outside our great walls. They may roar loud enough to make those walls less great, less impregnable. The Virgin cannot but abandon her guardianship over the unjust.'

As she spoke and I translated, I thought of her intervention some eight years earlier when she steeled her husband to face up to the Nika rioters and crush them. Samuel had mentioned the event in Najd but news of it had resounded noisily across Lebanon and the whole Empire at the time. She continued.

237

'Your destiny, O King, must include an all-important task. It must help my husband turn to the *real* power base of his kingdom, the south – Syria, Arabia, Judea, Egypt.'

'The strengthening of our links with the imperial city is surely part of my mission,' Emru said, weighing his words carefully, my translation assisting. But like me, he was still unable to negotiate a way between Theodora's reasoning and that of her husband. Samuel had pointed out a distinction between the two. It was now patently revealed. But I wondered whether Emru, like me, was considering the possibility that the Empress was playing the role of an agitator, testing Emru's loyalty to his new-found patron and his fitness for the mission he had vowed to accomplish. But that did not make sense. Why should the Empress herself set out to do something that could be done by a trusted agent or a court official? Why really, unless the Empress was infatuated with Emru and was using this as a dignified ploy to squirm her way into the fable of his bed?

The first thing a desert Arab thinks of when he sees a woman is her *han*. I wonder whether this is what all men anywhere think about in the heat or chill of their days.

Spurred by the wildness of the thought, I had a vision of the young Theodora on the stage naked but for a sparse loincloth round her hips. I heard her complaint that a woman's three natural openings were not sufficient receptacles for physical pleasure. Thus seized by these runaway fancies, I came to the conclusion that Emru's reputation as a rake had reached the now older but no less ravenous Empress; and there she was poised to offer this eastern libertine a banquet of fleshly delights in the shadow of the Sacred Cubicle.

In my profane thoughts I expected to be promptly dismissed to allow the two royals to 'continue their discussion in private'. Images of the young Theodora continued to stream and sparkle in my mind. I fancied her lying on her back, squatting on her knees, straddling, being straddled, gorging, being gorged, from Libya to Egypt, Syria to Rome, in brothels and boudoirs, in *howdahs* and hovels, for a *follis* or for free. How many men eased or rammed their lusts into her, how many tongues of mating did she hear or moan in, what sceptres of princes, swords of soldiers and canes of mendicants did she stroke and bend and beguile? But what of now? In my delinquent fancy, I was yet troubled, sobered, by the thought of the grave danger a relationship of this kind would pose for Emru, his political ambitions and very life. I shrank from that thought, just as Theodora's aristocratic clients in her days of debauchery shrank from her face in public – the craven and two-faced men we are!

But the Empress was soon to send my ill imaginings tumbling down a deep ravine. For, clearly as I was to know the once roving harlot had long emerged from her wild pilgrimages to settle down with a searing sense of mission, one that burnt away the lust of the flesh for a lust of a different fibre.

As she spoke on, she soared in my fickle and now dizzied thoughts. She soared, a Virgin Mother, an Amazon, a Zenobia, a Semiramis, commanding my silent apology and penitence. Still, fickle as my thoughts always are, the carnal halos of Salomes and the Bacchante and the Hetaira continued to hover around her in enticing helices.

'O King radiant with the radiance of the blessed East! The faithful of Syria and Arabia, Libya and Egypt, have long endured the harsh policies of the Church of Rome. Let me not speak of Arius the Egyptian. Let it be Nestorius the Syrian, Sephros of Antioch, the tragedies of their peoples, the burning down of villages, the massacres, the wicked taxes - all crying out to heaven. The very throne of Christ, the all-loving, is shaken. So why not Justinian's? It is especially so when he sees his treasury, topped up by Anastasius, depleted on wars in the name of our Lord, the Shepherd on the Mount. Justinian's waking dreams, for he seldom sleeps, visit the wrong places and embrace the wispiest of phantoms. The loathsome Cappadocian, guilty of the riots, has been reinstated. He has been made the Praetorian Prefect of the East. The one you have been sent to. The world thinks my husband gives me an attentive ear. But his ear is like a weathercock, and it turns with the wind that finds favour with his games. O King, you must help me anchor him to reason!'

'I shall do what I can to fulfil my Lady's wishes. They seem to serve the more enduring interests of your realm and my people,' I interpreted, adding the last phrase as Emru's own.

In any event, since his arrival in the city and his court audience, Emru had been showing himself more and more adept at diplomacy – one forged in his trials and sore need to further his cause. Samuel's celebration of the art had also helped. But I could not but reflect on the irony of a situation in which a poet was being asked to help bail out

239

a dreamer – if Justinian truly was one – out of his reveries. An added irony was the petitioning of a pagan to assist in a Christian enterprise.

'These are justly 'enduring interests'; but my eminent husband is not convinced. He humours me at best.'

'But what is it that I am asked to do? Is not striking the Emperor's enemy, the Persians' claw in Arabia, with a more assured sword the best service I can render His Serenity?'

'My husband is his own enemy. Burying the sword, disbanding the Legions, is the best service one can render him. This would find favour with our blessed Mother, who saw her own son fall under the blows of soldiers.'

'Fall only to rise! Isn't that the story?'

'True! It is true for a mortal also. *He* too rises if he drops the sword.'

'Even when gored by the sword? Is that how it is?'

I faltered at the translation, not wishing to risk Emru's recent diplomatic gains. But the pace of the exchange left me little time to adjust my interpreting back and forth. At the same time, I was beginning to enjoy the couple's intellectual fencing.

He persisted, sensing a gap.

She had merely paused. Her ear, unhindered by the perpendula of her crown, had been caught by the cry of a bird from the darkness beyond.

'But is not the man who wielded the sword (or is it the spear?) in the story but an instrument of the god who wished it to happen? Wasn't the devil in the other tale similarly used? How can one tell that an empire's spurning of the sword isn't a ruse for a better tackle?'

'You argue well. Fit for the Lyceum, though too bold for our times. The Emperor, with little appetite for sleep or food, spends a great deal of his time brooding. The walls of the palace echo to his footfalls pacing the halls at night. But it is more like the case of a child who cannot sleep before the festive day, thinking of the toys and the new clothes he will get the following morning. Justinian has already had his toys and corpses in plenty, Huns, Slavs, Hebrews, Saracens, Samaritans – not to mention his own subjects. It is all so futile, so wasteful! We must work for peace. The East is the breadbasket of the Empire. Its people are the intermediaries of much of our trade. If it were to incline towards Rome, not through coercion but through persuasion and mutual benefit, then we would have a leaner but fairer realm. It would be one that can endure for centuries, dispensing goodwill, justice, virtue.'

240

Coming from a former prostitute this was an impressive oration. – and a moving one to boot. Fantastic as it was, it did not ring hollow to me. But some doubts raced in my mind – they raced faster than the chariots in the Hippodrome. Why is Theodora baring her soul to us, so unreservedly, if baring it is? Here is the woman who, in former days, toiled to expose to best advantage the charms of her young body in the theatre. Wearing the thinnest of garments and the flimsiest of veils, she would prostrate on the stage with grains of wheat scattered over her body. A bevy of starved geese would be brought on the stage to pick up the grains, thus throwing her insubstantial raiment into tantalising disarray. When this was not enough for the now frenzied audience, she would part her thighs to provide the most intimate view possible. Thus had narrated Samuel, to the embarrassment of his noble wife Sarah and the merriment of Hend, Emru's sister. And here she was now, an Empress. But was she opening up to bless or to waylay and entrap? True, she was not in this instance wearing the heavy diadem of shared command, with its gold and jewels and pearls, on her head. Still, she held an invisible sceptre of power. And intrigue?

There she stood, a woman who knew men like no other woman. Who knew exactly what to say and what not to say, what to reveal and what not to reveal, what game to play with one man but not with another. An adept actress and harlot who had given the whole of her body to her clients, her soul probably to none. Might she be giving it now to her God and his kingdom for a share having learnt to share expanses and recesses, dreams and nightmares, with her clients and partners?

Whatever she was and regardless of her intents, there stood before us a most remarkable woman. She was one who had thrown modesty to a Gorgon-eyed wind, seized an empire with the strings of her loincloth and stitched a sainthood from brothel bed-sheets, triumphing over her low birth and the hierarchies of the scrotums and swords and *solidi* who rule the world. There she stood liberated from the hypocrisies of courtrooms and the brutalities of battlefields to forge a unique future for herself and probably for us.

Emru, cultivating an appetite for repartee, may have forgotten that this was an art Theodora was a master of since her days as a comedienne and stripper on the stage.

'I do not wish to quibble endlessly, Empress. But how will Rome convince the peoples, let alone the churches of the East, of her good intentions? Those churches themselves have their own internal jealousies and squabbles. Long have they split hairs and slit throats in competition for God's pleasure and a slice of his world. The church of my late mother is in Persia's purse. The church of my friend's mother here sports many a scar from Roman abuse. Then there are the noble and long tormented Jews and the pagans and others. They are worthy partners too. How will Your Serenity (and come to think of it how will I) convince them of the value of entrusting their hearts (and souls?) to the new Rome? What coinage can buy hearts and souls? Might they not say, Ah, this is Rome at her old tricks again! Just as she feels hard-pressed by the Persians she comes up with a pacifier for her wild children - only to cut them down or desert them when her troubles with the Persians or with some other enemy are over?'

Theodora, smiling through much of Emru's sermon, summoned up a serious face and said:

'I respect that, and I admire you the more for saying it. More than before I am convinced that you are the right man to help bring about the transformation I have in mind. It is a transformation that can be best led by a poet rather than by a dour politician or an army thug - or even a priest. Even Arethas, El-Hareth, of Syria, whom I still trust in many ways, cannot play that role. Certainly, the challenges are formidable. But we need to start somewhere. I suggest that on your way back to Arabia, you meet with John of Ephesus. I understand he is sojourning in Antioch. I have already confided some of my ideas to him. These were ideas I had discussed years ago with the most venerable Patriarch Timothy of Alexandria. You will find John a man of great understanding and sympathy. He has people who can assist in this effort. They hold positions of moral authority in Syria, Iraq, Samaria, Judea, Arabia, Yemen, Egypt, Libya, Ethiopia. As soon as you have made contacts and devised an initial plan, send me word. I may be able to come on an official tour of the region. I miss the East - 'Oriens' to Rome; to me something more. I may then discuss these matters further. Perhaps seal an initial agreement. I can then convince the Emperor to hold a synod, a new sort of synod, here. I wish it can include poets. But poetry in the Empire is almost dead. Greek poetry died with Menander; Latin poetry with Claudian. Perhaps I am dreaming here. Anyway, the Cappadocian thorn, the Emperor wanted you to meet, can then be tweaked out of my side. The Senate and the Archbishop will not be the insuperable barrier you might imagine. The Archbishop prides himself on his authority to place the crown on the Emperor's head; but his is a ceremonial role – mere theatre. Ah, the word, the *world*! The Senate, ever concerned about their benefit, will see the wisdom of peace making. The people – they will have better bread and less wars, though they will continue to have their entertainment at the Hippodrome. People have sold their sons and daughters into slavery and prostitution to pay taxes. Others have had their fingers crushed and their backs scourged by the tax collectors. Still others have opted to do unto their subordinates what the authorities have done to them, spreading a panto of tyranny and mendacity. Your own people will also be relieved. They will have their rewards, and they will have their pride and freedom. A dream? A dream?'

'Nay, but *wisdom*, to which I bow, as I bow to your beauty,' said Emru, bowing in earnest.

'I have had some of your poems recited to me. I like the rhythms and the freedom and the desert imagery. What do the women of Arabia feel about them?'

Emru seemed taken aback by the sudden turn in the conversation and by the question. But he answered with passion, 'Our desert women are free to choose their lovers, as men are, perhaps more than men. I believe they value their freedom and those who celebrate it. I have long celebrated freedom. This I have done with my brothers the *sa'luks*. Poets, lovers, warriors, they are the conscience of Arabia. We embraced and sang all manner of freedom. But there is more to embrace and sing now, and more to change.'

'I have done all I could to give women of the Empire rights under the Law. Not all change is good though. And what some men call change may just be the heavenly laws restored. O King, just be yourself. There is much nobility in what you have done and in what you will be doing!'

Theodora spoke the last two sentences in perfect Aramaic, the language of Yesu, the language of this 'history', repeating them in good Northern Arabic.

Emru and I were stunned.

Then, turning to me with her luminous eyes and sensuous nose, she said, also in flowing Yesu-speak, 'You have done a very good job being an interpreter and a diplomat. A double credit to your mentor and king. Would that you could work for me, helping my words as they travel in a new garment to another ear, another era perhaps. I believe the mission of the king will be favoured by your words and tact.'

I bowed my head and went down on my knees, tears rising to my eyes, while Theodora allowed Emru to put his lips to her dainty hand. With the other, she, advancing towards me, put a purse in my hand, but my hand withdrew as if bitten by an adder. 'For you to melt into ink', she whispered. An enigmatic smile in her eyes and a slight dance in her exquisite nose, she baffled me again as on the previous day with the mystery of her discernment.

And then she turned with her cultivated eyes to survey the dinner table and said, 'I too have a Syrian cook. My compliments to her and to your gracious hosts.'

Then she paused.

There was a horse's sneeze outside the gate. It was followed by the rush of a figure from inside the villa hurtling towards us. It was Yahya, the youth who accompanied us from Gaza, pale faced and shaking as he had never been even when facing and single-handedly defeating two pirate ships off Rhodes.

For an instant, the Empress was taken off guard; but the youth promptly knelt before her, his eyes for a second meeting and melting into hers. Reverently, most reverently, he kissed the hem of her skirt, even as he raised with his right hand a small ivory box, which she took with some reluctance. Then, gently disengaging her skirt from the youth's trembling lips and fingertips, she departed, leaving us her damask cloak on the floor and the scent of only a hundred, dazed roses.

COURT AUDIENCE

Two days before had seen a court official arrive at Yonah's villa to summon us to an audience with the Emperor the following day.

This had been largely arranged by our resourceful and well-connected host. Yonah's very existence and success in the city was a resounding triumph over the official intolerance of Jews in the Empire.

Emru had shrugged his shoulder then and told the courtier, 'It was time we had an audience with your king.' I modified the petulant sentence to suggest in my translation an expression of immense delight and gratitude for the honour given. I also asked whether I could be included in that privilege as an interpreter and adviser to the Arab king. 'His Majesty the Emperor has his own Arabic interpreter; but, certainly, your Excellency can come with his Highness to the court of the great Augustus,' was the deft answer. My appeal for the favour to also include Yahya as a member of the king's delegation was kindly granted.

The following day saw us leave four horses and two pedigree hunting dogs in the custody of the guards outside the palace. The horses, creatures of exquisite beauty and grace, were two stallions and two mares of the purest Arab stock traced to *Zul Iqal* and *A'waj* as I may have mentioned before. They had been ordered by Yonah for a client in the city several months before. But Samuel had instructed Yonah in a letter we carried with us to hand the horses over to Emru as part of the presents he would give at the Roman court. Other presents were also provided by Samuel through his agent in Gaza. These included, among others, the salukis we left with the palace guards. Both horses and hounds had been housed and looked after in a stable owned by Yonah north of the city.

Having divested ourselves of the larger presents, we ascended a flight of porphyry stairs in the company of two officials and an armed guard. The sacred palace is the apex of a plateau of marble palaces, pavilions, galleries, and chapels, ringed by and interlaced with towers and barracks and gardens, all overlooking the sea and encircled from the west by the oldest of the city's defensive walls - that of ancient Byzantium.

Our ascent was one to a heaven of pageantry, pomp, and colour. At almost every step and turn of our climb we saw, alongside the ever-present guards, people in striking dresses of sorts we had seen on the city's main thoroughfare, the Mese. Emru was clad in a white, gold-threaded silken *aba* fluttering over a cotton caftan held at the waist by an encrusted belt. These, and the simpler but neat robes Yahya and I wore, had been bought for us by Yonah at a Syrian shop on the covered market called the House of Lamps on the west side of the Augsuteum off the *Mese*. Four of Yonah's servants carried our presents to the emperor and the empress - twelve gold threaded Yemeni robes, a sandalwood box of myrrh and another containing Gulf pearls, and two swords of Damascus steel with handles embossed with precious stones - all provided by Samuel's agents in Gaza and Rome at their employer's instructions.

We were led into an anteroom by a gigantic Grand Usher, who scrutinised with dark unblinking eyes our features and garbs and presents. Yahya refused to give up a small ivory box inside a leather purse he had been strapping across his chest for inspection and would not leave it behind; so he was firmly denied entry into the throne room with us. Headstrong as he was, he left with Yonah's four servants, followed by the Grand Usher's look of suspicion and disbelief. Then the giant, cleansing himself of the latter emotion but not the former, said solemnly, 'Remember to prostrate at full length on the ground in homage to His and Her Serenity.' Prior to translating this to Emru I briskly replied, 'I am very happy to oblige, but my king shall be accorded the honour and rank he deserves in the Emperor's presence.' The man's voice modulated between naked scorn and partially clothed courtesy. 'The desert king does not carry his desert with him. May his petition to retrieve his dunes and cactuses be crowned with the Emperor's favour.' I was aghast at the man's tone and the extent of his knowledge of our affairs and the purpose of our mission. I turned to Emru offering a quick but gentler version. 'I must see him, at whatever cost,' he seemed to be speaking to himself, his face as pale as death.

After our presents to the Emperor were inspected, we were led, three attendants carrying our portable gifts on ornate trays, into the throne chamber, its immensity and glare sending me into a state of disorientation. I struggled to wrench my mind free from the battering of a sea of shimmering tapers and gleaming gold and marble. I narrowed my eyes expecting to be further assaulted by the collective gaze of hundreds of nobles and dignitaries, bishops and generals, courtiers and clerks, sitting in chairs or standing along the floor of marble and mosaic leading to the two glittering thrones at the end of the chamber.

But there were none of those, none to crowd the place with their gaze and regalia and body heat!

I did not have time to ponder the mystery of their absence.

The two thrones were jostling my eyes with the splendour of their design and the majesty and command of the two royals sitting in them.

The carved thrones themselves were elevated some three steps above the floor onto a platform of porphyry and adorned with gems and gold and ivory. Arching over each throne was a small dome resting on four marble pillars and crowned by a carved eagle spreading wings of silver.

The person sitting on one of the thrones was a man of apparently medium height and a decidedly stout build. He was clad in a white tunic under a silken but somewhat austere purple robe made brighter by a large round-shaped medallion on his right shoulder, a sunflower with a big ruby heart and leaves of gold ingots and pearls. The hem of his purple toga fluttered ever so slightly over the golden straps of his jewelled sandals. In his left hand he held a small globe with a white cross mounted on top of it, and on his head he wore a crown of gold studded with rows of rubies, emeralds and pearls. Under its lower side-rims wisps of rough greying hair peeped out somewhat petulantly. His lightly bearded face was round and ruddy, a smile or a grimace faintly inert at the right corner of his mouth – a forceful and somewhat grim presence but not indifferent or unwelcoming.

On his left, sat the Empress on a similar throne and in a somewhat comparable but more feminine and opulent regalia. Bedecked with jewels on her person and wearing a high and rich crown flanked by two glittering waterfalls of pearls, she shone, though a small woman, with her own aura and large penetrating but somewhat pensive eyes. Was this the same woman who in Samuel's account played Salome wearing a flimsy veil and a loincloth round her waist and dancing and parting her thighs to offer a better view of her well trafficked *Mese*? Was this the bear-keeper's daughter who had educated herself into an ingenious courtesan, whose *han*-cravings dozens of young men standing in a queue did not satisfy – or so she pretended for the business? I detested these images invading my mind at this time, and I shook my head to whip them away.

No, here was an Empress, wielding in her petite hands the power of life and death, happiness and misery, for millions of people. At this very moment, her power sat or roved in silent or trumpeted witness as bakers baked their breads, soldiers charged enemy columns, mariners sailed on distant seas, miners crawled through dark shafts, men spied on forbidden women taking their baths, mothers suckled their babes, prisoners faced their executioners, and gladiators confronted starved and bewildered beasts. A thousand thousand men and women doing a thousand thousand chores along a radius immeasurable, endlessly rolling with hills, whining with deserts, heaving with woods, sparkling with lakes, sweltering with cities, her power, and that of her consort, was there, cautioning, admonishing, promising, heartening, terminating. How can a human being, man or woman, cope with that weight, that universe, of power and responsibility and expectations? No wonder Justinian hardly ever sleeps!

The spectacle was overwhelming. I heard Emru, behind whom I was walking as usual, miss a step in his impatient stride towards the twin thrones. And yet he may have been calculating his next move, an instant of indecision which gave me enough time to further scrutinise the human frames that carried those weights coloured for the world's theatre in purple and decked with pearl and gold.

The man's body, though clothed and composed, radiated untamed, restless power. The stout fingers resting on the gilt arms of the throne tapped fretfully as if intolerant of the time being wasted in frivolous ceremonies, or on us. An image leapt to my mind - the tail of a gaudy panther I had once seen in the Hejaz crouching behind an *arta* bush as a young buck strayed from a herd, grazing. But this was a fleeting thought from a wilderness which did not fit into this most urbane of settings, one though presided over by a peasant soldier and a former circus dancer. Perish the thought!

But then I was seized by the eyes. Under their bushy, curved eyebrows, they fixed on the stately and yet-undiminished Emru, banishing me to the periphery of their interest. But they were an oriel into the man's soul. Intelligent, impatient, bored, mournful, indifferent, aloof, accommodating, they presented a mix of moods and impressions. Set in a ruggedly handsome face of some fifty and odd years, they were glowing with an authority that could cripple men of their resolve but also send them forth to all manner of deeds they had not imagined they could undertake.

248

As my thoughts galloped and spun wildly and I tried to rein them in, I saw Emru's towering figure ahead of me suddenly come to a stop over a square of the mosaic floor showing a deer with an arrow in its flank. He halted, swayed slightly as though drunken, one part of the shaft of the arrow in the deer's flank under his right foot. Then, opening his arms wide, the sleeves of his *aba* giving him the semblance of a stork about to take off, he advanced towards the Emperor. No doubt he had a smile on his face and was striding to embrace a fellow royal, a brother. Instantly, two equally towering guards barred his way, and the Grand Usher hurried along, scattering angry mutterings in his path. Emru brought his advance to a standstill and drew back a step, dropping his white wings to his sides. I seized the lull to slump upon a section of the hunt scene prostrating on all four in the most obsequious act of homage. I hoped I was fulfilling the Grand Usher' earlier instruction while distracting attention from Emru's well-intentioned gaff.

Time stopped breathing, or so it seemed to me. Then I heard the words 'Do arise now!' explosively hissed to me by the Grand Usher. I scrambled to my feet to see and hear Justinian, half obscured by Emru's broad back, speak.

'We welcome you, Majesty, and we extend our apologies for the time gone by since your arrival in our city. But we hope that some of that time was not in vain. We trust you have had the opportunity to acquaint yourself with the main attractions of our sacred capital.'

His words seemed to race ahead of the efforts of his Arabic interpreter, who had come in from the side, almost tripping in his rush. He was a young fellow, dressed in a monk's cowl and seemingly ill at ease with his task, stuttering and making a few mistakes in the translation as he began to essay it. Perhaps he was standing in for a more veteran interpreter. Sensing his difficulty, the Queen gestured to the Grand Usher. He hurried to the side of her throne, and bowing gave a dutiful ear to a compelling whisper from her. Soon *I* was charged with the task of translating the exchange. The young monk withdrew briskly, his cheeks aflame; and when he settled on an empty studded chair he threw me a vague look. I responded with a reassuring and apologetic smile, which I instantly regretted since it could be read as a sign of gloating. My face and ears burning, I shook my head to dismiss that thought from his head should it have reached him in that garb. There I was fumbling even before I started. How would I fare with the rest, I wondered!

'We are well acquainted with the essence of your mission here. We have it in our means to grant you your petition and restore your kingdom to you.'

Before I began my task of interpreting, I murmured my thanks to the Emperor and the Empress, expressing a wish that I might live up to their trust and the demands of the lofty mission to which they had raised me.

'We are confident that a student of the eminent Theodorus will not fail to shine under any roof,' said the empress, her words, gentle as they were, hitting me like a battering ram. How did she know? But I bowed my head low above the tesserae of the floor, tears bedewing my eyes with memories of my teacher and Sofia, strangely easing my tension.

'It is a higher summit, a dearer desire, to have the trust and affection of your Majesties than to have my kingdom restored,' said Emru, diplomatically, having listened to my translation of the Emperor's speech. Both of us knew that Rome's domains had never extended to Arabia proper. Rome's Phylarchs in Syria or Phoenicia or Palestine, even her 'Phylarch of the Saracens', did not have real presence in the Arabian hinterland. Rome had sent a succession of Ambassadors to Kenda, most competent ones like Euphrasisus and Abraham and Nonnosus, and had concluded a treaty with Emru's grandfather; still, Kenda and the Arabian interior kept their sullen independence. No doubt the Emperor knew of the troubles which the deputy of his Christian brother the Negus was facing in the Yemen. Doubtless he also knew that the Persians had strengthened their position there with the alliance Al-Munzer had forged with the Assads. But he also knew, as we did, that, though standing tall and puffed up with dreams, Emru had no army behind him in his own homeland. His family was cut down and his once-prevailing tribe was reduced to five ancient shields probably destined to rust in Samuel's fort.

'I present to your Majesties a small token of the yield of Arabia and the munificence of one of her most noble sons and princes, Samuel Ben Ored Ben 'Adiya, represented in Your mighty city by the gracious Yonah Ben Nanu. Captive as Arabia is at present, she waits with bated breath to enrich the world with the fruits of her freedom,' Emru addressed the royal twain, even as he half extended an arm towards the gifts upon the trays carried by the three attendants. I advanced towards one of the trays and placed on it four *houjjas*, rolls of parchments Yonah had given me detailing the pedigree and tribal ownership of each of the horses and mares we had left at the gate.

The Emperor gave the presents a cursory look, his ambivalent smile expanding at the right corner of his mouth. The court Usher dutifully murmured that four horses and two hunting dogs were tethered outside waiting to be inspected by the Emperor and the Empress.

'We thank the king and his associates. As Nation of Christ, we desire to prevail only by the Sword of the Truth. Long may that sword remain in Our hand. Long may the good war endure. And endure as it might, Our resolve shall not waver. Half a million of the best soldiers and mariners in the world stand guard of Our cities and shores, roads and borders. They guard the world which is free and bring hope to the one to be so enfranchised. But, inviolable as Our realm is, We leave room to diplomacy, and exercise patience. We exercise patience even as We are provoked by the barbarian hordes in the north and the brutal Persians and their coarse hireling in Iraq. At this very hour the Persian tyrant is fomenting trouble to end our Eternal Peace. But We shall stand firm. We have chosen to bear the duty and accept the honour of defending Our world, your world, Our Rome, your Arabia.

'We have golden memories of the mission of Rome's Ambassadors to Kenda. They have sown seeds which now lie dormant, dreaming to be nourished by new rain,' Emru said, benefiting from the Emperor's pause, my translation interposing, assisting. But I could not help thinking of the impatience and disdain with which young Emru had routinely treated meetings of tribal elders with foreign envoys.

'That shall be done. Your Majesty may well be the rain these seeds await. Arabia is too precious to be abandoned to the enemy. Her heart is yet to be won.'

'She will give her heart to those who give her her freedom back, though the ways of freedom may lead her into ways all of her own,' Emru responded, bravely and candidly, which I could not but render faithfully.

Here I saw the Empress lean sideways towards her imperial husband. Her eyes more lustrous, her features more sharpened, she whispered some words to the ear under the crown. Justinian nodded slightly, and said, somewhat stiffly, almost as if rehearsing a speech:

'We welcome all into Our fold. And We are prepared to welcome you as a future Phylarch of Arabia. The peace of your troubled land

251

and the hopes of your oppressed people lean on you – on Our coalition. Arabia's harmony and Ours must be one, the unity of Our Christian family inviolable.'

Emru as a Roman Phylarch over Arabia! That was a truly generous offer. Was it Yonah's contact at the court who proposed it? Was it the Empress's whisper that sealed it? Yet, did not the imperial twain know that Emru was a pagan in word and deed, his mother having been a Nestorian and a heretic in Rome's view?

The Emperor continued as Emru vibrated with anticipation and uncertainty.

'The Persian court, since the beginning of Our reign, has been in breach of treaties deviously concluded only to be profanely flouted. A nest of tyrants, it has not ceased to try to enlarge its domains at Our expense. Syria has often been raided and terrorised. But it remains largely secure under the faithful Arethas, Our Phylarch there. Your help in securing the heart of Arabia and its borders north and south, east and west, against the Persian terror will be vital.'

Emru maintained his quivering silence, while the Emperor, his eyebrows raised above his great eyes, paused for a response before continuing.

'The *Oriens*, Her Serenity the Empress never tires of reminding me, takes up fifteen of Our provinces. These include Syria and Palestine together with southern Anatolia and the region from the Tigris to Mare Nostrum, counting Cyprus. It is Our belief that the fellowship of truth and faith shall strengthen the existing bonds and craft new ones. Kenda's role, Arabia's role, shall be crucial. She shall benefit from Our system, as Our system shall benefit from her. Our laws shall lift her from her anarchy; her repose shall lift Us from Our disquiet.'

'Arabia united will certainly be uplifted. Noble as she is, she will be doubly ennobled to be an agent of harmony in the world. That is a destiny to aspire for. I have said that before. Her anger at being trifled with will be soothed by her sisterhood with Rome, with the world. My own anger, my own grief, will also be lightened by my brotherhood with you,' came Emru's belated response to the earlier announcement. 'Already the hearts of the Arabs are inclined to Rome, with whom they have been trading since times uncounted.' he added.

Justinian reflected on my translation, his head slightly bowed and leaning faintly towards his wife. Then he said, a wan smile fluttering then disappearing on his stout face,

252

'The honour shall be shared. Your Majesty's requirements shall be addressed. You shall avail yourself of Our Legions stationed in Palestine, when you need them. So shall your native horsemen, when they are back in the saddle, make themselves available in the war on the Persian terror – a war in which no neutrals shall have a place. By siding with that terror, your adversaries have made themselves adversaries of Ours. And it is in Our interest that you prevail over them, as it is your interest that We prevail over their patrons. Noble as the pedigree of your line, it is now bereft of steel, needed in a righteous cause. In the meantime, thousands of Our men with that steel shall await Our command at Caesarea. Its well-tested Proconsul has Our trust. So does Our Praetorian Prefect of the East, Our first minister. He is not with Us today. His presence was directly required in Ancyra. Nor is Our brave Belisarius at hand. Nor for that matter Our trusted chronicler Procopius.'

I did not dare or have time to look around, but the emptiness of the great chamber had already pressed on my chest and tantalised my mind.

The Emperor, his eyes shifting furtively to his wife's side, continued.

'But We need to show the importance We attach to your mission. Thus We decree that for the first year of your Phylarchate, your Kenda Basileia aside, shall be reprieved of raising taxes for Our State. You may though levy imposts for the promotion of your own rule. We shall further exempt you from any presentation on the formal assumption to your title. The Legions you shall need and as long as they are stationed in Arabia shall be provided for, salaried and provisioned by Arabia's lucrative trade, which We hope shall increase a hundredfold.'

I remembered Samuel's words. Here was Justinian shepherding the lamb of Yesu on the highways of the world. Here he was etching the tearful cross on more battle shields and tattooing it on more trade caravans! Here he was being generous to the roving nomads of Arabia!

True, Justinian was not born into the purple - did not grow into a priesthood. He was invested into office by rough soldiers on a shield in a circus, a man riddled with a medley of humours and re-moulded into a faith found to be handy and a mission calculated to be profitable. Deep are the tremors in my heart when religion dictates politics or when politics wears the mask of religion. And yet Justinian deserved respect. I thought as I looked at him pinned somewhat fretfully to his throne that he too was a Christ crucified - as I am crucified, though no Christ.

But I also thought of an Egyptian juggler I once saw in Bayroute. That man in a garish clown's outfit was trying to keep five pomegranates in the air all at the same time. Wasn't Justinian such a man, juggling a quinquevirate of Church and Senate and Army and Merchants and People? Under the skin of these pomegranates, however, there were seeds that jostled bitterly for room and harboured their own sweetness or sourness – and their own maggots.

There were no members of the Clergy sitting on the inlaid chairs in spectacular vestments and under magnificent mitres as should have been their custom, described to me by my beloved mentor in law and diplomacy so many years ago. We had seen them, members of the Clergy, in the Great Cathedral, where they were transformed into icons of opulence and pageantry unlike the more humble monks and priests we had regularly seen hurrying along the streets of the capital in sombre and austere garments. In the cathedral at the time, the Archbishop sat in his *phelonion*, richly embroidered with crosses and with an equally luxuriant square piece of embroidered material hanging from his girdle. Round his shoulders he wore a fine strip of red cloth also decorated with crosses; a tall staff with a decorated ivory head nestled between his legs. What thoughts, visions, lusts, lust-denials, did the staff pick up between those legs?

Nor were any Senators there in the throne chamber. *Those* we had also seen in the Senate a few days earlier, courtesy of an associate of Yonah's. They had sat or stood in simpler togas as they deliberated and orated in the house. Listening to them I thought they were far removed from the ancient Greek and Roman ideal. They seemed to me as a body of men engaged in the pursuit of their own interests and inevitably those of the palace. Coming from families and professions connected to the establishment that ran the Empire, they were not expected to take decisions unfavourable to Justinian.

The Merchants? They were not in the chamber. They were everywhere, though pretending not to be anywhere. But their own sway was also felt all along the *Mese* and side streets; in the hawkers' shouts, the jingling of the *solidi* and the *folles* and the *nummi*, the betting on the charioteers and the gladiators, and along the Golden Horn in the mariners' hopeful songs and the groaning of the tethered ships.

The People, described by a senator during our visit as a beast with a thousand heads (or was it two, blue and red?), were certainly nowhere to be seen here. They were outside, far outside, leading the low life imposed upon them while daydreaming of the Hippodrome, where they could place their meagre bets on race horses or on men and beasts expected to rip each other's guts in public. Woe to the city if those daydreams were not given a seat and a gory spectacle. And woe to an Emperor if he would not season his immoderate taxes with the *qat* of the Hippodrome. Eight years before, Justinian had his wife to save him.

The thought of the *people* made me wonder yet again as to why this ceremony of ours was being conducted in the absence of the usual court audience. Was it a mark of confidentiality, gravity, the exceptional nature of the mission entrusted to Emru? But what if it was a mere dress-rehearsal by Justinian and his wife for someone else, the Syrian king for instance, our attendance being a mere sideshow, a comic relief, a charade, an indulgence, not meant for the official record? But, what if it were indeed a genuine act, one protected from the prying eyes and ears? And yet, was Emru paying any real attention to the implications for his people and his own rule should any of these plans come to pass? He responded somewhat dreamily, 'I thank your Serenity for your largesse. It will not go amiss. Arabia will rise to her destiny.'

'It is a small matter,' said the world Emperor. 'Our alliance is meant for larger things, weightier gains.'

A commission for Emru's appointment as a ruler for Rome over Arabia was presented by the Master of the Rolls and the Emperor signed it in intriguingly crimson rather than purple ink. A banquet was promised.

Accompanied by a more subdued and deferential Grand Usher with his bunch of keys, Emru left the throne chamber. He held the Roman gift of a Trojan horse proudly in his right hand. I followed, haunted by the silence of the chamber and, more forcefully, the clamour in the Empress's eyes.

A KINGDOM TO RETAKE

Four days later we left the world's capital.

We proceeded with a mounted escort early in the morning from our guest lodgings in the Imperial complex. We had been housed there after the investiture of Emru as a Phylarch, the ceremony having taken place in a small and dimly lit room. We had most reluctantly bidden farewell to Chava and members of her household, preferring to have remained in their hospitality, though overwhelmed by it. Her husband's prudence and connections in the city had spread for us a plush carpet into the court - uncertain and unfathomable as that court's designs and its rewards might be.

A mystery and a calamity had attended our last day at our hosts' villa. Young Yahya, who had accompanied us from Gaza and distinguished himself so brilliantly in a battle with pirates off Rhodes, was snatched from the villa by a band of men. The Syrian cook was the first to become aware of the noise made by the intruders and came at them with a roll pin. But she was thrown against a wall and became lost to the world. The youth, though seized while asleep, had clearly put up a fight as there were smudges of blood and several broken teeth in the room he had occupied. We all hurried out of our rooms into the garden to see his body being thrown by some half a dozen men over the croup of a horse's saddle and galloped away with by a burley rider, partly hooded. The man was surrounded by some dozen others on horseback, one placing before him in the saddle the youth's sandalwood chest. Our shouts to them to halt rang out to no avail in the pre-dawn air, speckled with shrieks of cockerels interrupted from their leisurely orisons. Emru fetched a carving knife left on the table in the garden, but the marauders had disappeared into the co-conspiring darkness.

Lo! I have failed to give an account of our sea journey from Gaza over the fourteen days previous to our coming ashore at Smyrna. Here is a summary.

Nothing untoward had happened after our departure from the Gaza quay on board Samuel's merchant ship the *Adara*. We had streamed away from the shore attended by the valedictions of Aharon and the tears of Yahya's grandfather. The tears of our desert-brother Al-Ward had sparkled fiercely in his hawk eyes. They seemed reluctant to leave their source in his big heart and drop on the sand of Gaza, much as he had humbled himself to the sands of Arabia and consorted with them for our benefit. How can we ever repay or pay enough tribute to that *sa'luk* prince, that Emir of a man - he disdaining, ever mocking, the title of a king?

The three men stood on the shore in the growing haze, the old man stooping, until we could see them no more.

My own tears resurged in my eyes like a burning fount as we sailed a day later by Bayroute. The captain had navigated somewhat close to the coast at the request of Emru. The king, knowing something of my attachment to the city, also wished to make up for not supporting, not wholeheartedly, my plea for a stopover at Petra during our land journey from Tayma.

Bayroute lay in the distance like a ripe lover unreachable, the green-blue mountains behind her a pillow plump with the down of dreams. Was I fated to be severed from Sofia, whose villa on a hill facing the seafront I fancied I could see? But were not the eddies of fate also spurred on by the upheavals of my own soul? Could I ever be a master of my saddle, a skipper of my dhow?

The ship ploughed on, the toss of the waves preventing me from putting ink to paper. The captain had promised a brief halt at Cyprus and then at Rhodes. At the orders of Samuel, passed on to him by Aharon, he was to take us by the shortest route to the Golden Horn, discarding the safer but slower coast-hugging course usually taken by trade ships. For the first few days, however, he sailed, at Emru's request, not far from the coast, hence I was able to feast and scorch my eyes at the sight of Bayroute in the distance.

Soon we had other worries. The captain, a squat and muscular but quick-witted and agile Tyrian man named Nazrat, told Emru that he had observed a smaller ship following our own not long after our departure from Gaza. She was later joined by two larger ships as ours veered to the west leaving the beguiling sight of Bayroute to fade away in the heartless glare. The smaller ship also vanished, with the silhouettes of the two larger ones becoming more relentless, ominous.

The plan for a breather at Cyprus was swiftly thrown overboard. The captain felt a double urgency to abandon the plan so he could make up for the time he had lost hugging the coastline. He also wanted to gain on the two ships, nakedly showing themselves to be in hot and ill-intentioned pursuit.

Yahya, our young ward from Gaza, had been a distinctly silent passenger. He had sat on the foredeck, rarely giving the coastline to the east any notice, preferring to direct his large, penetrating, albeit somewhat pensive, hazel eyes at the northern horizon. Though of a slight frame, he was a handsome youth, with a princely bearing and delicate sensuous features, an elegantly upturned nose giving him a special distinction. He had come onboard at Gaza with a large sandalwood chest carried by a servant of his grandfather's. On board the ship, he was never seen without a belt strapped across his chest from which a leather purse dangled and which he was in the habit of opening, often before sunset, to take out a small ivory box he would open and look into thoughtfully for a minute or two.

This mild-mannered, wistful and slender youth was transformed into a towering warrior when our pursuers closed in for the kill. The pirates, for want of a better word, seemed to have had nailed to the wooden floor of each of their foredecks a siege engine, a catapult or a ballista, I could not tell at first. They began to unleash missiles on us as the pirate captains realised he could not gain on our ship. For, though, heavier with cargo, the *Adara* was fitted with a wide lateen sail, a Gulf invention unknown in the Roman Sea. The ship herself had been designed after the sleek dhow shape and fitted with the rigging and the unerring eye of a *kamal* to hold her own in any race for trade and profit – and at times for dear life.

The chase took us past the island of Rhodes, and despite the head-turning manoeuvres performed by our skilful captain, some missiles hit the ship, injuring three of our sailors, with one stone smashing through the starboard hull near the water level, allowing water to seep in and slow the ship down. The neighing of the agitated horses and the barking of the *salukis* mingled with the roar and splash of the waves, the groaning of the rigging, and the hubbub of human alarms – the heart-drumming vibrating in my ears alone. Two pigeons in a bamboo cage dangling from a projection on the mast had cooed peacefully as their cage swayed gently during the first phase of our journey. They had been the object of attention and pampering by Emru, who regularly offered them titbits of bread and dried fig. Now they beat their wings furiously against the ribs of the cage as it lurched madly with the ship's surges and dives - the barking of the dogs and the whinnying of the horses and the clatter of their hooves down in the hold unsettling us further. It was then that the two assaulting ships came perilously close to our ship. Emru stood on the after-deck with a drawn sword in his hand and a sad grimace on his face, expecting the pirates, if pirates they were, to board our ship and sink his dreams of an Arab kingdom to the bottom of an alien sea.

It was then, as I stood with a heart about to burst or crash next to Emru, that I turned and saw young Yahya emerge from the bowels of the ship carrying his cumbersome sandalwood chest between his arms. Ever so calmly, he opened the chest and bent over, sifting through the contents. A minute later a missile landed in the sea next to starboard and splashed with water the right side of his face. Anon he was standing up, wielding in one hand a short stout bow and a sheaf of thick arrows. In the other hand he held an earthenware vessel, which he cradled securely as the ship bounced and lurched. He then shouted to the ship's cook, who had come on the deck to take part in defending the ship, to fetch him a bowl of fire. When he acquired this, he asked me to hold the earthenware basin, which had a dark and foul-smelling solution inside it, and the fire bowl. Soon he was tearing up his shirt and with a small knife cutting it up into strips. These he dipped into the solution inside the earthenware basin and tied neatly round the heads of the arrows. He did all this at great speed and seemed to me like an adept circus performer. He then stood with his bow on the right-hand side of the ship and took aim. As the nearest pursuing ship came within a distance of twenty feet from our ship's side, he dipped the head of his arrow in the bowl of fire, took aim, and released the arrow. Our eyes and the wild eyes of some twenty men with swords arrayed at the nearer side of the marauding ship followed the flaming arrow as it shot over their heads and lodged itself in the grey square sail of their ship. All eyes stayed on the sail as it became engulfed by flames which almost instantly billowed to the blue sky. More flaming arrows soon followed, lodging themselves in the sail and in various places on the deck, creating little islets of fire and flurries of panic among the pirates. One arrow lodged itself with its flaming arrowhead into the chest of one burly buccaneer. Strangely, the water which the pirates poured from buckets upon the fire only made the flames rise higher as though the flames were feeding on the very water meant to douse them.

The *Adara* was taking in water whenever it swayed to starboard; but the distance between her and the pirate ship was increasing. And then the latter shuddered to a halt, rolling from side to side; her sister ship halted beside her to offer help.

We all came up and gathered around the young defender cheering and embracing him. But he steadily kept his alert posture with the bow and an un-torched arrow in his hand. His large hazel eyes continued to study the two pirate ships, a column of smoke rising from the stricken vessel, in the now receding distance. 'There is still life in them, in the second ship,' he murmured, impassively.

Before long, he was proven right. By then, our captain had attended to his injured sailors and inspected down in the ballast the hole in the side of the ship. Now he was negotiating the Aegean islands and contemplating laying anchor at one of them to repair the hole. I in my turn, still shaken to my wet sandals, was trying to reflect on the splendour of the isles and the seaways blessed and burdened with the legends of the ancient Ionian gods and goddesses, heroes and heroines. Then the grey square sail of the second ship came into view.

So we pressed on. The pirate ship, wary of the flaming arrows, kept a safe distance, though sending hopeful missiles from her ballista every now and then. But we were now sailing through much trafficked waters, and before long the pirate ship fell behind and out of our view. In a day and a half we ditched at the crystalline port of the city of Smyrna, home of the martyred Polycarp and the immortal Homer. Poseidon and Demeter had looked after the city's commerce in the past. Now a Jewish community survive there, their dainty synagogue coexisting with the ruins of the pagan temples and the new churches that had borrowed their marble from the older shrines.

As we limped like a wounded dolphin into the port, the captain, who, throughout the journey, did not need to lift the *kamal* dangling from his belt, let out one of the two pigeons in the cage. The bird soared out of his hand, a message folded and tied to its left leg. Five days later, riders with a trail of pack mules sent by Yonah arrived to pick us up. An engineer came with the party. We were to learn later that he had the ship repaired, which allowed her indomitable captain to steer her along with her precious cargo into the Golden Horn with fitting dignity.

Yahya rode with us, but would not let go of his sandalwood chest. He tethered it himself, heavy as it was, on the back of a stout mule, whose bridle he kept in his hand as he rode on a horse beside it. He had a new shirt, but the belt with the bulging purse was still firmly strapped across his upper body. When, on our way north we rode under the weeping rock face of Niobe on Mount Sipylus, Emru questioned him on the fire he had unleashed upon the pirates (our captain was of the opinion that those were not pirates but killers paid by someone to waylay us). The youth said he would tell us but only in the strictest confidence. I was impressed with the gentle quality of his voice and eloquence as he spoke, not being a loquacious fellow. The mixture, he said, was an invention of an alchemist who lived in Baalbek, the City of the Sun, which I had visited when I was in Lebanon. He confided to Emru, no doubt out of respect for him as his guardian, that the alchemist in question had inherited the formula from his own father and had lately given it to his son to continue to improve on it. Yahya's father had promised the young man to have the invention taken to Rome, where it would be promoted as a possible weapon for use in naval warfare, with material benefit to the young alchemist. Yahya intimated that his father had also looked upon this as a means to help Yahya's own mission in Rome. About that mission, Yahya, instinctively touching the purse dangling from his belt, said that it was of a much greater import than either commerce or war, though he needed to exert great effort before he could fulfil his 'quest' and rise to his 'destiny'. I saw a sparkle of fellow-feeling in Emru's eyes as he listened to the youth.

A few days later, the sight of the city's domes and fortifications in the distance from the Asian shore filled our hearts with awe. Surely, it should fill the heart of a conqueror, should he exist, with despair.

After taking the ferry, we entered the Metropolis over a drawbridge and through a massive gate above which a gilded inscription read: 'Christ our Lord, Guard Your City from All Strife and War. Overwhelm and Crush the Power of the Foe.'

May that protector also offer the young Yahya his safeguard and may he foil the youth's enemies whoever they might be! After the abduction, Yonah and Emru made desperate solicitations and inquiries about the youth without success. What secrets did Yahya, wary as he was at first but increasingly impatient, reveal to a sullen or solicitous ear? What enticing darkness or blaze was in the small ivory box the youth had kept close to his body only to surrender it so readily and reverentially to the Empress? Surely something far more important than the trade in that fire-oil, however prodigious that might be, must have seized his mind and the mind of his father as he had lain dying in Gaza.

Emru was formally instructed to proceed to Ankara to meet the Praetorian Prefect of the East, whom the Emperor had praised and the Empress maligned. He dithered, troubled by doubts and misgivings, which I may have stirred in part, regarding his assigned role in Arabia. Also, he had promised Yahya's grandfather to guard the youth and deliver him safely to his destination. Then a cryptic message was handed over to Yonah apparently by the same lady who had delivered to me the Empress's earlier message. This one read, 'The youth has reached his home. Do not fear for him.' May the Virgin Mother join with her Celestial Son to accord him the protection he needs in the Metropolis of Intrigues!

ROME, MY ROME

I sighed my farewell to Rome as Emru and I pulled back from her along her *Mese*. It was like a man (Emru in my fancy?) withdrawing from one embrace to enter, re-gorged, another. In any event, Emru's promised kingdom was beckoning with honeyed arms and silken thighs from across the rough roads of Galatia. Only then would he break and fulfil all vows, only then.

All along the *Mese* which links the Augusteum in the west to the Gate of Charisius in the extreme east and north, we rode, escorted by a mounted soldier, probably an under-officer of the *Logothete* of the Drome or foreign ministry. Yonah graciously rode with us. The *Mese* was busy with its daily traffic: the rich on white horses or in painted carriages pulled by mules with gilded trappings, others – porters, strollers, slaves, shoppers, priests, mendicants – loitering, plodding or ambling along. The air reverberated with shouts of riders and carters and cries of mountebanks and stall keepers peddling their wares under the porticoes on the sides. Various tongues and moods of the world also floated by, hawking, haggling, cursing, propositioning, begging... Greeks, Macedonians, Dacians, Scythians, Slavs, Armenians, Illyrians, Goths, Syrians, Egyptians, Arabs. Costumes of every cut and fabric flowed or rushed or swaggered along the regimented path, the silk of China, the cotton of Egypt, the fur of Armenia, the gauze of Gaza...

Behind us retreated, though still towering, the Grand Cathedral and the Temple of Holy Wisdom, dominating the heights of the Augusteum. It was consecrated only three years earlier on the ruins of an older basilica. And there it squatted on the chest of the city like a red-skinned Sphinx, magnificent and morose with its pride and sorrows and riddles. Some three weeks earlier, Emru had listened rather impatiently to Yonah's account of its history and the marble columns shipped from the unguarded glories of Egypt and Delphi. We were then standing under its dome and within its nave. We were like ants which an impish boy had trapped underneath a cracked bowl allowing some tantalising light in. Emru, his impatience reaching a pitch, dismissed the building as a monstrous hunchback endlessly brooding, a dark-crimson mole, a tumour, cunningly designed to demean Man, split his vision, and drain his earthly vitality. I thought of my mother and my uncle when a kindly priest pointed to where splinters from the cross on which Yesu had been crucified were encased in an ornate crucifix of gold and silver and pearl. Though my rebel uncle would have let out, as Yesu himself might have done, a howl of outrage, my mother would have nailed her very heart to those splinters.

We were leaving all that behind our backs, various splinters and panaceas in our hearts. We proceeded north of the circus, which Emru had visited on the third day of our arrival to watch the races. We trotted past the palaces and courts nearby onwards to the *Argyropratia*, where the silversmiths of the city live and work. We pressed on past the circular Forum of Constantine, with its distinctive marble floor and arches and gallery of pagan and Christian statues, but more prominently and splendidly the brave figure of Constantine as a sun-god beaming from the top of a central pillar. More mundanely and practically, to the east, in the *Artopolia*, lay Constantine's promise to the city, the Bakeries, which supply the metropolis with its bread, the wheat transported on ships from Egypt and Lebanon's Beka' valley.

We pressed on, as if revisiting, though less leisurely, the landmarks to which Yonah had first introduced us after our arrival in the city. We rode through the rectangular Forum of Theodosius, with its university and library, blessed with the tomes of my dear mentor. I had inquired after him there and was told he was in Bayroute working on an 'Index' to the great Codex he had helped write. Blessed, O blessed may his stellar home be! The central column in the Forum is dedicated to the victories of Theodosius, with another gallery of imperial figures. To our right we could see again the stately Aqueduct of Valens, towering so gracefully on its many arches and carrying the sweet water so vital to the life of the city. Further to the east, my eyes lingered upon the spot dedicated to the three sons of Constantine as they came together for their last meeting after the death of their father. Here they stood in marble as true brothers united in their filial grief before they set out to rule the provinces of their father's Empire. In flesh, which had long melted into the all-forgiving earth, they lived on to turn their swords against one another in a fratricidal pursuit of power, a fate not unlike that which befell the sons of many an Arab king afflicted by the same disease.

Soon, we were riding under the gateway to the forum of *Amastrianum*, with its overarching symbol of Justice, forewarning those who may cheat in weights and measurements. The forum itself was crowded with statues of gods and dragons, being a place of public execution for low-cast criminals. Beyond it, the *Mese* stretched in a north-easterly direction towards the Gate of Charisius.

Rome, Constantinople, Byzantium, the jewel and terror of the world, was now behind us. As we glided away from her envied and overpowering embrace, I turned my face to cast a last look. The Theodonian wall was, no doubt to remain so for centuries, tall and defiant, arrogant and reassuring, achieving its point of filling the heart of a conqueror, should the womb of a woman deliver such one, with desolation but also with a fatal attraction. In the interval, how would a man pacing in the shade of a wall several miles long, five yards thick and ten yards high feel but like a cockroach?

I felt a vague sadness rising within me. The city that had ensnared my fancy during my youth and education in Arabia and Lebanon had already become part of my own personal history, my emotional and spiritual mosaic. It was a part I could never renounce. The weeks I spent within her walled and veiled sanctuary they too had become part of my being. I knew I would miss that city, even with the anguish of her stones, the boom of her semantrons, and the madness of her circus factions; yeah, even with the eerie circling of her gulls and the wiles and riddles of her court.

Like her Empress, perhaps like Bayroute, she was a saint and a temptress, Christian and pagan, a bastion of the West and of the East, a bestower and a plunderer, a healer and a hydra. Glittering with palaces, basilicas, statues and pleasure gardens, she was also a-gleam with spears and swords, tainted by the blood of petty criminals, intoxicated by the lust for empire and the greed for trade, her backstreets beckoning with forbidden pleasures and daggers and poisons for hire and sale. But she is also the city of the unique Modius of Wheat crowning the gateway to the Forum of *Amastrianum*. Would that that same icon of just measurement be employed to deal more equitably with the rest of the world, a world that lies beyond her and from which she draws her bread and recruits and on which she works her magic? She is also the home of libraries and seminaries, monasteries and hospitals, orphanages and poorhouses, dedicated to the love of the Christian God and charity to all people. Might she be the great mother and sister who would lift Kenda from her quicksand and the East from its vagrancy? Like myself and like Emru, if not also like many others, she is an abode of contradictions, as we all are within the walls and dreams and nightmares of our individual souls.

AN ENCOUNTER WITH A SKY DWELLER

I had heard Chava mention a hermit who lived on top of a column not far from the city. I shared with my gracious hostess a fascination with mystics, both my dear mother and uncle having been mystics of sorts. Stylites or pillar-dwellers are not uncommon in Syria, where they originated. I had wasted an opportunity to see one outside the city of Tripoli in northern Lebanon when I was in that dear land. My interest in the mystical path had been further fired up by my reading of such authors as Philo of Judea, Iamblichus of Syria and the great Plotinus, a tradition in which Mithra joined hands and hearts with Orpheus, the Nazarene later to embrace and forswear them all.

There had always existed in the East men and women who believed their place in heaven could be bought only by a denial of the earth. They lived in caves or in deserts or on top of pillars, shunning human fellowship and the claims of their own flesh. Chava's own Syrian cook narrated, on some authority, that one ascetic had once gone into a bath of naked women to prove that he was thoroughly impervious to the stirrings of his flesh. Emru, who had been listening to the cook's fable, ascribed another impulse to the ascetic's visit. He himself, ever since his ill-fated oath, had been tethering his balls to some stern talisman, baffling me with his self-control, tortured as I am in mine.

My mother and uncle had presented Christianity to me as a simple creed, one which spoke to the heart through love and charity and selfless service. It was one which saw no distinction between master and slave, priest and layman, God and the world, fallen and damaged as the latter may seem to be. Though severe and unbending in its dismissal of carnal love and wealth and war, the creed was one in which my mother and uncle somewhat freely forged their own laws and churches, my mother's in personal transcendence (with her Yesu and Saints), my uncle's in a rebel's rage against tyranny and injustice. I was never sure why my uncle had broken with the church of his native Lebanon and that of Rome. I believe it had little to do with the big raging questions about Christ's nature; more I think with the simple life he wanted the church and its representatives to follow. Interestingly, though a great devotee, as I too became, of the Saint of the *Confessions*, he did not approve of his *City of God*, which he deemed unfortunate. In all events, through much of my past life, I was also claimed and reclaimed by the sunny deliriums of Emru, my vain wooing of the Muse, and, so, so briefly but indelibly, by the favours of a goddess in Bayroute. Throughout, the enigma of an oracle marking my birth continued to steer and waylay my life.

During our stay in the city, Yonah had pointed to the imposing complex of government buildings called the *Hebdomon*, where emperors are crowned by the Patriarch of the day. He said that a hermit by the name of John used to live on top of a column in that complex scores of years earlier and that from time to time that column was occupied by an ascetic dweller. A column outside the city on the western side of the Bosporus, Yonah added, had been inhabited by a celebrated monk of a previous century, a Saint Daniel, who lived on that column for some forty years until his death at an advanced age. Now, the top of the column was occupied by an ascetic called Elias.

With the Theodosian walls behind us, we rode until we could see the column in the distance. It was a moderately high structure on top of which stood a small shelter, first erected, Yonah told us, for the benefit of Saint Daniel by the Emperor of the time after the stylite had almost frozen to death during a snowstorm. It was yet a small affair since neither the saint nor the space on top of the column would allow for a more lavish structure. That same monk, Yonah said people believe, was responsible for holding back a huge fire which had claimed the city for a week. The fire petered out only when the saint, to whom the people fleeing the blaze appealed, prayed for God to make the fire cease.

When we arrived at the foot of the column, the hermit was sitting outside his shelter listening to a crowd of pilgrims, mostly women, craning their necks and raising their voices to speak to him. There was a ladder laid on the ground near the column. But, though at a height of some fifteen steps, the stylite could hear and be heard quite clearly, the stillness of the wind helping the exchange. The women became silent when they saw us. Observing our foreignness and the token military escort we had with us, they timidly withdrew a space, allowing us the privilege of talking to the hermit with little interruption.

I greeted the hermit on behalf of Emru, my king, I explained. He, a balding man with a slight, sun-scorched frame and huge eyes, nodded courteously. I further made clear that we were here to learn and be inspired on our journey to our lands, thereafter through life. We hoped he would not mind our untutored questioning. I had a hundred questions to put to him, not all philosophical or mystical, some involving mundane things about eating and drinking and defecating on such an elevation. But I cried out, making an effort not to sound false or sarcastic:

'Give us of your lofty wisdom, O dweller of the heights, fellow of the angels!'

'Wisdom can also walk on the earth, for the lizard and the tortoise may not be deemed less wise than the sparrow and the eagle. And I am not yet high or worthy enough to hang out with angels!' His voice was ethereal but steady and penetrating. It had a note of good-natured humour and disarming humility, which made me assume more earnestly the posture of a pilgrim and supplicant.

However, unable to rid myself of my inquisitive drift and feeling I was in my element, I asked him, after translating his response to Emru, why he had chosen to live his life in this peculiar way.

'What other way is less peculiar?' he rejoined.

'Well, you could have led the life of a monk in a monastery. It would have given you a life of peaceful contemplation and uninterrupted service,' I answered, thinking of my uncle and jumping ahead of Emru, whose humour of the moment remained phlegmatic.

'Perhaps that kind of peace, that kind of activity, within fat walls no longer draws God's ear. The walls' occupants presume they are God's elect. They presume too much. I wish to woo the divine ear with my wind-buffeted soul! But maybe it's the rich diet of the monastery that doesn't suit my constitution! After all, a stuffed belly is the darkest dungeon to the soul. And then there's that hard roof above their heads. I can't stand roofs! Nor books! Not anymore!'

'Then we shall be content with your words alone, for words may yet heal the sick at heart,' said Emru, half-stepping out of his apathy and humouring him, having given ear to my translation and been drawn to the pull of words.

'The serpent of brass Moses fashioned for the healing of the people cured all without speaking!'

'But,' I barged in, asking leave of Emru as I knew the biblical story, 'that machine, the snake, was made to possess all virtue. We are men, made of flesh...and *need* words!'

'The fewer the words the better! Was not the thief on the Cross saved by a single utterance, while Judas, the Apostle, who was full of his own words and those of the silver-tongued count, lost all? The world is already too clogged with words...and few use the runes of the heart!'

'A few words, runes, from you may be enough. They may give us the remedy, the knowledge, we seek!' I did not wish to argue further, though I had the appetite for it. I hoped I was speaking for Emru's needs.

'The knowledge of the Cross is etched in the pain of the Cross. If men are not taught by silence they will not be taught by speech. However, I say to you, both, be no slaves to glory, but become all flame!'

'That's a bit tough, isn't it? And may take a while!' I said, Emru's smile allowing me the reins for the free run I wanted.

'Not in the divine kiln; the switch would be instantaneous!'

'But we, made of flesh, hate to see our essence melted away before our journey is done, before our ship has tamed the waves!'

'Your essence is not of the flesh. First find your true ship then worry about the waves!'

'I hate ships, save those of the desert, cleaving sand. But, for the sake of the argument, what load, if any, should a man place on the back, the deck, of the ship you speak of?' Emru asked, and I interpreted back.

'One loaf of heaven and the hunger for another!'

'Isn't that too little, or, perhaps, too much?' Emru persisted, light-heartedly, beginning to enjoy the intellectual swordplay.

'Why should you feed your burdens and forfeit your buoyancy? The body is a slave, the soul a sovereign! Make your body lighter with the bread of heaven and your ship swifter with the breath of God.'

'And the hunger...is it of the soul or the loins?' Emru queried, less playfully.

'There was a man who ate a lot of food and remained hungry, and another who ate little and was satisfied. The one who ate much and was still hungry received a greater reward than he who ate little and was satisfied. Such are the ways of God, and of Love!'

'So it's best for a man to resign himself to the pains of unrequited love!' I translated.

'And to the joys. The untouched is stroked. The master is held by the slave. The wounds are revealed to the seekers!'

'And the wounds have been revealed to you?'

'I'm still unfit to be given that honour!'

'But you carry your own wounds, I suppose!'

'These are but scratch marks. Their shine fades like grass under a blazing sun, unlike the wounds of the privileged!'

'Who are the privileged, and what have they done to be granted the honour?'

'I can only repeat. They're those who've entered the roaring furnace and cooled it with their dew. They've been to Egypt and given food when famine held the sceptre. They've been to the stubborn sea and taught it wisdom with a staff. They've been into the pit and tutored its wild beasts to fast. They've been to the harsh desert and made it blossom with pillars.'

'Too many prophets, too many saints, too many paths! Who should a man follow? Which path should he take?'

'The prophets, the saints, are but as different trees bearing different fruit. But they're all nourished by the same water, which feeds every human heart. And all the roads come together in the end.'

'But, again, that takes time!'

'As base metals are rarefied in the divine Kiln, so in God's garden roses blossom to the touch and never shed their holy blush. And yet, Father John the Short had to water a dry piece of wood for three years in the desert. He stayed with it until it came to life and bore the leaf and fruit of patience!'

'Perhaps mine has!' said Emru, by way of concluding the interview rather than through sheer conceit.

'Our age is a storm. It loves nothing more than uprooting trees and hammering on brickwork. It may be the vanity of that brickwork which whips its fury!'

'Ah, that's a good image, the storm, uprooting in order to plant change!' Emru reflected. Perhaps he was recalling the scene of a desert flash flood in one of his poems. Might the long-submerged poet come up for a gulp of sunlit air?

I was impressed with the stylite's ability to argue using some of the words of his fellow sky-seekers – simple or arcane as they are. He himself, having referred to books he had lost patience with, may have been a cleric or a scholar. I did not know what I should offer him in return for his troubles, knowing he would be offended by the offer of money. I said, 'Your leather shirt is already in tatters, and winter is not far off. May I give you my cloak for it to be blest upon your shoulders?'

''If we wear the heavenly robe, we shall not be found naked'!' he said dreamily.

'And what if wicked men rather than the rushing wind rob us of that robe?' Emru suddenly interposed. I had given up on gaining more of his attention and was trying to conclude the interview.

'Why does man trouble himself in a house that is not his own? Father Makarius, while in Egypt, came upon a man looting the few worldly goods he possessed, putting them on an ass's back. Father Makarius went up to him and helped him load the stuff on the back of the animal. He then bade the thief farewell with a good cheer, saying, 'We have brought nothing into this world, and we can take nothing out of it, the Lord gave and the Lord has taken away, blessed be the name of the Lord.''

'Should a man do nothing to stop wickedness or keep it at bay?' I asked, my interest renewed, given license by Emru's resurgence.

'A band of wicked men descended on Father John the Persian. He brought a basin to wash their feet. The men were baffled and began to do penance.'

'The world is a basin, one that overflows with blood. I do not see how men, good or wicked, can be transformed so suddenly and by one lone act of what you call goodness,' Emru said, regaining his impatience, and cynicism.

'Look into your own memories, old and fresh, and you shall see that very *transformation* having come to pass, *coming* to pass. But, Ah, I agree. There's much confusion, much *seeming* confusion. When the heart of one Abba became filled with peace, he became too content with it. He thought about it. Soon he was praying for war to revisit him. He knew his soul needed the anguish that had disciplined him. So he begged the Lord to give him 'strength for the fight', the fight within!'

I admired the man's honesty and doggedness, typical of the ascetics whom he echoed and seemed to outdo, subtle in his artlessness.

'What of *my* fight, will it continue?' Emru asked. I knew he was troubled by the choices and decisions he had to make or were being made for him.

'As long as you remain a fugitive from God!'

'God doesn't interest me. He's too vague and remote. I don't *see* him!'

I feared the force of these words on the hermit, but he responded, nonplussed, 'Be on the watch, and He'll come to you!'

'We've no need for one another. Your God will deem me fallen anyway!'

'The fallen mourners are more blessed than those who have not fallen and are not mourning over themselves! God Himself descends. He descends to the humble as a stream flows down from the hill into the valley.'

'So I should start mourning for myself to be in his good books! Nay, I'm a warrior and, laughing, shall claim my victory!'

'Even so. You may be a fugitive from heaven, but the dice may roll to your benefit. And your benefit may be other than the one you think it is. God himself is a hunter. He stalks with a fishing rod, His hook a cross, His bait His own flesh!'

Emru was content to leave the hermit with that image of the deity as hunter and quarry. But as we bade farewell to the lone, sun-and-star-scorched man on top of the column and retreated, my neck stiff, my jaw aching, Elias murmured, rather merrily, to Emru or to me I did not know, 'Be a flame, even when the flood comes. Even when it shall crowd your throat with its silences. Even…' But then the women, who had simmered at the periphery of our banter with their winged idol, surged towards the base of the column raising their voices to be given as much hearing as the foreigners had been privileged with.

As the sky dweller was being reclaimed by his devotees we said goodbye to Yonah. His eyes were moist as he embraced us, repeating that he was sending the *Adara* after her new freight had been loaded at the Golden Horn to wait for us at Smyrna. There she would remain however long it took us to cover the distance from Ankara to the coast. The ship would then carry us to Pieria for our suggested appointment with John of Ephesus at Antioch. The kindly Chava, our tireless hostess of the previous weeks, had prepared for us, when we had called upon her to bid her farewell, enough bundles of meat pies and stuffed vine leaves and aubergines, sweets and dried fruits, to provide for a journey to China. Again, Yonah assured us that he would continue to search for Yahya and send us word about him.

DEATH AT ANKARA

I invoke the Saints of the *Confessions* and the memres and the power of the prophecy and all the forces of life to help steady my hand as the wings of death buffet these last pitiful pages.

We entered the town of Ankara eight days after our departure from Rome. Our journey to that town had been dictated by the Emperor's wish for us to meet John the Cappadocian. As Praetorian Prefect of the East, he was in the town on a business related to reports of Iraqi troop movements on the Syrian borders. As the Emperor himself had hinted, Al-Munzer had picked up a quarrel with Al-Hareth, Rome's client-king of Syria, over a piece of pastureland near Palmyra curiously called here *Strata*. Rome had already sent two envoys, Yonah had told us. One was an army officer dispatched to study the military options. The other was an administrator of the Royal Treasury sent to judge whether the dispute could be resolved by Roman gold. Apparently, Al-Munzer was providing his Persian patron with a pretext to break a peace treaty the Persian king himself had concluded with Justinian some eight years earlier. The spectre of war hung over the heads of men though it had its source in their very souls, or at least the soulless ambitions of a few.

To reach Ankara, we had to travel on a rolling landscape of hills and rivers and valleys dotted with beautiful hamlets and monasteries, castles and ancient settlements, to which we did not afford to pay due reverence, and which I cannot pay now. At the entrance to the town, we were met by an official who seemed to have been awaiting our arrival. He told us that the Prefect had left a day earlier for Edessa to insure that its defences were adequate. He further handed Emru a letter advising him to continue with his journey south without delay. He also delivered unto him a suit worked in golden and silver threads. As a Phylarch of the Emperor, Emru was requested to wear it without delay. It was a codicil to his investiture.

However, as we stood outside the gate of the Governor's palace, a mounted soldier galloping through the courtyard brought his horse to a steaming halt beside us. He announced that he was carrying an urgent dispatch to the Prefect of the East from the Governor of Edessa. A sentry standing outside hurriedly escorted him up the steps and into the interior of the building. The face of the official speaking to us turned red. I pretended not to have noticed. As I turned to convey my suspicion to Emru, I saw his great eyes widening, seized by some scene behind my shoulder. Then I saw his lips giving tongue to the astonishment of his eyes. 'Kubeysa!' he murmured. I turned, and saw the profile of a tall, slightly stooping man emerge from some exit behind the palace. He was being helped by three attendants, the four clad in flowing *abas*. One of them, a man of a slight build, bent down to assist the older man to get on the back of a grey horse. I did not see clearly the face of the older man, now lifted into his saddle and ready to trot off. But the slightly built man who had been assisting him happened to turn his gaze towards us as he was adjusting his *aba* before riding his own horse. 'Elba!' my lips moved on their own accord, my eyes smitten, unbelieving. The man, obviously caught unawares, quickly turned his gaze away and spun into the saddle, the others following, spinning or clambering, into their own saddles. Fleet as he was, I caught a flash of a stabbing eye and a furtive, sneering grin, one of spite and triumph, a murderer's grin, on his vile features. And then they were gone, the clanking of the hooves of their horses on the cobbles hammering into my head like a shower of nails, the flash in the eye like the quill of a porcupine rattling in my heart.

The encounter left me swaying upon a precipice. The party of four were of the Asad tribe. Elba was the assassin who killed Emru's father, and Kubeysa, the Asads' emissary who had petitioned Emru for a disingenuous peace after the murder! Or so I had come to conclude, wishing to absolve Emru of his own imprudence!

Now, though, Emru seemed unmoved, dismissing the men's presence as a non-event. Perhaps they had come to beg for money, he said. But I was far more mistrustful, and worried. Here were murderers and apologists for murder, my early sympathy for Kubeysa's peace mission eroding with the same naiveté that had created it. Here they were, I thought, allies of the Persians, curiously at ease at the heart of Roman rule of the East. What robes of fakery were they wearing? What foul brew were they stirring?

But Emru was in high spirits. He seemed to have reined in all doubt. He had been a fool in the past, he said, but now he had a 'fool*proof* plan', he added. The pack mules were close behind him, the Imperial seal of his appointment in his belt, the Phylarchate suit upon his arm, the *Adara* at anchor or gliding in the Bosporus raring to give his hopes a wind-favoured lateen sail.

So he turned to head for Smyrna, at some three hundred miles to the east and south. Ankara did not exercise any more hold on his mind. After all, the town's only landmark, next to the Governor's palace, was the church of Saint Paul. The locals, Yonah had told me, believe that the Saint had visited their town during his travels through Galatia. They also claim that another great Christian icon, Saint Peter, had earlier blessed their town with his holy footfalls. When I reported this to Emru he laughed and declared himself as yet another 'Christian' idol gracing the town since he too was on a 'Christian' mission. When we had earlier ridden past a building that looked more like a pagan temple than the basilica into which it had been converted, he noted that the pagan gods had their way of travelling through time, be it under new names. I asked what manner or name he would choose to travel by in the company of King Time. A 'fellow king?' I suggested. 'Perhaps just a traveller, a *sa'luk*, if Time was generous enough to allow me my feet. But I don't know if that madly-galloping mate was the best of fellow-travellers. You should do better, treading more cautiously, and craftily,' he quipped.

We lodged for the night at an inn recommended by the official, who again petitioned Emru to put the suit on. When Emru did so at the inn later in the day, the suit flowed upon his magnificent body, shimmering in gold and silver. A pin perhaps carelessly left at its neck caught at his skin and drew blood. 'A small prick for a big kingdom,' he joked.

However, the cut hurt and became inflamed. That night Emru, in escalating pain and fever, but with a mind somewhat affected by the encounter with the stylite, was paid a visit by his long-estranged Jinn-Muse. She was in a sombre and cynical mood, with which he tussled and prevailed upon, composing the following verses:

What is a man? A hooded hawk?
A caterpillar's dream?
A fly delirious on some dregs?
A gurgle in a stream?

A whirl of dust in a desert?
An ever-creaking wheel?
A canter on a dying star?
A wound that will not heal?

I've been all that, entwined with life,
At one with all her moods –
The howling dust, the heaving breasts,
And all their sisterhoods!

In the morning, we set off, Emru insisting on travel despite the fever that had driven its claws into his body. He was hoping to reach Smyrna and the *Adara* in less than ten days. 'Blue vomit' or not, he would then disembark near Antioch, he hoped. I was hoping for a stopover at Bayroute, my yearning to return to the city of my love and education being all consuming.

The official who brought the suit insisted on escorting us, pack mules following. But as we reached a hillock, just outside the city, Emru crumpled in his saddle. I eased him down and laid him at the foot of the hillock. I appealed to the official to gallop back to the city to fetch a doctor. He went at a slow trot. He never came back.

An hour or so passed. Emru's breathing quickened, then his pulse waned. His mouth became dry and his pain relentless. Yet, despite his increasingly laboured breath, he extemporised the following verses, his Jinn-Muse reasserting her sombre mood as she was bidding him farewell, he hanging on to his natural defiance:

A claw…descends…or crawls within
To rip…a man's…entrails
And like…a storm…ransack his…deck
And tear…his…puffed-up sails.

The man…who wants…to ride…the wind
And toss…to earth his…cloak
Desires Death to use…his blade
But in…a…single stroke!

For Death…has loitered with…intent
Knitting a…yellow shroud,
His needles in the man's…green veins
An insult to…the proud!

If Death…is game…as is this man,
The contest…will be brief…
The man…will get his…flying ride,
And Death…the fallen leaf!

Then he said, 'I remember…a pearling diver. I was…perhaps seven… or eight…at the time. My uncle…Salamah took me…on board a…ship he owned. He had a…fleet of them…ships…in the Gulf. I remember…I was sad…sad…at first…to leave Najd and…leave you. Do you…remember? It is so…vivid to me now. I wonder…why it should be so…here…and… now…so far…so far…from the Gulf…so far…from Najd. The diver… never came up. I waited for his…glistening…shaven…black head to… pop up…the turtle shell clips…in his…nostrils…his hand…holding the…oyster basket. They…he…never did. Perhaps he…strayed…from the line…and…was…carried away…by the current. Perhaps he…swam away…under the water…with his catch. They have huge…lungs…these divers. They expand…these lungs…with their ache for…their own lost… green kingdoms. Perhaps…perhaps he was attacked…and…eaten…by a shark. But the water was…not stained. It was not. I remember. For days…months…afterwards I kept thinking about what…might have happened…to him. Did he make it…back to Africa to rule there…a king…with a crown of…pearls round his head? Or was he…snatched away by…a…mermaid, and…lived…with her in a…cave? Aeons of… incandescent bliss…forever…perhaps? An old…sailor there…one from Iraq…I think…told me a…story of a…king…a king…who searched for…the secret of…everlasting life and found it…in a plant at the… bottom of the sea…only for it…to be taken away…taken away by…a… serpent while he dozed. You may have heard it yourself in…Lebanon or Iraq. You have been to…Iraq…have you not?'

I said that I had been to his uncle's tribal land. It had by then shrunk away from the Gulf waters. He continued with his musings, I wishing him to stop to save his strength.

'Anyway…I kept thinking…of the pearling diver…I'm thinking of him…now…He seems to be so…important…now! What do you think…happened…to him?'

'We used to play story-telling when we were children. Do you remember? So here we are at it again. Your mermaid story is charming. Its finish is perhaps the best for the diver, short of homecoming, which is also excellent, but challenging as all homecomings are. The tale of the king and the snake is interesting as well. Sad, but true to life, for all time perhaps. But I'd vote for the mermaid story. I'm sure you agree that the love of a woman, real or imagined, is cubits above the trials of a philosopher-king weighed down by the yoke of rule.'

'The love of...*women*,' he sought to correct me, grinning faintly. 'In any case...we have a...woman here...in the story...an un...usual woman...a mermaid. Her tail may...however...get in the way. It might offer no way at all! That is unless...the diver himself...became...a merman. Still, the crown...the...turban...the...headache...of a kingdom is...a temptation...a torment...a...madness...when the man...wearing it...tries to...knock a hundred...hundreds...of squabbling tribes into one...one...nation! The great Abu Karib suc...cee...ded in...this some...what...a hundred...more?...years...ago? The Elephant Road from...Zafar to...Mecca still stands as...proof. The Ka'ba wearing Kenda's black...Would that it...could...wear the black...the infinite colours of...*poetry*? Might Al-Munzer...make...the Arabs...one? Will the Persians...wait for him to...roll out all...his dreams? Will the Romans allow...us to...roll out ours...we...underlings? Samuel...what would you do? Where are you? And...Al-Ward? And Hend? Ah, the snake in...the...stylite's...story...and the...other...story. I believe he was right...the snake...in stripping Man of his...delusions. Already I feel his...coils tightening...round my...own...fancies. Let it...be so!'

'You have no delusions, my king,' I said desperately. 'You never had! Fancies are another matter. They become a poet.'

'I've had...several...of...the...first sort. And...you know...that. But do not...call me...king. You've not...forgotten my...name...have you...you old yarn-spinner...word-bender?'

The official who had accompanied us to the hillock then abandoned us had casually said that a young lady of a foreign noble family had died at that same spot and was buried on the hillock. He had indicated her grave at the top of the elevation carpeted with six-pointed yellow flowers. Emru had expressed interest in the lady's story.

He now said, 'I shall call on her...tonight! There may not...be a canopy of...silk...or stars above...our heads. But the turf will be... roof enough...the earth a...steady bed...the flowers garlands...the caterpillars wedding guests. I shall promise her eternal devotion. That is unless...another comely woman is...buried...next to us. But...until that time...our bones will make better...music than the...choir of... Saint Sophia.' Then he turned with his gaze towards the grave of the woman further up the hill, and extemporised the following verses:

We were...but strangers...you and I.
Apart we lived...abreast...we lie.
A rendezvous...decreed...by Chance
As she...performed...her...random dance;
This hill...to be...our home...and mart,
From whose...grey hold...we shall...not part.
And here I shall...perfect my rhymes
For you...my queen...of future times!

'No! The lady should fear no...competition. But I will not...deny her if she...wants to have a...threesome,' he said, smiling in his pain.

Then he said, 'I shall leave...you to your...pen and...paper. But may you...journey beyond them...to...some happiness in this...world. You have been so... unjustly...shackled to...my...misfortunes...my ineptitude. Ah! All the men who died! I...wonder...whether your... father...got my...father's...dying wish...right. Why the son with... the...mask...of...stone? May your...Arabs...my...Arabs...be...ever... cursed...blessed...with...impotent...kings!'

Then he bade me divest him of the Phylarch's suit and clothe him in an old *aba*, which I fetched from a box on one of the mules. He also asked me to dispose of the Imperial decree or, in a second breath, take it to Antioch and give it to John of Ephesus, and listen to what he might say. But only if I felt inclined to do so and ventured that far. He wanted Theodora's plan to be conveyed to John, who might take it further by other means. And should I ever return to Arabia, he wanted me to pass on his love and gratitude and regret to his sister Hend and Al-Ward and Samuel. The signet ring of Kenda, which he alone and without my help, which I could not give, he eased from his finger, wishing it to be conveyed without its nightmares to Hend. Then a fit of bloody coughing seized him. It did not let go until it had sucked his life away.

After the labour came the calm. Emru lay on his left side, curled on the ground, as though he was bestriding the winged mare of Death, spurring her on. Pain-free and taut and handsome still, he had his large eyes staring outwards, his luxurious black hair, wet from his past exertions, pushed back as if buffeted by the winds of eternity as he sped into their vague embraces.

He had escaped and triumphed over pain and betrayal. Old age would never lay a crooked finger on him. The vengeance he had sought he had made redundant; the kingdom he had ventured to restore he had outgrown. He had shed his mortal garb and donned the raiment of myth. No more would he need to trek the desert paths and clamber over the brooding dunes to solicit the approval of men and the favours of women. His venture will be embellished with a thousand golden threads by every generation. His verses will be recited by the amorous and the forlorn, the weary and the hopeful, the vulgar and the learned. They will be recited around campfires and lovers' Ka'bas, and in cells and seminaries. They will be engraved on lovers' keepsakes and emblazoned on the shields of warriors, scornful of war though he was.

At least that is what I think will happen, though, of course, nothing of this may come to pass, and his story and poetry may well fade into the Oblivion he had deified and perhaps feared.

And yet beyond the pain and wonder of dying men, will the God of his mother or the gods of his father stand up in their old-time halls to receive him, weaned from the brilliance and brittleness of his flesh, into their heaven or hell? Or would Oblivion, blissfully shambolic and non-judgemental, be the supreme arbiter and the final host and comforter? Or, rather, would he, the poet, having breathed his own life-force into the pompous transience of his world and times, take his own place among the gods as another life-giver and immortal? Let the centuries rush and lurch and tumble above his grave. Let them boast and sneer and cast out. His words shall hoist their saddle onto the back of Time itself and dig their heels into its flanks. They will not – let me plead with my scorched throat and my dying pen – be thrown off by the speed of the flight or awed by the fleeting horizons.

Take pride, my king, my brother and nemesis, that you have gone into the earth with your bloom tried but unblemished and your daring voice loud and joyous in the air. The kings you have seen and those who have feared your recklessness and wild dreams, the mandates and dominions you have won and lost, mocked and bungled, will shrivel and sink into the hissing sand. Those that will continue to live will breathe through the seasons because they were touched by your laughing fury and etched into your sprinting poems.

When a man dies, barriers tumble down before him. Loosened from space, he becomes everywhere. Delivered from the sundial, he grasps all hours. By bodily fading away, he assumes all bodies. By moving back, he draws nearest.

As the cold wind of Galatia swept over my head and rattled my ribs, I reckoned that the pastures of Najd were now lush with *basat* and *khitmah* and *naima*. Children will be running around after the goats and the foals and the butterflies. Maidens, fresh and untroubled, will be dipping their dainty toes into the pool at Jouljoul, their virginal breasts scorning the stars and scorching the passions of the lads spying on them from behind palm trees or in their dreams.

Ah, no more will the fragrant breeze of Najd brush your cheek as you ride your white mare. No more will the eyes and hearts of the women of Najd and the Hejaz and the Yemen flutter or dance or stand in judgement as you breach their sanctuaries and submit yourself to their beatitude or banishment.

But where are these women now? Where are their sweet throats to raise their keening, dark and arrow-sharp, against the sky? Where are their slender, nimble hands to sweep away the indifferent blueness and spread the cloth of mourning over the widowed, re-wedded, earth? Where are they, the fond women, to scatter the funereal ash in the wind, streaked, riotous, with the silken wings of their shorn, long-treasured tresses?

I raised my face to the sky, my jaw tense and shaking like a fist, bruised, to punch a hole into the sullen mantle of the god who toys with the sun and the moon and the multitudes beneath them as they snatch their gulps of life from each others' throats. Only a pitiable groan slunk out.

The moment I heaped the last scoop of earth upon his grave, a flock of wild geese flying southwards, passed over my head, the beats of their stout white wings faint but regular and resolute. In the clouding blue sky, they seemed like a gigantic arrowhead released from some titanic bowman in the autumnal north. A lone shriek from one of the birds rang out in my ears as a dirge and a lampoon.

Is this why Fatimah of the Taghlebs went into labour in Al-Sharaf and rejoiced over the birth of him, only for his full-grown body to fertilise a hillock in far-flung Galatia some thirty and more years later?

I did not want to leave him having been so long fettered to him as a drunkard is fettered to his wine or a lover to his mistress or a slave to his master. A part of me, much of me, lay under that freshly dug heap of hunched earth. My youth and mission and a life of adventure I could not have lived without him. In truth, he may have been the pouring of water, heavenly or subterranean, which jolted a seed within me into flower so that I might attend to its seasons. A chained, untrained gardener, I mutely mutinied within my irons, albeit taking secret pride in their clang and glint and durability.

I did not want to leave him, my better, harder, braver self, in that pit. There was a hole in my heart swelling up to my mouth with the taste of alien dust. And yet, strangely, sickeningly, I felt relieved. It was as if a burden had lifted from my shoulders. Now that the rosebush had suddenly, inexplicably, withered, the attendant did not need to stand guard with the water jug in his hand. Now that the galley had sunk, the bondman could leave his oar and swim back to his native shore. Now that the tavern had forever closed shop, the drunkard could turn to more sober pursuits, as might a lover driven from the fragranced door limp away with a dart in his heart. Now that the Idol had succumbed to the earth, the worshipper could seek new gods or forswear all.

I am done with quests, whether those ordained by gods or dreamt up by men. The pen I carried for years like a cross I shall break anon; the china paper I have long wrapped myself with like a winding sheet I shall consign to a crypt. Both have served their purpose. I have served mine.

This concludes the saga of the King Emru Al-Qais of Kenda, who was born in Najd and died and was buried on a hill outside the city of Ankara in the year 540, written by his subject and chronicler, devotee and friend, Jaber Ben Rabi'a Ben 'Amr, who must now learn to live in freedom and silence.

POSTSCRIPT

MY NAME IS JULIAN SON OF THEODORUS OF BERYTUS. I WRITE UNPROMPTED
TO SEAL A CHRONICLE WRITTEN BY A MAN TO WHOM I AM JOINED BY
GRATITUDE AND AFFECTION.

THE MAN GEBER BEN RABI HAD COME TO BERYTUS IN THE YEAR 551 OF
OUR LORD. HE ARRIVED SOME TWO OR THREE MONTHS AFTER THE GREAT
TREMOR WHICH TOGETHER WITH THE GIANT WAVE HAD RAVAGED OUR
CITY AND KILLED MY PARENTS ALONG WITH TWO THIRDS OF THE CITY'S
INHABITANTS. I WAS PLUCKED OUT OF THE RUBBLE OF OUR HOUSE THE
BROKEN BODY OF MY MOTHER PROTECTING ME FROM A FALLEN BEAM BY
A BAND OF LOOTERS. LUCKILY IN THE CIRCUMSTANCES TWO OF THEM
SPED WITH ME TO AN ENCAMPMENT OF SLAVERS ON THE SLOPES OF THE
MOUNTAIN RANGE EAST OF THE CITY. BY THIS THEY SAVED ME FROM THE
CUFF OF THE WAVE THAT FOLLOWED THE QUAKE. FROM THE MOUNTAINSIDE
I WATCHED WITH HORROR AND ANGUISH THE DEADLY SURGE THAT FINISHED
THE FELONY OF THE EARTH. THERE THE CITY WAS TO LIE DIMINISHED TO A
SWAMP OF DEBRIS ITS MARBLE BALCONIES AND REDBRICK ROOFS MANGLED
ITS UNIVERSITY AND SCHOOLS OVERWHELMED ITS NOBLE PEOPLE REDUCED
TO FLOATING CORPSES ABJECT BEGGARS AND MURDEROUS BRUTES.

MY BENEFACTOR THE MAN NAMED GEBER SPARED NO EFFORT TO
TRACE ME. HE HAD ENQUIRED FROM THE FEW SURVIVING NEIGHBOURS
ABOUT MY PARENTS AND WAS SHOWN THEIR GRAVES NEARBY. I WAS TOLD
HE HAD MOURNED BITTERLY AND LONG UPON THEM. BUT WHEN HE WAS
INFORMED THAT THEIR ONLY CHILD HAD SURVIVED HE SOUGHT ME OUT
WITH UNBENDING RESOLVE. HE WAS A MAN OF MEANS AND TACT AND WAS
ABLE TO TRACK ME DOWN TO MY FIRST 'SAVIOURS'. THESE LED HIM TO THE
SLAVERS TO WHOM THEY HAD SOLD ME AND WHO IN TURN HAD SOLD ME TO
AN OLIVE GROWER IN AKKARE.

FOLLOWING THE QUAKE AND THE DELUGE CIVIL ORDER HAD BROKEN DOWN
ALMOST THROUGHOUT THE REGION. FAMILIES DISPERSED. AFFILIATIONS
DISSOLVED. VOWS MELTED. I WAS HAPPY TO BE DELIVERED OVER TO HIM
OUTLANDISH AS HE SEEMED. HE HANDED OVER A BLOATED BAG OF COINS
TO THE OLIVE GROWER IN A DETACHED AND CEREMONIAL MANNER. YET
HE WAS A PERSON OF GREAT COMPASSION. A TOTAL STRANGER HE CLASPED
ME TO HIS CHEST WETTING MY CHEEKS WITH HIS TEARS. HE HAD HASTENED
TO BERYTUS FROM MESOPOTAMIA BREAKING HIS GOLDEN CHAINS HE SAID
AFTER HEARING OF THE EARTHQUAKE TO SEEK OUT MY FATHER. HE HAD
BEEN A STUDENT OF HIS MANY YEARS EARLIER.

283

I HAD ALREADY BEEN VERY PROUD OF MY FATHER THE ILLUSTRIOUS THEODORUS. HE WAS CELEBRATED IN OUR CITY AND EMPIRE AS A GREAT TEACHER AND JURIST. DURING HIS LIFE HE WAS REGULARLY VISITED BY OFFICIALS AND DIGNITARIES AND WAS TOO OFTEN PREOCCUPIED BY THEM AND BY HIS STUDIES AND TEACHING. EVEN SO HE GAVE ME AND MY MOTHER MUCH CARE AND LOVE WHENEVER HE HAD THE TIME. I MYSELF WAS A PRACTICAL BENEFICIARY OF HIS POSITION AS I STUDIED LAW AT OUR FAMOUS LAW SCHOOL NOW RESTORED IN STRUCTURE THOUGH NOT IN STATURE.

THE SCHOOL WAS MY FATHER'S GREAT LOVE AMIDST WHOSE COLLAPSED COLUMNS HE MIGHT HAVE PREFERRED TO DIE RATHER THAN UNDER THE BEAMS OF HIS VILLA. GEBER WAS TO ADD FURTHER DEPTHS TO MY YOUTHFUL ADMIRATION OF MY FATHER AND PRIDE IN HIM. THIS HE DID BY INTIMATING TO ME MANY DETAILS OF MY FATHER'S LEARNING MUNIFICENCE WIT AND PIETY. GEBER HAD ALSO KNOWN MY DEAR MOTHER WHOM HE DESCRIBED AS THE MOST GRACEFUL CHARITABLE AND VIRTUOUS OF WOMANKIND.

GEBER WAS A MAN WITH TOO MANY MEMORIES WHICH SEEMED TO WEIGH HEAVILY ON HIS HEART. OVER THE YEARS THESE BALLASTS SURFACED FROM TIME TO TIME TO LINGER ON OCCASION BRIEFLY AT OTHER TIMES MORE LEISURELY ON HIS LIPS. THEY FED THOUGH NEVER TO FULLNESS MY IRKSOME CURIOSITY. 'I WAVER BETWEEN BEING A SILENT MONK AND A BLATHERING OLD SOLDIER' HE WOULD SAY. BETWEEN HIS SILENCES AND EFFUSIONS I CAME TO KNOW THAT HE HAD SERVED AS A LIFE COMPANION AND CHRONICLER TO A KING OF AN ARABIAN PEOPLE CALLED THE KENDES. HE HAD TRAVELLED WITH THAT KING TO OUR ILLUSTRIOUS ROME WITH THE DREAM OF UNITING THE ARAB PEOPLES UNDER ROMAN PATRONAGE. THE ARABIAN KING HAD BEEN UNSEATED BY ANOTHER ARABIAN PEOPLE WHO HAD MURDERED THE KING'S FATHER AND WERE ALLIES OF THE PERSIANS. IN ROME, THE TWO MEN SOUGHT THE HELP OF HIS EMINENCE THE GREAT IMPERATOR CAESAR FLAVIUS JUSTINIANUS AND HER MAJESTY THE MOST SAINTLY EMPRESS THEODORA...BOTH NOW DECEASED AND MUCH MOURNED. THE GREAT JUSTINIANUS WAS OF COURSE THE MOST AUGUST AND MOST WISE SOVEREIGN WHO HAD EMPLOYED MY FATHER ALONG WITH A SELECT COMMITTEE OF EMINENT JURISTS INCLUDING THE RENOWNED TRIBONIANUS AND THEOPHILUS TO COMPILE THE CORPUS JURIS CIVILIS. THIS WAS THE GREAT CANON OF LAWS PARTS OF WHICH I WAS TO READ AND PROUDLY QUOTE FROM DURING MY LEGAL STUDY AND FLEDGLING LEGAL PRACTICE.

GEBER AND HIS KING HAD LEFT ROME CARRYING THE PLEDGES OF THE PURPLE COURT BUT ALSO SCARRED BY ITS INTRIGUES SO SAID GEBER. SURELY IF THESE TOOK PLACE THE DEVOUT JUSTINIANUS HAD NO KNOWLEDGE OF THEM. A YOUNG COMPANION OF THEIRS WAS SNATCHED IN ROME AND

POSSIBLY MURDERED A SECRET HISTORY BURIED WITH HIM. GEBER WAS TO BURY HIS OWN KING ON A HILL IN GALATIA. THE DREAM OF UNITING THE ETERNALLY FEUDING ARABIAN PEOPLES WAS ALSO INTERRED WITH THE KING WHO WAS ALSO A MAKER OF VERSES. ENVOYS OF THE ARABIAN PEOPLE HOSTILE TO THE KING HAD BEEN SEEN IN GALATIA. THEY MAY HAVE BEEN SENT TO TURN THE EMPEROR'S HEART AWAY FROM GEBER'S KING PROMISING A BETTER ALLIANCE WITH ROME. BUT SOMEONE IN THE IMPERIAL COURT THOUGH NOT THE EMPEROR AND MOST CERTAINLY NOT THE EMPRESS WHOM GEBER ADMIRED MAY HAVE SEEN IN THE KING'S ENTERPRISE A THREAT INSUFFERABLE.

SUBTLE ARE THE WAYS OF COURTIERS AND FICKLE AND DECEITFUL ARE THEIR PLEDGES. MY OWN FATHER WHOSE WORK ON THE *CORPUS* HAD BROUGHT HIM VERY CLOSE TO THE COURT OFFICIALS WAS NEVER TAINTED BY THEM. THEY SUCCEEDED THOUGH IN USURPING OR CROWDING HIS TIME AND OUR MOMENTS WITH HIM.

GEBER HAD PLEDGED HIS LIFE AND PEN TO THE CAUSE OF HIS ROYAL FRIEND. IN THIS HE SAID HE HAD BEEN 'DRIVEN MORE BY THE POWER OF HUMAN LOVE AND LOYALTY THAN BY ANY OTHER COMMAND'. HE WAS NOW FREE TO LIVE OUT HIS OWN LIFE EVEN THOUGH HIS LIFE HAD JUST BEEN DENIED A MAJOR PURPOSE. NOT TOTALLY FREED YET HE DISEMBARKED AT ANTIOCH TO DELIVER A MESSAGE ON BEHALF OF THE SAINTLY EMPRESS THEODORA AUGUSTA. HE THOUGHT THAT THE PURPOSE OF THE LETTER MIGHT STILL BE ACHIEVED IN SPITE OF THE DEATH OF HIS KING. HE HOPED TO TRAVEL LATER TO BERYTUS WHERE HIS TRUE HEART LAY HE SAID. BUT HE WAS OVERTAKEN BY THE PERSIAN INVASION OF GALATIA AND SYRIA LED BY KOSRO AIDED BY HIS BRUTAL DEPUTY EL-MUNTER OF MESOPOTAMIA. GEBER WAS DRAGGED FROM THE ENVIRONS OF ANTIOCH AND TAKEN TO THE NEW EDESSA IN EASTERN MESOPOTAMIA. THIS WAS A TOWN KOSRO HAD BUILT SOME NINE YEARS EARLIER AND POPULATED WITH THE PEOPLE OF OLD EDESSA.

SPOTTED BY THE WILY PERSIAN FOR HIS KNOWLEDGE OF TONGUES AND COUNTRIES GEBER WAS INVITED TO PURSUE THE STUDY OF PERSIAN ART AND FAITH IN NEW EDESSA. IN LATER YEARS HE BECAME TRUSTED ENOUGH TO BE ALLOWED TO RUN A SUCCESSFUL TRADE IN SILK SPICES AND HORSES WITH ARABIA EVEN WITH OUR ROME. STILL LATER HE WAS BROUGHT CLOSER INTO THE COURT AND TRUST OF KOSRO EVEN AGAINST THE JEALOUSY AND SCHEMING OF THE MURDEROUS EL-MUNTER. AIDED BY THE VETERAN PERSIAN AMBASSADOR IZADH-GOUSHNASP GEBER WAS TO SERVE AS AN AMBASSADOR BETWEEN THE COURTS OF ROME AND KTESEPHON DURING THE LAST TWO YEARS OF HIS LIFE IN NEW EDESSA PLAYING A ROLE IN THE EXCHANGE OF LETTERS AND NEGOTIATIONS WHICH LED TO THE RELATIVE PEACE OF THE FEW YEARS FOLLOWING THE OUTBREAK OF HOSTILITIES.

ALL THE WHILE HE WAS WISHING TO BE RELEASED FROM HIS OBLIGATIONS MUCH THAT HE VALUED SERVICE IN THE CAUSE OF PEACE BETWEEN THE TWO NATIONS. WHEN THE NEWS OF THE QUAKE REACHED HIM IT GAVE HIM THE COURAGE TO PLEAD TO BE DISCHARGED FROM THE KING'S SERVICE. HE NEVERTHELESS PROMISED TO FULFIL TO THE BEST OF HIS ABILITY A MISSION HE HAD BEEN ASSIGNED AS AN ENVOY TO THE ROMAN GOVERNOR OF LAODICIA.

AS DEFINED BY GEBER A TRUE AMBASSADOR IS ONE WHO SERVES THE CAUSE OF PEACE BETWEEN TWO KINGS RATHER THAN THE POWER OF ONE OVER THE OTHER. AS SUCH HIS MISSION IS LOFTIER AND MORE VALUABLE THAN EITHER SOVEREIGN. HE MAY STROKE THE JEWELLED DAGGER IN HIS BELT AS BIDDEN BY HIS MASTER TO IMPRESS HIS HOST. HE MAY ESCORT A CHEST OF GOLDEN SOLIDI TO HELP WIN HIS HOST'S FAVOURS OR SEAL AN AGREEMENT. BUT HE SHOULD NOT ALLOW TERROR TO INFORM HIS PEACE BID OR GREED TO DICTATE IT. NO FLATTERER MUST HE BE TO HIS EMPLOYER BUT AN HONEST COUNSELLOR A RESTRAINT TO HIM WHO LUSTS AFTER WAR AND A SPUR TO HIM WHO BLUSHES BEFORE PEACE. SO GEBER HAD SAID RATHER ORNATELY. BUT HE HAD ALSO ADDED THAT A TRUE AMBASSADOR MAY YET MANOEUVRE HIS KING BY MAKING HIM BELIEVE IN A GREATER GLORY AS A MAKER OF PEACE RATHER THAN AS A CAPTOR OF SCORCHED FIELDS AND HAUNTED CASTLES. THIS GEBER HAD SAID GIVING CREDIT TO HIS TEACHER MY FATHER IN ALL HE HAD SAID.

WITH HIS ACCOUNTS OF OTHER LANDS AND TRADITIONS GEBER EXPANDED ON MY LARGELY LEGALISTIC STUDIES AND ASPIRATIONS. TO THESE I HAD BEEN DRIVEN IF THE TRUTH IS TO BE TOLD MORE BY MY REGARD FOR MY FATHER THAN BY MY OWN LIKING. GEBER'S TALES AND THE VERSES HE RECITED (WHICH I SUSPECT HE MADE UP DESPITE HIS CLAIM THAT HE WAS NO POET) INJECTED INTO MY MIND AND SPEECH A SYMPATHY FOR THE GENTLE ARTS COMPLICATING MY VIEW OF HUMAN NATURE AND REALITY. MY ACADEMIC AND LEGAL ACHIEVEMENTS WERE QUITE MODEST AND DESPITE MY BEST EFFORTS I DID NEVER DEVELOP THE APTNESS FOR THE LEGAL PROFESSION I WAS EXPECTED TO HAVE AS MY FATHER'S SON. I AM ASHAMED TO CONFESS THAT AN OLD LADY WHO SOUGHT MY OPINION ON A LEGAL MATTER WENT AWAY SAYING I WAS NOT GOOD AT PUTTING TWO AND TWO TOGETHER. THIS WAS AN OCCASION WHEN I WOULD HAVE PREFERRED TO JOIN EUELPIDES AND PISTHETAERUS ON THEIR FANTASTIC JOURNEY TO THE DOMAIN OF THE BIRDS THAN REMAIN IN A HARD-HEARTED AND LITIGATION-ADDICTED CITY.

I WAS TO RECEIVE CONSIDERABLE SUPPORT FROM GEBER. UNSUITED AS I WAS TO THE RIGOURS OF THE PROFESSION IN A TORMENTED COUNTRY I WAS EASILY PERSUADED TO ACCEPT GEBER'S OFFER TO MANAGE A TRADE HE HAD SET UP I SUSPECT FOR MY BENEFIT. IN PREPARATION FOR

THAT HE HAD EXCHANGED LETTERS WITH HIS FORMER PARTNERS AND CLIENTS IN MESOPOTAMIA ROME AND ARABIA. HE ALSO SENT A LETTER AND A HANDSOME GIFT TO THE PERSIAN KING THANKING HIM FOR HIS GRACIOUSNESS IN RELIEVING HIM OF HIS DUTIES IN CONSIDERATION OF HIS 'NEW FAMILY COMMITMENTS'. HE CHOSE FOR THIS MISSION A MAN FROM ELUSA CALLED HELAL WHO HAD BEEN BRIEFLY ASSOCIATED WITH MY FATHER AT THE SCHOOL OF LAW BUT WAS SAVED BY GEBER FROM SOME DIFFICULTY AND TRAINED AND EMPLOYED BY HIM AS A SECRETARY. INTERESTINGLY THE CHIEF MINISTER OF THE PERSIAN KING REPLIED WITH A LETTER INVITING GEBER AND HIS 'NEW FAMILY' TO LIVE IN KTESEPHON AS HONOURED CITIZENS. AMBASSADOR IZADH-GOUSHNASP ALSO SENT A PASSIONATE PLEA TO THAT EFFECT. GEBER COURTEOUSLY BEGGED TO BE EXCUSED FROM THAT KINDNESS CITING PERSONAL REASONS.

GEBER I MUST CONFESS HAD HELPED SOFTEN MY HATRED FOR THE PERSIANS THE FOREMOST ENEMY OF OUR ROMAN STATE. HE HAD PORTRAYED KOSRO AS A MAN OF REFINEMENT AND COURTESY IN HIS GENTLER MOODS. HOWEVER HE DID NOT GLOSS OVER THE MONARCH'S HARSH PRACTICES WHEN PURSUING HIS DREAMS OF CONQUEST OR SETTLING ANCIENT SCORES WITH ROME.

OF GEBER'S OWN RELIGIOUS BELIEF I CAN VOUCH THAT HE KNEW THE FUNDAMENTALS OF MANY FAITHS AND SEEMED TO SYMPATHISE WITH THEM ALL WHILE ELUDING THEIR AIRS AND CLAIMS OF EXCLUSIVITY. HE HIMSELF HAD BEEN BORN TO A DEVOUT CHRISTIAN MOTHER WHO SPOKE THE LANGUAGE OF THE SAVIOUR IN WHICH GEBER WROTE HIS CHRONICLE. AND HE ALWAYS HELD A SPECIAL AFFECTION FOR THE CLERGY HIS OWN UNCLE HAVING BEEN ONE OF THEM AND FOR NUNS HIS OWN MOTHER HAVING BEEN NEARLY ONE HERSELF. BUT THOUGH A MAN OF ACUTE REASON HE NEVERTHELESS BELIEVED OR SAID HE BELIEVED IN THE POWER OF SOME WOMEN BE THEY PAGAN OR CHRISTIAN TO READ THE FUTURE PERHAPS THROUGH READING THE PRESENT OR THE MINDS OF MEN. WHETHER HE WAS SAYING THIS TO EDIFY OR AMUSE ME I ALSO CANNOT TELL.

HOWEVER HE WAS SERIOUS ENOUGH TO INTIMATE TO ME A WISH TO HAVE HIS CHRONICLE STOWED AWAY AT THE PAGAN TEMPLE IN AFKA. HE SEEMED TO BELIEVE THAT ITS PRESERVATION FOR POSTERITY HAD BEEN PLEDGED BY A PRIESTESS OF ASTARTE WHO HAD ALSO BEEN IN THE SERVICE OF THE BLESSED VIRGIN. HE TOOK ME ONCE TO THE SITE OF THAT TEMPLE ON THE ROCKY HEIGHTS SOME TWENTY MILES WEST OF BYBLOS. THERE HE SHOWED ME A SECRET CRYPT WHERE HE WOULD DEPOSIT HIS CHRONICLE IN THE SAFEKEEPING OF THE TWO GODDESSES AS HE SAID. I CANNOT ALWAYS TELL WHAT HIS FEARS WERE BUT HE SEEMED TERRIFIED BY SOME MENTAL DECAY WHICH HAD AFFLICTED HIS UNCLE IN YEARS PAST. 'THE WORST THING THAT CAN HAPPEN TO A PERSON OR A PEOPLE IS THE WEARING AWAY OF

THEIR MEMORY GUILEFUL AS MEMORY MIGHT BE' HE HAD SAID. THE TOME HE WISHED TO SAVE WITH CELESTIAL HELP WAS A SORT OF HISTORY OF HIS PEOPLE A 'RECORD OF THE EYE AND THE HEART' A 'SPECK ON THE WING OF TIME' A 'TESTAMENT OF FAILURE BUT ALSO OF HOPE' HE HAD DECLARED.

HE HAD CHOSEN TO TRAVEL TO AFKA I MAY NOTE ON A PARTICULAR DAY. IT WAS THE FIRST DAY OF THE SPRING IN THE SECOND YEAR HE ARRIVED PROMISING ME A JOLLY SPECTACLE. BUT WHEN WE ARRIVED AT THE PLACE AFTER A HARD CLIMB WE WERE MET BY A DREARY SILENCE SAVE FOR THE TUMULT OF THE WATERS ISSUING FROM A GROTTO IN THE ROCK FACE THE GROTTO ITSELF RESEMBLING AN ENORMOUS TRAGIC MASK HOWLING. IN THE DIN GEBER LIFTED HIS VOICE WITH AN APOLOGY. HE MENTIONED SOMETHING ABOUT A CERTAIN GALA HE HAD WITNESSED THERE WHEN HE WAS A STUDENT IN LEBANON.

NOW HE STOOD A FORLORN FIGURE ROCKING BACK AND FORTH NOT FAR FROM THE EDGE OF A CLIFF. HE MUST HAVE BEEN DIZZIED MORE BY THOUGHTS COURSING THROUGH HIS HEAD THAN BY THE SHEER PLUNGE TICKLING HIS TOES. BUT LO AND BEHOLD AN OLD LADY SUDDENLY APPEARED BEHIND US. PLUMP AND SOMEWHAT STOOPING BUT DISTINGUISHED-LOOKING SHE WAS ACCOMPANIED BY A GIANT OF A MAN WITH A MILITARY BEARING.

IT DID NOT TAKE ME LONG TO RECOGNISE THE WOMAN AS LADY AMELIA A CLOSE FRIEND OF MY DEAR MOTHER'S AND A FREQUENT CALLER ON OUR OLD FAMILY HOME. IN THOSE DEAR DAYS SHE WAS THE PATRICIAN WIFE OF THE GOVERNOR OF BERYTUS ONLY TO MYSTERIOUSLY DISAPPEAR FROM THE CITY LEAVING ITS GENTEEL WOMEN TO WHISPER IN THEIR SALONS WHISPERS WE CHILDREN WERE NOT SUPPOSED TO HEAR. I RECALL THAT HER HUSBAND AN OLD MAN EVEN THEN AND LATER DECEASED CAME TO OUR VILLA AT THE TIME TO SPEAK TO MY MOTHER. IT WAS RUMOURED THAT MY MOTHER WAS THE LAST PERSON TO HAVE SEEN HIS WIFE BEFORE HER DISAPPEARANCE. I SUPPOSE MY MOTHER SAID NOTHING FOR HE EMERGED FROM HER AUDIENCE MUTTERING SOMETHING ABOUT WOMEN BEING 'CARVED IN THE STONE OF THE SPHINX'. HER COMPANION I ALSO RECOGNISED ALMOST IN THE SAME BREATH. HE WAS A FORMER CAPTAIN OF THE GUARDS WHOM I HAD OFTEN SEEN BEFORE AT THE HEAD OF THE MOUNTED ESCORT TRAVELLING WITH THE LADY'S CARRIAGE WHEN SHE CAME TO VISIT MY MOTHER. IN FACT I USED TO STAND AT THE BALCONY GAZING IN WONDER AT HIS GLITTERING REGALIA AND THE SPLENDID HORSE HE RODE A FEARSOME SWORD AT HIS SIDE. HE TOO HAD VANISHED WITH HER SO MANY YEARS BEFORE.

AT AFKA WE BECAME AWARE OF THE COUPLE'S PRESENCE AS THEY ASCENDED TO OUR PLATEAU. THE CAPTAIN WAS ASSISTING HIS LADY WITH SO MUCH CONSIDERATION SHE LOOKING PENSIVE. SHE STARTLED LIKE SOME WILD AND NOBLE ANIMAL CAUGHT OFF GUARD AS SHE RAISED HER GAZE AND SAW US. REGAINING HER COMPOSURE SHE GAZED MOST INTENTLY INTO

Geber's face her gaze feeling his features. Anon she uttered a loud cry and rushed almost stumbling away from her companion's loving custody and over the rock-strewn ground between us to embrace Geber with great passion and a flood of tears. He responded with his own tears mumbling 'Dear Lady Amelia dear Lady Amelia Sophia's son Sophia's son!'

She turned towards me with a tearful cry and took me in her ample arms rocking me against her liberal bosom and repeating through sobs 'Sophia my darling my darling Sophia darling Julian Julian my darling. You were just a little boy a darling little boy when I last saw you. All now you're a man a most handsome man with your dear mother's eyes' and so on and so forth. She then told us between sniffles and gasps how she had travelled with her spouse from their self-exile in Samaria to check on my parents after hearing of the blow that had struck Berytus. She had arrived there to see our villa in ruins. There were no people around in the wake of a smaller tremor that had just taken place. Most of the remaining inhabitants had retreated to the mountains fearing a new deluge. She had then travelled she told us eastwards to Damascus where her husband Catallus had a cousin. Both were wary of staying in Berytus devastated as it was with mobs and vigilantes ruling the streets. They were also chary as a result of some old problems that had arisen out of their elopement and Catalus's desertion from the army. They had been leading a somewhat modest but contented life in Samaria. Geber later offered Catallus a trade partnership.

Lady Amelia had known Geber when he was a student of my father's and a guest at our house. Now on her way back from Damascus through the Lebanon mountains she had opted to visit Afka at a time when the festival which Geber had spoken about would be taking place. I surmised that the occasion had some meaning for her and her husband as for Geber.

Though no festival came to pass this reunion was by far a greater reward for the threesome. They offered their supplication to the grounds and the ruins which they deemed holy or made so by some event of their youth. We descended the mountain and drove back on the coastal road to Berytus some forty miles away. The good lady and captain were invited by Geber to stay for as long as they wished at our villa which he had by then rebuilt redecorated and refurnished to the best taste. But the devoted wife and husband never truly at ease in the city preferred to travel back to Samaria. The captain proved to be a trusted and

SUCCESSFUL TRADE PARTNER FOR US IN THE YEARS THAT FOLLOWED UNTIL HE CONVEYED TO US THE SAD NEWS OF THE PASSING OF HIS BELOVED LADY SOME SEVEN YEARS LATER AND HIS WISH TO RETIRE FROM THE TRADE.

GEBER WAS A MAN WITH AN ASSORTMENT OF CONTRADICTIONS AND A BUNDLE OF MYSTERIES. HE WAS MERCIFULLY AWARE OF HIS OWN CONTRARIETIES AND WAS ABLE TO NOTE SIMILAR ONES IN OTHERS. THE LATTER HE DID WITHOUT MALICE. I SUSPECT HIS INTENTION WAS TO RESTRAIN MY ZEAL TO PASS 'JUDGEMENT' AND PRONOUNCE 'VERDICTS' ON PEOPLE I HAD BUSINESS OR QUARRELS WITH.

HIS PATRONAGE OF ME WAS AN ENVY TO MANY OF MY PEERS. BESIDES THE WEALTH HE HAD BROUGHT WITH HIM GEBER HAD IN THE SPAN OF FEW YEARS BECOME A PROMINENT MERCHANT PLACING ME IN A SECURE FRONT SEAT WHEN THE BUSINESS HAD BECOME WELL ESTABLISHED. HE HAD TRIUMPHED OVER THE GENERAL DESPAIR OF THE COUNTRY FOLLOWING THE QUAKE HELPING TO RE-IGNITE IN THE PEOPLE OF LEBANON THEIR INBRED LOVE FOR LUXURY AND COMFORT AND SPUR THEIR DESIRE TO LEAVE THEIR MISFORTUNES BEHIND. AT HIS BIDDING (WHICH SOON BECAME MINE ASSISTED BY THE DILIGENT AND VERSATILE HELAL) CARAVANS PLODDED THE WASTES BETWEEN LEBANON AND ARABIA AND SHIPS PLIED THE WAVES CARRYING THE FINEST GOODS BETWEEN THE LEBANESE PORTS AND THE GOLDEN HORN ALEXANDRIA SYRACUSE OSTIA CARTHAGE AND EVERY EAGER PORT.

AND YET A CYNICAL MAN LOOKING AT OUR RELATIONSHIP MAY HAVE COME TO THE CONCLUSION THAT GEBER'S INFLUENCE ON ME WAS NOT SO BENIGN. HIS PATRONAGE ENTICED ME AWAY THE CYNIC MAY HAVE ARGUED FROM MY FATHER'S LEGACY AND PROFESSION AND WEAKENED MY RELIGIOUS AND PATRIOTIC SENTIMENT. NOT IN THE LEAST. I REMAIN STAUNCHLY LOYAL TO MY FATHER'S HERITAGE AS TO OUR GLORIOUS ROMAN STATE AND A LOVER OF LEBANON JUST AS MY FATHER HAD BEEN AS DOUBLY CONFIRMED BY GEBER. GEBER HIMSELF BY THE BY ASSURED ME THAT THE CHRONICLE HE HAS WRITTEN BEARS NO ILL WILL TO OUR STATE NOR TO OUR CHURCH THOUGH OFFERING A GLIMPSE INTO IMPERIAL POLICIES CONNECTED TO HIS ARABIAN KING WHO IS THE CHRONICLE'S CHIEF PURPOSE. IN ANY CASE GEBER WISHED HIGHER POWERS TO DECIDE WHEN THIS 'INTIMATE RECORD DEFICIENT AS IT IS' WOULD REACH WHOEVER MIGHT BE INTERESTED IN PERUSING IT.

HERE I MAY ALSO NOTE IN PASSING THAT THOUGH A READER OF PEOPLE'S IMPERFECTIONS GEBER NEVER SPOKE DURING THE YEARS I SPENT WITH HIM ABOUT MY PARENTS EXCEPT WITH THE UTMOST LOVE AND REVERENCE. THIS HE DID TO THE EXTENT OF PORTRAYING THEM AS COMPLETELY ABSOLVED OF ANY HUMAN FRAILTY EXCEPT PERHAPS EXCESSIVE GENEROSITY TOLERANCE COURAGE AND DEVOTION TO THEIR FELLOW HUMAN BEINGS.

GEBER AS I SAID EARLIER WAS NOT WITHOUT HIS OWN FAILINGS AND INCONSISTENCIES. CHIEF OF THOSE WAS HIS EXCITABILITY AND GENERALLY MAUDLIN DISPOSITION. THE RAWNESS OF HIS FEELINGS WAS RATHER ODD IN VIEW OF THE REAL HARDSHIPS HE HAD EXPERIENCED AND THE SKILLS HE CLEARLY HAD POSSESSED TO A HIGH DEGREE IN DIPLOMACY AND TRADE. IT MIGHT HAVE BEEN DUE TO HIS HAVING USED UP MUCH OF HIS ABILITY TO DEAL WITH LIFE'S PROBLEMS AND WISHING TO INVEST THE LITTLE HE STILL POSSESSED IN TRIALS THAT LAY AHEAD. NONETHELESS HIS EYES SEEMED NATURALLY PRONE TO BE FLOODED WITH TEARS IN TURN FLOODING ME WITH EMBARRASSMENT. EVEN MY DEAR MOTHER WHO HAD THE TENDEREST FEELINGS WAS TOO LOFTY TO DISSOLVE LIKE A CONE OF SALT UNDER A DRIZZLE. GEBER'S TEARS FLOWED FOR THE BRAVE BELISARIUS AS THEY HAD DONE FOR THE WILY EL-MUNTER AUTHOR OF HIS PEOPLE'S RUIN. PERHAPS IN THEIR DEATHS HE ALSO SAW THE SHADOW OF HIS OWN PASSING. BUT I THINK DEATH POSED NO TERROR FOR HIM THOUGH IT MUST HAVE ADDED TO THE PATHOS HE SAW IN MEN'S LOT ON EARTH. I SUSPECT HIS GREATEST FEAR IN LIFE WAS TO BE SEVERED FROM HIS MEMORIES. HIS GOD DID NOT SEEM TO HAVE A FIXED ALTAR OR HARBOUR OR NAME. HOWEVER HE MAY STILL HAVE HOPED TO SAIL THE SHIP OF HIS HEART INTO AN ANCHORAGE WHERE ALL WAS RESTORED. SOMETIMES I WOULD CATCH HIM LOOKING AT ME AS IF TRYING TO SEE UPON MY FACE THE LINEAMENTS OF MY PARENTS AND BY ASSOCIATION THE LINEAMENTS OF HIS OWN YOUTH.

HE SHARED MY LOVE FOR BERYTUS. THE CITY HAD BEEN TO HIM A LIVING BEING A MOTHER AT WHOSE BOSOM HE HAD FOUND NOURISHMENT FOR HIS MIND AND SOUL. BUT THE BERYTUS HE HAD COME BACK TO WAS NOW A BEREAVED MOTHER SHATTERED BY THE DEATHS OF HER CHILDREN AND DIMINISHED BY THE DESTRUCTION OF HER SCHOOLS AND CATHEDRALS AND GRANARIES. MY OWN DEAR AND SAINTLY MOTHER HAD MANY YEARS BEFORE FOUNDED A HOME AND SANATORIUM FOR THE DESTITUTE. THIS GEBER HAD REVIVED AFTER THE FIRST TREMOR. HE LATER FOUNDED ANOTHER IN THE BEAUTIFUL CITY OF SIDON WHERE THE LAW SCHOOL WAS MOVED AND RESTORED THOUGH ONLY IN MASONRY AS I MAY HAVE NOTED EARLIER.

BUT IT WAS IN BERYTUS THAT GEBER MADE HIS CHIEF CONTRIBUTION TO THE COUNTRY. NOT ONLY DID HE DONATE GENEROUSLY FOR THE RESTORATION OF THE CHURCH OF OUR LADY OF THE ROSARY IN THE CITY CENTRE AND THE CUSTOMS HOUSE AT THE HARBOUR. HE ALSO SOUGHT AND OBTAINED SUBSIDIES FROM TRADE AND DIPLOMATIC ASSOCIATES IN VARIOUS LANDS TO HELP WITH THE REBUILDING OF THE CITY. HIS TRADE VENTURES ENLIVENED THE SPIRIT OF THE NATION MOTIVATING PEOPLE TO DWELL ON THE LIFE AHEAD RATHER THAN THE SPECTRES HAUNTING THEIR MINDS AND FOOTPATHS. AND THOUGH HE MADE SUBSTANTIAL PROFITS

HE ALSO CREATED OPPORTUNITIES FOR COMMERCIAL ACTIVITY IN THE COUNTRY AND RENEWED THE CONFIDENCE OF FOREIGN TRADERS TO INVEST IN HER RECOVERY HOWEVER WARILY BY SOME.

ON A MORE PERSONAL NOTE GEBER I MAY HAVE MENTIONED STARTED REBUILDING MY PARENTS' HOME ALMOST IMMEDIATELY AFTER HIS RETURN TO THE CITY. HE HIRED THE BEST MASONS AND IMPORTED THE HANDSOMEST STONES AND MARBLES TAKING PAINS TO REPLICATE THE OLD STRUCTURE EVEN BRINGING FURNISHINGS FROM ROME AND DAMASCUS AND THE YEMEN TO REPRODUCE THE LOST ONES. THIS HOWEVER DID NOT SLOW DOWN HIS CHARITABLE WORK DONATING TO ORPHANAGES AND HOSPICES AND SECURING EMPLOYMENT FOR THE UNWAGED EXPRESSING REGRET AT TIMES THAT HIS CAREER HAD TURNED OUT TO BE WITH THE AFFAIRS OF THE RICH.

MUCH THAT I LOVED MY PARENTS I RARELY ACCOMPANIED GEBER TO THEIR GRAVES WHICH HE WAS IN THE HABIT OF VISITING NOW AND AGAIN PARTICULARLY AS THE SUN WAS DIPPING OR HAD JUST DIPPED INTO THE SEA. I REMEMBER HIM SITTING ON THE PUNGENT GRASS GAZING OUT FROM THE HEIGHT OF THE HILL AT THE TINGED AND DARKLY BREATHING SEA IN THE DISTANCE. THE WAVES WOULD BE BREAKING ON THE ROCKS BELOW PERHAPS MURMURING TO HIM MORE ABOUT DROWNED SAILORS THAN TRIUMPHANT ARGOSIES. ABOVE HIM THE SWALLOWS AND THE SWIFTS WOULD BE RETURNING TO THEIR NESTS THE GULLS REELING SLUGGISHLY THEIR HUNTING WATERS DIMMING WITH A DYING GLOW OF SUN-BLOOD. THEN THE BATS WOULD EMERGE IN STRENGTH FROM THE CREVICES OF TWO GIANT ROCKS JUTTING OUT OF THE SEA (AND WHICH LATER SANK BACK INTO IT) TO CROSS-STITCH THE BLANKET SWEEPING OVER THE CITY. GEBER HIMSELF OFTEN DREW MY ATTENTION TO THESE THINGS.

SOME TWO YEARS AND A HALF AFTER HIS RE-ARRIVAL IN BERYTUS GEBER ARRANGED FOR MY ENGAGEMENT TO THE LOVELY MARIA DAUGHTER OF THE RENOWNED JUDGE NAZARUS WHO HAD SURVIVED THE QUAKE. GEBER PRESIDED OVER THE WEDDING CEREMONY SPARING US NO EXPENSE OR CONSIDERATION. THE FINEST EMBROIDERIES AND RAREST GEMS ADORNED OUR GOWNS. THE BASILICA GLITTERED. THE VILLA VIBRATED. THE GUESTS WERE REGALED WITH FRAGRANCED WINES AROMATIC SHERBETS PISTACHIOD CREAM CAKES MIXED KERNELS ROASTS AND CASSEROLES OF EVERY KIND. MUSICIANS PLAYED ON THEIR HARPS AND PIPES AND KITHARAS AND GAY YOUTHS DANCED AND ROLLICKED. BUT IT IS THE WORDS OF THE PRIEST WHICH STILL ECHO MOST DISTINCTLY IN MY MEMORY. AFTER INVOKING THE EXAMPLE OF OUR LORD WHO HAD BLESSED THE WEDDING IN CANA THE PRIEST APPEALED TO THE SAVIOUR TO CONSECRATE THIS MARRIAGE ALSO. AS THE 'INCARNATE WORD OF GOD' HAD BEEN IN GALILEE SO MIGHT HE IN BERYTUS TOO 'GRANT JULIAN AND MARIA A PEACEFUL AND LONG LIFE AND

CONJUGAL CHASTITY AND THE BLISS TO SEE THEIR CHILDREN AND THEIR CHILDREN'S CHILDREN'. BUT WITH THE PRIEST'S INVOCATION OF CHRIST'S 'INVISIBLE PRESENCE' TO BLESS US AND GIVE US 'DEW FROM HEAVEN AND THE ABUNDANCE OF THE EARTH TO SHARE WITH THOSE IN NEED' I ALSO INVOKED THE PRESENCE OF MY PARENTS A PRESENCE THAT WAS AS 'VISIBLE' TO ME AS THAT OF THE MUNIFICENT GEBER.

SHORTLY BEFORE MY MARRIAGE GEBER CHOSE TO MOVE OUT OF THE SMALL SEA-FACING ROOM HE HAD LIVED IN SINCE THE RESTORATION OF MY PARENTS' HOUSE. HE OPTED TO RESIDE IN A VILLA NEARBY WHICH HAD BELONGED TO HIS MOTHER'S FAMILY AND WHICH HE HAD BOUGHT AND REBUILT. NOT LONG AFTERWARDS HE CONVEYED TO ME THAT HE WANTED TO TRAVEL TO THE LAND OF HIS BIRTH IN ARABIA. NEWS OF HIS FATHER'S DEATH HAD REACHED HIM YEARS BEFORE IN MESOPOTAMIA BUT HE HAD ALSO WANTED TO SEE A HEBREW ARAB PRINCE ONE SAMUEL BEN EDI WITH WHOM HE HAD BEEN TRADING EVEN FROM KTESEPHON AND MORE LATELY FROM BERYTUS. TO THE SAFEKEEPING OF THAT PRINCE GEBER'S KING HAD ENTRUSTED HIS OWN SISTER PERHAPS THE LAST WITH GEBER IN THE LINE OF A ONCE TEEMING PEOPLE. BUT GEBER ALSO HAD OTHER DESIGNS.

EVER SINCE HIS RETURN FROM PERSIA GEBER HAD WANTED TO TRAVEL BACK TO ARABIA IN ORDER TO STAND IN REMEMBRANCE AT HIS FATHER'S GRAVE IN HATRAMOT AND THE GRAVES OF HIS MOTHER AND UNCLE IN THE NEARER CITY OF PETRA. HE ALSO WISHED TO RECOVER THE FIRST PART OF THE CHRONICLE HE HAD STARTED WRITING MANY YEARS BEFORE AT THE BIDDING OF SOME ORACLE. HE HAD TRUSTED THE SAME HEBREW PRINCE WITH HIS PRECIOUS TOME AS HE WAS TO TRUST ME BEFORE HIS DEPARTURE WITH THE SECOND HALF OF THAT HISTORY CONCLUDED THE DAY HIS KING DIED AT ANCYRA. GEBER HAD DOWNED HIS WRITING TOOLS ON THAT DAY. HOWEVER HE STILL HELD THAT HIS MISSION WOULD NOT BE COMPLETE WITHOUT UNITING THE TWO HALVES OF HIS CHRONICLE AND HELPING TO SEE TO ITS PRESERVATION FOR POSTERITY AS HE HAD BEEN TUTORED HE SAID.

SEVERAL YEARS WERE TO PASS BEFORE GEBER COULD FULFIL HIS WISH. A COMBINATION OF MILITARY SKIRMISHES UPRISINGS AND REVOLTS (DESPITE THE PEACE TREATY GEBER HIMSELF HAD HELPED CONCLUDE) CONSPIRED WITH SMALL-SCALE TREMORS AND TWO PLAGUES IN THE REGION TO BAR HIS ROUTE TO THE SOUTH. IN THE MEANTIME MARIA AND I WERE BLESSED WITH THREE CHILDREN ON WHOM GEBER DOTED LIKE AN ADORING GRANDFATHER. THEN A LETTER ARRIVED BY SEA FROM ARABIA SENT BY ONE OF SAMUEL'S SONS ONE NAMED SOREH. IT SPOKE OF AN ILLNESS THAT HAD STRUCK THE HEBREW PRINCE AND OF HIS WISH TO SEE GEBER. A SHIP WOULD TAKE HIM TO GAZA FROM WHICH HE WOULD TRAVEL ON LAND ESCORTED BY GUARDS TO SAMUEL'S CASTLE SOME FIVE HUNDRED MILES AWAY.

GEBER HAD LONG HANDED OVER THE DAILY MANAGEMENT OF HIS BUSINESS TO ME AIDED BY THE NOW ANCIENT HELAL AND RETREATED INTO HIS SMALL VILLA WITH AN ELDERLY COUPLE SERVING HIM. AND YET ON THE MORNING OF HIS DEPARTURE I STOOD AT THE QUAY WITH MY WIFE AND CHILDREN FEELING FORLORN AND BEREFT. BUT LIFE WENT ON FOR ANOTHER TWO YEARS. AND THEN HE CAME BACK ARRIVING BY LAND. HE WAS ACCOMPANIED BY AN OLD BUT MOST STATELY AITHIOP WOMAN WHOM HE INTRODUCED TO US AS HIS OLD NURSEMAID. SHE HAD TRAVELLED WITH HER HUSBAND AND THREE GROWN-UP SONS AND THEIR FAMILIES. THEY LATER BOARDED ONE OF OUR SHIPS TO ALEXANDRIA.

ON HIS RETURN GEBER WAS VISIBLY WORN OUT BY HIS TRAVELS AND THE ENCOUNTERS HE HAD HAD. THE MARK OF A WOUND ON HIS UPPER CHEST TESTIFIED TO ONE INCIDENT HE DID NOT EXPLAIN. HE HAD ALSO AGED CONSIDERABLY UNDER ARABIA'S SUN WHICH HAD CRACKED HIS SKIN AND BENT HIS BACK AS IF AVENGING ITSELF ON THE YEARS HE HAD ESCAPED ITS DOMINION. BENEATH THE TAN OF HIS FACE AN OMINOUS PALLOR LURKED. BUT HE WAS MOST HAPPY WITH MY CHILDREN NOW FOUR IN NUMBER EMBRACING AND NUZZLING THEM THE YOUNGEST IOSEPH SQUEALING AT THE STRANGER. AND YET AS EVER HE WAS LIKE AN INDULGENT PATRIARCH LADEN WITH EASTER GIFTS EVEN FOR LITTLE IOSEPH ANTICIPATING MARIA'S RUNAWAY FONDNESS FOR CHILDREN THOUGH NOT DURING HER DELIVERY OF THEM. FOR ME HE HAD A SHEAF OF INTERESTING STORIES.

HE HAD SUCCEEDED AS I HAD PRAYED HE WOULD IN GETTING BACK THE FIRST HALF OF HIS TOME FROM THE TRUSTEESHIP OF THE HEBREW PRINCE. THE PRINCE HAD YEARS BEFORE DONE SOMETHING THAT HAD GONE DOWN IN THE LOCAL HISTORY AS AN ACT OF EXCEPTIONAL CHIVALRY NOBILITY AND MADNESS. DURING GEBER'S FLIGHT WITH HIS ARABIAN KING SAMUEL HAD OFFERED THE FUGITIVES AN ASYLUM IN HIS CASTLE. HE LATER PLEDGED TO PROTECT THE KING'S SISTER AND SAFE-KEEP SOME KENDE HEIRLOOMS. BEFORE THEIR DEPARTURE HE ALSO PROVIDED THE TWO FUGITIVES WITH THE MEANS TO TRAVEL BY SEA TO ROME WHERE HIS AGENT IN THE CITY AND LATER OUR OWN ASSOCIATE THERE THE GALLANT AND RESOURCEFUL YONAH HELPED THEM PLEAD THEIR CAUSE AT THE IMPERIAL COURT. AFTER THE TWAIN'S FLIGHT HOWEVER AN ARMY OF EL-MUNTER LED BY A LIEUTENANT OF HIS ONE NAMED BEN ZALOUM LAID SIEGE TO SAMUEL'S CASTLE. REALISING THAT THEIR QUARRY HAD ESCAPED BEN ZALOUM ASKED FOR THE KING'S SISTER AND THE HEIRLOOMS TO BE HANDED OVER TO HIM. FOR HIS BARGAINING ASSET HE HAD BEEN DARKLY LUCKY TO CAPTURE ONE OF SAMUEL'S SONS A LAD NAMED HOZ. THE LAD HAD VENTURED OUT TO INQUIRE ABOUT A TROUP OF HORSEMEN WHO HAD ASKED FOR DIRECTIONS BUT TURNED OUT TO BE A VANGUARD OF BEN ZALOUM'S ARMY. FINDING THE CASTLE INVIOLABLE THE BESIEGERS THREATENED TO KILL THE YOUTH IF THE

GIRL AND THE HEIRLOOMS WERE NOT SURRENDERED TO THEM. POSITIONING HIMSELF AND HIS TROOPS UNDER THE WALLS OF THE CASTLE BEN ZALOUM PUT A DAGGER TO THE YOUTH'S NECK WHILE THE YOUTH'S FATHER STOOD ON THE WALL. STILL SAMUEL DECLARED THAT HE HAD GIVEN HIS WORD TO THE KING TO PROTECT HIS SISTER AND FAMILY TREASURES AND WOULD NOT GO BACK ON THAT WORD BE IT AT THE PERIL THAT WAS STARING HIM IN THE FACE BELOW THE WALLS. HE SAID HE DID NOT WANT HIS DEARLY LOVED SON HARMED AND WOULD OFFER EVERYTHING IN HIS POSSESSION BARRING THE GIRL AND THE HEIRLOOMS IN EXCHANGE FOR HIS SON'S RELEASE. THE HEARTLESS BEN ZALOUM SLIT THE YOUTH'S THROAT UNDER HIS FATHER'S GAZE EVEN THOUGH THE SISTER OF THE ARABIAN KING HAD THROWN HERSELF FROM THE WALL DYING TO RANSOM HIM. THE ATROCITY LOST EL-MUNTER AND HIS ALLIES SYMPATHIES THEY HAD BOUGHT WITH GOLD OR CARVED OUT WITH THEIR SWORDS. SAMUEL'S NAME BECAME PROVERBIAL THROUGHOUT ARABIA. NEWS OF HIS DEATH CONFRONTED GEBER AS HE ARRIVED AT THE CASTLE. SAMUEL'S WIFE HAD EARLIER WASTED AWAY AFTER HER SON'S DEATH.

FOLLOWING A SOJOURN AT SAMUEL'S CASTLE WHERE THE HEIRLOOMS REMAIN GEBER TRAVELLED ON TO PAY HIS RESPECTS TO HIS FATHER'S GRAVE IN HATRAMOT. THERE HE FOUND A REMNANT OF HIS ONCE PROUD PEOPLE. THEY HAD NOW SUCCUMBED TO THE RULE OF THE RISE AND FALL OF NATIONS. A CRONY OF HIS A DESERT POET AND A LEADER OF INSURGENTS HAD DIED BUT GEBER WAS ABLE TO TRACK DOWN HIS SON WHO WAS NOW FOLLOWING IN HIS FATHER'S FOOTSTEPS. AND AFTER CHANCING UPON HIS OLD NURSEMAID AND SAVING HER AND HER FAMILY FROM BONDAGE THEY HAD FALLEN INTO GEBER VISITED THE GRAVESIDES OF HIS MOTHER AND UNCLE IN PETRA ON HIS WAY BACK HERE. IN ALL THIS HE SEEMED TO ME LIKE A MAN FRANTICALLY DOING PENANCE OR TRYING TO ATONE FOR A SIN HE HAD COMMITTED IN YEARS GONE BY. INTERESTINGLY THE SIN THAT HAD WEIGHED DOWN ON HIM LIKE A CROSS IN THE VIA DOLOROSA OF HIS SOUL TURNED INTO A GALLOPING THOROUGHBRED IN ARABIA.

LESS DESPERATELY BUT MORE REMARKABLY HE HAD MANAGED UPON HIS RETURN FROM HATRAMOT TO HELP SHAPE HISTORY IN MEKA. THIS IS THE CITY TO WHICH PAGAN ARABS TRAVEL IN THE WAY CHRISTIANS JOURNEY TO ROME AND HEBREWS TO JERUSALEM. THERE WAS A TWINKLE IN HIS WEARY EYES WHEN HE TOLD ME HOW HE OVERSAW THE HANGING UP OF A POEM COMPOSED BY HIS KING ON THE EAST-FACING WALL OF THE TEMPLE IN THAT CITY. THE POEM GEBER HAD HAD EMBROIDERED IN GOLD ON A PIECE OF BLACK DAMASK AND HAD IT SEWN ONTO THE HEAVY CLOTH THAT COVERS THE WALLS OF THE TEMPLE. I DO NOT KNOW HOW GEBER WAS ABLE TO ACCOMPLISH THIS FEAT IN VIEW OF THE MILITARY AND POLITICAL FAILURE OF HIS KING AND THE RUIN OF HIS PEOPLE. I SUPPOSE GEBER'S POWERS

OF DIPLOMACY AND HIS FRIENDSHIP WITH KOSRO NOW THAT EL-MUNTER HAD DIED HAD PLAYED A ROLE. HE MAY HAVE BEEN HELPED BY THE MORAL DOWNFALL OF THE KING'S ENEMIES IN ARABIA WHOSE MEANNESS AND BARBARITY WERE NOW CONTRASTED WITH THE LOFTINESS OF SAMUEL'S GALLANTRY AND THE TRAGIC NOBILITY OF THE PRINCESS'S SACRIFICE. THE ARABS' WAR-WEARINESS AND THEIR INSANE LOVE OF POETRY MAY HAVE ALSO LENT A HAND. GEBER'S KING WAS REPORTEDLY A MASTER VERSIFIER THOUGH I SOMETIMES WONDER WHETHER THE LINES GEBER USED TO RECITE TO ME IN TRANSLATION WERE PARTLY HIS OWN AS THEY SOMETIMES CHANGED IN THE TELLING. IN ANY EVENT GEBER HAD SAID THIS ACT FOR HIS KING IN MEKA WAS MORE MEANINGFUL TO HIM THAN A JOURNEY HE MIGHT HAVE MADE TO A DESOLATE HILL OUTSIDE ANCYRA. MORE GENERALLY HE HOPED THAT THE PRACTICE OF CHOOSING POEMS OF DISTINCTION AND PLACING THEM ON THE HALLOWED WALLS OF THE TEMPLE IN MEKA WOULD CONTINUE. HE HOPED IT WOULD DRIVE THE ARABS TO COMPETE WITH ONE ANOTHER WITH VERSES RATHER THAN WITH RAIDING PARTIES CAPTURING HEARTS INSTEAD OF CATTLE AND SPEAKING IN THEIR OWN TONGUE RATHER THAN IN THE TONGUES OF ROME OR KTESEPHON. THUS WOULD THEIR QUARRELS DIVISIONS AND HUMILIATIONS BE TRANSMUTED INTO FAIR CONTEST HARMONY AND DIGNITY. AND THUS WOULD THE 'TRUE KINGS AND QUEENS' OF ARABIA RISE AND TAKE THEIR FITTING PLACE. IN ALL THE ABOVE HE NOTED THE INFLUENCE OF MY FATHER'S ETHICAL AND DIPLOMATIC TEACHINGS THOUGH THE PASSION WITH WHICH HE SPOKE WAS CLEARLY HIS OWN. DREAMER OR NOT HE HAD REMARKED TO ME YEARS EARLIER THAT ONLY A POET COULD UNITE THE ARABS THOUGH THE HELP OF AN ARCHANGEL WITH A FLAMING SWORD MIGHT COME IN HANDY HE HAD ADDED WRYLY.

A DREAMER HE CERTAINLY WAS IN SOME WAYS. HE HIMSELF HAD ONCE COMMENTED ON THE IRONIES AND AMBIVALENCES OF HIS SITUATION A 'HISTORIAN TURNED ROMANCER OR THE LATTER TURNED THE FORMER'. ON ANOTHER OCCASION HE DESCRIBED HIMSELF AS 'ONE BIDDEN TO CATCH THUNDERBOLTS ONLY TO CHASE AFTER BUTTERFLIES'. EVEN AT THE HEIGHT OF HIS 'MISSION' HE ALSO TOLD ME HE HAD BEEN MORE LIKE JONAH A RELUCTANT AND AT TIMES TESTY MESSENGER. MUCH OF THAT TESTINESS HE CONFIDED WAS MORE TO DO WITH HIS FRUSTRATION AT WHAT HE DEEMED TO HAVE BEEN A SIEGE IMPOSED ON HIS LIFE AND AGGRAVATED BY 'COLLAPSES AND BETRAYALS FROM WITHIN'. OVER THE YEARS HOWEVER HE HAD CLEARLY MANAGED TO PURIFY HIS SOUL OF THE BITTERNESS AND DOUBTS ASSOCIATED WITH HIS 'MISSION' THOUGH NOT ALL THE SORROW AND GUILT THAT HAD COME WITH IT. SOMEWHAT LIKE MY OWN ILLUSTRIOUS FATHER HE GREW TO SPURN POLITICS WITHOUT DERIDING IT. AND LIKE MY FATHER HE WAS LARGELY UNTOUCHED BY THE HUBRIS AND DUPLICITIES OF

POWER RATING TRUTH AND REASON AS THE WORTHIEST OF PURSUITS. MY DEAR FATHER'S STRICT SELF-DISCIPLINE AND SELF-RESTRAINT MAY HAVE ELUDED HIM HOWEVER. AND YET I WAS CONSTANTLY STRUCK BY THE MAN'S EMPATHY WITH THE IMPOVERISHED AND THE VAGRANT EVEN WITH SOME OF THOSE WHOSE IDEAS OR ACTIONS PUT THEM OUTSIDE THE BOUNDS OF THE LAW AN EMPATHY I WAS SOMETIMES UNABLE TO SHARE. BUT IT WAS CLEAR AFTER HIS RETURN FROM HIS LAST JOURNEY THAT HE WAS IN A STATE OF ALL-EMBRACING PEACE HAVING MADE HIS RECONCILIATION WITH ALL GODS AND MEN AND HAVING PERFORMED PILGRIMAGES TO ALL HIS SHRINES AND FULFILLED ALL HIS 'MISSIONS' SAVE ONE.

I DO NOT KNOW WHY I AM DRIVEN TO RECORD THE ABOVE OR WHY I SEEM TO BE ADDING MY TESTIMONY TO GEBER'S OWN. FOR A START I CANNOT TELL IF HIS TESTIMONY IN A LANGUAGE ARCANE TO ME IS AN ARTEFACT OF FANTASIES OR AN HONEST ACCOUNT AND TRIBUTE. MY OWN IMMORTAL FATHER CERTAINLY NEEDS NO PRAISE FROM ME OR FROM ANY OTHER. PERHAPS I AM MOVED BY A SENSE OF JUSTICE OR A PASSION FOR COMPLETENESS WHICH I SEEM TO SHARE WITH MY BENEFACTOR INCOMPLETE AS HE WAS. OR PERHAPS I AM LED BY SYMPATHY OR LOYALTY NEITHER OF WHICH GEBER HAD ASKED FOR. OR MAYBE I AM LURED BY HIS MYSTIC BELIEF THAT HIS CHRONICLE WOULD SURVIVE AGAINST ALL ODDS AND I DESIRE TO PARTAKE OF THAT IMMORTALITY THAT HAPPY ILLUSION ENTERING HIS DREAMS AND INVENTIONS THOUGH NOT THEIR DARK RECESSES.

SO INVITING WAS THAT SERENE SMILE HE HAD IN HIS SUNKEN CHEEKS AFTER HIS RETURN HAVING OFFERED ALL POSSIBLE SACRAMENTS AND ACCOMMODATIONS. HE SEEMED TO ME LIKE A SURVIVOR AT SEA WHO HAD SWUM FOR DAYS BUT NOW FLOATED WITH A PRAYER ON THE PILLOW OF A WAVE TAKING HIM TO A CUSHY SHORE. COULD I SHARE SUCH PEACE SUCH SENSE OF ACHIEVEMENT SUCH TRANSCENDENCE AS I AM ENTERING THE TWILIGHT OF MY OWN YEARS? HE HIMSELF HAD ONCE SAID THAT GROWING OLD WAS THE WORST INDIGNITY AND THE CLEAREST PROOF OF A DESPOTIC PROVIDENCE. HE SAID HE ENVIED HIS ARABIAN KING FOR MANY THINGS BUT MOST FOR DYING YOUNG. WHEN I ARGUED THAT OLD AGE GAVE A MAN WISDOM HE SAID HE WOULD TRADE ALL THE WISDOM OF MEN FOR AN HOUR AT MY FATHER'S MORNING CLASS OR AT MY MOTHER'S DINNER TABLE! THERE HE SAID FOREVER LAY THE PATRIA OF HIS HEART AND THE PERACTIO OF HIS BEING. I THOUGHT HE WAS NOT BEING WHOLLY SERIOUS BUT RATHER AS ALWAYS OVER-SOLICITOUS TO ME AND TO THE MEMORY OF MY BELOVED PARENTS. AND YET WHO CAN GIVE A RULING ON THE TRUTHS AND RUSES BRAWLING INSIDE A MAN'S HEART?

DURING HIS LAST JOURNEY GEBER MADE AN EFFORT TO SEE A PRIESTESS WHOSE ORACLE HE CLAIMED HAD SKETCHED THE COURSE OF HIS LIFE AND HAUNTED IT. SHE STILL LIVED PEOPLE SAID. SOME FASCINATION

297

HAD DRAWN HIM TO HER THE NEARNESS OF HIS OWN DEATH PERHAPS HIS
WISH TO CHASTISE EXTOL TEST HER HE COULD NOT TELL. HE TRACED HER
TO A PLACE CLOSE TO AN OASIS TOWN CALLED NAGRAN WHERE HE HAD
BEEN INFORMED SHE WAS LIVING AT A MONASTIC ENCAMPMENT IN THE
TRADITION OF THE DESERT MOTHERS. THIS HOWEVER WAS AN UNUSUAL
PLACE AS IT ACCOMMODATED WOMEN FROM ALL FAITHS CHRISTIANS JEWS
AND PAGANS. HE LOITERED AT THE GATE AND IN THE NEARBY OASIS TOWN
SENDING ONE MESSAGE AFTER ANOTHER TO HER NOW KNOWN AS AMMA
SILVIA. ALL THE TIME HE WOULD KNEEL IN HIS FANCY BEFORE HER SHE
AGELESS AND STATELY WITH FLOWING RED HAIR OR A CRONE SHRIVELLED
AND SUNKEN WITH FEW DESPERATE WISPS OF THE FADED RED ON HER SCALP.
EVEN THEN HE WOULD DRAW NEAR HER AND WHISPER OF HIS LIVES AND
LOVES AND DOUBTS AND LEAVE HIS TEARS ON HER GLEAMING OR SKELETAL
KNEES. THEN HE WAS INSPIRED TO SEND HER TWO SPECIFIC QUESTIONS
APPEALING TO HER WEAKNESS FOR ORACULAR EFFUSIONS. THE LEADER OF
THE COMMUNITY AN 'ABBESS' CALLED AMMA SARAH EMERGED A FEW DAYS
LATER TO SEE HIM AFTER SENDING WORD TO HIM IN NAGRAN. SHE HANDED
HIM TWO PARCHMENTS TWO ORACLES SHE SAID WHICH HAD COME FROM
SILVIA WITH A NOTE. THE NOTE SAID THE ORACLE GIVEN TO HIS FATHER
IN ARABIA WAS MEANT TO REASSURE AND GUIDE, RIDDLING AS IT WAS.
THE NEW ORACLES WERE IN RESPONSE TO HIS TWO QUESTIONS AND WERE
MEANT TO AMUSE AND PROVOKE, THEREAFTER TO REST IN A TEMPLE OR A
CHURCH ON MOUNT LEBANON. WHEN GEBIR OFFERED TO SEND INTO THE
ENCAMPMENT A TEAM OF CAMELS LADEN WITH GIFTS AND PROVISIONS HE
WAS FIRMLY ASKED BY THE 'ABBESS' TO LEAVE AND NEVER TO RETURN. I
TRANSCRIBE THE 'ORACLES' HERE NOT KNOWING THE PURPOSE FOR WHICH
THEY WERE SOUGHT. GEBIR HAD MENTIONED THOUGH THAT THEY DEALT
WITH ISSUES LARGER THAN THOSE OF HIS PERSON AND HIS TRIBE. I COPY
THEM HERE ONE AFTER THE OTHER WITH SOME DARK AMUSEMENT OF MY
OWN THOUGH UNABLE TO FATHOM OUT ANY MEANING IN WHAT APPEAR TO
BE LINES OF VERSE OR CONFIRM THEIR AUTHENTICITY KNOWING SOMETHING
ABOUT GEBER'S WOOING OF THE MUSE AND HIS DREAMING OF IMPOSSIBLE
DREAMS.

HENCE THE FIRST:

The gods look down with lofty grief
As time prepares to turn a leaf,
Which will see them rejoin the earth,
In whose entrails they had their birth,
To rest, though restless, as one clan,
Whose deathless God began in Man.

Beneath the sun a Palm reborn
Will grow to weave a parchment torn
And rouse the four, blood, bile, and phlegm,
As spurred by stout Jerusalem
And moved to tears by soulful Rome,
To rise and fall beneath one dome.

A stitch will burst and woe will flow,
But joy shall not forsake the show.
And proud dynasts of priests, they, too,
Will see the old bestow the new
And incense burn in halls to be
Reclaimed from hoary masonry.

The desert wind will rage thenceforth
To meet the wind that rules the north,
And neighs of steeds and swirls of steel
Will fan the breeze that drives the keel,
Whose deck will boast of silk and spice,
While soars the laughter of the dice.

I hear it hiss, the laughter, hark!
An infant crackle in the dark!
How soon? The gods? They may not know;
The arrow, cocked, now bites the bow,
Its archer Time, its eye a scroll,
Its start and end the human Soul!

AND THE SECOND:

Belqis shall journey once again,
To meet her one, and brace the twain,
And stir anew his wistful bed,
Anointed with her virgin red,
And, in the haze of incense, breed
A fellowship that will not yield,
Through thick and thin, belief and doubt,
The calm, the torrent, and the drought,
Even as rabble-rousers howl
And smithies fume beneath the cowl
And tyrants sit on thrones of spears
Dreaming their men's and their own fears,

Until the gods, behind their bars,
Shall hear the One re-call the stars
And close the Book, for it to start
More starry cycles of the heart!

THE ACCOUNT OF HIS QUEST FOR SILVIA HE NARRATED TO ME AS I SAT
BEFORE HIM ON THE DAMASK CUSHIONS PILED UPON THE MARBLED FLOOR
OF HIS VILLA'S BALCONY THE SLY OLD SUN UNRAVELLING UNTO HER RUSSET
LOOM ANOTHER THREAD OF OUR DAYS THE SEA BREATHING OUT INTO OUR
CHESTS THE TANG OF THE GARDEN AND THE SULPHUR OF THE PIT.

GEBER'S OWN TOMB LOOKS OUT TO THAT SEA HEAVING AND MURMURING
IN THE WEST. BUT IT ALSO LOOKS OUT TO THE EAST AND THE NORTH AND
THE SOUTH ALL HAVING BEEN THOROUGHFARES OF HIS TRIALS AND JOYS.
HE DIED AN EXILE PERHAPS A STATE HE RELISHED AND IN A LAND HE LOVED
LEAVING NO WIFE OR OFFSPRING SAVE THE AFFECTION AND GRATITUDE WE
OWE HIM AND THE BENEFITS OF THE TRADE AND PROPERTIES WITH WHICH
HE ENDOWED ME AND MY FAMILY ALONG WITH THE PEOPLE AND THE LAND
HE LOVED.

AND THERE IS OF COURSE THE CHRONICLE. NOW THAT ITS FIRST AND
SECOND PARTS WERE JOINED AND ITS AUTHOR HAD REJOINED HIS MEMORIES
TRUE AND IMAGINED IT WAS TIME TO FULFIL HIS PERHAPS ONLY PERSONAL
WILL AND TESTAMENT. THIS WAS TO TAKE THE TOME TO ASTARTE'S TEMPLE
IN AFKA AND TRUST IT TO THE 'SAFEKEEPING OF THE GODDESS' AS HE
HAD WISHED. HE HIMSELF HAD ONCE AVERRED THAT THE MERE ACT OF
ASSEMBLING MEMORY BE IT OF ONE SOUL OR ONE NATION WAS ENOUGH OF
AN ATONEMENT FOR FAILURE ELSEWHERE. HE DID NOT KNOW HOWEVER
THAT A CHRISTIAN CHAPEL HAD IN THE INTERVENING YEARS BEEN BUILT
IN AFKA USING THE TEMPLE'S ANCIENT STONES. THE PROJECT HAD BEEN
MULLED OVER FOR A LONG TIME BUT WAS RUSHED THROUGH THREE YEARS
AFTER THE QUAKE. THE PEOPLE WERE LED TO BELIEVE THAT THE TREMOR
WAS A PUNISHMENT FOR SOME LACK OF PIETY ON THEIR PART. A LINGERING
PAGANISM WAS SINGLED OUT AND THE AUTHORITIES MOVED TO EXTIRPATE
IT ROOT AND BRANCH. MOTHER ROME HAD DOLED OUT BURSARIES TO HELP
WITH THIS SCHEME PARTICULARLY SINCE A SERIES OF SMALLER TREMORS
TOOK PLACE AFTER THE FIRST ONE AND MORE ARE STILL FEARED EVEN NOW.

SO I HAVE BEEN DITHERING OVER THE TOME FOR YEARS. GEBER HAD
SAID HE HAD LEFT THE CHRONICLE AS HE HAD WRITTEN IT. HIS WISH TO
'RINSE' IT (A WORD HE FEARED LIKE THE WORD 'FIRE') OF YOUTHFUL RAGE
HAD BEEN SUBDUED BY HIS LOYALTY TO HIS OWN 'TRUTHS'. BUT NOW AS
GREYNESS HAS PREVAILED UPON MY TEMPLES AS HAVE FURROWS UPON MY
BROW THE CAPTAIN OF ONE OF OUR SHIPS HAS BROUGHT MORE DISTURBING
NEWS. THE ABYSSINIAN RULER IN THE YEMEN WHO IS A VICEROY OF HIS

EMINENCE THE EMPEROR JUSTIN THE SECOND NEPHEW AND HEIR OF THE GREAT JUSTINIANUS HAD STARTED TO ASSEMBLE A LARGE ARMY WITH WHICH TO MARCH ON MEKA. THE VICEROY WAS DUE TO MARCH WITH HIS TROOPS BEHIND A WAR ELEPHANT WITH THE INTENTION OF KNOCKING DOWN THE PAGAN TEMPLE IN THAT CITY. THE SKIPPER SAID THAT THE VICEROY LOOKS UPON THAT TEMPLE AS A RIVAL TO A GRAND BASILICA WHICH THE VICEROY HAD BUILT IN THE YEMEN WITH THE AIM OF TURNING THE ARABS AWAY FROM THEIR PAGAN PRACTICES TO THE TRUE FAITH. UNWITTINGLY HOWEVER IT WOULD RIP DOWN GEBER'S TRIBUTE TO HIS POET KING SEWN INTO THE CURTAINS OF THE TEMPLE. PERHAPS IT IS TIME TO GIVE UP MY CUSTODY OF GEBER'S TOME AND LET ASTARTE AND THE MOTHER OF GOD LOOK AFTER IT. SURELY GEBER A MAN RESPECTFUL OF THE AMBIGUITIES OF LIFE AND THOROUGH WITH ITS IMPERFECTION WOULD BE FINALLY COMFORTED AND REASSURED BY SUCH GUARDIANSHIP HOWEVER FLAWED OR CAPRICIOUS TO OTHERS. IT WOULD ALSO PUT AN END TO MY EVER-NAGGING ITCH TO ARRANGE FOR A MORE LEARNED LOOK INTO THE CHRONICLE MUCH THAT I FEAR WHAT I MIGHT LEARN.

AS FOR THE CHRONICLER HIMSELF HE HAD ONCE WISHED TO BE BURIED 'AFTER MY VAGRANCY IN THE SUN HAS ENDED' NEAR THE GRAVES OF MY PARENTS. 'PERHAPS NEXT TO MY TEACHER YOUR FATHER' HE HAD SAID IN HIS LAST ILLNESS. HE HAD ENUNCIATED THAT SOMEWHAT SHYLY NOTING THAT THIS WAS 'YET ANOTHER FUTILE DREAM' OF HIS BUT ONE WHICH HAD SUSTAINED HIM ON THE WAY FROM ARABIA TO THE 'HOMELAND OF HIS HEART'. NONETHELESS I HAD HIS SUN-AND-DREAM-RAVAGED BODY INTERRED NEXT TO THE GRAVE OF MY MOTHER SO THAT SHE WOULD BE FLANKED BY TWO MEN SHIELDING HER FROM THE SCHEMES OF THE INSCRUTABLE SEA.

301

NOTES ON THE POEMS

Listed below are notes to the generally free adaptations of the poems of Imru ul–Qais and other verses cited in the text.

The *Diwan* or collected Poems of Imru ul Qais listed in the Select Bibliography, serves as a main reference, and is cited below as *Diwan*. Other sources are cited by their author's surname.

p. 27. Preface, *Diwan*, p. 30. Also see *Diwan*, pp. 27–28, 259–62; 300–1; 346–47; 393; 446

p. 47. 'Urwa, pp. 51–52; 119–124. Also see Hifni and al–Shahhal on *Sa'alik* 'Socialism', respectively pp. 341–50 and pp. 28–30

p. 85. *Diwan*, pp. 73–80; 101–12; 242–44; 305–7

p. 91. Brock, *Studies*, pp. 58–59

pp. 92–93. See ibid., pp. 74–89

p. 134. Frazer, p. 9

pp. 135–36. Ibid., pp. 9–10. Also see pp. 223–59

pp. 139–40. Al–Samaw'al, p. 80. Also cited in Sirat Ibn Hisham, 3/31

pp. 141–42. *Diwan*, pp. 287–88

p. 171. *Diwan*, pp. 287. Also see verses in praise of another Tayy ruler and host, p. 468

p. 175. See 'Urwa, pp. iii–v, 127–28. Also see Hifni, on overall *Sa'alik* attitude to despots before and after Islam, pp. 44–47, 313–17

p. 200. See Ali, vol. 5, p. 404

p. 219. *Diwan*, p. 424; also see pp. 181–84

p. 219. Ibid

p. 219–20. Ibid., pp. 494–95

p. 220. Ibid., pp. 106–9

p 221, Ibid., pp. 70–80

p. 221. Ibid., p. 486; pp. 360–1; 481–2

p. 221. Ibid., pp. 359–61

p. 221. Ibid., pp. 66–69; 358

p. 222. Ibid., p. 457

pp. 222–23. Ibid., pp. 60–63; 271–3; 487–8

p. 237. Al–Samaw'al, p. 66

pp. 237–38. *Diwan*, p. 60

pp. 238–39. Ibid., pp. 67–81. Also see Al–Rabi' bin Dhab''s poem in praise of Al–Samaw'al, Preface, *Diwan*, p. 44

p. 285. *Diwan*, pp. 170–9

p. 337. Ibid., pp. 222–6

p. 338. Ibid., pp. 237–8. Also see pp. 115–6

p. 341. Ibid., pp. 410–2

BIBLIOGRAPHY AND
FURTHER READING

Al- Aspahani, Abu al-Faraj, *Kitab Al-Aghani*, 11 vols, eds. A.Z. Safwat, A.S.M. Harun, M. Saqqa, Matba'at Dar al-Kutub al-Misriyyah, Cairo, 1927-1938

'Ali, Jawad, *Tarikh al-'Arab qabla al-Islam*, 10 vols, Baghdad and Beirut, 1950-1973

Al-Samaw'al, *Diwan*, ed. by Wadhdhah al-Samad, Dar al-Jil, Beirut, 1996

Al-Shahhal, Radwan, *Imru ul-Qais: Kabir Shu'ara' al-Jahiliyyah*, Matabi' al-Buhayri, Beirut, 1962

Al-Zawzani, Al-Husayn bin Ahmad, *Sharh al-Mua'llaqat al-Sab'*, Dar al-Qalam, Beirut, n.d.

Augustine, Saint, *The Confessions*, transl. by Charles Bigg, Methuen, London, 1998

Blunt, Lady Anne, *The Seven Golden Odes of Pagan Arabia, known also as the Moallakat*, translated from the original Arabic by Lady Anne Blunt; done into English verse by Wilfrid Scawen Blunt, privately published, London, 1903

Brock, Sebastian, P., *Studies in Syriac Spirituality*, Anita, Poona, 1988

Brock, Sebastian, P., *From Ephrem to Romanos: Interaction between Syriac and Greek in Late Antiquity*, Ashgate, Aldershot, 1999

Browne, Lewis, ed., *The Wisdom of Israel*, M. Joseph, London, 1949

Browning, Robert, *The Byzantine Empire*, Weidenfeld and Nicolson, London, 1980

Frazer, Sir James George, *The Golden Bough: a Study in Magic and Religion*, Part iv, *Adonis Artis Osiris*, vol. 1., 3rd ed., Macmillan, London, 1913, 1990.

Graves, Robert, *Count Belasarius*, Cassell and Co., London, 1938

Hawi, Iliyya, *Imru ul Qais: Sha'ir al-Mar'ah wa al-Tabi'ah*, Dar al-Thaqafah, Beirut, 1970

Hifni, 'Abdul Halim, *Shi'r al-Sa'alik: Manhajuhu wa khasa'isuhu*, Al-Hay'a al-Misriyyah al-'Ammah li al-Kitab, Cairo, 1979.

Ibn al-Kalbi, Hisham, *Kitab al-Asnam*, ed. Ahmad Zaki Pasha, Matba'at Dar al-Kutub al-Misriyyah, Cairo, 1924

Ibn al-Kalbi, *Ansab al-khayl fi al-Jahiliyyah wa al-Islam wa akhbaruha*, ed. Ahmad Zaki Pasha, Dar al-Kutub al-Misriyyah, Cairo, 1946

Ignatyus Afram I, Patriarch, *Kitab al-lu'lu' al-manthur fi tarikh al-'ulum wa al-adab al-siryaniyyah*, 2nd ed., Aleppo, 1956

Imru ul Qais, *Diwan*, edited by Abul Hajjaj Ysuf bin Suleyman bin 'Isa, revised by al-Shaykh ibn Abi Shanab, al-Sharikah al-Wataniyyah li-al-Nashr wa al-Tauzi', Algiers, 1974

Jacobs, David, *Constantinople: City on the Golden Horn*, Cassell, London, 1971

Gollancz, Hermann, transl., *The Book of Protection*, H. Frowde, London, 1912

Procopius, *The Secret History*, translated with an introduction by G.A. Williamson, Penguin Books, 1966, 1983 reprint.

Serjeant, R.B. *South Arabian Hunt*, Luzac, London, 1976

Shahid, Irfan, *Byzantium and the Semitic Orient before the Rise of Islam*, Variorum Reprints, London, 1988

Shahid, Irfan, *Byzantium and the Arabs in the Sixth Century*, vol. I, Part 1: *Political and Military History*, Dumbarton Oaks Research Library and Collection, Washington, 1995

Tuetey, Charles Greville, *Imrulkais of Kinda, Poet*, Diploma Press, London, 1977

'Urwa ibn al-Ward, *Diwan*, sharḥ Ibn al-Sikkīt Ya'qūb ibn Isḥāq; edited and annotated by 'Abd al-Mu'īn al-Mallūḥī. Wizārat al-Thaqāfah wa-al-Irshād al-Qawmī, Damascus, 1966

Ward, Benedicta, transl., *The Sayings of the Desert Fathers: the Alphabetical Collection*, Mowbrays, London, 1975

GLOSSARY

aba:	'*aba'a*, traditional Arab cloak
abal:	'*abal*, Arabian fruit-bearing shrub found in sandy deserts; its twigs are used as firewood which produces smokeless fire. Also '*arta*
Abqar:	'*Abqar*, fabled valley and abode of the Jinn, associated with poetic inspiration
abyar:	wells and underground cisterns
aflaj (sing. *falaj*):	underground system of irrigation
Algol:	bright star in Perseus
aman:	solemn pledge to grant sanctuary and protection
arfaj:	'*arfaj*, perennial aromatic herb
arta:	See *abal*
asafiri:	'*asafiri*, secret language imitating bird-sounds used by children in their play
bah:	sexual desire, potency
barjeel:	windcatcher, wind cooling tower and ventilation system
basat:	wild plant
basileia:	kingdom
dalul:	fast and hardy dromedary
dhow:	Arabian sailing vessel
dhoweila:	wild Southern Arabian plant
Drome:	Byzantine equivalent to Foreign Ministry
dromon:	warship of the Byzantine navy
efreet:	demon
Eram:	fabled lost city of the rich and powerful tribe of 'Ad, mentioned in the Qur'an
farsakh:	Arabic for ancient Persian parasang, unit of length or distance
follis:	pl. *folles*. Roman and Byzantine bronze coin

Gehenna:	Hebrew term for Hellfire
ghada:	wild bush
ghaf:	flowering desert tree
ghazw:	tribal raiding
grammatikos:	teacher of grammar
hamah:	the spirit of a murdered person transformed into a bird which clamours for revenge
Hanif:	pl. *Hanifs* or *Ahnaf*, follower of the faith of Abraham
harmal:	perennial herb with medicinal properties
Homs:	a puritanical sect in pre-Islamic Mecca
houjja:	pedigree chart of a thoroughbred horse
howdah:	roofed and curtained structure placed on the back of a camel for the use of women in travel
houbara:	Arabian bustard
hurrah:	prized breed of South Arabian camels
kanab:	wild high-ground plant; ash from its roots is used to make kohl
kamal:	old navigation instrument used to help plot the latitude of a ship
kashkoul:	medley, jumble, also an untidy assortment of amusing tales and anecdotes
Khidr:	*Al-Khidr*: the immortal Green Man mentioned in Middle-Eastern folklore and alluded to in the Qur'an
khitmah:	South Arabian plant
khuweira:	wild South Arabian plant
khuzamah:	lavender
kilit:	evergreen shrub of Southern Arabia with medicinal properties; its berries are eaten raw or roasted
Korban:	Hebrew for a sacrificial offering
Kum:	South Arabian herb
kumayt:	horse of a reddish-brown colour
kutenun:	desert plant
lazzah:	physical pleasure
Logothete:	Byzantine official

majnun:	madman
manakh:	resting place for caravans
marhala:	stage of a land journey
marwaha:	cooling fan, here dance in which dancers turn their heads this way and that way
marzaha:	Yemeni folk dance
mawwal:	type of traditional Lebanese song
memra:	pl. *memre*. Syriac homily in verse
mikveh:	Hebrew for a ritual bath
Mizar:	star in Ursa Major
naima:	perennial Arabian herb
Nisan:	April
Nummus:	pl. *nummi*, Roman and Byzantine copper coin
phelonion:	outer vestment worn by a priest of the Eastern Church
Phylarch:	Byzantine title given to an allied Arab ruler
peractio:	Latin for completion, summation
qabbadah:	holder, woman adept in sexual stimulation
qamat:	(sing. *qamah*): height of a person as a unit of measurement
qit'a:	short poem
qomqom:	bottle in which Solomon (in popular legend) imprisoned a rebellious Jinn
qassis:	South Arabian plant
qat:	small shrub cultivated in Yemen, its leaves used/ abused as a stimulant
quinquevirate:	Latin for a body of five
rakh:	wild South Arabian plant
Rhetor:	teacher of rhetoric
rob:	flowering plant; grows rapidly in the rain
saker:	large falcon
sa'luk:	member of a group who defied tribal laws in pre-Islamic Arabia

samhari:	strong and well-made lance or spear
sarooj:	decorative Yemeni flooring made from burned clay
sayyidah:	Arabic for lady
semantron:	instrument struck to summon worshippers to prayer
senna:	shrub with various medicinal attributes
Shamal:	north-westerly wind
sidr:	fruit-bearing Arabian tree
simoom:	cyclonic sand storm
soheet:	South Arabian bush, whose wood burns brightly and without smoke
Solidus:	pl. *solidi*, Roman and Byzantine gold coin
Sumr:	South Arabian tree
tahr:	wild goat-like mountain-climbing mammal of Southern Arabia
tesserae:	mosaic flooring
tijarah:	trade
walwala:	wailing for the dead
zahra:	Southern Arabian plant
zamil:	Yemeni folk song
zerutret:	Southern Arabian desert plant
zuger:	desert plant

ACKNOWLEDGEMENTS

This work was an idea and an urge for many years. But it took the loving pestering of my wife Ranam to make me start work on it in earnest some seven years back. The gratitude I owe her must however be shared by a number of people who had inspired my interest in Imru ul-Qais and contributed to it and to my life generally.

My mother, Isaaf, and my father, Atef, who were career educators and occasional authors, had instilled in me early in my life an abiding love for Arabic poetry and for its indisputable king, Imru ul-Qais. Even when I was a child of ten I had memorised the king's *mu'allaqah*, though by no means sufficiently aware of its subtleties and boldness. In the game of *musajalah* I played with my parents, along with my sister and brother or with my school friends, lines from Imru's ode often came to my rescue. The game, meant to entrench us into the classical tradition while building up our memory, repartee, and inventiveness, consisted of recalling (sometimes making up) at a moment's notice a line of verse beginning with the letter ending the line just recited by another player.

One striking feature of Imru ul-Qais' poetry and that of his contemporaries was that it had come down from or was associated with a very rich pagan epoch that had coexisted with an equally rich Christian and Jewish tradition in the Arabian Peninsula. Interestingly, the predominalty pagan and hedonistic features of that poetry did not prevent it from being endorsed as a model of literary excellence by successive generations of poets and critics during the Islamic era. The poetry of that period itself went on to evolve in many innovative ways influencing poetic traditions in some other parts of the world; but the poetry of pre-Islamic Arabia remained a foundation and a polestar.

To this day, poetry occupies an exceptional position in Arab culture. The Arabs call it their *diwan*, implying that it is their truer collective register and *deeper* history – truer and deeper (in the Aristotelian sense) than their political and other official histories and a more profound and ennobling expression of their ideals, yearnings and frustrations, with the interface (and tension) between poetry and politics enduring as an ever topical and challenging subject for debate and creativity.

The remarkable qualities of Imru ul-Qais' poetry aside, the man himself, with his triumphs and failures, restiveness and conformity, reality and legend, has emerged through the ages as a metaphor and icon for Arabs, making an understanding of him, however elusive, helpful in gaining an insight into the Arab character. But he is also a universal man and a composite man; and like Tennyson's Ulysses, he is part of all he has met or has been foisted on him. This work, too, with its range of interests, characters, settings, moods, and genres, is similarly part of a much larger and unresolved encounter.

To my parents, my sister and brother, wife and children, teachers and students, friends and colleagues, too many and too precious to name them all, along with the various authors, historians, biographers, and commentators I read over the years and more specifically for this undertaking, together with my very accomplished but ever patient and nurturing publisher, Naim Attallah, I owe 'what I can ne'er express, yet cannot all reveal'. At Quartet Books, David Elliott's own patience and editorial wisdom, along with the expertise and friendliness of the team at 27 Goodge Street, Gavin James Bower, Grace Pilkington, and Josh Bryson, I also acknowledge with much gratitude.